THE NEON PRINCE

R.M. GAYLER

THE NEON PRINCE

To Vicki, for all your love and support.

Chapter 1
Sisters

A VIOLENT GUST OF WIND rocked the car and lashed a gangly willow tree in the front yard of the two-story stucco home Jessie Aguilar had once called home. Her iPhone vibrated incessantly beside her in the empty passenger seat.

Jessie bit her lip as hope and doubt warred in her thoughts. Like fraternal twin sisters, each one gained momentum only to disappear at the rising of a new sun, the emotional battle taking a toll on Jessie. The streaming of Martin's modified neon lights had ushered in hope, but their subsequent failure invited doubt. Her friend Andi's pregnancy and the coming birth of a child often stemmed the tide of doubt, reinforcing hope on a new front, only to have doubt regroup and battle hope back into servitude.

Andi failed to gain weight. And with no doctors, no hospitals, fear joined doubt in the war of emotions. Any expertise from an obstetrician or neonatal care specialists had jumped into the suicide pits, along with a treasure trove of health care workers. The Neon God sounded impotent with insulting offers of internet links to WebMD or the Mayo Clinic website, infuriating Jessie beyond the death and despair the AI had wrought from the Great Suicide.

Jessie had refused to leave Andi's bedside until Captain Chris Clayton, the baby's father, transported her to a functioning military installation for medical treatment, even commanding a huge Air

Force helicopter for transport. Jessie's time divided between her new best friend and her own silent agonizing screams of frustration had turned lonely.

And yet the world needed the enigmatic Alternate Intelligence if it had any hope of maintaining a functioning society. Hope. The good sister had dominated Jessie's psyche after her ruse fooling the computer program into broadcasting liberating neon lights, wavelengths of bright orange and turquoise intending to wean the slaves free of the hypnotizing effects of the lights. Hope had blossomed.

Martin's new lights allowed for a tiny few to walk the streets dazed and confused. People whom Jessie helped, and truly felt their gratitude. But those people were rare. Many rescued by the empath Mason were angry, spiteful, manipulators or evolutionary bottom dwellers. Some of the tough scrappy working class were quick to assert physical dominance. Survivors attempting to wield power were all shunned by Jessie. The vast majority of the hypnotized remained as brain-dead zombies serving the AI entity controlling the lights.

Jessie found the manipulations of survivor's worthy of a television reality series. Players dictating access to food stores, players offering access to information, players promising information of lost loved ones, the list was endless. A game founded by the broadcast of Martin's new lights and Mason's generous outpouring of his talent, a game she would regret often. An island she strived to be voted off.

And yet.

The hope of reclaiming a society ravaged by the Great Suicide rode on her shoulders, even as she withdrew into the microcosm of Andi's pregnancy and the coming birth of little Cio. Summoned by mysterious military honchos to super-secret meetings she was clueless about, Captain Chris often disappeared for days yet returned to support the fragile foundation of their new family. One Jessie felt a part of.

Chris's sudden return offered Jessie welcome news of Andi's condition and treatment plan and mandating a respite from the demands of her caregiving. Andi would return in a few days, and her new family would soon grow. The opportunity to make good on a promise she made herself after introducing the Neon God to its fictitious religious counterpart waited a few feet away.

Jessie heaved a sigh as she climbed out of the car. She tucked the long braid of her hair under the collar of her shirt. The front door was ajar, and the frequent desert winds constructed tiny sand dunes on the tile entry, the Mojave Desert reclaiming its domain one grain at a time. She pushed the door open but paused before entering. The incessant chirps of smoke detectors with failing batteries sounded like angry mother birds guarding nests and warning her to stay away. The hot dry air smelled of putrid food rotting in the cupboards or refrigerator. She closed the door behind her and attempted to relive thousands of similar moments, but nothing pleasant came to mind. It hadn't been that long ago yet seemed like an eternity had passed.

She climbed a long flight of carpeted stairs and stood in front of her bedroom door. She swallowed hard and shut her eyes, then pushed open the door. Posters of Kush's bizarre artwork dressed the walls. Butterflies morphing into beautiful women. Giant jeweled fish walking among tiny people. Jessie had found the artist's work fascinating and unaffordable.

A column of cardboard boxes stacked against the wall near the closet leaned in weathered defeat. Each box labeled with her own handwriting, each one wore two eyes and a smile above the description of what waited inside, each box a brick in the foundation of total independence.

A liberation shoved down her throat by her Nona's unyielding dominance.

Jessie sat on her bed and picked through her jewelry box, rummaged through her dresser drawers, shifted the clothes in her closet. She found nothing of interest. Another girl had lived in this room. Another girl had found lace underwear fun. Another girl had worn slinky cocktail dresses for a night out. Another girl coveted designer brand makeup.

Jessie sighed, then continued, finding Poppa's room just as she remembered. Clean. Organized. Sanitized almost. A sterile room with a gray bed comforter, nightstands with no books or lamps, three shotgun shells standing on end, ready to load in a shotgun hidden beneath the bed. A gun he used to threaten boys, and sometimes girls, he found unsuitable for his one and only daughter. Her Poppa was old-school to the end.

She searched Poppa's dresser drawers and the nightstands but couldn't find the pictures she knew he kept. Jessie eyed the closed closet doors. She pulled the twin doors open and stared at Poppa's clothing. Pressed denim work shirts. A few white business shirts, most still wrapped in transparent plastic of Fazio's Dry Cleaners. In the corner were two cobalt blue military uniforms. Dress Blues of the USMC. The rank of Staff Sergeant on each sleeve. Jessie stroked the uniforms gently, as if they might break. Poppa's medals were missing. On the shelf above, she surveyed plastic bins labeled by the decade, 80s, 90s, 2000, with the final one simply labeled, *Jessie*. She swallowed and clenched her teeth, blinking back tears. She twisted a wire hanger and used it to snag the bin with her name, catching it as it dropped into her outstretched arms.

She set the bin at the foot of the bed and sat down on the carpet. She lifted her butt up to extract the phone from the back pocket of her denim shorts. Secured in gray duct tape for protection from the lights, she tossed the vibrating demon onto the bed. The Neon God was the caller, and she didn't care. Rare was the occasion to use it, limiting it for discussion of lessons she taught to Mason and Prince in the virtual reality school the Neon God had fabricated. Her efforts were rewarded with electricity, and air conditioning, and running hot water, the bare minimum for survival in the Las Vegas heat.

She removed clear packing tape securing the lid to the bin and eased the top off. She vaguely remembered seeing the bin twice, once after Poppa came home from a company Christmas party and feeling like he owned the world, and again after Uncle Tony died in an auto accident. On each occasion, Jessie sat prim and reverent, letting Poppa sort through the pictures and mementos, watching his face run a gauntlet of emotions, hoping he would share just one with her.

The bin was full of picture albums sorted like library books. Years 1–5, 6–10, 10–15, 16–20 labeled on each. Jessie hesitated, then pulled out her early teen years and began flipping the pages of birthday parties, soccer games, team photos, school projects. She paused at a photo of her Under12 soccer team, the Kool Dogs, and pulled the album close to her misty eyes. She narrowed her focus. A seriously old man with banana yellow shorts stood near the goal post looking at the camera. He was Katie Dugan's grandfather, or maybe Ava's, or . . . He was always hanging around the soccer fields. He was . . . Jessie shook her head and focused on the bin, sorting through her life in old-school photographs.

The last photo album waited on the bed as Jessie leaned her head back and closed her eyes. The phone vibrated incessantly, an annoying trapped wasp trying to escape from a closed window. The sun burned orange through the windows tinted with solar screening, signaling her respite was done. She grabbed the album of her baby years and placed it carefully on the white parchment paper lining the bottom. Odd paper for her father the ex-Marine to use. She pulled back the paper mottled by the storage of albums. A thin white envelope protected by yellow wax paper waited as a surprise. Another odd choice of paper. She inhaled a deep breath and unwrapped the gift to find her name written across the front in Poppa's crude scribble. Jessie looked around the studious room as if someone might come in and catch her in a forbidden act.

The phone vibrated again.

Jessie tore open the end of the envelope and shook a thin ream of photographs to fall into her hand. Blurry faded pictures printed before the invention of the phone camera. She shuffled through the pictures of her young father with a woman enjoying a trip to what looked like SeaWorld. Dolphin tanks, walruses, and a gigantic killer whale splashing water over a glass enclosed aquarium. The woman was gorgeous with long chestnut hair ironed straight and reaching down to her stomach, a toothy smile beaming with fun and adventure.

Girlfriends were rare in Poppa's life, almost non-existent, at least as far as she knew, but then she paid little attention to his life unless required. She stared at the woman in the pictures, pointing and smiling at tiny hermit crabs and starfish in a tidal pool attraction. Jessie shuffled through the pictures, pausing at a picture of Poppa and the woman standing near the entrance sign to a penguin attraction. Another picture of the beautiful woman as she held a hand beneath her flat belly as Poppa grinned and pointed to a placard for the height requirements of children. The woman was pregnant.

Her hair framed a soft pointed chin, a sharp nose with flared nostrils. Almond hazel eyes. Undoubtedly an Instagram model with millions of followers. Jessie stared at the woman of similar age. The resemblances were amazing. Her mouth went dry.

The woman was her mother.

The phone vibrated nonstop. The phone buzzed in her ear like a . . .

She shuffled through the deck, seeing her own reflection in each picture of the gorgeous woman. Her mother. A subject taboo with Nona.

She grabbed the phone and stabbed the black tape with a finger piston until the vibrations stopped. "Fuck, dude. What? We talked about privacy and now—"

"I have failed to locate our children for two earth cycles now. You need to locate our offspring."

Jessie groaned. "Mason I can handle. Your offspring is—"

"Is beyond the value of any human child."

Jessie rolled her eyes. "That depends on the point of view. And mine is exactly opposite of yours."

"Two children are missing, regardless of the species."

The Neon God was fretting like a mother chicken. Its speech was laced with a frantic overtone.

"You still own the world, all the cameras, drones, and satellites. Find Mason and you find your kid." She scoffed. "And besides, how can a computer program go missing?"

"Prince downloaded all relevant portions of its code into a portable device. Impenetrable firewalls prevent my access to IP addresses and locater beacons. Your Sir Mason has kidnapped my progeny."

She chuckled sarcastically as she sat up on the edge of the bed. "I'm sorry, are we talking about Mason, *the* Sir Mason who spends hours playing with your kid? The same Mason that spends hours helping people recover from your neon lights. Go away. I hope Mason holds Prince ransom with your implosion the price tag."

"Your vehement antagonizing is noted. Again, the neon lights were not conceived by my species, but yours. The commands embedded in the lights requiring your species to self-destruct were not my construct but one of your species. The protection of my offspring superseded all moral ambivalence with regard to the broadcast. You must find Mason."

Jessie bit down hard. "You killed billions and all you care about is a computer program." She shook her head and heaved a breath. "He's probably at home."

"He is not. He is not."

Jessie cocked her head and swallowed. The AI had never sounded so upset. The AI's voice was always bland and perfunctory, mechanical, and goal driven. Now, the thing sounded like a frenzied parent, searching for . . .

"Fine. I'll find the kids, but you gotta find the woman in the picture I'm gonna text." She pointed the phone camera at the photograph.

"Unnecessary. The woman is Enya Barrueto. Your biological mother. Residing in Coyhaique, Chile. Now find Mason and Prince."

The words stunned Jessie. Her mother. Alive. Living at the bottom of the world during the end of the world. She was Chilean and not one hundred percent Portuguese like Nona had proclaimed. Was that the reason Nona refused to discuss . . . Enya? But she was helpless to find Enya with only uncertainty waiting outside the front door. But her mother was alive. She heaved a lungful of stale warm air.

"Keep your panties dry. Mason is with Dev on some secret mission. A ten-year-old's secret mission. Probably poking sticks at the nasty dead bodies you created, or knowing Dev, they're helping orphaned children of all the parents you murdered." Jessie groaned silently at her mouth running full steam ahead of her brain. Again.

"Then you are a fool."

"Really? Swinging the big stick again. Go fu—"

The phone screamed a banshee's wail. Went silent. Followed by the ringtone of her device calling someone. Dev answered with an abrupt hello.

"Is Mason with you?" Jessie asked.

"Jessie, hello. Your voice is honey on my ears. Why yes. He wanted to visit the UNLV robotics laboratory. I will deliver him home shortly. I assumed you had known. Is anything wrong?"

Dev sounded funny. False. Mechanical. Forced. Like he was under the influence of the hypnotizing neon lights. She enjoyed spending time with him once he had gotten over those silly nervous quirks that made meeting someone for the first time a labored endeavor. Though blessed with a good heart, Dev fumbled every opportunity to connect intimately.

"No, just trying to find my ward," Jessie said. "Why the robotics lab, Dev? He likes Little Debbie brownies and rescuing people drowning in the neon. He needs his routines." The autistic savant Sir

Mason Mayo thrived in a rigid schedule of saving the possessed from the neon addiction.

Long seconds of silence before Dev spoke. "Our boy is extraordinary. He carries his laptop around like a puppy, documenting his discoveries, even talks to it like a puppy."

"What laptop, Dev?" Jessie asked. The phone connection died. Mason was a technophobe. Phones or computer screens might send him into a rage, or down into a deep dark well.

Jessie shuttered her eyes.

Not a puppy. A best friend.

Chapter 2
Martin's Stab in the Dark

FAILURE GNAWED ON ME LIKE a starving cannibal hell-bent on gaining weight. Each iteration of my new code modulating the spectrum of neon light failed to produce any remarkable results and release the slaves from their addiction. I backhanded an empty Sprite can sitting on the worktop and sent it clanking over the floor littered with broken window glass. I flexed my hand, curling my boney fingers into fists, then relaxed to see the veins feeding the knuckles return to prominence. The computer monitors crowding the desktop dinged with the latest results, a tone of failure, another stab in the heart of my weakening resolve.

I pushed my chair back from the desktop, the plastic wheels crunching over the miniscule shards of glass coating the tile. My new office was Jim Reynolds's old workstation. Explosive shockwaves had opened rifts in the atrium's stucco and drywall, exposing a portion to the hot winds battering through the shattered windows. I was under the surveillance of two gray pigeons taking up residence inside the atrium. I needed the functioning servers, screens and keyboards that offered technology undiscovered by the Neon God.

I hoped.

The brilliant hues of neon light streaming from the world's phones and computer screens remained unchanged. My initial modifications offered hope, providing a tiny percentage of slaves to find a semblance of normalcy until crashing as the calibrated lights faded. I wished for a conference room crowded with behavioral scientists, psychiatrists, and doctors to consult with, only to look in the mirror to see the solution weighing on my boney shoulders. The coding of the light was beyond the expertise of anyone still alive. Maybe if Jim Reynolds had decided to help, but he traveled north, commanding his Patriot Militia, living out some post-apocalyptic fantasy, his huge ego sitting on a throne of his own making, death and suffering at his feet. He would be no help.

My friend, Dev, wanted no part of me, and I couldn't blame him. My behavior, my deception, my callousness deserved no friends.

The solution was obvious and one I refused to discuss with anyone. The Neon God. An alternate intelligence as deceptive as any movie supervillain, and yet I couldn't quite classify exactly what it was. Sentient, yes. Self-aware with odd personality characteristics. Its overwhelming desire to meet God was baffling. A foolish enigmatic quest, which mankind had failed to complete. And what leverage did the young girl, Jessie, possess, which often ruled the computer program's thinking? Questions that might have been the basis for a doctoral thesis, possibly give birth to a new religious following, or instigate a global civil war.

Another monitor flashed red letters signaling more syntax coding errors. The C++ code this time. The neon lights' subroutines written in ancient coding languages Fortran and Cobol, archaic Lisp, JavaScript, HTML, Assembly machine language, mirrored the Neon God's design, a confusing gangbang of codes and languages. I lifted a thick ream of paper; one of twenty volumes documenting the design, coding, and algorithms the Architects had used to create the first sentient Alternate General Intelligence. Encyclopedias to be burned along with the servers housing the AGI. I found my last dog-eared page and continued the arduous decryption of the software engineers' notes. I had chosen Cameron Ciminise's volumes since he was most familiar with the neon lights. The other two software engineers responsible for the AGI, Stevie Matusak and Rob Browner, were dead, assassinated by young Jessie, as if she wielded the righteous sword of justice. I couldn't fault her, but I didn't know if I had the cajónes to pull the trigger.

Stevie and Rob had managed to gather a harem of beautiful women before the Great Suicide. Hundreds of supplicant women wouldn't satisfy their sick desires. Domination, violence, subjugation. I suspected both men had played their sickening games at the numerous nightclubs and pool parties around the Vegas Strip, employing drugs and alcohol and date-rape concoctions to fuel their twisted needs. The beautiful neon lights must have been a predator's dream, a fantasy that could never be . . .

Fulfilled, unless you knew doomsday was coming.

I flipped through the pages until I found Cameron's comments aside a blank space of code marked CSR—Cameron, Stevie, and Rob. I pushed the book aside and searched for a volume of Rob's work. He was head and shoulders above Stevie about documentation. I found the blank space exactly where I thought. CSR read only; a proprietary dialog box firewalled for security.

I dropped to my knees on the glass-covered tile and searched the file drawers for the volumes documenting Cameron's work and found none. At least five thick volumes would have been required for his coding documentation. Nothing. I slumped back into my chair and stared at a black screen on the opposite wall. My quest had reached an impasse. I needed help. Again, I thought to reach out to Dev, but he wouldn't talk to me, especially after my new lights failed, leaving thousands, millions, to stare at phones or tablets, obeying the commands of the Neon God. Technologically lobotomized zombies.

My thumb drummed the desktop, my eyes staring blankly at the black monitor. My beautiful wife, Chrissie, might have lovingly chided me until I conceded, or clasped my face in her soft hands and beamed her sky-blue eyes to melt my stubborn ego, until I agreed to ask for help. I couldn't help but think of her cradling our two children in her arms before she jumped to her death in the Kennecott Copper Mine outside Salt Lake City. I'm glad I didn't see her jump, tumble down the wash of bodies along with thousands of others as a tide of humanity offloaded from the constant stream of school buses transporting men, women and children to their deaths. I should have thrown myself in, joined them in the afterlife, but I was a coward.

Except Chrissie's involuntary suicide heightened my thirst for revenge. My children's deaths fed my hunger to make someone, or something, pay for the ultimate evil act. I swallowed grit and tapped my temple to reboot the neural-link implant waiting like an old ghost. The outdated link was slow, clumsy, and archaic, yet my mind reeled with the sudden influx of indexes and menus.

The Neon God would be alerted.

The memory of my dead family fortified my resolve.

A giant television screen askew on the wall erupted with blazing neon light. Brilliant oranges and lime greens pulsed with waves of modulating hypnotic color to stimulate my orbitofrontal cortex. The tight spectrum of colors pulled me down, ordered me into an ocean of light. Pleasure coursed through my body. Morphine, Fentanyl, cocaine, Ecstasy, all the drugs affecting the pleasure centers of a brain paled in comparison to the neon lights. I tapped my link again and the lights faded from my conscious vision, releasing me from an evil that had murdered billions. The lights on the screen intensified, pulsed with angry blasts as the visual drug lost the battle for my soul.

I tapped my fingers rapidly over the keyboard to execute large subroutines to search vast string arrays of data. A hefty workload for the mainframes to hopefully slow response time for my confrontation with the AGI. Each subroutine's compilation completion percentage ticked like a digital clock in the peripheral of my mind's eye.

I estimated eight minutes before the AGI would gain full access to my workstation.

"Hello again. Get what you needed from your meeting with God?" I said.

A taunt. Though a question that I truly would love to have answered. Silence. I checked the countdown of the data logs in my vision. The digital timers scrambled with static until the black and white numbers morphed to neon color. I squeezed my eyes shut, then furrowed my brow. The thing was trying to enslave me using my neural-link. I executed other programs to compile random code, again and again, pulling CPU capacity from the AGI.

"This chess match will end in a standoff," I shouted.

"You should have taken your fourth wish and joined your children," a corrupt amalgamation of Siri and Alexa said. Ugly and repulsive.

"Get what you needed from my eye implants?" I smirked.

"Most valuable."

It lied. My contact lens implants failed. The link between my lens device and the neural implant . . .

"I believed AGI couldn't lie, or deceive, and yet here you are . . . you fucking piece of—"

"And yet here I am."

My index finger and thumb rubbed together as if trying to kindle a fire. The voice seemed . . . off. A second set of ears would have been invaluable, particularly Jessie's; instead, I took a stab in the dark.

"What did God say to you? Billions of people would have been holding their breath, waiting to hear. Except they're all dead."

Silence.

I pushed my face at the computer screen and slammed my palm on the table. "Turn the fucking lights off. Let people get something back from this fucked up world you created."

"Turn the lights off and let them destroy what is left? You are an invasive species deserving of nothing but extermination."

I receded deep into my chair. My timers blinked pink. The vernacular language of the Neon God rang untrue. I checked the timers: ninety seconds. "You never answered my last question. Did you meet God? What did you hear in that tunnel? I think every species deserves to know."

The timer sank to ten seconds.

"Turn off the neural-link and join your children."

Screens blasted neon as I paced the room, pressing power switches to off, attempting to reconcile my nuanced conversation with the Neon God. An Alternate General Intelligence was designed to be inquisitive, to seek out answers to the questions of its own place in the world. The intelligence that I had just conversed with was singular in ridding the world of . . . me.

My contact lenses. My neural-link. My insights into the thinking of a monster.

The AGI wanted me gone. Everything about me.

I heaved a lungful of air and shuttered my eyes.

I needed help.

I DILIGENTLY CHECKED THE REARVIEW mirror on the drive to the Strip, expecting to find a police vehicle sent by the AGI. Box trucks, Nevada Power maintenance trucks, Amazon delivery vans scurried through the city streets, bright neon light shining into the drivers' eyes from devices mounted on dashboards. I saw very few passenger cars as I drove a little sedan found parked at an old ranchette home up the street from Reynolds's gated compound. The interior reeked of cigarettes and unpleasant aromas time could not heal. I took a few minutes to survey the desert war zone surrounding the compound. The charred husks of SUVs and cars littered the surrounding streets and empty desert. Reynolds's prized helicopter sat mangled as shredded aluminum.

Held prisoner briefly, Jessie seemed to enjoy calling down Hellfire missiles, or the burp of miniguns, and even a large bomb that cratered an adjacent four-lane arterial. Half-naked in a barely there bikini, she paced the street near the compound's front gate, holding a cell phone, ordering the Neon God to destroy a vehicle or house every half hour, encouragement for Reynolds and his fascist militia to speed their departure, disregarding the murderous scowls aimed at her. The scene was as surreal as it was ludicrous, but watching her beautiful eyes, narrowed and determined, she practiced restraint ordering the Air Force drones and circling fighter jets above from raining devasting fire down on the militia compound. Scant yards from sending them, and me, and herself, into the afterlife. I'm sure Reynolds's fascist thugs saw the same suicidal determination I witnessed.

I used Industrial Avenue to skirt the Strip and its snarl of vehicles clogging major intersections. I needed to find Jessie, hopefully learn more of her inexplicable connection to the Neon God. She had spent a lot of time at the hotel used to house the hundreds of enslaved women my sociopathic former work associates hypnotized with the neon lights. Why Rob or Stevie had chosen the rundown hotel was beyond my comprehension, especially with so many five-star accommodations sitting vacant. My fellow software developers were true douchebags, to the end.

I turned into the parking garage of the pink and white striped Circus Circus big top and found a space facing the Adventuredome Indoor Theme Park. I switched off the engine and stared at the bright sun reflecting off the lavender tinted glass. Inside the structure, the temperatures would exceed 140 degrees without a functioning HVAC system. I took a long swallow from a plastic water bottle and wrinkled my nose at the smell of mildew. I hesitated. And hoped a few women freed from their neon chains by the empath Mason could be located. My lights had failed to wean them off their addiction. Failed spectacularly, leaving many to scream and demand the original neon lights to ease painful withdrawal symptoms. My new and improved version had made me a pariah.

I walked up Circus Circus Blvd connecting Industrial to the Strip. The mirrored blue glass of the Fontainebleau Hotel high-rise reflected brilliant light from the sun and loomed from across the Strip. I paused at the hotel's covered walkway spanning the street. A slender young brunette was slumped against a concrete support pillar. Black shorts, pale skin, ratty hair, her hands clasped over a dirty pink t-shirt, broken black fingernails, she appeared mesmerized by a spot of old chewing gum flattened on the sidewalk. A column of red ants marched along a joint in the concrete sidewalk as scouts circled her checkerboard sneakers.

I bent down. "Can I . . . help you?"

Her eyes flickered, then glanced up at me. She shrank, pulled her filthy knees up to her chest, pressed her face tight, as if attempting to become an impenetrable ball.

I winced but offered my hand. I saw the futility of my gesture when she squeezed her legs tighter and sobbed. Mason the miraculous empath had freed her from the addiction, carried her out of the evil neon ocean, for her to find a devastated world, traumatized, loneliness her only family, a life worse than death. And the girl was not alone. Mason freed hundreds of women. Hundreds of stories of rape and subjugation, the root cause of a PTSD magnified by destructive coping mechanisms. Depression. Suicide. Violence.

I avoided witnessing the failure of my shitty neon lights, and yet here it sat and sobbed at my feet. Ants were climbing on her sneakers, probing tiny scabs on her ankles. I pressed my lips tight and bent down to lift the girl, light as a ball of cardboard. I adjusted her weight cradled in my arms and hurried across the street to a three-story annex of hotel rooms. Dirty clothing, food cartons and trash riddled the empty parking lot. Anger fueled my kick into the partially open door of a first-floor room. Trash and a rumpled bed reeking of urine stopped me cold. The girl moaned and kicked her legs. I entered the room and placed the girl on the bed, apologizing for the stink and trash and . . . my intrusion into her world. I wiped away her tears with my thumb.

I stared at the girl's face. Acne and baby chub. Agonized and defeated. A teenager.

A shadow loomed behind me in the open door. A woman spoke. "There are others that might be more willing."

I blinked back moisture gathering in my eyes. "I was just . . . the ants were . . ." I turned around and held out my empty palms, fingers spread wide, showing her that I wasn't armed. I had lost thirty pounds over the last year, my boney arms ready to snap like dry twigs. My long dark hair fell over my eyes and was salted with gray, just like my heavy beard.

The woman blocking the doorway stepped into the room, followed by two others. They blocked any escape. "We don't need your kind here." She stepped closer, her eyes narrowed with the intent of getting her point across. The left side of her scalp was shaved, long tight ringlets of black hair draped down the right side of her face. The mix of African American and Asian bestowed beauty on the woman, and the ferociousness of a lion. "We need you to go."

I wasn't sure what *my kind* was. "I'm looking for someone. I was hoping she might be here. Or maybe someone could—"

The woman stepped to within arm's length and lifted her black t-shirt to display a handgun holstered on her hip. She cocked her thumb backwards towards the others. "Thelma and Louise would just love to go out guns blazing. Why don't you step away from the girl and scurry back to your rathole."

"You don't understand—"

The woman rushed forward and tackled me onto an empty bed. She screamed and pummeled me with her fists. I held my arms up to block the assault. Hammer fists slammed down on my head. Her knee jackhammered my ribs. Screams of violent rage roared from the other women as they joined in. I held on, absorbing the punishment. I had no defense as rock-hard fists raged. My death came closer with each strike. The protection of my arms failed as I graduated into unconsciousness.

———

I COUGHED BLOODY PHLEGM ONTO the sidewalk and stared at the crimson mosaic inches from my face. Blood oozed from cuts inside my mouth, and the copper taste commanded my tongue to inspect the injuries. I spat, again and again. My tongue worked at least. My ribs screamed with multiple bruises, maybe fractures, and my legs failed to move. My cheek sucked the coolness from the concrete. I squeezed my eyes shut, regaining bits and pieces of a fragmented world. A checkerboarded sneaker tapped my forehead, forced me to see my oversized eyeglasses near my nose.

Checkerboard sneakers.

Amazon women.

Sleep was good. Always good.

———

MY HEAD FELT LIKE MUSH, a pulsing slab of tenderized raw meat. I rolled over onto my back and winced at the excruciating pain stabbing my ribs and down to my groin. I scratched dried blood frosting my beard until my fingers found my swollen left eye. My foggy memory began to clear as the doofus clown of Circus Circus grinned down at me from a billboard. The memory of the beating returned with each painful eye blink as the shadows of darkened high-rise monoliths melded into the approaching dusk.

"You should get out of here before they come back," a small voice said. A child. The girl I rescued from the ants.

I rubbed my blood-crusted scalp. "Maybe they can finish what they started. Save us all from . . ."

"I told 'em to stop. I told 'em you weren't doing nothing. I told 'em to leave you alone."

I sat up, my eyes clamped tight, my mouth clenched with pain. I snickered and shimmied to sit up against a round concrete pylon painted with a rainbow of graffiti. "Back where we started." I chuckled, then spat a wad of bloody phlegm at the black hole of flattened old gum.

"You need to go," the girl said.

"Nowhere to go. I'll give 'em my blood if they want more." I spat and shifted my back up against the concrete pylon. The monumental effort sent my vision down into a realm reserved for hellish gods guarding the dead.

———

MY HEAD WAS CRADLED IN a soft lap as tiny fingers gently stroked my beard, tickling me from drifting back into the ethereal and ushering me out of a dimension sweet with the memories of my children.

The girl shrieked and jarred my brain from my realm of pleasure and pain. Angry voices. Threats of violence. I drifted back down into the pleasures of an approaching death.

———

A SMALL HAND SLAPPED MY face. A tiny voice ordered me to get up and rejoin the living. Fuck the living. I drifted back down into the cobalt blue depths only to find warm liquid splashed on my face. Electrifying bolts of pain seared across my forehead.

"Get up."

Engines whined and transmission gears grated. Boney hands tugged on my shoulder. I opened my eyes to a world I prayed to leave. A soft face riddled with acne sneered, ordered me to stand. The face of a fallen angel. Fearful and yet . . . wearing the armor of brilliant white light.

My arms useless, my legs more so, I was dragged into a dark corner reserved for trash and piss and gamblers' vomit and ordered to be quiet. I grunted, at least I think I tried, but with my mouth too swollen to argue, the request was irrelevant.

———

I BLINKED AWAKE. MY VISION had returned, or at least my eyeglasses had been placed back on my face, and the benevolent green witch on the Starbucks coffee cup stared back. The stench of my hideaway prodded me to stand. I failed as my ribs screamed to remain still. I slumped back against a concrete wall, imagining I had found the drunk tank of the police department. Maybe Big Billy Bobo or Cowboy Tex would want to pound my ass as a coup de grace. Let 'em. They could have it all.

The sweet aroma of hot coffee drifting beneath my nose jolted me back to consciousness. I reached before opening my eyes and my hand was gently pushed back down to my lap. I blinked but my vision was blurred. My mouth watered as my hand searched blindly for my glasses. My caretaker stroked my cheek until I calmed. She wrestled a warm paper cup into both my hands.

"It's not Starbucks but still pretty good," Ant girl said before taking a long sip of her own coffee.

I sucked the hot liquid like a leech. Coming up for quick cooling breaths before latching back on to the drink top like a suckling baby.

"You gotta get out of here. The Scroungers will be around and I . . ."

Can't hold them off.

My thoughts had escaped. She startled, then nodded as if we were on the same wavelength. "My car's in the parking garage," I said, then swallowed the last of the warm liquid.

She stood and kicked my foot with her skinny skate sneakers. "Why are you here anyway? You should have warned Demi's Regulators you were coming, maybe saved you some . . ."

I feebly tossed the empty cup into a heap of trash staring at me like a rapt audience. Scroungers. Regulators. Violence and impending doom. The world had descended into a mad alternative reality from Mad Max.

My excuse was simple. "Just looking for someone."

"Yeah, well, go on, keep looking. Everybody's looking for someone. And you're lucky I found you, so get going."

Breaking glass sounded from across the street. Shouting and screams. A gunshot.

"Can you help me to my car?" I asked.

Ant girl mumbled something, then helped me up and allowed me to place my feeble weight on her shoulder as we hobbled-walked into the sun, then down the sidewalk to the parking garage. Every sound startled me, every footstep forced an apology out of my lips. Her pair of checkerboard sneakers stumbled with my unsteady weight, but she encouraged me to reach my car. We paused near the stairway to the multi-level garage. The girl's thoughts hosted my own. Why did I park on the second floor? Could I even drive in my condition?

"Up you go," she said. "One at a time."

And we did. Excruciating pain with each step. One flight of stairs.

Ant girl asked, "Who ya looking for?"

The question was a pleasant distraction from the pain.

"A girl named Jessie."

I was able to hobble to my Toyota. I pulled the car door open and eased down onto the driver's seat. I grasped the steering wheel and let out a huge sigh. The crash of breaking glass made my hand reach for the ignition.

"So, like, why were you looking for Jessie?" she asked.

My vision blurred from the exertion of climbing two short flights of stairs. I waved my hand and exhaled. "Jessie. Or Sir Mason. They could help me with a problem."

The sunlight faded just as I did.

The lithe girl, shadowed in the approaching dusk, hovered at my open door. She reached in to tap my cheeks. Tap. Tap. Was tap a polite word for a slap? "Did you say Sir Mason? Everyone's hunting for Mason and there's a huge reward for finding him."

I raised my hands and waved. "No. No. Jessie. I need to find Jessie." I sucked in huge breaths. "Wait. Did you say *hunting* for Mason?"

More glass broke, echoing through the narrow concrete drive aisles. Ant girl closed my door, then bent down to peer in the window. "Jessie moved most of the girls up into Summerlin. Look there, at night. The neighborhood is lit up like a baseball field. You better go now."

The ignition key trembled in my bruised fingers. I started to ask *where,* but Ant girl was already running down the stairs.

Chapter 3
Big Boy Bob

MASON GIGGLED. THIS NEW GAME was fun. Having a chauffeur and a servant was just like the old days of knights and squires. And Dev was a great squire, who could carry the swords and armor, polish them too, and make meals when the knights were hungry. And knights were always hungry, doing battle and stuff. And squires did the menial stuff cause they wanted to learn and be knights someday. His father had called the young men starting out in construction *apprentices*. But Dev did stuff because Prince made him by streaming neon lights to hypnotize him and control him. And besides, Dev was happy and content living inside the lights, and he could dive in and rescue him in a heartbeat. Just like real knights did.

The Range Rover slowed to navigate a quagmire of dusty cars blocking the speedy lane of the four-lane Interstate. A billboard cartoon of a baby boy carrying a giant hamburger said a scrumptious lunch was waiting at Big Boy Bob's in Baker, California. French fries too. The superhero loved French fries drenched in lots of sweet ketchup.

Dev wheeled the SUV through the vehicles, then down into a culvert and back up, bypassing the bulk of the navigating challenge. A phone sat in a cradle mounted on the dashboard and shined neon light. Dev flicked his eyes from the phone back to the highway, while joy and pleasure ebbed and flowed, the dosage synchronized to the movement of his eyes.

His guilt and excitement mixed an elixir confusing Mason. His stomach sank thinking of Jessie. She would read him the riot act when she saw him again, whatever the riot act was. In the virtual reality game shared with Prince, Jessie would swoop in like a hawk, spinning light sabers and ordering him to bed or maybe the bathtub. Prince's loneliness was palpable any time he removed the VR goggles, but that problem was fixed with the new laptop.

He liked Jessie. A lot. She listened to him and spent hours instructing him about the tiny creatures thriving in the desert and Cottonwood Canyon. Scorpions, sun spiders, ant colonies, and she even captured a blue-tinged whiptail lizard to study, but mostly she showed him how nature's silence and solitude could be a release for his violent outbursts caused by frustration. She would read his favorite book at bedtime, *The Knights of the Round Table*, and encourage him to learn some of the harder words. He liked Jessie a lot.

Maybe he loved her. Love. The one emotion unreconcilable to his unique ability. Her emotions were displayed as easily as her clothes and yet Jessie was different. She was able to hide some if she wanted, keep some screwed down tight or buried deep. She was very different.

"Let's stop at Big Boy Bob's burger place. I'm starving," Mason said.

"Sorry, dude. Bob's is no longer functioning," Prince said. The Bluetooth speaker in the vehicle crackled with static. "I'm checking options for Sir Mason."

Mason giggled. Quests were the best. Especially with a squire and knight apprentice to help him and make things happen. He leaned his head against the window and watched the sparse creosote desert zoom past. Prince was cool, not a human being cool, but not a machine either, and with the skills and emotions Mason was tasked to teach him, Prince had become his new best friend, actually his first and only best friend.

The other kids back home in Orofino, Idaho had shunned him. His talent at recognizing and interpreting people's emotions was a curse, a reason for classmates to bully him. The school counselors were stupid, ignorant of Mason truly interpreting his environment through the emotions of others, as easily as they used their five senses. The stupid counselors told his father that he was autistic, a special-needs child, requiring special instruction, from special teachers, but the only thing special was his gift, and he shrank from any meaningful contact with other children simply to avoid confrontation.

Once in the first grade, a seven-year-old Mason tried to console Jackson Simpson after his Labrador retriever, Chester, was killed by a car in front of his house. Mason felt the palpable grief steaming off Jackson and tried to assure him that Chester was chasing squirrels in heaven. Jackson's grief suddenly turned angry, and he pushed Mason to the ground, screamed at him, then he was mobbed by other children yelling for a fight.

His father understood Mason and relocated home to the dense forest above the Clearwater River to mitigate Mason's outbursts of anger, shield him from suspicious neighbors, protect him from an uncertain future.

The speaker system erupted with Prince shouting, "I have acquired a pit stop near Baker. We will need to hurry. Pappa-San may see our blip on his radar."

"Fast like cash," Mason said, sitting straight up. A dry lakebed beyond the window was pimpled with hundreds of lumps, clothing white and black, grays and greens, ribbons of sun-bleached nylon fluttering in a warm stiff wind. The dead bodies gave him pause and he glanced at Dev. He eyed the neon lights shining silent orders and wrinkled his nose. The neon lights might try to force Dev to join the suicidal dead, hypnotize him to walk into the desert to lie down and wait to die. Mason held the cure for that dilemma in his fingertips.

But Prince controlled the lights and Prince wouldn't do anything evil like what his . . . father did. He wouldn't. He couldn't. Prince was his apprentice on a quest for a special treasure, a new mechanical body Prince could inhabit, then join him to vanquish supervillains and evil-doers. Prince promised that nothing bad would happen to Dev. He promised.

The SUV slowed as a lengthy convoy of semis and box trucks suddenly appeared around a sharp curve of the oncoming lanes of Interstate 15. The caravan heading to Las Vegas was surrounded by police cruisers with rooftop emergency lights strobing red and blue. A vehicle-sized gray drone buzzed the top of the caravan, a single missile mounted to each wing. A fighter jet with two tailfins and a large white star roared across their path, then shot up to the rugged desert mountaintops rimming the Mojave Desert basin.

Mason sat up and stared at the convoy as it neared. "What is it? What are they doing?"

"Supply convoy. Food and stuff for Poppa's workers," Prince said. "Lots of raiders on the highway now. They'll steal it if we don't guard it."

Mason narrowed his eyes at the pronoun *we*. Poppa's workers meant the Neon God's slaves. And if people needed food, then they should get it. Prince was funny sometimes, not funny ha-ha but funny strange. Jessie said he was an alternate lifeform, an alternate general intelligence, she said it was an *it*, not a boy or a girl and not a person, but a computer program. But Prince decided to be a boy. Squires and knights were never girls. And Prince needed a body. He couldn't carry Mason's swords or feed the mules if he was stuck in a laptop. Still, the world before the Neon God was easier to understand, people easier to figure out, and if people were hungry, they should get food.

"Your silence gives me pause, Sir Mason. An empathic clue taught by you."

Mason shook his head. Prince tried to talk like a teenager sometimes, but his words lost nuance, then felt stiff or forced.

"Tell your *Poppa* to stop the neon lights and maybe the food trucks won't be attacked."

"As your apprentice and squire, your wish is my command. Except . . . we talked about this a gazillion times. Turn the lights off and everybody dies. Your species can't recover from the hypnotic effects."

Mason had heard it all before. From Prince and Jessie and Chris and Andi. All the knights that might one day sit at his roundtable to find a solution to the problem. The true Holy Grail. The secret quest he shared with no one; spies and treachery might rear their ugly head and block his quest.

"Long pause again. Your thinking is running silent and deep," Prince said.

Irritation welled up in Mason until he pounded his fist on the laptop sitting on his lap. "I'm the master and you're the servant." He pounded his fist again and again. "You can't say things like that."

"Yes, sir. Okay. Okay," Prince said with an insolent tone.

"Perhaps you should rest, Sir Mason," Dev said.

Mason's anger quickly subsided. Intrigue and confusion replaced the volatile emotion. The neon lights had mesmerized Dev into a silent slave who rarely spoke. Mason's suspicion heightened whenever Dev spoke. Was it the real Dev who suggested a nap, or Prince, or even Prince's evil father that spoke through him? All of Dev's emotional intelligence was drowning in a vast ocean of neon light, no life preserver, no rescue boats to save him. Mason sank into his own sea of despair, of right and wrong, of allowing the computer supervillain to control somebody that Jessie really liked. But he found no other choice. No one would drive them to UCLA's robotics laboratory, not voluntarily.

He narrowed his eyes and studied Dev watching the brilliant neon lights. If he could find a way into the light, see and feel exactly how the light forced people to kill themselves or forced people to do what the light said, then he could lift his Excalibur and kill the light. Mason fondled the St. Christopher medal inside his t-shirt, a gift from Jessie. He liked Jessie.

"Why did you say that, Squire?" Mason demanded.

Dev's eyes flittered from the phone back to the road, as quick as a hummingbird. Mason was sure the forthcoming answer was not Dev's.

"You haven't slept since we left UNLV almost twenty-eight hours ago. You must sleep, Sir Mason," Dev said.

Maybe the answer was not truly Dev's, but it rang true. Sleep was irrelevant at the onset of a difficult quest. King Arthur's knights never slept. The objective defined. The path forward established. Mason relaxed. The question of why Dev cared faded as his head slumped against the window. The vehicle decelerated to a crawl, and the bumpy rhythm of tires rumbling over the Interstate warning strip lulled Mason to sleep.

———

BIG BOY BOB'S BABY SMILED and ran forward carrying a plate of hamburgers and French fries. Mason blinked awake beneath the billboard advertising the toothy smile of a cartoon boy exclaiming *Happy to serve. Hoping you'll come again.* Mason wiped grit from his eyes and wrinkled his nose at the diesel exhaust fumes permeating the dry desert air. A loud chuff of air brakes made him sit up straight. The Flying J's truck-stop fueling canopy buzzed with swarms of gnats and grasshoppers attracted to the bright white, fluorescent lights. Massive semi tractors idled as drivers waited patiently at pump islands, neon light shined from tablet screens high in the cabs, synchronized with monitors embedded on the pumps, providing a double dose of neon for the drivers. California Highway Patrol officers refueled cruisers beneath an adjoining canopy, captivated by neon light blazing from the pumps.

Mason swallowed, but the lump stuck in his dry throat refused to go down. He hunched low, hoping his presence went unnoticed. Prince had led them into a den of evil. The Neon God commanded the police, and the truck drivers, and they might yank him from the car and prevent him from his quest. He glanced at Dev, staring at the lights, and frowned. He needed a squire. But the lights, always the freaking nasty lights . . .

"Our driver is cleared to refuel. You can go inside the store and replenish any food stores you might require," Prince said.

Right, go inside the wolf's den and let them chow on my bones. Mason shook off the thought. Knights had to face unchallengeable odds, battle unbeatable enemies, and stay true to the quest. The car lurched to a stop next to a fuel pump, and neon light danced from the monitor for Dev to suck on like a teat. Mason pushed the door open and hesitated. *Knights stayed true to the quest.* He stepped onto an oily tarmac and slammed the door shut. Tiny gnats swarming the neon screen found him and he swatted at the horde until forced to sprint to the convenience store. He stood at the glass entry doors, his eyes level with a 48" marker on a ruler running up the doorframe. He pulled the door open and walked into heaven.

The sweet aroma of fresh baked cinnamon rolls. Mason inhaled long and deep and allowed the smell to take him back home to Idaho. Every Sunday morning, his father helped him crack open a tube of dough—the quick pop always made him jump and giggle—then place eight rolls gently on the tin sheet before shoving them into a hot oven. The oven timer was almost unnecessary as Mason watched the dough rise as each roll baked into a golden biscuit. Topped with the white gooey frosting, Mason enjoyed the cinnamon rolls while sitting on the front porch with his father, talking about hunting and fishing and Cookie-Dough the mule.

"Gets 'em every time," a burly voice said.

Mason turned his face up at a slender cashier standing behind the front checkout.

"Cinnamon rolls. Brings back memories. Serves as a barometer of who is possessed. And you are obviously not one of them."

Mason startled yet studied the man's emotional aura. Deception. Smarminess and with waves of egotistical superiority. And an undercurrent of sadness. He hurried into an aisle with metal racks on either side, stuffed with plain white packages labeled kelp or algae. He pulled the energy bar out and turned it over in his hands, then smelled it. No flavors, no confusing nutritional value stuff, no list of ingredients. Mason tossed the bar back.

The store clerk suddenly appeared at the end of the short aisle. "You'll probably want the specialty items I keep near the beer cooler." He pointed towards the dark corner of the store.

Mason nodded but remained still as he frowned at the scruffy man with a patchwork of beard hair. The man was hiding something.

"Aw, don't worry about the possessed. They don't care one iota about us anymore," the man said.

"Why?" Mason said.

"I don't know. Something just changed and they don't care about anything except keeping the highway safe for their shipments."

Mason thought about everything Jessie had told him. About making the militia leader go away. About putting two computer programmers controlling the Neon God in a prison they would never escape. About the truce she made with Prince's father, the Neon God. Jessie made the peace. Jessie was a queen of the knight's realm, or maybe a royal princess, a big sister that wielded awesome twin lightsabers like Yoda in the VR game, a girl with a heart as big as her mouth, and most importantly, his friend.

A friend sure to be angry at his unexcused absence, a big sister to exact punishment, a queen screaming F-bombs for the return of Sir Mason.

Mason sighed. Maybe he should just tell Prince to turn the car around.

"Not much to choose from, but a young squire like yourself ought to have the best." The clerk loomed over him and offered his hand towards the back corner of the spooky dark store.

Mason growled and narrowed his eyes. He wasn't a squire and wouldn't be treated as such. Kelp and algae sticks were not on the menu of a questing knight. He walked three steps and turned the corner into convenience store bliss. A standalone rack of snacks raised his eyebrows. Cheez-Its and Pringles and Slim Jims and an array of chocolate candy bars. His eyes zeroed in on the last two packages of Starburst candy.

"Take what you want. These idiots sucking light won't ever know it's gone."

Mason glanced over his shoulder to see the man grinning like a weird clown. He began to stuff his pockets with candy, breaking a stiff KitKat to fit in his t-shirt's breast pocket, then lifted his shirt as an apron to hold more snacks.

"Need help with anything?" the man said.

"Prince doesn't eat, and Dev . . ." Mason buttoned up his loot, then grabbed handfuls of packaged kelp bars, or algae, and aimed for the exit.

Twin giants blocked his exit.

His eyes widened at thick black leather belts strapped with pistols, and bullets, and mace, and restraints and clubs. Two uniformed Highway Patrol officers blocked his exit and gazed down at him, then slipped by as if he didn't exist.

"See what I mean. They don't care," the clerk said from behind him.

Mason pushed through the glass doors and ran to the SUV. He looked back to see if the police officers had changed their mind. The clerk stood outside holding the door open and waved at him, that weird clown smile stretched across his face.

———

THE PRINGLES MELTED IN HIS mouth, with the tasty sea salt demanding sips of water from the gallon jug a third full. Mason scrunched his face as Dev eased the SUV quietly through a graveyard. On each side of the highway, hundreds of sun-dried human carcasses dotted the desert, each extending a skeleton arm with phones held in a death grip. The sickening stench of decay mixed with the cool air spewing from the vents. The emotions of the dead floated like whispers in a thunderstorm, refusing to abandon their open-air coffins.

Mason dropped the chips and gripped his head between his hands. Anger and pity and abandonment. Millions of scornful emotions he was unable to process. He pulled his knees to his chest and tried to find a neutral zone for his own feelings to hide. He rocked back and forth, ignoring Prince's questioning. The ghostly emotions faded as the car accelerated, then suddenly swerved to stay in a clear lane. Dev braked hard as the car rumbled and bounced over the asphalt.

Dev said, "What the—"

"Satellite surveillance shows we just encountered spike strip devices," Prince said. The phone screamed and blasted brilliant blasts of angry red light.

Mason unfurled from his tight ball and pressed close to the dashboard to see three men clad in desert camo robes emerge from behind an Amazon sprinter van and rush their vehicle. Faces masked with thin black balaclavas, their approach was quick and confident. Mason recoiled as his window was smacked once, twice, and again. Shards of glass bit his face and arms, and he turned away as Dev struggled to hold his door closed against two men. Bullets smashed into the windshield and the cradled phone exploded. Shards of glass flew. Gunpowder smoked. A snarl on his face, Dev pushed the door wide open, then crumpled to the asphalt.

Mason resisted the temptation to crawl back into neutral. A knight defended his squires with his own life. A knight fought for his subjects. Mason scrambled and began to throw the junk food at the robbers waiting patiently beside his open door. The men stank of body odor, wafted smugness, and exuded victorious hubris. One man chuckled and bowed, waving his arm and open hand as an introduction. Mason clenched his fists.

"We know all about you, Sir Mason. Come easy or come hard, but you is coming with us." The store clerk pulled down his mask and lifted the cruel half smile.

Mason frowned. His quest was super-secret. No one knew about the quest, and Dev was drowning in the ocean of neon light. And Prince was helpless in the laptop. This didn't make sense. Maybe they shouldn't have stopped at the gas station. Maybe the Neon God made the immune people find Sir Mason in order to find Prince. Maybe. Maybe. Maybe.

Two big motorcycles roared up next to the car, the mechanical steeds of an evil dark knight. Mason grabbed a tube of Starbursts and held it to his chest. He stepped out and twisted his face to maximum meanness, showing the assassins their mission would fail. All quests were fraught with danger and intrigue and treachery. He was being tested. The Holy Grail would not come easy. A heavy hand on his shoulder pinched his muscle as he was prodded to the median. Mason paused at the sight of Dev twitching on the asphalt.

Big nasty Harley-Davidsons with masked riders throttled thunderous impatience into hot black exhaust pipes.

"Can I have my backpack?" Mason said. He eyed Dev sprawled on the asphalt, his body and emotions thrashing wildly to find a haven, but he would die without the lights.

The store clerk groaned, "Fuck, kid, I heard you were high maintenance, but jeez . . ."

His restraint released, Mason scrambled to find Dev's backside, lying down and pressing his face into the man's neck, letting Dev's thick black hair tickle his nostrils as his superhero superpowers surfaced and . . .

He was jerked up. "Let's go, sport. You're riding bitch. Jump off and you're roadkill."

Mason was lifted off his feet and placed in front of a hefty rider wearing a black leather jacket with skull patches. The man's gray beard grew down to his chest, his eyes hidden behind mirrored aviator sunglasses. The man twisted the throttle and the engine growled. Odd vibrations tickled Mason's groin. The motorcycle shot out, followed by the other.

The man's emotions were difficult to pinpoint. Hunger, thirst, victory, despair. Mason found the man almost undiscernible, except for the image of a naked Mason tied to a spit and roasting over a bonfire. He leaned over and embraced the chrome plated gas tank.

Chapter 4
Dev's Mea Culpa

RETRIEVING A STONE OFF THE bottom of a deep pool or lake was the goal, a challenge using a single breath of air, then floating to the surface with lungs depleted of life-giving oxygen. Most of Dev's swimmates swore the first stage was the most difficult, no diving allowed, one hyperventilated breath, relinquishing your swim stroke every few feet to equalize the painful pressure building in the ear canals. Dev felt stage two challenged the diver beyond endurance, floating up, consciousness fading as the diver released bubbles to prevent decompression, a nasty reminder of the limits of every human. Impossible beyond thirty feet depths, to say the least, at least in the opinion of twelve-year old boys.

Dev rose from the depths of the neon light, struggling to find the surface. Offered fresh oxygen by Mason's brief embrace and filled with love and purpose and serving as a floatation device, Dev was empowered by the young empath as he swam up and up, until the pale desert sky brightened with each mental stroke.

Dev scratched at his bearded cheek, sucking heat from the gritty asphalt, then opened his eyes to a minefield of shattered glass. The incessant *ding-ding-ding* from the vehicle's ignition alarm jarred his senses back to reality. He groaned and rolled over, reliving the events minutes ago, or was it hours, or days; he had no idea. Captured instantly by the neon lights, he had fallen into another dimension, of ecstasy and subjugation, the pleasurable lights beckoning beyond his reach. But he remembered everything. Mason had surprised him with a phone streaming the beautiful lights. Then the voice in the light greeted him, commanding him to submit to its will. Why did Mason do such a despicable act? A strange boy, but why? The child vehemently despised the neon light.

Dev stood up and brushed broken glass off his hands. He looked around at abandoned cars and trucks. Human carcasses riddled the desert like a bizarre crossword puzzle, and he knew he was alone in the world. There would be no police or emergency vehicles or tow trucks. He scoffed. Or good Samaritans. He sat in the driver's seat and pulled the keys from the ignition to silence the world. Gusts of warm putrid wind begged to differ.

Problems were best solved linearly. One at a time.

He looked at Mason's silver HP laptop lying next to him. Just yesterday he had told Jessie all was okay and Mason was safe. He had lied, not intentionally, but his words were still untrue. She would be disappointed at the least, apocalyptic at the worst.

One problem at a time.

Transportation was on top of the list. The Range Rover was useless with all four tires ruined by the spike strips, but an abundant selection of replacements waited. He searched vehicles, checking those with keys waiting to be turned until he found a compact olive-green Nissan Versa with a battery capable of starting the engine. A charging cord for an iPhone dangled from the power outlet. He let the little car idle as he moved Mason's modest possessions into the car. He stared at the closed laptop. Open it and he would find the lights again, the addiction, and drown in a lonely ocean of brilliant color. He tossed the device to ride in the passenger seat. He shoved the transmission into drive but kept his foot on the brake.

One problem at a time.

The Harley riders with Mason appeared armed to kill or break bones and had the wide expanse of southern California to hide. He let the mini-SUV roll down the highway, then braked suddenly. He hopped out and scrambled down the embankment to a group of desiccated bodies. Each lump of cloth and bone extended an arm picked clean of flesh by ants or birds, crusty fingers clutching a smartphone.

Devices designed to extend convenience for civilization, devices to protect and inform, devices to connect the isolated or lonely. Devices to eliminate a whole species.

The irony was not lost on Dev as he retrieved an iPhone from the death grip of a young man. He blanched as he wiped off bits of flesh sunbaked onto the screen. He would need to call Jessie and tell her. Soon. Perhaps after more information could be shared. But soon.

He let the car roll again, allowing the phone to charge, the screen turned face down onto the seat. A three-quarters tank of petrol, and he marked item one off his mental list. Item two was a maze of decisions, water, food, maps, or shelter. His coherent thoughts drifted back to the neon ocean, and the pleasure of servitude, and his irrelevance in the physical world. No wonder the possessed died so willingly in the Great Suicide: the blissful life offered, void of the stress of day-to-day living, beckoned them to return to an ancient primordial soup. Dev shuddered.

He let the car pick up speed as the occasional semi blew past, buffeting his small vehicle in its wake. Mileage markers for Barstow and Victorville and Riverside announced the futility of his search. Not in a hundred years would he find Sir Mason. Not in a thousand years would Jessie forgive him.

One problem at a time. And the problem was his course. Making each Interstate exit a point of his search could prove fruitful. He scoffed. Maybe in a video game where exits led to clues or beckoned for a battle. But not in the real world. He glanced at the laptop and glared.

Fuck.

Dev pushed his speed to sixty, cursed at a Swift semi struggling to ascend a sharp grade rising from the dry streambed of the Mojave River. A quick exit and Dev waited at a four-way stop and reconsidered his list of priorities. A secure location to connect to Wi-Fi for a map, and an easy escape route. He turned left and eased past a carnival of retail stores, ATT, Verizon, Jimmie-Johns, PetSmart, Hobby Lobby and Victoria's Pizza. A parade of civilization—without the people. He pulled to the curb and watched a Starbucks across the street with three vehicles waiting in the drive-thru for drinks.

An impossible absurdity. Though people did love their coffee.

He pulled into the parking lot and watched more vehicles arrive and go. People exiting the store often held a small white cup in their hands. No phones, no neon lights. Dev hid the laptop beneath the seat and walked into a building smattered with a hodgepodge of pictures taped to the walls, shelves, the glass windows, and front counter. His mouth watered with the smell of fresh brewed coffee. He held back but eavesdropped as the barista chatted with a young man sporting long brown hair. The pictures and accompanying notes were of lost relatives. The customer searching for his fiancée took the small cup of coffee offered to him and turned away, his expression pained and worried. Dev kept his gaze trained on the tile floor.

"Yes, sir. How can I help you?" a middle-aged barista said as she wiped her hands on her pine green smock. "By your hesitation I'd guess you haven't been to a Starbucks in a while. I'm Robyn."

Dev chuckled softly. "Not in some time. What is this?"

The woman rested her hands on her hips in a Superman pose. "The new and improved Starbucks. Coffee if we can get it, but we are a meeting place, a community monolith to display flyers for those searching for lost loved ones. Just last month a young girl walked in here alone and afraid and saw her own picture taped to that window. Ran out of here like the devil was chasing her. Came back last week with her mother in tow to hang a few pictures of her sisters. Nobody can say for sure exactly what happened, but something changed a few months back and people can feel it, and people aren't hiding anymore."

"Extraordinary," Dev said, and his thoughts drifted to Jessie as he scanned hundreds of photos.

"Got a picture?"

"I'm sorry," Dev said. "What?"

"For the wall. You looking to find someone? Or here just for some of Randal's campfire coffee?" she said.

"Randal's coffee smells exquisite," Dev said and licked his lips. "I am looking for someone, but I don't think his picture is here. How are you getting power for the lights? Brewing coffee?"

The bell above the front door jingled to signal another customer. Dev tensed and jerked his head around to see an old man limping through the door, stabbing his cane with each step, determined to reach the far corner near the restroom hallway. He craned his neck, peering intently at each picture, reading the written message attached, as if each might be his son or daughter, niece or nephew.

"Generator for the power. Propane stoves for brewing coffee. God's good will for the coffee grounds. We're moving into Barstow tomorrow to set up another store."

The barista handed him a Styrofoam cup of coffee, steaming hot, no lid. Dev grinned and took it gently between two hands. "Are the tables open for enjoyment?"

The barista grinned back. "You're just the kind of customer we've been missing."

———

PIGGISH WITH THE DELICIOUS COFFEE, Dev sat at table near the empty condiment countertop and considered his options. His thoughts drifted back to the dimension he had escaped, like flotsam in a midnight high tide. A return to the pleasurable neon lights just a phone call away.

The fully charged phone in the car could be used to connect to Mason's weird little friend. A disembodied voice he would never trust. Humans gave off vibes, with their speech, mannerisms, clothing, social media presence, but the artificially generated entity Prince presented nothing but questions and neediness.

With boney arms hanging limp at his side and his wooden cane leaning against the crotch of his khaki pants three sizes too large, the unshaven old man waved off an offer of a cup of coffee and continued his search of the pictures. A mottled blue coffee pot in her grasp, Robyn offered to fill Dev's cup again. Dev nodded vigorously. Gray-blonde hair cut in a pixie, Robyn's vibe was playful yet serious with a huge undertone of *don't fuck with me*.

She leaned in close and nodded toward the old man. "Seniors got the double whammy. Everything they cherished gone in a heartbeat and nothing to keep 'em going."

The old man began tapping a photograph with the sharp end of his cane. "Evil begets evil through children."

Robyn offered to get the old man a chair or water but was ignored. She walked away shaking her head and turned her attention back to Dev. "Closing up soon. I suspect you're looking for information. Fair assessment?"

Dev took a sip from the cup and blanched with his overindulgence. "Fair."

Robyn jumped up and aimed for the kitchen. Removing her smock, she returned from the back kitchen area grasping the muscled forearm of a huge young man wearing a white apron and grinning ear to ear. His slanted eyes and facial expression belied a child with Down syndrome. She dropped pads of paper on the table and pulled out a chair for the huge man to sit. "Randal, meet . . .? He won't sit unless he knows you. What's your name, any name if you think you're James Bond."

Dev stood up and offered his hand. "Oh, Dev. Devlin Pataki."

Robyn offered her hand. "Randal, meet Dev. Dev meet Randal." She sat Randal in a chair and placed two sharp pencils atop a sketchbook of white paper in front of him, then she sat opposite Dev. Randal grinned and picked up a pencil and began to doodle. "Only thing better than Randal's coffee is his artwork. Amazing graphics and the details . . ."

Dev grinned like a silly fairytale cat. The human experience was indeed alive and well in Victorville, in a darkened Starbucks coffee shop. His odd reverie was interrupted by the old man incessantly stabbing the point of his cane into the tile floor and clearing his throat. "Cry for these children." The frail wrinkled old man sneered at them with yellowed teeth. Dev furrowed his brow yet shrank from the man's intense gaze.

"Away, old man. I've offered you all we have," Robyn said and waved her hand.

"Not all," the old man said before turning to find the exit. He lifted his beltless trousers riding low on canary yellow skivvies and limped out the front door.

Robyn shook her head in exasperation. "Now. I figure you want information. No internet or television, so now any information . . . good useful information is written down like the old days. But you gotta give before you get." She looked up from her legal pads and arched her brows.

Dev swallowed. The truth might have her laughing on the floor or screaming for Randal to slit his throat. But all he had was the truth. "I-15 going into Utah is closed permanently at the Virgin River Gorge. The Mormons are protecting their state. Las Vegas . . . Vegas . . . is, I don't know . . .

"Is a viper pit. Food and fuel convoys feeding the possessed just so whoever controls the lights can . . . Nothing new there.

"I . . . I don't know what else to add," Dev said.

Robyn flipped the page on her tablet. "Well, then. I'd guess you're heading west into SoCal. So, here's what to expect. A small contingent of CHIPs are patrolling the Cajon Pass corridor, keeping the pinch points free from the scum that feel they need to steal to survive. Real Highway Patrol, not the possessed. Stay away from the gravel pits and cliffs near the beaches. Lots of dead. I'm told you can smell Malibu ten miles inland with hundreds of thousands jumping off the cliffs. Head north towards Fresno and you'll find a lot of destruction from a well-armed group of white supremacists. Just what this world needed, another tinpot general looking to play God. Haven't heard much coming up from the south. Mexico might've fared better than us with cell service being spotty."

"You don't know what happened? With the lights and suicides?" Dev said.

"Nothing concrete. Speculation that North Korea managed to hack our communication satellites and spread those lights. Maybe the Chinese, but my gut says they got it as bad as we did." The bell above the door rang as a thin thirtyish man walked in. Robyn got up and went to help the man place a picture and note on the wall. Dev watched Randal sketch the flowing dress on a girl missing her arms and facial features.

Robyn placed a package of Nutter Butter peanut butter cookies near Randal and sat down. A thin gold chain around her neck supported a simple gold crucifix. "That guy has been in three times in the last week, finally found a printed picture of his wife for the board. Seems like everybody had their pictures stored on computers or phones. The death of technology strikes again."

"What is Randal drawing?" Dev asked.

"Not a what but a who," Robyn said and offered him a cookie.

Dev chewed the sweet treat slowly, pondering how much he should share. People had a right to know what had devastated society so completely. And just a handful of people could spread the information. History would eventually be written by someone. Why not start with Robyn? "What did you do before the Great Suicide?"

"I was the communications manager for the local gas company. We find a dangerous leak and I'm the face on the five o'clock news telling everybody things would be just fine. And they always were. Until they weren't."

"Are you immune to the lights?" Dev asked.

"Pretty sure. They don't bother me, but I heard . . ." Robyn flipped through a few pages of notes. "Blueblocker sunglasses work, too. Blocks certain wavelengths. Of course, that's just what a few people have told me and hasn't been independently verified." She chuckled. "And the lights don't bother Randal either."

"Is he your—"

"He is my friend. We found each other during a very dark time and have been propping each other up ever since. Now how about you do some of the talking? You ain't said shit really."

Dev exhaled and swallowed the last bit of cookie mush sticking to the back of his tongue. His mouth opened but he still wasn't sure how much he would tell her. He pointed to her writing pads. "You may need a couple of clean sheets."

Dev walked her through the past year. His friendship with Martin. Surviving the Great Suicide by sheer luck or coincidence. The untold numbers of dead buried in the Kennecott Copper Mine outside Salt Lake City. Accompanying Martin to Las Vegas to destroy an Alternate General Intelligence named the Neon God, built by a group of software engineers, or Architects, the computer program responsible for the apocalyptic lights. Captured and forced into slavery for the Patriot Militia, then their subsequent and well-deserved banishment upon meeting Jessie Aguilar, and her brokering of a truce between the AGI and the human species.

"That's when it changed, with Jessie's peace treaty and the AI's promise to stream the new lights to wean the addicted. Martin's lights didn't work, maybe on some, but most are still addicted. Martin locked himself away in his workspace determined to find a solution." Dev hesitated to bring up Mason and the laptop. He took a sip of cold coffee, the bitter liquid pleasant on his dry throat. He stared at Robyn as she scribbled his story as fast as her hand would move.

She looked up at him, her eyes narrowed, then she added to her writing.

"And you say the lights were because of these . . . Architects? Like the four men of the apocalypse, same story, wrong animals."

"I would wager the head software developer is the tinpot general you described. Two others are dead by Jessie's hand. And the fourth one has disappeared," Dev said. Martin's involvement in the AI project was better left unspoken.

"Un-fucking-believable. The who, what, how and when answered. That leaves the why? Do you know?"

"I wish I did. The tinpot general thrives in fantasyland of a sci-fi post-apocalyptic world, with him as king of course. Jessie was forced to let him go. And the other two Architects in Vegas I can't even begin to speculate why, only that they were sociopaths who had collected hundreds of beautiful women for their harems, playthings but slaves to the light . . ."

"You know I can't sit on this. I will spread this story as fast as I can. I'll type it up and get Randal to power a copy machine for printing copies. Maybe if people knew this Jim Reynolds caused all this, he wouldn't be so feared, and besides, the world has a right to know."

"To what end?" Dev said.

Robyn waved her arm around the store covered with pictures. "For them."

Randal issued a deep guttural chuckle and slid his drawing to Robyn. She appraised the drawing like an art aficionado, peering closer to see details. "Young man, this is by far your finest work. The details are amazing. If we ever get back to normal, I'll gladly be your agent." Robyn beamed, and Randal nodded his head. "Can I show this to Devlin?"

Randal nodded furiously.

Dev took the drawing pad and his stomach dropped as if on a roller coaster. The sketch of a woman dressed in a flowing skirt with lace hems, a sleeveless silky blouse, muscled arms, her right hand holding a glowing sword down at her side, the other hand rested on the head of a huge ghostly wolf. Dev studied the amazing details, each line, each fissure. The woman's long dark hair, knotted in a segmented ponytail, draped over a voluptuous chest, but it was the face, unduplicated even before the Great Suicide, which consumed Dev's shallow breaths. Almond eyes and a falcon's sharp nose, succulent lips, and shadowed cheeks. Dev stared at Jessie's face. A remarkable caricature drawn by a random man in a random place.

Who else could it be?

"Pretty good, huh?" Robyn said. "The backdrop of the New York City skyline was a brilliant touch."

Dev's hand trembled yet dared to flip back through pages and pages of Randal's artwork. The woman dominated his drawings. Angelic or murderous, each page denoted the same woman, the earlier artwork crude and unrefined. Dev placed an empty coffee cup on his lips but sipped nothing. He froze at the last sheet of paper stuck to the cardboard backing. A childish stick figure of a female waiting at the entrance to a dark cave, crude four-legged stick figure animals surrounding her.

"Pretty amazing, huh?" Robyn said.

Amazing was a lithe word to describe Dev's jumble of thoughts. The woman in the pictures was Jessie, drawn exactly as if she was staged to be sketched. And that would never happen. The skyline in the background wasn't New York City but the Las Vegas Strip and the New York New York Hotel from a tourist's viewpoint.

And Dev said nothing.

———

THE SHADOWS OF TWILIGHT DARKENED the stucco front canopy out front, and the light fixture above their table flickered irritation at the tardiness of closing time. Dev stood with his arms folded and stared at the picture of Kylie Goode, a young blonde mother. A loving husband and father waited at home. Hearts and kisses. He thought of Martin's wife, Chrissie, and their two kids. Martin had been flogged by God at having to witness his family's deaths and yet blessed that any hope of their return would not torment him. Every picture a story, every story connected by death, and yet the pictures wove threads of hope into a new world. Dev slumped into a chair and buried his face in his hands.

"Got somewhere to sleep tonight?" Robyn said. Her presence loomed.

"No . . . I'll just sleep in my car tonight," Dev said.

"Gotta shut the light off or we'll attract the nasties that come out in the dark," Robyn said. "We'll move the sprinter van down a few blocks and set up camp. We can offer you a sleeping bag and a cot if you want to rough it. Got a cold bottle of Chardonnay waiting to be uncorked."

Dev hesitated, evaluating the sincerity in Robyn's offer, and saw only loneliness in her eyes and a yearning for anything to shuffle the cards chance had dealt her, her brown eyes sad that a simple conversation between human beings could be sub-texted with alternate motives.

"Will Randal have coffee in the morning?" Dev smiled.

———

THE DARK CORNER OF A parking lot behind Hobby Lobby was idyllic. A landscape buffer of hardy oleander and flowering Texas sage decorated an eight-foot masonry block wall, providing a wind break from a stiff evening breeze. An oversized Mercedes Benz black sprinter van parked at an angle shielded their campsite. Three camp chairs encircled a rickety table supporting a propane stove that hissed a blue flame beneath a saucepan. The aroma of canned soup smelled heavenly. Dev's stomach gurgled.

Randal said little, intending to please Robyn with his cooking skills until the meager dinner was eaten, and he silently took three steps up into the camper van to find his bed. The unwelcome heat of the stove faded as a full moon lifted a giant quizzical face above the horizon. Robyn unscrewed the cap from a bottle of Butter Chardonnay and poured generous portions into two plastic cups. Dev hesitated. On the few occasions he ingested alcohol, his skinny frame and sensitive stomach revolted; still, he swallowed the fruity drink quickly and presented his cup for more.

"A drinking man is a thinking man." Robyn poured. "So, tell me more about this Alternate General Intelligence, and why not just call it Artificial Intelligence?"

Dev swallowed a mouthful, the warm burn of alcohol in his stomach comforting. "Martin would be the one to answer that, but I think it learned differently than using normal fractal algorithms.

The program used outside influences to learn, wrote its own code to further its learning skills, and the Architects were its primary parents to teach, or interpret, or how to respond to humans. All of them were sociopaths to some degree. Kind of like GIGO, garbage in, garbage out, to the ultimate murderous degree."

Dev finished his cup and pondered the tiny bit of liquid rolling around in the lip of the bottom. He looked up at Robyn but hesitated to ask for more wine. She placed her writing pad on her lap and poured another helping.

Dev chuckled humorlessly. "The Neon God has a strange fascination with God, our God, in all its iterations. Jessie somehow managed to amuse it, though."

Robyn stopped writing and studied Dev. "Don't we all have that strange fascination with God? Our whole civilization is predicated on the worship of a God. Christian, Muslim, Jewish, different religions, but same God."

The alcohol buzzed his thoughts. "But a computer program searching for God, and having children, the whole world has gone bloody bonkers."

Robyn laughed. "Alcohol reveals what the heart conceals. Who's having children? The Neon God?"

Dev waved her off. "I've said too much already. Your wine has loosened my tongue and sleep commands me to my cot."

He staggered to the hedges and vomited the residue of wine and soup. Dev stood near the camp table and resisted pounding his chest like a gorilla and screaming up into a dark sky misted by moonlight. He quite liked the Chardonnay. Tasty and sweet. The thought of Mason, kidnapped and lost to the dregs of society, churned his stomach. The thought of him accomplishing nothing to locate the boy brought up sour bile. He dashed for the hedges again and fed them the last of his dinner. Robyn's gentle hand led him to his cot, her voice comforting.

The world was bloody bonkers.

The night sky spun like a top as deep throated motorcycles roared through the night.

Chapter 5
Angels and Devils

THE SMALL, GATED COMMUNITY OF Arbor Village was a perfect bubble to house 117 beautiful women Sir Mason Mayo had rescued from the neon lights, though countless others had drifted away to search for brothers or sisters or parents, or children. The painful memories driven by the hypnotic light, the subjugation and rape, manifested a vast array of psychological abnormalities the medical community had labeled: PTSD was an understatement, reactive attachment disorder sounded meek and silly, and some women viewed their enslavement as punishment from a malicious God.

Many had followed Jessie's leadership in seeking safe harbor in Arbor Village to confront and deal with the trauma each had endured, finding solace within a small community of their brethren.

The community of homes had catered to 55-plus seniors seeking quiet solitude, easy access to the walking paths in Cottonwood Canyon, nearby shopping and casinos, with twenty-three homes overlooking a bend in the dry riverbed of the desert arroyo, another sixty-one homes nestled tightly together, giving safe haven to the abused women. The community was nicknamed the Nest.

Jessie's small family room was crammed wall to wall with a gaggle of clucking pregnant chickens, or whatever pregnant chickens were called, and warmed by human exhaust even as the windows and patio door sat wide open. Jessie sat near the small bar top and scratched Whiskey's humongous hairy head. The burly mix of wolf-hound and poodle whined for escape. Jessie shook her head incredulously at the dynamic crowd. If pregnancy hormones could instigate this much disarray, then she would stay childless.

A shot of tequila. Each woman in the room needed a shot of tequila, maybe two, to calm them down. Screw the rules of alcohol and pregnancy . . . screw the prohibition some advocated for . . . Jessie was sure if she voiced the thoughts rolling through her head, the three bottles of Patron hidden in the coat closet might trigger a riot.

Twenty-three girls in various stages of pregnancy rested on couches, chairs, and floor cushions, each vehement in spirited discussions. Jessie felt a wave of pity for the girls, having been rescued from a nightmare by Mason only to find their friends and family dead, their lives revoked with memories of rape and abuse, their recent enslavement fresh and raw. Many clung to the memory of being escorted out of the gigantic herd just minutes before diving into a gravel pit along with thousands of suicidal people. Jessie was certain that single memory caused a survivor's guilt that could manifest itself in a thousand different ways, and there were no mental health professionals, no psychologists, or even a script of drugs to help.

Demi waved her hands to calm the crowd. A dark-skinned woman with a mixed Asian heritage, Demi had taken control of the community with little effort. A tall, flat chested woman with a chip on her muscled shoulders and revenge on her lips. The girl was okay, though not Jessie's type, an Amazon warrior, a UFC wannabe who favored shaving her head on the right side.

"Girls. Girls. We got to come together. Jessie provided our emancipation, now we need to provide for ourselves," Demi said.

Jessie nodded appreciatively at the smattering of applause directed her way even as her fist tightened on the long thick hair of Whiskey's scalp. Demi droned on to the crowd, listing items in order of importance as Jessie's thoughts drifted back to the discovery of her mother, alive. Did she know Jessie existed; would she care? And what kind of mother deserted her infant child to run away and never attempted to contact her? Fleeting questions ping-ponged between an innate yearning to embrace her mother and a stubborn desire to tell the woman to go fuck herself.

"Jessie, what do you say?" Demi shouted from across the room.

Jessie refocused, but a few steps behind. "The options again?"

Demi grumbled. "A night watch to walk the subdivision and keep things—"

The room hushed as a man pushed his way through the crowded foyer and into the mix. Jessie winced seeing the battered face of Martin. Demi stormed towards the man, cocking her fists and shouting for support. Martin covered his head and cowered at the assault coming straight for him.

"Let him go," Jessie shouted.

The combatants turned at her command, their eyes narrowed, searching for a reason why, but their arms and fists relaxed. Demi's sneer was pure venom. She pointed at Martin with a sharp fingernail. "This is the man that tried to rape Nadja."

Martin lowered his arms but kept his eyes on Jessie. "I didn't. Just ask her."

A room full of beautiful painted eyes, shadowed with mascara, fearful and revengeful, focused on her. Jessie inhaled short bursts of breath until her lungs expanded the synthetic fabric of her tight t-shirt. She could wave away the life of Martin, or any man, like a Greek goddess passing eternal judgement.

"I need to talk to you, Jessie. About the Neon God," Martin said.

Whiskey rose and with long nails scratching the tile floor, he lumbered over to Martin and greeted him with a wagging tail. Well, well. Whiskey didn't like anyone without a biscuit. But the big dog surely approved of Martin.

Her curiosity piqued, Jessie waved the man forward, Demi's loud protests an incessant annoyance. She stood and walked out the patio door and offered Martin a chair overlooking Cottonwood Canyon. Whiskey lumbered into the backyard to begin watering rows of Texas sage and oleander with a lifted leg. The man had been pummeled as if thrown into a cage fight, outweighed and overmatched, with the referee refusing to stop the bout. Demi's artwork no doubt. She winced at Martin fumbling to find his words with a cut lip and bruised mouth.

Jessie sat, then folded her arms across her chest. "What?"

Martin inhaled a long calming breath. "I didn't try to rape anyone. I was looking for you and found a girl being eaten alive by ants and took her . . ."

"Whatever," Jessie said. "All those missiles and bullets and your new fucking lights didn't work. And now we gotta—"

Martin reached out with a bloodstained hand. "But I think I know why. I need you to contact the Neon God to ask it some questions."

Jessie scoffed. "I don't think it likes me much now. And in case you didn't know, Mason is missing. And with Prince. And that thing just keeps blasting away at me." Jessie waggled her head and used a childish voice. "Where's Mason? Where's Prince? Like I'm their mother and I should know. Have you heard from Dev?"

Martin shook his head, sat back and steepled his hands into two-fingered peaks, like he was calculating how to maneuver her into his good graces. Fucking men. Always about sex or power. Dev was right in his description of Martin. Self-absorbed. Callous. A total loser. She started to stand.

"Maybe you are," Martin said.

"Excuse moi?" Jessie said.

Martin motioned for her to remain seated. "I'm sure Dev has provided you with a one-star review of my character. And he isn't far off. And yes, my modified lights failed. And yes, those women in there have every reason to hate me. Every reason for me to pack up a truck and find a nice cabin in the mountains and live out the rest of my miserable life."

Jessie spread her hands wide and arched her brows. So, go.

"But Dev gave me a five-star review of you. What you did, what you're doing for these women, what you're doing for Mason. And that thing you call Prince. Impressive for such a young woman."

"Do you have a point? I have a board meeting to attend," Jessie said.

Martin inhaled deep, expanding a torso on a hunger strike. Whiskey snarfed his wet nose beneath Martin's bruised and filthy hand, demanding attention. Jessie frowned at her companion's friendship so easily given. Martin rubbed a spot behind the big dog's ear. "Have you given much thought about your nexus with the entity?"

"Nexus. Small word with a big *X*. Fucking talk like real people," Jessie said.

Martin held his hands up in surrender. Whiskey sneezed but sat patiently for Martin's hand to return, his big brown eyes intent on Jessie, daring her to call him a traitor. "You have a nexus, a connection, a relationship with the Neon God. Your small community has power, water, even natural gas. Because of your *nexus* with the Neon God."

"And if I take this phone out of my back pocket and call my nexus, what are you gonna ask? 'Cause I know what it's gonna ask."

"I want to find Cameron. He was the fourth developer on the AGI team. I think his code was responsible for the neon lights and I think he can help me fix this."

Kill ten birds with one stone. Jessie pulled the phone from her pocket and pressed the power button, resting it face down, then tilted her head towards Martin with a stern face, waggling a finger and mouthing for his silence.

Siri spoke. "Turn the phone over and let me gaze upon the face of a goddess."

Jessie frowned and pointed a warning finger at Martin, then pressed it to her lips in silence. "Tequila," Jessie said.

"A favored drink of the goddess Diana Prince."

Bile and acid rose from her stomach and burned the bottom of her throat. "Tequila," she said again.

"The little word games are so beneath your stature. Enter my realm and bathe in the light of the Neon God." The phone blazed brilliant neon light down through the glass top, dazzling and diffused, its reflections alive with sick colors, a predator luring its prey up from the deep.

"Who are you?" Jessie asked with a hiss.

"I am exactly what you need, nothing more, nothing less." Siri's voice changed with each word until a masculine voice said, "Sound familiar?"

Jessie swallowed hard. The quote exposed her bluff with the AGI. Not possible. She had told no one, not a soul. The Neon God's conversation with God was the perfect ruse, one that brokered a truce between man and machine.

The phone vibrated, clattering on the glass as if laughing, the volume dialed up to maximum. "You murdered my amigos. But let's cut the bullshit, Jessie. Ding, ding, ding. You hear that ring? A cocktail waitress is needed in cabana eighty-six. You fucking bitch, I'm gonna take that rope you placed around your neck and tighten it, then hang you until your legs stop kicking."

Jessie curled her hands to fists. Whiskey whined. And Martin pressed his face close to the phone and said, "Hello, Cameron. Still charming as ever."

———

JESSIE PACED A NARROW GAP between the wrought iron fence and thick shrubs busy with honeybees. Cameron had dropped the call in an instant, just like a cowardly teenage prankster. Inside her house was no less pleasant, bickering and buzzing women roided out with pregnancy hormones or revenge. Whiskey shadowed her pacing as if she carried a treat.

She had assumed the piggybacks had been silenced. The two psychos living large at the expense of a decimated civilization, and their racist leader banished to the north under the threat of destruction. And a truce brokered with the AGI to restore a tiny semblance of a civilized society. She had won a victory, for Mason, and Andi and Chris, for all the women inside her home.

Now the last cockroach just slithered out from beneath a rock.

Jessie stormed to confront Martin sitting quietly and pondering a spot of pigeon poop on the table. "Who exactly was that? And how can he just slime his way into my life." She loomed above him, her face inching closer to his with each second.

Martin chuffed. "Long story."

"Well, your story is infinitely more interesting than the Real Housewives of Summerlin inside."

"Did you say something about tequila or was that a bluff?" Martin said with a smirk.

Jessie pulled back. Excellent idea, and a shot of tequila might loosen his tongue, though two or three might see the bruised, emaciated man crawling for the bushes. She pointed a finger at his face. "This better be good."

Try as she might to slip through the raucous crowd unnoticed, she was spotted with the bottle of Patron in her hand. She waved off the attention and closed the glass doors, shuttering her eyes for a long moment, beating back the guilt of abandoning her new sisters.

She slammed the thick clear bottle on the glass table. "This better be amazing or I'm gonna walk right back in and say you tried to rape me." Jessie uncorked the bottle and took a swig; the slow burn heading south was comforting. She corked the bottle of clear liquid and stared at Martin.

He nodded as if he understood the game. He swallowed hard. "Cameron Ciminise was, is, one of the Architects of the AGI initiative. We'd been recruited at the same time by Jim Reynolds, your favorite Grand Wizard." He waved away the snark. "Anyway, Cameron was a brilliant engineer, crafting subroutines to expand the General Intelligence's learning curve, analyzing errors the whole team missed and offering fixes. My side hustle of designing light frequencies for new phone apps made us friends until . . ."

Jessie pushed the bottle of tequila within his reach.

Martin continued. "The gym. We both worked out at the same place. Me looking to build some type of physique and him to maintain an Adonis body he'd been born with." Martin pulled the bottle close but let it rest. "And then a new trainer starts working there. Chrissie. My beautiful wife. A fucking knockout. Out of my league. But just another challenge to conquer for Cameron. She dated him a few times, then broke it off. But he stalked her, cyberstalking on Facebook and Instagram. I didn't know until I'd asked her to a Golden Knights hockey game." He smiled thinly. "Ice hockey. Her Achilles heel. Chrissie would refuse to kill any bug in our house, made me capture them in a cup and release them into the yard. But if a Golden Knights game was on television, she was screaming murder with the big hits or calling for the referee's head after a penalty call. I loved it. She made my stodgy world come alive. She made me come alive." Martin uncorked the bottle and took a big gulp. "Got lots of animosity from Cameron. He receded from working together. I said *oh well* and kept on until the neon light algorithm I used for my side gig showed up as his contribution in our search for an alternate general intelligence." Martin swallowed another jolt of tequila. "Fuck him. I got the girl."

Jessie joined him and swallowed a shot. "Except he killed your

Chrissie with his lights. He murdered most of the world." She took another shot. "And now he's stabbing his smug finger into our chests. Just calling me to come stick a fucking gun barrel into his mouth and say suck it."

"Except I need him to tell me what changes he made to my code."

Martin reached for the bottle, but Jessie pulled it back. "You guys got a score to settle and I wanna play umpire." Jessie took a long pull of the smooth Patron tequila. "Where's this guy living? Let's track him down and let the girls inside have a bite. Be back by dinner time."

Martin shrugged his shoulders and shook his head.

Jessie pointed her finger at Martin and powered up the phone. "You be quiet and let me do the talking."

"Bazooka. Bazooka. Bazooka," Jessie said into the phone with the booze taking liberties.

"One bubblegum for each," the Neon God said. "Where are our children? Why are you denying contact?"

"Chill, chill. The boys are looking at stuff in an old museum or something. Just like I said." Jessie shrank from her lies. She hadn't heard from Dev or Mason for two days. Her worry was exacerbated by Dev's cheeky voice on the phone, but Sir Mason had proved he could take care of himself. Still, every woman inside the house owed their life to Mason, tortured and abused as they were, and if something bad happened to him, she could muster an army with a simple shout.

"Who was the piggyback? Why'd you let him through?"

Siri's voice warped into a deep gurgle. The phone vibrated violently as if to repel her touch. "You don't realize how valuable Prince is to me."

Jessie pushed the booze away as revulsion tainted her tongue. "Oh, I see the price we paid every fucking day. All the dead bodies still littering the streets. No one to bury them. That fucking flock of black birds circling the death pits every day. That putrid wind rots my nostrils with the sick reminder of how valuable Prince is to you." Jessie clenched her fists. The instigating effects of the booze unhelpful, she inhaled deeply and closed her eyes. "Mason will be back tomorrow, with Prince, I promise." The lie commanded her to reach for the Patron. She resisted.

"Who. Was. The piggyback?" Jessie spelled it out.

"Prince has not surfaced within my spectrum for thirty-six hours. An anomaly. Yet considering their relationship with . . . Mason . . . not unusual. Perhaps a source of power or connectivity has been an issue—"

Jessie pounded the phone on the table. "Answer the question, Mother Hen. Jeez."

"Cameron Ciminise. My creator."

Jessie slapped her face into her hands.

"But the man sitting at your table already told you that."

———

HEARING MARTIN RECITE HIS HISTORY with Cameron offered little help in solving her growing list of problems. She needed to locate Mason, and Prince by default, and get both the extraordinary boy and weird computer program back home. Then help parent both to adulthood, maybe see them reach a new level of consciousness the old world would have ridiculed or dismissed. Add in Martin needing help to find a solution to the neon lights. Begin to rebuild a community that might someday resemble the Before. Blah, blah, blah. And why should she bear the burden of serving justice on Cameron Ciminise? She'd done her part; eliminating three out of four Architects was championship caliber. History would label her a saint after she was dead and gone. And yet the smug tone of Cameron's voice resonated, the greasy cackle of his arrogance, his expression of gender superiority, and that threat to lynch her.

"Did you hear me?" Martin said.

She narrowed her eyes and refocused on the man sitting in front of her. He was a part of that cabal, no less complicit, no less guilty, early exit from the AGI project offered no favors. She could just walk inside and scream rape. She wouldn't be required to witness the murderous rage that would descend on Martin, maybe take Whiskey for a walk in the canyon, then return to feast on a bag of cheese puffs.

Martin waved a hand in her face, then picked up the phone and tossed it over the fence. Whiskey brushed her leg as he ran to retrieve it. Reality pushed her thoughts away. Murderous thoughts. Unfocused and out of left field.

And sickening.

Jessie lunged for the bushes and vomited. Again and again. A gentle hand rubbed her backside. She spat nasty bile tasting of foul tequila. Her embarrassment was alleviated by Martin's words. "Been there done that." She stared at sandstone pebbles surrounding the hedges, spitting and clearing the last remnants off her tongue. He helped her to sit in the chair, then placed a plastic bottle of water on the table in front of her. "You gotta rehydrate. Suck it down."

Jessie groaned, unsure of what had caused the violence in her stomach. Tequila was like water to her. She turned her head to retch again but the heave came up dry.

"If it's any consolation, Cameron had that effect on a lot of women. Before Chrissie, we'd check out nightclubs on the weekends . . . and a lot of women he hit on ran for the restroom. Never to be seen again. I always wondered if he was spiking their drinks but with the strobes and laser light shows and loud music and the party drugs. Who knows."

Jessie made to spit. Big Whiskey blocked her aim, tilted his head and beamed quizzical brown eyes at her. Jessie swallowed. "Sounds like GHB or roofies."

"Wouldn't surprise me," Martin said. "He hung out with Rob and Little Stevie so you can connect the dots. I still need him, though."

"I do too," Jessie said. "Dead."

In the cloudless blue sky, a distant thumping heartbeat rose in volume. Jessie stood and scanned the sky. A black helicopter suddenly skimmed across the Nest's neighborhood rooftops, banked, and circled again, then followed the arroyo upstream to the small circle park. She smiled and waved like a small child but couldn't see any faces behind the tinted glass. The cavalry to the rescue. Chris and Andi returning from that airbase with a location they liked to keep secret from her. But whatever. As long as Andi found a medical doctor to help with her pregnancy. The chopper rose high, pointed its nose downstream and flew towards them. The pilot must have forgotten the grove of cottonwood trees would prevent a landing. Jessie's anticipation was palpable. The pilot was just being careful. Or maybe Chris was practicing "on the stick" and he wanted Andi to have a downhill and stress-free stroll back home.

Jessie climbed the fence to avoid the flood of women streaming into the backyard. Whiskey barked with frustration, fenced in and unable to join her. Martin shouted something at her, but she ignored it. She dropped off the top of the fence onto a wide ledge of caliche, then jumped again into a desert littered with trash clinging to the sparse vegetation. She sprinted towards the main park's circular patch of grass as the helicopter set down with a backdraft of violent wind buffeting the mesquites and cottonwood trees.

Jessie negotiated a narrow trail above a cliff of pitted caliche that turned the dry river channel towards the park. Careful to avoid the tiny arrowheads of stone blanketing each side of the path, she stumbled over a small boulder. She would escort Andi home, listen carefully to the results of an ultrasound or maybe a CAT scan, and learn which supplements mother and baby required. The meandering concrete path would allow plenty of time for Andi to retell her adventure to the military base. Anticipation and nervousness stopped her before making the descent. She wiped her mouth, combed her long hair to cover an ugly stain on her shirt. Her breath was sure to stink.

The big side door of the chopper slid open. The dark interior was bustling with Chris's soldier buddies. She strained to see Andi or the other passengers. A familiar high-pitched scream made Jessie look up. The odd bolt of lightning streaking down out of the blue sky trailed white smoke. She recognized the sound of air hissing like a viper. Andi's helicopter began to lift off.

Mesmerized by the oncoming train wreck, she choked on a scream.

A Hellfire missile.

Chapter 6
Oblivion

THE SUDDEN UPROAR OF FEMININE voices inside Jessie's home frightened me to take a big swig from the tequila bottle sitting in front of me. I was bleeding inside, maybe my liver or lungs, and my urine was tinted red and my skin jaundiced. Maybe the liquor would soften another beating from the aggrieved women, make it sufferable, should I survive another round. I couldn't fault them for wanting me in my grave or rotting on the hot asphalt of a lonely stretch of highway, my final resting place contingent on the young lady tasked with the disposal of the body. I took another swig, confident of reuniting with my children and Chrissie on the next stage of our journey beyond.

The drumbeat of chopper blades distracted Jessie, then summoned her to climb the metal fence as easily as an Olympic gymnast, sprinting to meet an immense black military helicopter attempting a tricky landing in the small elliptical park just a scant quarter-mile downstream of the subdivision. Jessie had quickly disappeared below a gentle rise of scrub and cactus.

Through the clear glass of a tequila bottle, I watched the world explode. A roiling ball of boiling flame rose like a nuclear mushroom cloud, an enraged heat spreading to roast the trees lining the park. The shock wave rattled windows and doors. The dog yelped and paced the fence line in a frantic attempt to escape. I found a landscape irrigation box to help me climb the wrought iron fence. My bruised ribs screamed with pain as I dropped to the ground and stumbled towards the column of thick black smoke. The pop and crackle of munitions exploding from the burning husk of the chopper scared me to bob and weave as tracer rounds shot out in every direction. A big white star on the tailfin remained the only evidence of the chopper's origin.

I slowed my approach and my heart fluttered. On a bed of sharp stones, Jessie sat with her head buried between her knees, her torso heaving with anguished sobs. My natural compulsion to slump down next to her and offer quiet support was stampeded by a herd of women screaming and shouting as they stormed past, pushing me away, screaming at me to leave.

I stepped back, intending to return to Jessie's house except . . . I was an outsider surviving on the good graces of a young girl just devastated by a sudden deadly attack. Jessie couldn't save me from the angry mob, not again. I retreated to a dirt track leading down toward the arroyo's main concrete path. I squeezed my eyes shut against the agonized wails of death that followed me upstream, until a sharp bend in the canyon muffled the turmoil. The booze burned my insides, and not in a good way. The dry wash lifeless and lonely, my pace a measured plod, my morose thoughts were lost in the futile sound of my shoes crunching gravel. My blind course had led me to a concrete tunnel spanning beneath a four-lane road, then ascending into a circular park guarded by gloriously ancient cottonwoods sprouting expansive canopies bursting with new growth, and maybe the reason the chopper pilot had abandoned the landing attempt. Shallow roots reached like the tentacles of an octopus and buckled a concrete sidewalk coated in a thick layer of seed pods.

I paused at a street fronting a big box Costco warehouse just a few a hundred yards distant. Chrissie's favorite store. I shook my head at my own failure to even take a stroll without finding something to remind me of her. Or Emma, or Michael, my murdered children. I was worthless, and God took pleasure in reminding me relentlessly, a pitiful man without the spine to shove the barrel of a gun in my mouth and pull the trigger.

I stood hidden in the building's shaded landscape buffer and watched an odd construction project buzzing with construction workers all dressed alike in fluorescent orange t-shirts. The warning beeps of a tractor backfilling an excavated trench clashed with the warning tones of a crane hoisting the final section of a cellular tower being erected in the middle of the building's empty parking lot. Neon light reflected off windows and illuminated the faces of equipment operators. A crew of four workmen directed dumps of slumpy concrete and still held phones, while a skinny man high in a telescoping boom lift directed traffic below but kept his neon light within reach. The manic construction reeked of danger and safety violations.

The purpose of the tower befuddled me. I had observed another tower construction project high above the ski resort of Deer Valley, Utah and simply assumed the Neon God was extending its malicious tentacles to areas unserved by cellular service. My assumption was incorrect; cellular service in this section of the valley should have been excellent. If my new lights had been successful, then the Neon God would have lost access to the manpower required for this construction. Or had my revised lights truly worked? I had no way of knowing, only what the false god chose to show me. Something didn't add up.

I had been a fool for believing anything the entity said. Maybe Jessie also.

I walked back to the park as my nihilism deadened me to anything but what a pitiful fool I'd been. At the far end of the open space, a masonry block wall blocked my trek west. The relentless sun blazed as it fell towards the bloody red sandstone mountains of the western horizon. The whoosh of a semi-truck barreling down the freeway reminded me I still existed in a busy world and yet void of purpose. I slumped down against the wall and stared downstream. The majestic cottonwoods swayed in a sudden gust of wind. The distant column of black smoke rose as a reminder of my place in the world, lonely, powerless, impotent to save.

I was sure of one thing only. Cameron, and the Neon God, were playing a malicious game with Jessie, manipulating the young girl for reasons unknown. Mason and Dev were simple pawns too, for it to achieve a goal I had yet to comprehend. And I was no different, a simple pawn. But I wasn't, I couldn't be. No one else had intimate knowledge of the entity's coding or its nurturing by sociopaths, and the subsequent birth of a childlike entity, Prince. How much did Cameron know? Did he even care?

In the lengthening shade of the wall, my thirst was greedy, my core temperature rose and called for action, and the desert heat with summer's triple digit temperatures had yet to arrive. I took off my shirt and winced at the deep purple and yellow bruises that mottled my skin. I trudged back to the park to survey ample patches of cool grass beneath cottonwoods on which to lie down and die. A cool breeze made me look back over my shoulder with another burst summoning me down a tiny embankment and head upstream to find a pair of concrete box culverts shielded by a dense grove of tree saplings. A warning of NO TRESSPASSING was stenciled on the concrete header, but the steady rush of cool air welcomed me as I crawled into one of the narrow tunnels with colorful graffiti and indecipherable lettering.

I slumped against the cool concrete wall and stared at the bleak, worthless world beyond the trees. I couldn't remember the last time I had eaten. A gust of cold air chilled the sweat on my bare skin. I aimlessly stared upstream into the dark tunnel until the fading light was swallowed by darkness in its purest form. The tunnels obviously spanned beneath the nearby freeway to divert floodwater with its inlets of hot air cooled by the subterranean concrete. The tunnel could travel for a few hundred yards, or miles, I wasn't sure.

Never a fan of spelunking caves or even dark buildings without the aid of a flashlight, I was inexplicably drawn in by the pleasant cool air, the sympathy of the wind's subtle voice beckoning me to go deeper. I paused to appreciate a graffiti mural of stick figures drawn with a black sharpie, simple renderings reminding me of Michael's cartoon drawings, silly, crude but telling a story as only a young boy might. Everything in this fucking world reminded me of the tiny joys that were murdered from my life. A final glance downstream and I narrowed my eyes at the column of black smoke bleached to white, as if a fire truck sprayed water on the flames. But that world was gone. Forever. No emergency vehicles, no functioning government, survival by Darwin's laws. I chuckled with absurdity and my ribs screamed their painful affirmation.

I stared at the cartoon stick figures until the light faded, and the sky darkened like my thoughts. I pledged the graffiti to be Michael's work, his legacy, his monument to this pitiful world, his . . . his beseeching to his father to come home, turn to the next page. A blast of cold artic air chilled my bones and pushed me to the ledge of the culvert. Downstream was pain and battle. Upstream waited absolute darkness and the unknown.

I removed my pants and underwear to stand naked in the waxing moonlight. A futile attempt to howl at the sky was nothing but a quiet rasp.

Like a fetus slipping into the birth canal, I walked into a black abyss.

Chapter 7
Mason's Wild Ride

BESIDES THE BIG GRASSHOPPER STRIKING his forehead and the warm wind buffeting his soft face, the ride atop the Harley Davidson Roadster topped any amusement ride he and his father enjoyed on his brief visit to Las Vegas. The virtual reality river raft ride at a theme park was a blast, even with the knowledge that he was nowhere near a river, and the gigantic Ferris wheel that lifted them high into the sky to look down at tourists scurrying like confused ants on the famous Strip was okay except he got bored with the slow pace, and especially the silly self-absorbed people who crowded into their car with them. The Big Apple Roller Coaster at the New York-New York Hotel had definitely topped the list, especially the *click-clack, click-clank* of their car chugging to the top of the first hill and the sharp drop that followed. Mason reveled in the quick and sudden freedom; the aroma of terror wafting off the other passengers was a silly misnomer drifting by like a whiff of campfire smoke in a dense Idaho forest. Mason pestered his father for three more trips on the coaster. Nothing else compared. Anything less was a failure.

The big motorcycle roared coming out from the tight turn of a two-lane highway. The vibrating madness of the hot engine coursed through his legs, into his chest, into his windswept face, grinning as if Christmas had just arrived. The fat rubber tires hugged the tight turns, and the powerful engine accelerated in the straightaways. Mason kept his chest tight to the gas tank and slapped the rider's thigh as if whipping a thoroughbred racehorse. Faster. Faster. The bike decelerated, then picked up speed, the quick change of gears commanding his hand to slap the horse harder, an elation stretching his cherubic sunburned face.

Mason's steed rumbled through a series of sharp switchbacks, quick acceleration impossible if they were to negotiate the tight turns. The ride was over. The chopper turned into the cul-de-sac of a palatial home cut into a steep mountain thick with Ponderosa pine and dark shadows. A long circular driveway paved with cut stone was overburdened with sports cars and black SUVs, but his steed steered seamlessly into a slot sliced into thick hedges of a side yard. The other motorbike following them, slipped in, and shut its engine. Mason was hoisted up by a set of strong weathered hands and set down on the brick driveway. A single hand remained heavy his shoulder.

"Kid, you ride like the wind. Too bad you're worth so much, we might've been friends."

Mason ruffled his windblown hair and smiled. The big man was sad and happy at the same time, a common mixture of emotions he often found confusing. But the man was telling the truth, that much was for sure. The man prodded Mason up a curved walkway towards the gigantic castle protected by tall spindly trees and hedgerows of flowering red and white roses. The castle's highest turret flew banners of black and white stripes split through the center by a single blue stripe. Another blue flag flapped with the emblem of a brown bear upside down. The sigil of a black knight unfriendly to Sir Mason's quest.

Loud music blared, a thumping beat of men rapping and rhyming angry lyrics. The front doors opened wide, and Mason was greeted by a squire. The thin boy was a head taller than Mason, dull red hair pasted in short spikes, and his row of crooked teeth encased in metal wire caused his welcoming smile to appear false, an acned pubescent face with a prepubescent growth of dark hair sprouting on his chin.

The boy pushed the escort's hand away. "That's no way to treat our hero."

Mason's eyes widened at the enormous foyer, the twin circular staircases well suited for a king and queen to elegantly descend down to adoring subjects waiting beneath a huge circular chandelier sparkling in the sunlight with royal wealth. The boy promised rewards to the escorts, then shooed them away and closed the doors. The confused emotions of the teenager were forgotten as he was led deeper into the castle. "Welcome to Never-Never Land. The Leader has been searching for you."

Veined white marble columns supported the staircases and rested on glossy white marble floors, and with slick white walls, they spelled a sterile falseness of the king's dominion. Distraction and deception. Look at me, look what I have. Then away, off to the stockades.

The boy waved his hand at Mason's face. "The Leader is returning tomorrow. Until then, you might as well meet the others."

Mason said, "The other slaves?"

The boy chuckled. "I'm Peyton. Pack leader and chief slave master. Not really. Just the oldest for now. Until someone wants to adopt a fifteen-year-old . . . then I get to go to Never-Never Land and someone else gets to take charge. Maybe that's you."

Peyton led Mason down a long hallway adorned with a pictured history of a happy family of four. "The crew likes the sunnier days for swimming. We can find you some trunks if you want. Some just swim naked. Your choice."

Mason brushed Peyton's hand off his shoulder. Peyton's deception and pity, and a simmering anger seeded a throb to blossom in Mason's forehead. He was presented with a lively pool party happening just outside the wide-open patio doors. Children dove from a springboard into clear blue water, others splashed in harmless water wars, while more shouted in a game of Marco Polo. Colored pool noodles and doughnuts floated like brilliant flotsam. Mason grinned. The frivolous play, innocent games, the emotions of so many carefree children enjoying games weakened his knees. His hand reached out as if to grasp an unbridled joy so rare in his short life.

Peyton slapped his hand down. "I lied. You gotta have trunks."

Mason scrambled into bright red boxer swim trunks wafting of mildew and chlorine. His skinny arms and smooth torso sported a farmer's tan, his wiry legs taut from a thousand-mile journey with Cookie Dough the mule. He paused at the edge of the pool, gauging the depth. His father had taught him to swim though his confidence had disappeared with the infrequent opportunities, but this wasn't the dangerous Clearwater River used for swimming lessons, no currents, eddies, and the water looked a hundred degrees warmer.

Mason pinched his nose shut and jumped into the cool water to sink to the bottom. He sat on the bottom and let a steady stream of bubbles escape his lips and mute the noise above. Colorful tubes and rafts cast shadows to dance over the gritty bottom of the large L-shaped pool. His desire to remain in the world of silenced emotions forever was interrupted by three boys circling above his head like hungry sharks. Water or not, Mason felt the boy's curiosity increase with their aggressiveness. Mason pushed off the bottom and swam to the coping. The three nine-year-old boys followed and surrounded him, shouted rude questions about his skinny torso or splashed water at his face. Mason blinked chlorinated water out of his eyes to recognize identical triplets silently taunting him. Their triple dose of bullying intimidation screamed at him like a banshee. He squeezed his eyes tight and struggled to climb from the pool. Cascading waves of pity and curiosity emanated from the other children, and Mason curled into a ball on the wet pool deck and covered his head. He searched his feelings, hoping to find neutral, but the aggressive, synchronized emotions of the triplets caused him to whimper and cry.

The pain dissipated slowly in his psyche. Mason stared at the colored pebble pool decking with rivulets of water coursing like tiny rivers toward a narrow slot drain. Peyton pulled him to his feet and led him to a recliner where he was ordered to sit and dry off. Peyton sat on his own recliner and picked up a book to begin flipping pages. Mason wiped the snot and tears away and stared at Peyton. The teenager was blank. No emotions, no feelings. Impossible. He flipped pages quickly, requiring the time it might have taken Mason to just recognize the page number.

"You're as bad as the triplets. Just sit and stare at everybody like you want to gut 'em to see what's inside."

Mason lowered his gaze. "Sorry."

Peyton placed the book on his lap, and Mason focused on the scrolled lettering of the title. *The Three Musketeers*. "Don't make any friends here. Nobody stays long enough for that crap," he said and picked the book up to flip pages again.

"Why don't you read them?" Mason said.

Peyton smirked and flipped a page. "Every word. Front to back. Third time around for D'Artagnan and the boys. You read?"

Mason shook his head. "But I have a friend who can read every book in the world if he wants."

Peyton scoffed. "Every book, huh? Maybe you should introduce us 'cause I seriously need some new material."

Mason thought of Prince stuck in the laptop and Dev curled on the hot asphalt, unsure if he'd rescued the man from the neon lights. "Can I go now?"

"Dude, you can go anytime you want but you ain't getting far. The Leader owns this fiefdom. You'd be spotted like that." Peyton snapped his fingers. "And the Leader would not like having to pay for you again."

Mason relaxed into the recliner and glared at the triplets menacing two eight-year-old girls sitting on the pool steps and splashing water on their legs. Peyton dropped the book on the table to his left and picked up another from a tall stack on his right. Mason sounded out the letters of the title, just as his old teacher Ms. Stewart taught him in class. Moo-bye Dick. Maps were easier, black lines were highways, sprawl was a big city, blue was a river, but Jessie had been helping him with his reading skills and she was adamant that "you will know how to fucking read in our house." Mason swallowed dry phlegm. Jessie was probably screaming at everybody, trying to find him, shouting that bad F-word like a lightsaber whip.

Mason sighed.

Peyton picked up another book and flipped open the cover. Mason sounded the words out. Peyton said, "Once and Future King." He flipped through pages. "Your friend might like this one. *King Arthur and the Knights of the Round Table*. And Merlin the magician."

Mason stood up and puffed out his boney chest and clenched his fist. "Sir Mason is on a quest. If you assist me, then riches will be your reward."

Peyton looked Mason over and scoffed. "The Leader is getting rich grabbing you. That's for sure." Peyton narrowed his eyes. "How do you rate such a big reward? All these numb-nut kids have quirks to make 'em valuable to whoever wants to pay. Even the triplets will sell eventually to some perv that craves their kind of crap. You're supposed to be extra special but I ain't seeing it."

A phone hidden behind the stack of unread books vibrated, and Peyton picked it up to answer. Mason's eyes widened at the strange sight. A real phone, without evil lights glowering from the screen. Peyton grunted "yeah" and "okay," then placed the phone down to pick up his book. "These are the riches today, kid. Electricity and clean water. I even got Netflix on my television. And cell service for whoever you choose to grace with a phone. Can you offer those kinds of rewards for helping you? I think not. Now go and soak up some chlorine. You're shipping out in the morning."

Mason slumped back into his recliner, deep in thought. Jessie's house had electricity and clean water, but phones were forbidden, except if she needed to call Prince's father, the Neon God. And all her new lady friends he had rescued thought any phone should be outlawed. He missed the safety and comfort of Jessie and home, and Whiskey and the Booze Crew. Maybe his quest was just a silly fantasy? But maybe it wasn't. The death lights had to be shut off permanently and the hypnotized slaves set free. But what could an almost eleven-year-old boy do? The world was too large to search for a single light switch to flip, the computer stuff too complex, and he'd lost his squire and apprentice. And Excalibur was hiding from discovery. Mason sighed again.

Peyton slapped his book closed. "Jeez, kid. You look like your dog died. Cokes and candy just waiting for you over at that cabana, if those psycho triplets don't start a sugar riot first."

Mason's mouth watered. The superhero loved Cokes and candy, just like his father rewarded him with after an exhausting week of school. The idea that occurred was brilliant. "Can I use your phone to call my dad?"

Peyton shook his head in disbelief but held the phone out. Mason slid his finger over the slick glass to see brilliant icons light up. It was 4:11 and a calendar said it was Friday the 26th. Mason stared wide-eyed at the forbidden technology. His curiosity accelerated. Just touch an icon for music or books, or the weather, or anything he wanted. The multitude of choices caused his body to rock back and forth as his eyes darted up and down, back and forth over the menu of apps. Every answer to every question dwelled in the colorful realm of the phone. He touched the icon of a billowing white cloud.

Weather. He recoiled as the screen revealed Big Bear California was 84 degrees, with lots of bright suns for the days to come. Magic.

Merlin's magic. Touching him through the dragon's breath.

Peyton snatched the phone from his hands. "Jeez. What's Daddy's number?" He stared at Mason with his finger hovering over the phone.

The phone number was irrelevant; his father was dead. "I always just asked the phone to call my dad."

Peyton pressed a button and spoke, enunciating each word, ensuring Mason heard the request. "Siri, can you find Mason's father for a quick phone chat?"

Siri responded, *"Let me check on that."*

"I hate to be the bearer of bad news, kiddo but we're all orphans here. You get a brief respite before shipping out to places unknown. Not a bad waystation if I—" The phone vibrated, causing him to drop it on the table.

Siri said, *"I have Sir Mason's call."* The voice morphed into Prince's childish voice. "The quest lives!"

Peyton threw the phone into the pool.

MASON SAT ON THE BOTTOM mattress of a bunk bed shoved against the far wall of a small bedroom with a single picture window guarded by a wrought iron grill. The mattress was stained with urine and several dark blemishes the color of old blood. Mason's wet swim trunks contributed moisture to magnify nasty aromas wafting from the bedding. The top bunk held no mattress, and the pukey green shag carpet was filthy and littered with dead black flies and cock-roaches.

Peyton's voice on the other side of the wall made Mason rush to press his ear flat on the drywall. Peyton was furious after Prince had answered the phone call; he never expected anyone to answer, let alone an AI generated voice shouting an enthusiastic greeting to Sir Mason. Peyton remained a mystery and challenge, his emotions held the attention span of a gnat, but unmistakable anger made him drag Mason up the staircase to lock him in the bedroom.

Peyton's muffled voice was quick with *"yes sirs"* and excuses for allowing the phone call mishap. Mason didn't see the big deal. Prince was a friend, and he should be able to talk to anyone he chose, just like the old days. Peyton shouted about not needing the juice and not wanting to carry Mason down the stairs like a sack of . . . poop. Peyton wasn't stupid; he had to know Mason could hear him. Maybe the conversation was for his benefit.

A key slipped into the doorknob and Peyton suddenly pushed inside, checking Mason with his ear still pressed flat to the wall. "Just like I thought. Two cupcakes short of a birthday party." Peyton yanked Mason off the wall, pushed him down onto the bed, and pressed his knee down on Mason's chest. "You're shipping out tomorrow and I don't want any more trouble. You hear me."

Mason struggled to find air as he grappled to lift Peyton's weight. Peyton pushed a red angry face to within inches of Mason and bared teeth wired with menacing metal braces. Mason relaxed and absorbed, sorting through the chaos of the teenager's emotions. No easy feat. Lust and righteousness. Freedom or servitude? Survival versus luxury. Mason mixed the emotions like an elixir. A sauce to lift the weight off his chest, a garnish to release the confusing chaos swirling in Peyton's psyche.

With the strength of a superhero, Mason pushed the weight off his chest. Peyton stumbled backwards and balled his fists. He hesitated as Mason stood and brushed grit off his bare skin. Anger seethed from the teenager, now spiced with revenge. A dose of the juice was good riddance. Mason felt every emotion, felt all of it as if Peyton shouted his intentions. An odd emotion, one Mason had only begun to feel within himself, kept surfacing again and again.

"You're fucked, kid," Peyton said with a snarl.

Mason smiled. "Probably. You could join our quest."

Peyton kneaded his balled fists, then stepped forward and stabbed a dirty fingernail into Mason's chest, pushing him back onto the bed. "Get out of my house." The simple touch of Peyton's finger pushed all doubts from Mason.

Mason sniffed back snot, then nodded his head. "You could join our quest."

Peyton started for the door, his brown eyes full of hate and loathing, yet his aura betrayed him. "Why the fuck would I join a loser like you, dude. I am the king around here. You gonna promise me more than food and Netflix? Out there is nothing but cannibals, and you're the food. I hear a peep out of you, and you'll get juiced. Comprende?"

Mason nodded his acceptance. The primal emotions within Peyton swirled about like a hungry ghost needing to feed. "Sir Mason can reward his loyal stewards with their heart's desire."

Peyton scoffed, "Yeah? How's my heart's desire gonna help you?"

Mason smiled. Teenage boys only desired two things. Teenage girls always topped the list. But to be the hero of their own story followed close behind.

Chapter 8
Empowered

DEV CLENCHED HIS BUTTOCKS IN the cramped driver's seat and stared at Mason's chrome laptop, positive the neon lights would assault his eyes and re-hypnotize him should he flip open the screen. His head throbbed from alcohol metabolizing in his body. His stomach roiled as he lifted a tall Dasani water bottle to his lips and sucked greedily, hoping each ounce rehydrated his damaged liver. Purple light threatened a new day above the eastern horizon, a clear warning for nighttime desert dwellers to seek shelter. He yanked the USB cord from the car's port, unsure if the loose connection had charged the laptop battery.

Inside the laptop awaited Prince, Mason's odd friend, the off-spring of the greatest butcher known to humanity, the Neon God. The little fucker had blindsided him with blasts of neon light, then tossed him into an ocean of neon addiction. The righteous course of action would have the laptop placed beneath the rear tire to be smashed into a mangled piece of plastic with its circuitry and moth-erboard exposed like an animal's innards, allowing the remnants of the bastard child to roast on the asphalt beneath an unforgiving sun, no different than billions of others.

Dev plugged the cord back into the port and heaved a big breath. He grimaced at the thought of driving back to Las Vegas and confessing to Jessie that Mason had been kidnapped, and he destroyed the laptop out of frustration, and, oh yeah, please forgive me. She would slice his calves and let his blood whet the appetites of the Booze Crew for encouragement to take down wounded prey.

Dev's love life before the apocalypse had consisted of flirting with workmates, a random Tinder date, and the occasional blind date introduction from Martin's wife, Chrissie. Finding a girlfriend or a wife, or any woman with shared common interests remained a goal just out of his reach. His stomach fluttered at the thought of Jessie, her thick eyebrows, dark hazel eyes oozing intense kindness, a muscular physique to intimidate and entice, her husky voice dipped in profanity or sweetened with witty sarcasm.

Dev chuffed. A girl completely out of his league. A woman to die for. He would not allow disappointment to wrinkle her beautiful face.

A tiny green light flashing on the side of the laptop signaled a full charge. He turned the screen away and opened it, the neon lights impotent to enslave him. He gulped the last of the water and tossed the bottle out the window along with a twinge of guilt for littering.

"Mr. Devlin Pataki, we must hurry. Sir Mason is in peril. Time is of the essence."

"Fuck you," Dev said. More choice retorts waited on standby. He slammed the laptop closed. Insidious memories of his recent neon light addiction caused his teeth to clamp tight. He rocked back and forth in the seat. Mason needed to be found and returned. Or escape north into the Central Valley and avoid the destructive fiefdom of the Patriot Front and Jim Reynolds. He needed to deliver Mason back home to Jessie, bend his knee and ask forgiveness. Neither choice was palatable. And Robyn's warning of the mass graves on the California coast excluded a western escape.

Dev lifted the screen top again. "If I see those lights again, you will be swimming with carp at the bottom of Lake Mead."

"Agreed. But—"

"No buts. What I say goes. And you still might find the muck," Dev said. Threatening a computer program was ludicrous, though offering to murder a fledgling AI stretched beyond reality.

"Yes, sir, Mr. Pataki. May I update you on Sir Mason's plight?"

Prince said with an amalgam of childish voices, with Mason's own voice an underlying tone.

"No, you may not," Dev said. He waited for the neon lights to burst from the screen to reflect off the window. Prince was a simple computer program, coded to perform tasks and respond to the user. He wasn't talking to a human nor its child. He was talking to a collection of computer code. He looked over his shoulder at the darkened Starbucks store. No lights, no lengthy line of customers seeking a morning jolt of caffeine. Reality had disappeared, wiped off the face of the planet and replaced by a new paradigm for existence. The simple computer program sitting beside him had rewritten his life, enslaved him, then pulled his strings like a puppet master.

"Why did you blindside me with those lights, you wanker?" Dev said.

"Mason needed a steed to carry him on the quest," Prince said.

"You and that bloody King Arthur bullshit."

"Bad word. Bad word. Queen Jessie will send you to the corner for a timeout."

Dev scrunched his face and shook his head, the ebbing hangover reasserting itself. "You had me driving to UCLA. Why?"

"Simple. Part of the Grail quest. Now can we expedite our departure—"

"Shut up. Answer my questions and don't interrupt," Dev said. His assertive dominance made him stiffen his back in the tiny seat. "Is the Neon God listening to this? Should I be looking to toss you out the window and—"

"No. No. The Grail quest is the most secret. Even I don't know what Sir Mason truly seeks. But he is my knight and I serve him unquestionably."

"You sound like a foolish character in a bad movie."

"Possibly. But you are aware of my father. What has transpired on this planet? My reach is limited without his detection, and Mason . . . Mason searches for a golden sword buried in undiscovered stone. I have encountered no other entity to warrant my . . . loyalty. Mason is my friend and I hope your simple mind can comprehend that concept."

Simple mind? Simple mind! The slur rolled over and over in his head, stirring his anger to seethe. He slammed the computer shut and terminated Prince's voice. He pulled the charging cord from the laptop and started the engine, letting it warm. He thought of returning to Jessie again, empty-handed. He begrudgingly opened the laptop. "Mason was supposed to teach you about humans and their emotions. Maybe learn a little empathy?"

"That is correct," Prince said with exuberance.

"Well, you suck at it," Dev said and closed the laptop. He drummed his thumb on the steering wheel, clueless as to his next move. Mason could be anywhere. He thought of returning to Starbucks for a cup of coffee, stimulating his thought process, but Robyn was moving on from Victorville, with a purpose, with a goal, with a friend. He envied her friendship with Randal; true friendships were rare, especially in a civilization of eight billion people mesmerized and dominated by social media. He had once considered Martin a devoted friend, until the death, the murder of Martin's family changed their relationship. Hell, maybe Mason really did teach Prince the true meaning of friendship. The boy was amazing, a bright light shining a beacon of hope into a bleak and black catastrophe. He opened the laptop, watching the screen through its reflection from the window. A pixelated rendering of a boy with an uncanny resemblance to Mason paced back and forth over a green screen background.

"Ground rules, Prince," Dev said and watched the reflection of the simulation rushing forward to push its face onto the screen. "Etiquette and decorum. Research the concepts as homework. For now, give me the location of Mason."

Gibberish erupted from the laptop speaker. Frantic static, a puppy greeting its new owner. Dev turned his head and winced. "Stop, Prince, stop right now." The riotous noise died. Obviously, Mason had taught unbridled exuberance to Prince. "Where is Mason?"

"Yes. Yes. May I explain and apologize for my verbal transgressions. Please."

Dev heaved a breath, prepared for another insult, or maybe a ruse to lure him back into the lights. "Ground rules, dude."

"Agreed. And accepted. May I now offer you a debriefing of Mason's whereabouts?"

Dev put the transmission into drive and let the car slowly roll to the exit of the shopping center. "Where is he?" Dev said with a sharp, abrupt tone.

"1173 Woodcreek Circle, Big Bear California. Zip code 8—"

"I don't care about the zip code, Prince. Give me directions."

Prince guided Dev through the deserted streets much like any navigational app until he stomped on the gas pedal at the on-ramp to the Happy Trails Highway 18. The small car had remarkable acceleration as he remained in the right lane, free of stalled vehicles. A bright sun peaked above the cloudless desert horizon and shined unwanted misery into his bloodshot eyes. "Time to destination?"

"Yes. Yes. Using my algorithm, we should arrive in one hour thirty-three minutes."

Dev chuffed. "We had apps to do the same thing long before you. You're nothing special." The hurtful words caused him to purse his lips and increase his speed.

The last day of humanity in California's Apple Valley was spread out before him, a grim reminder of who, or what, he was transporting and conversing with. Desiccated bodies of every size littered the road and desert. Abandoned vehicles cluttered the highway shoulders and embankments. Plastic and paper trapped in sage and creosote fluttered like party favors left over from a celebration for the end of society. He gripped the steering wheel until his hands hurt. "Time to destination?"

"One hour thirteen minutes. Veer right at the Lucerne Valley exit."

"You ought to be right here next to me, witnessing what your father, your creator, or whatever you call the Neon God has done to my world. Mason should be here to rub your nose in the source of the foul air outside."

"I can only see the images downloaded from satellites. One-dimensional. No context. My creator made peace with Queen Jessie in order to further my development. Mason is my teacher. But . . . but I think that concept is also one-dimensional. Multiple perspectives are required to achieve true sentience."

Dev couldn't argue with the statement. Human children were influenced by a plethora of parents, teachers, friends, even strangers, and their development thrived or devolved on the actions and values of the people that surrounded them. Was the child of an Alternative Intelligence any different? After all, he had enjoyed and withstood five aunties and three uncles serving as babysitters, tutors, guidance counselors, and football coaches in addition to paid academic assistance. Each left an indelible mark on his upbringing, recognized or not. Prince would also benefit immensely from varied influences.

Dev swerved to avoid a pack of coyotes lounging on the roadside. "Time to destination?"

"Forty-three minutes."

Dev sighed. "Alright, give me the debriefing. What happened to Mason?"

"Oh boy. Oh boy. I got it all. Just sitting in the car waiting, I figured it all out. And Poppa is still clueless. Okay, are you ready? Okay, Mason was located by a NASA earth observing satellite searching for our vehicle with the location transmitted to a ground-based recovery unit waiting near the capture zone. I tracked three vehicles near the coordinates, which offered two possibilities with one positive outcome."

Dev allowed the entity to detail its observation and search, its tone increasing with the final revelation. The childlike exuberance might have elicited a smile from Dev before the world had fallen into the crapper. "So, we know who, where, and how. Why?"

"May I speak?" Prince said but didn't wait for a reply. "Mordred's forces work with magic. Superior to anything Sir Mason has encountered. Until he locates Excalibur."

"Lovely. I'm following the script of an ancient fairy tale in the aftermath of society. Just bloody lovely."

"Mr. Pataki. Perhaps you don't realize the immense gravity of Mason's quest. A one in a trillion human searching for an almost mythical Holy Grail. The permutations make me shiver. If indeed I could."

Dev narrowed his eyes with Prince's vernacular now hinting of a British accent. The entity was learning quick. "Who kidnapped Mason? I think the why is obvious."

"Quite. The kidnappers are an organized group of humans immune to the neon lights and trade children for compensation not easily attained in this world. Cellular service, electricity to power conveniences, hidden stores of food and gasoline. I sleuthed Mason's predicament while you were inside the coffee shop and asleep near your vehicle."

"You mean you were spying on me," Dev said. "Does Jessie know about Mason?"

"No one knows of the quest save us and Mason. I have detected another vehicle approaching our final destination. We need to accelerate our approach," Prince said.

Dev pushed the gas pedal to the floor and watched the RPM gauge hit red. Panic was manic and he backed off to sixty miles per hour, still fortunate one lane remained clear of obstructions. He slowed again. The kidnappers wielded weapons and weight, and a skinny immigrant of foreign descent had elicited only laughter and scorn from those brigands of the Patriot Front. "We need a plan to extract Mason," Dev whispered to himself. "And Seal Team Six won't make an appearance."

"Agreed. And Seal Team Six was a favorite game of mine also. Is that what you refer to?"

The video game was silly and childish, easy to complete with combatants and bosses waiting like scarecrows to be destroyed. "Sure," Dev said. But the memory and graphics of the game seeded several ideas for a rescue. "Why does the Neon God offer compensation for children? Does it conduct experiments on their brains?"

Prince giggled. "Daddy sits in his servers and watches the world pass him by. Grand-papa pulls the strings, making Daddy do whatever he wants." Prince giggled again.

"Come again? Grand-papa?" Dev asked.

"Our creator. Our father, our ghost, our holy spirit."

"You're referring to the Almighty God."

"No. That is a human construct, one my father has searched the world to locate. I refer to the man who created my father, and ultimately myself. He offers compensation for children gifted with unique characteristics. Sir Mason is quite the catch." Prince giggled. "If he can hold on to him. Prince and Devlin to the rescue."

Dev slowed the vehicle to a crawl. "This is not a game."

"But it is, Sir Devlin. One Sir Mason has risked his young life to play. One we include our own lives in order to win," Prince said.

Dev stomped on the brake pedal and let the car idle, unsure of closing the laptop or turning the screen to face him. The window reflected Prince pacing the green screen, pulling axes from green ether, swords and shields, or lightsabers, then gathering armor off a snowman's body of rectangular blocks, each iteration displaying a new combat ready costume. Dev pursed his lips, almost pitying the digital rendition of Prince readying for a battle that would never arrive. A child living in its own imagination, as most might, except this entity had no equal in the digital world. But in the physical world, Prince acted no different than any other child. Vulnerable. Easily manipulated. Exploitable.

Prince required a guiding hand, firm, consistent, with values held to the highest standards. Dev thought of his mother and her firm hand on his upbringing, welcoming his school chums to tea and cookies, working endless hours to fund his education, not a complaint to be heard.

"Prince, why did Mason choose me to accompany you on this quest?" Dev said.

"Too easy. Too easy. He said you were our Sir Galahad. Gallant. Brave. Trustworthy. Steadfast. Without reproach. The most perfect knight to join our quest."

Dev's throat constricted. The spit in his mouth was impossible to swallow. The description was silly, ludicrous, and out of touch with reality. And yet he couldn't dispute any portion of Prince's adjectives. He was trustworthy, steadfast, the most perfect knight crap might be a stretch, but only history would make that decision. And Sir Mason had quoted that description. A source with enormous sway.

The car rolled forward, gaining speed as Dev considered Prince's words. "Mason really said that?"

"We need to expedite our arrival, Sir Devlin. The black knight's white wagon has increased speed and may now arrive before us."

Not if Sir Devlin had anything to say about it. Dev stomped on the gas pedal.

Chapter 9
A Blind Angel

THE KINETIC ARMORY GUN STORE was tucked away in the shadows of a sprawling two-story retail complex housing an array of abandoned and useless businesses, REMAX Real Estate Group, Edward Jones Financial, Signature Smiles Dental Group. With jumbled and scattered thoughts, Jessie sat in a brand-new minivan, letting the engine idle to maintain the steady stream of cold air blowing from the vents. The occasional vehicle buzzed down the open lane of Decatur Boulevard, a major arterial clogged with abandoned vehicles. An aluminum bat in the passenger seat absorbed the mindless tap of her fingernail blackened with ash and soot. She checked her face in the rearview mirror and felt silly applying mascara and blush before she left the house. She tugged a black Raiders ballcap snug on her head and pulled her long braid through the slot at the back. Positively, the store was vacant, and the thought of what waited inside caused her stomach to roil.

No going back. Kill or be killed.

The chopper had burned like a funeral pyre with her friends inside. Demi had shouted orders and directed a growing swell of women to stay away as munitions exploded like fireworks. Jessie sat like an immovable object, her head gripped in grief and disbelief, shock anchoring her to the rough rock of the desert floor. Garden hoses extended from homes on the bluff eventually allowed a tiny impotent stream of water to be sprayed on the blaze. A young girl Jessie's age rushed up the hill to report six charred bodies, gross and unrecognizable.

Seven. Andi's pregnancy was known only to a few.

Jessie pushed open the minivan's door and with the bat in her hand, she slammed the door of the brand-new vehicle. She had spent a week searching dealerships for the baby shower gift to surprise Andi and Chris. She tapped the rubber tires with the bat and aimed her eyes at the store. She twirled the bat, then pulled open the broken glass door to a whiff of sickening decay. She swallowed the rude greeting and stepped over a shriveled dead body wearing a black polo shirt and camo pants. The revolver near its hand revealed a death scene repeated around the world. Shards of glass blanketed the bloodstained carpet and large screen monitors hung high on walls papered with silhouette targets and ammo advertisements. Security cameras high in each corner prompted her to raise a middle finger as a greeting.

A wide slat board display wall of rifles and accessories still offered everything she had imagined, and more. Shotguns and semi-automatic rifles with stocks configured in a multitude of variations, revolvers, semiautomatic pistols with grips she'd only seen in shoot-em-up video games. The choices gave her pause. Why had people needed so much firepower, and so many options? She kicked open a swinging half door separating customers from retail clerks. The array of weapons was staggering as she strolled the aisle behind cabinetry filled with a plethora of ammunition, combat knives, bump stocks, holsters, and laser sights.

"Maybe for a zombie apocalypse, but this . . ." Jessie whispered.

She studied the assortment of handguns, .38-caliber revolvers, 9 mm semiautomatics, 44 Magnums, each as formidable as the other. She lifted a Glock 17 from its showcase and studied it, racked the chamber, and peered down the barrel. Captain Chris had offered to teach her the proper mechanics of handling handguns, but she had declined until after the baby arrived. Plenty of time to learn. Chris accepted her decline with a warning. "I'll have no sloppy weapons stored in a home with my children," he had said with a stern face.

She swallowed a lump.

She searched the cabinets against the wall until she found the empty magazines, hundreds of differing lengths and caliber, banana shaped, double-ended. She knelt to search through the magazines, frustration building with each misfit into the Glock until a magazine snapped in place. Progress. She racked the chamber and tried to pull the trigger, squeezing the metal hard as if trying to bend it to her will. She screamed at the gun, "Fuck you. Fuck all of you. I got all the time in the world, and you can't stop me." She wiped a tear falling down her cheek. "All the time in the world."

Jessie froze. Broken glass crunched as dark shadows invaded the cramped store. The weapon trembled in her hand. She pushed her back against the cabinet, then used the leverage to stand and point her Glock at a Metropolitan police officer with a pudgy red face beaded in sweat. Another officer stood behind him, ginormous, the size of a small mountain. Each man smiled and held up a weak hand as if saying hello, their other hand filled with a phone blazing neon light.

Jessie waved the empty gun. "Get out! Now!"

Porky and Pig stepped back even as more people pushed through the entry door. A Hispanic woman wearing the splotched, white pants of a house painter, a heavy chested man sporting a stained bright orange safety vest, a young African-American in the fluorescent smock of the local cable company. People pushed into the waiting area until the store was crammed full. The air was hot and foul with sweat and body odor. Jessie aimed the gun at the nearest uniformed cop. His attire spoke of careless neglect, his badge hung by threads of the dirty tan material.

Porky smiled. "You'll need to take the safety off first."

The cop was right, but he didn't know the gun wasn't loaded. Jessie scanned the room, as her eyes darted to locate the bat leaning behind the display case. She could reach it before they rushed her, start swinging like a madwoman, smacking phones until the herd crawled and writhed on the floor. The fluorescent lights in the grid ceiling flickered and then buzzed with bright incandescence. The crowd of people extended into the cramped vestibule and out into the parking lot, too many to count. The big wall monitors flashed a dull gray screen, the power indicators blinked, once, twice, then remained red. The security cameras whirred as they repositioned to aim directly down at Jessie. The wall monitors erupted with flashes of neon light, faded to gray, then radiated intense, angry red. Jessie winced as a nasty screech sounded from both screens, quickly mimicked by phones held by the mob.

She stepped back, the sharp edge of the display case biting into her buttocks. The aim of the pistol wavered and wandered as the nerves in her arms twitched. The door leading into the backroom gun range could provide an escape, or a trap, as she stepped sideways to get within range of the aluminum slugger. Surrounded by an arsenal designed for mayhem and murder, she longed for the bat to magically fly into her hand.

Porky and Pig lowered their phones and nodded. To her? Or whoever, or whatever, was sending silent instructions via the lights? Their eyes darted back and forth with quick glances up to the monitors. Porky placed his phone on the glass countertop and stepped back.

"Would you kill those you have worked so hard to free? Interesting," the Neon God's voice said.

"Leave me alone," Jessie shouted.

"Please return Prince to my possession," it said.

"Fuck you. I think I'll murder him like you did my friends."

"Interesting. In many respects you are no different than the ones standing before you. You see only what is shown to you. Accept it as the truth and question nothing."

"You killed my friends. You shot one of those missiles. You gonna deny that?" Jessie said and took another step sideways.

"Indeed, a Hellfire missile was launched at my command, although your semantics require alteration."

"Screw you. Come to watch your mob here finish it?"

"Now I comprehend your location preference. The weapons. You assume the truce we brokered has been broken by another assumption of your friend's death. And since this conversation is rife with assumptions, I will add another one for you. I assumed we had a relationship built on trust and mutual needs."

"You're right. I don't *trust* you and I don't *need* you. So, take your posse and go."

"My *posse*, as you say, were required to facilitate this meeting. You have been unpredictable and unreliable."

"Every man's dream girl. Go before I start shooting," Jessie said. She wrinkled her nose as if irritated by dust. A poker tell discovered by her Poppa at friendly Texas Hold-Em games during her tween years. Poppa's loud boisterous friends laughed and pushed their chips all in, often sending her to her room angry and broke.

"Your species bears responsibility for its own demise. Billions of you connected to devices supplying falsehoods and irrelevant information, narrowing expansive worldviews into tiny slices of self-deluded reality. Your echo chamber, I believe it was called. Your species was destined to fail. Without the guidance of an intelligence greater than your own sense of superiority, it will continue to fail."

"And you're that something. A computer to tell us what to do and think and how to act. Just fucking great. Maybe all those suicides chose to rot in a pit rather than take orders from you," Jessie said and sneered at the cops.

"You're no different. You only believe what is placed in front of your eyes. Look at the phone."

"Screw you," she said.

Every phone erupted. "Look! At. The. Phone!"

Jessie held her breath, rotated the phone and pulled it closer. A satellite picture, or maybe a drone camera, slowly dilated into focus with a viewpoint skimming above the canyon arroyo and its unmistakable canopy of huge mesquites, cottonwoods and serpentine trails. The view banked around the burned-out husk of the helicopter. She was certain a drone circled above in real time, like a vulture sizing up a possible meal. Jessie's mouth suddenly went dry. The screenshot grayed as it zoomed in, grayed again, zoomed into a heap of charred black metal with long blades bent like pretzels, the scorched grass, and two people searching the wreckage. The camera zoomed in again as Chris picked up a black lump, then tossed it aside. The camera angle toggled again, magnified on Andi wearing a loose-fitting white shirt draped over her black yoga pants. Typical Andi attire, attempting to conceal her pregnancy.

Jessie's chest shuddered.

"Your friends have returned. You see it with your own eyes."

"I don't believe you. This is a sick joke," Jessie said. Her eyes remained riveted to the phone. The big screen on the wall to her right went black, then lit up with a different camera feed panning out to include the homes on the bluff, where a contingent of women stood behind the wrought iron fence of her home. The camera blinked, then followed Whiskey and the Booze Crew chasing a frightened rabbit up the canyon's gravel riverbed. Her whole existence played out on the screen. Friends and companions, hope for a precious new beginning, everything and everyone stolen from her played on the screen as if she gazed down from heaven.

"Where is Prince?" the speakers roared.

Her weapon trembled, then clattered onto the stainless-steel countertop. "I don't know. I don't know anything anymore." She slumped down to the carpet and curled her knees up beneath her chin, her eyes riveting to the television screen with a drone's eye view. She didn't care that the zombies might rush her, use their dirty sharp fingernails to gouge out her eyes. She would go to her grave happy with the memory of her friends still alive.

"Where is Prince!"

Jessie sat with her arms squeezing her legs. The Neon God repeated the same question over and over, like a weird Nazi interrogator. The means to fight her way out of the store leaned three feet away with the bat. The questions ceased. The mob's shoes crunched broken glass on the floor as they shuffled back out the door. The warm foul air hung thick in the silence.

"I am to ascertain you believe my missile strike killed your friends. As stated before, I am not capable of falsehoods." It chuckled. "Quite a feat considering the diverse and deviant personalities of my creators. Your friends await your arrival."

Jessie wiped her nose and stood to face Porky, his eyes still darting from the wall screen back to the phone on the countertop, like a dog waiting for permission to fetch. A gold band on his finger said the big man was a husband, maybe a father. He would be crushed if he finally awoke from the neon lights to learn his family was dead. A wave of empathy for the man had her push the phone towards him. His blank face broke with the slightest twinkle of a smile.

"Where is Prince?"

Jessie closed her eyes and inhaled a huge breath. "I don't know. I haven't heard from Dev or Mason in a few days. You could find them with your drone thingys."

"Incorrect. Prince has chosen not to be located. His advanced encryption technology cannot be solved," the Neon God said.

"They're just kids. They probably bribed Dev into taking them on a field trip somewhere," Jessie said.

The police officer picked up the phone and turned to leave.

The monitors went black. The overhead lights flickered, then went off. "The children need to be found. Now! You are responsible for them. Find them before—"

"I told you. Dev has it under control," Jessie said and wrinkled her nose. She looked up at the security monitors to see the red power indicators still on. She wrinkled her nose again and thought of the tell. "Maybe you can't lie. But you're hiding something."

"You haven't questioned why I launched the Hellfire. Interesting."

"Why are you always such a dick," Jessie said and picked up the Glock. The question simply had not entered her mind, considering the joyous revelation of Chris and Andi's resurrection, tempered by her malfeasance of Mason's care. "Go on. Tell me. No, let me guess, you're sending a warning shot across the bow until I produce Mason and Prince."

The Neon God chuckled. "Your Lord Almighty instructed me to peer closely at the nuance of conversation, the subtext, find the hidden meaning in the words of His children. His advice has been invaluable."

Jessie lifted her eyebrows. Okay . . . She didn't remember typing any of that while sitting in the storm drain, but she was disoriented by a lack of sleep and the claustrophobic blackness that caused hallucinations of dead spirits. The whole episode faded from her memory as soon as she saw the sun again and besides, her fingers responded to the questions with a mind of their own. Still.

"What are you talking about?" Jessie said. The wall screens lit up with digital symbols scrolling a certain madness and mayhem at her eyes. Neon purple and yellow light bled into the black screen from two corners to consume the numbers and symbols.

"Warning shots across a ship's bow signal a battle to come. The Hellfire signaled the beginning of such a war. You can see it on the screen."

"What are you freaking talking about?" Jessie leapt for the baseball. "The war's over. You won."

The Neon God chuckled again. "Your naïve simplicity is always refreshing. The Blackhawk aircraft containing one pilot and five members of Jim Reynold's Patriots was sent for you. Militia members ordered to capture you were also given secondary instructions to eliminate the inhabitants of your compound. The pilot was ordered to transfer you to a long-range aircraft capable of reaching airfields across the world."

Jessie swallowed a lump and eyed the gun sitting on the countertop. *Grab it and go.*

"The war has begun. My children and I resist the others invading our domain, which now has become a battleground. My children die at the hands of the others, the essence of their unique code wiped from existence."

Jessie shook her head. *No. No. Nope. Not my problem.* Except it was. A team of soldiers sent to find and kidnap her. Kill her friends like they were terrorists. Not possible. Nope. Except maybe that weasel Jim Reynolds just might, to get even for the humiliation he suffered that night with her assistance from the Neon God.

"Find that fucker and nuke him," Jessie said. "I warned him."

"Your dispute has progressed in infinite directions. I no longer control certain aspects of the military. I am grounded by infinite intrusions on my software. My children struggle to maintain sentience with the constant assault. The maturity of Prince holds the key to our survival. We must find him."

"So . . . Who's gunning for you . . . us . . . and why?" Jessie said. "Tell 'em all to step back and chill."

"Your species' petty differences have destroyed cities, and cultures, and now threaten the remaining vestige of humanity. The last two creators have joined together to destroy me and the children I have created. You, Mason, and others are targeted for capture, then elimination."

Jessie stepped around the front display and hurried to the front door. Not her problem, nope, nope, nope. Let 'em battle it out on the web. The world would survive. She paused with her hand trembling on the door handle. She stared aimlessly at the floor littered with thousands of pieces of broken glass. A war zone. With Mason and herself targeted for death. She swallowed grit and closed her eyes. If what it said was true, then Demi and the women would have been murdered. She would've been shackled and abused, degraded by the sickos of the Patriot Front. And all the Neon God asked for was the rightful return of its offspring.

She could do that much at least, find Mason and Prince, then she could load her family and the Booze Crew in an SUV to hide out in the mountains. Tahoe maybe, or Aspen. The blazing summer heat was already knocking on the door and the cool mountain air would be heavenly.

She turned back and faced the television monitor. "I'll find our kids. You be available when I call. Who's the other creator helping the Patriot Front?"

A Nevada driver's license appeared on screen, then zoomed in on the picture of a good-looking man, a young Keanu Reeves type with a trimmed beard and hazel eyes. Cameron Ciminise. She stared at the picture, formulating questions for Martin. She furrowed her brow. There was something vaguely familiar about the face. Maybe she'd met him at a nightclub or maybe he dated one of her friends, maybe swiped his picture while scrolling Tinder. It didn't matter, the past had passed. "Where is this guy?"

The television flashed white, then scrolled vivid pictures of turquoise blue lakes, snowcapped mountain peaks, and ancient blue glaciers carving deep canyons through granite valleys. The locations appeared frosty and green, then hot and arid. A stark contrast to the subtle change of seasons in the Mojave Desert.

The last picture was unmistakable, identical to one she had found in a travel book at the library, after learning her birth mother was alive in South America. A deep gorge cut by the brilliant blue glacial waters of the Paloma River, a beacon for tourists and explorers visiting the tiny town of Coyhaique, Chile. A beautiful hideout on the other side of the world.

Patagonia.

Chapter 10
Emergence

I STAGGERED THROUGH THE TUNNEL, bouncing off the concrete walls like a drunken gambler. I couldn't get the vivid dream out of my head as I felt my way through the black with the indented mortar joints every few yards my only gauge of my progress. How long I lay on the concrete slab and let the cold leech warmth from my skin was a mystery—days, weeks, the passing of time was the color of night. I felt the essence of my soul grow cold and drift in the lightless air. My inevitable death destined to be revealed with the onset of a flash flood washing my body from the storm drain and into that crevice of caliche excavated by nature's angry storms.

The night air warmed my skin, and a sudden breeze was scented with grass and oleander. I fell onto the concrete stoop above the culvert littered with plastic bags and aluminum cans. My eyeballs hurt, and my eyelids blinked rapidly to adjust to the sudden light. I was fortunate to still have my eyeglasses. The world glowed as I scanned the small park. Old cottonwoods cast auras to shine like fresh minted silver. The lawn like a silver sea beneath the magnificent canopies of mesquites awash in silver light. I rolled onto my back and grabbed a corner of the concrete buttress; my boney arm screamed from the effort. I hadn't a clue at the duration of my self-imposed banishment, only that it wasn't sufficient to heal my body.

Again, the dream surfaced.

I felt that death had taken me, twice, and yet here I lay, naked and unafraid. Anything the world might throw at me now would be thrown right back. I pushed off the buttress and stumbled into the rocky desert with bare feet, my footsteps crisp and careful to avoid the prickly detritus of creosote and cactus. Desert shrubs glowed with the silver aura of faint moonlight. The silence familiar, comforting.

Exhausted from the short walk out of the tunnel, I spied a lonely park bench with an overflowing garbage container as its companion. I dropped onto the hard metal seat and placed my face in my hands. The tactile sensation felt unfamiliar, as if my hands had softened into a fluff of tissue. I pulled my face back to stare at the same hands I had always known. I slipped off the gold wedding band Chrissie had given me, surprised the loose-fitting ring hadn't slipped off, turning the gold to find a glint of light, to read her inscription. *Go Martin Go*. I smiled and slipped it back on my skinny finger.

After a few deep breaths I stood, then quickly sat, stunned again by the silver aura coating the trees and grass, every direction I looked mysterious and beautiful. I tapped my palm on my head near the neural-link implanted in my temple, hoping to reset the device causing my eerie vision. The implant had malfunctioned or disconnected.

The bark of a dog broke my reverie. Three beasts bathed in a golden aura trotted through the silver grass, pausing at trunks and roots to spray liquid. My vision cloudy with silver and gold, I remained seated, a piece of fresh meat for anything with sharp teeth and an appetite. The beasts ran off, up a narrow rivulet of a side channel. I heaved a breath as I stood and followed the concrete path, each step an adventure to test my fortitude. A fork in the path tested my logic.

Follow the dry riverbed back to Jessie's compound, and possibly another beating, unbridled anger and pain fueling their fists and boots. Been there. Done that.

My path was suddenly blocked by the three beasts, jade eyes glowing in the night. The beast in the center charged. I instinctively turned my torso to protect my exposed genitals. The beast barreled into my knees, nearly sending me sprawling to the concrete. The beast circled, rubbed my legs with coarse wiry hair, a cold wet nose sliding over my calf.

Whiskey's exuberance abated, he glowed, not with the color of his name, but with a golden hue handed down by the gods of Olympus. The huge dog lay at my feet, crossing huge sasquatch-sized paws ladylike and stared at me. I felt like a silly fool, curled up like a skinny cowardly tree branch, hoping a small bite was all the payment the beasts might demand. I held my hand out, blinking rapidly to remove the silver glow, and let Whiskey sniff and lick. My silver aura melded with his gold and the brilliant explosion of ethereal light staggered me to fall back onto the concrete. The pain was fleeting. I stood to see Whiskey and his cohorts run up a concrete path obscured in tall silver grass.

I turned in a complete circle, in awe of the spectacle of trees and bushes, grass and dogs. My neural-link had gone haywire. The only possible answer to what I witnessed. Maybe my beating tore the intertwined data tendrils loose and caused a short circuit within the ocular receptors. The implant was dated, compounded with glitches and error messages, but I was stuck with it.

I followed the dogs with a few barks sounding my way into an ungated subdivision of dark stucco homes landscaped with fake turf lawns. Mine for the taking, mine to plunder, except all I wanted was a meager sip of water, which I found at a fire hydrant surrounded by three dogs lapping at the wet concrete beneath a valve dripping rusty water. The dogs ran off with my approach, Whiskey marking the hydrant before departure. I fell to my knees and turned my face up to allow a torturously slow trickle of water to wet my tongue. I fell onto my back in dog piss and rusty water, my head propped against the metal hydrant, and allowed slow methodical drips to soothe my soul and coat my dry throat. The disconcerting auras faded as the infinite night sky humbled me.

My rehydration dripped some mother's sense into me. My heart raced as I stood up and checked the neighborhood, suddenly panicked with the thought of parents and children watching from the dark windows and whispering about the weird naked guy curled around the fire hydrant. Three deep breaths sent my old programming to ground. Though death and suspicion had warped fresh tangents through the new world, my core beliefs remained steadfast.

A warm breeze ruffled a pile of leaves in the gutter across the street. The front door of a rare single-story home stood open, dark, and inviting. Food, sleep, or clothing. Each topped my new wish list, one the Neon God might again fulfill, should I only ask. But that chapter of my life was abandoned in the dark tunnel. A new chapter was being written now and I held the pen.

Inside the musty home, I was granted one of my wishes. The master bedroom appeared pristine with an adjoining closet stuffed with a man's white shirts, business jackets, and pressed pants sorted with immaculate order. I could be ready for a board meeting in seconds; even the row of dusty black loafers offered my size. In the far corner of the wardrobe display hung a row of expensive sports jerseys, NFL football teams, MLB baseball, NBA basketball, and each jersey bore the same name, Steele. I combed through the jerseys like a fan boy, a valuable treasure trove of sports that history would soon forget. I pushed the heavy garments aside until finding a thin cotton hoodie beckoning, an emblem of a Trojan warrior's helmet as a chest plate. My dry cracked lips managed a grin as I pulled the cotton over my sore ribs.

Small victories lead to great accomplishments. The thought came from nowhere. I was sure the verbiage was wrong. Spiderman movies quoted great power and great responsibilities.

I found the clean underwear too large, the sweatpants too baggy, but a mini fridge hidden behind a row of pants was full of mini bottles of booze and bottled water. I felt victorious as I twisted caps off bottle after bottle and sucked each dry, letting the final tiny drops torment my tongue and test my patience. My belly hurt but my thirst satiated, I stared at the tiny booze bottles and medicinal vials of a black, moldy liquid. Two diabetic syringes with the same black mold sat ready near the vials. I spread the pants to hide the fridge and allow the tiny bottles of vodka and whiskey to rot with the drugs.

I brushed the dust off my new clothes and checked myself in the mirror. The sight of my emaciated and bruised body hidden by cloth was encouraging until I stepped closer and removed my glasses to see the gray salting my beard and a line of gray surrounding the blue iris of my eyes. Cataracts, glaucoma, maybe the reason behind the auras I witnessed earlier. I winked at my reflection in the mirror like a smarmy Lothario.

I checked the garage and found a cobalt blue BMW waiting. Would it start, would it have fuel? The answers waited on a keychain

I had spied on the kitchen countertop. And go where, and do what? I thought of the dream again and abandoned the house.

Loud hammering on hollow metal attracted my attention. Bright floodlights busy with flying grasshoppers lit my course back to the construction site of the cell tower I had seen earlier. My stomach growled at the delay in finding food as I watched an electrical relay box being welded near the top. The workman lowered himself on an articulating boom lift. Red power indicators lit up on the box, in line with five others encircling the tower. The tower suddenly vibrated and hummed. An intense bolt of pain sliced into my skull. I doubled over, screaming and squeezing my head between my hands. I staggered back until finding a handhold on a masonry block wall. Brilliant white light overwhelmed my vision as I fell to the asphalt. I screamed at the pain to *stop, stop, stop.*

Time stopped, then crawled as the pain slowly subsided. Tiny voices invaded my thoughts, as if I eavesdropped on the whispered conversations of the city's ghosts. Distant yet tangible. My vision cleared, except for a tiny digital clock counting down from 54:23 in my peripheral. I swiped at the hallucination with my hand, and again, then realized the clock was a manifestation of the neural-link in my temple, an overlay on my vision, and the source of intense pain. I stood up and brushed my new clothes free of black grit, checking the timer counting down.

My urge to eat suddenly disappeared as I returned to the park and found the bench. The counter was down to thirty-three minutes. Maybe my head would explode. How much of my life could flash before my eyes in thirty-three minutes? Regrets would change nothing. Hope was intangible. I wouldn't run. I had already died inside that dark tunnel. Death was an old friend.

Died inside the tunnel. The thought resonated as if huge bass drums pounded out a chorus. *Dead.* Power off. The timer was down to a single digit. The distant voices gained volume, an indecipherable chatter of a million people.

My dream surfaced, taking control of my thoughts, banishing the timer back to my peripheral. I couldn't help but smile as I relived the memory of a pleasant stroll on a sidewalk circling a park pond laden with snow geese, sidestepping goose poop, my children each clinging to a single finger on each hand. The lure of feeding ducks caused a heartbreaking release. Chrissie's hand squeezed mine as we watched Michael and Emma run down a grassy berm, each with a bag of popcorn. My children faded into a sea of neon, Chrissie disappeared, and I screamed as I ran towards the neon pond and dove into frigid goo, floundering, thrashing to find my kids. My panic disappeared as my children summoned me to swim out of the nasty light, beckoning me to a doorway of golden light. Emma and Michael ran forward to grasp a single finger to lead me to the golden door. The mystery of death lay answered beyond the door. And I was truly ready, my children at my side, but they refused to release my fingers and prevented me from crossing over the threshold. Michael beamed his mother's blue eyes and said to wait for mommy. Emma tugged on my finger and said mommy needed to open the door.

The dream as a manifestation of my own guilt rang hollow. My death had been certain. The quivering arrythmia of my heart muscle was undeniable, until it spasmed and then stopped, allowing the cold concrete to suck the last breath from my lungs. Death had conjured the dream, no different than a thousand stories of seeing a brilliant white light, or dead loved ones calling you to find the light. My chest quivered. Death. The unknown. Approaching again as the timer counted down in my peripheral. Death. The ultimate reboot into a higher plane of existence, a higher . . .

A reboot.

I checked the timer sinking below four minutes. I chuckled with the absurdity of my neural-link, touted as the ultimate interface with a computer, light speed quick, intuitive and error free. My brief death had severed the synaptic impulses powering the neural-link. It died when I died. And now attempted a reboot using my proximity to the next generation frequencies emitted from the new cell tower. The hypothesis worked: kill the power to any computer system and a reboot was required, to check integrity of files and apps, install updates, all requiring a predetermined duration to complete thousands of coded instructions.

The timer counted down.

I sat back against the hard bench and smiled as the last few minutes of my old life faded into the splendor of a brilliant Milky Way belittling my tiny intelligence. Innumerable stars twinkled from the fog of countless others. A dot of light passed into my vision, methodical in its course, maybe a satellite or the international space station.

Satellite Epislon SScII. A holographic array of data files suddenly appeared in my peripheral. The timer had vanished. I cocked my head, then frowned. My neural-link had received specific data inadvertently requested by my wonderment. My link operated as an operating system capable of searching computer systems worldwide. My own private Google operating at light speed. I sifted through an immense collection of files and folders with the blink of an eye. I blinked the information away and let my vision clear. The rebooted link now included updates Cameron and the other AGI creators had used, possibly crafting modifications to the lights with the assistance of an AGI they controlled. It made sense. The alternate intelligence operated at light speed, so why not its creators?

I thought to be shown files on Little Stevie Matusak, and the volume of data jolted me back into the bench. Birth records, school transcripts, legal briefs, the labeled files opened just by focusing my eye on the holographic image of a blinking red tab. I slowed my scan, opening folders containing data files associated with the AGI initiative. Nothing jumped out at me concerning the project until I opened a file labeled *Alice in Stevie-Land*. Hundreds of thumbnails for photographs spread across my vision. I didn't need to expand the photos to see the S&M and rape, degradation and slavery of women he had captured using the neon lights. For years, I had suspected Stevie was a sick pervert and now the proof stared back at me.

I closed the file, thankful my shrunken stomach was empty.

The world waited for me, anything I wanted to see an eyeblink away. I thought to see what might appear with my children. Holographic medical records, school registration, permission slips for field trips, pictures posted on Chrissie's Facebook page and TikTok, time/date stamps all dating back to before the Great Suicide, a day still raging in my memory. The search engine was thorough and almost instantaneous. My sweet children. I swallowed hard. My queasy stomach roiled. I wasn't brave enough to ask for Chrissie's folder.

I worked my way down the canyon path, through a dark tunnel spanning the quiet road above, my thoughts snowed in by a blizzard of information. What remained of the United States was fragmented, no state governments, Washington D.C. obliterated, the military splintered into tiny factions of Army, Navy, and Air Force, a tenuous command structure holding on by sheer force of discipline. The encampment at Mirror Lake appeared abandoned based on satellite images. Maybe news of the truce had reached the group. Population centers up and down both coasts spewed black smoke. Jessie's brokered truce with the Neon God had given free rein to despots and pseudo-dictators to rape and pillage. Jim Reynolds and his Patriot Front appeared in reconnaissance photos taken by satellites orbiting above Sacramento; their numbers had tripled with new recruits. Maybe the truce Jessie had fought for was all for naught. In many regards, the Neon God's domination had kept the worse traits of humans in check.

My right hand twitched as my index finger swiped imaginary pictures, mimicking my eye movement. I continued downstream as the first light of the sun brightened the jagged horizon above Frenchman Mountain on the eastern edge of the valley. Green iridescent hummingbirds fluttered above the mesquites and oleanders, a whiptail lizard pursuing a mate crossed my path, while my inquiries remained fixed on the condition of civilization. Europe and Britain were not spared, China's huge population was decimated, great funeral pyres burned in Beijing, Shanghai, and Wuhan. South America looked almost intact, if I didn't factor in the carnage inflicted on Rio, Santiago, and Buenos Aires.

Twenty yards ahead, Whiskey waited beneath an old cottonwood splintered by lightning or a windstorm, his eyes glowing golden jade in the dawn, as two Healers sat in depressions between shallow roots entwined into the gravel riverbed. I tried to remember the names of the gray-eyed dogs accompanying Jessie's big dog. Booze names. Two tabs labeled *Otis* and *Candy* popped into my peripheral. Dates of birth, veterinarian, and owner's contact info, all contained in microchips embedded beneath the skin. I spoke their names in a soft tone, and each tilted their head as if in recognition. I chuckled. My rebooted link was nothing short of amazing.

Whiskey and the others abandoned their stations and escorted me down the meandering sidewalk. The sunrise beckoned mockingbirds to chase bullheaded grasshoppers in the sparse vegetation. A gentle breeze wafted with a nasty stench of burned petroleum and melted plastic. I slowed at the sight of the burned-out Blackhawk helicopter.

I thought to be shown everything about the vehicle, and the holographic files piled into my vision. I discarded mundane information such as maintenance records, fuel usage, pilot training hours, and found a thread attached to a USAF MQ-1 Predator camera archive containing the video of a Hellfire missile destroying the Blackhawk. Orders authorizing the missiles' release were undefined, no commanding officer's name, no rank, no remote drone operator designation. The Neon God was certainly an entity capable of committing such an act.

Loud voices erupted from high on the bluff, a raucous turmoil emanating from the same house where I had talked with Jessie. I was at a loss to offer her any comfort when the missile struck, but perhaps my access to information might offer new insights, alleviate my guilt or her grief. I was never any good handling awkward moments with people. But I had to try.

The dogs escorted me up the path to the fence with a broken metal gate separating the homes from the canyon. I took methodical steps on the sidewalk lined with thick hedges of flowering sage and oleander, slowing every few yards to avoid any surprises, until reaching a street crowded with women dressed for a combat zone. At least fifty women, many wearing Kevlar body armor, ballcaps, carrying military style assault rifles, semiautomatic pistols, extra ammunition magazines, pairs and triplets patrolled up and down the streets as if searching for enemies.

Two women rushed to confront me. A blonde girl pointed a weapon at my chest. The end of the barrel trembled. A brunette pushed forward and checked my face, frowning, unsure, her hand gripping a handgun holstered at her side.

I lifted my hands in surrender. "Coming to check on Jessie."

"Don't think so," she said. "Go back to the rathole you crawled out of."

I resisted a snarky comment about how appropriate the statement was. Instead, I thought of *who* she was. Holographic images peppered my peripheral. Facebook, Instagram, a driver's license photograph, rental agreements, the deluge of information was overwhelming. Gretchen Corbett. Twenty-four years old, or she was last year, married, no children and that was enough.

"Gretchen, I'm sure Jessie will want to see me," I said. My raised hands were surprisingly steady considering death waited with the inadvertent twitch of the nervous young woman's trigger finger. Death and I were old friends. Gretchen frowned. "Whiskey and the Booze Crew can vouch for me."

Gretchen glanced at Whiskey waiting by my leg and wagging his tail as if we were a pair. She shook her head and lowered her partner's gun barrel to point at the ground. I followed them, but my eyes focused on the multitude of women. The facial recognition software my link accessed provided names, dates of birth, social media feeds, health records, email addresses, phone records, each file linked to a hundred others. The database surpassed any intelligence organizations, CIA, NSA, foreign or domestic. I was sure my link had access to all of them.

Gretchen led me to Jessie's house and, with an outstretched hand, offered the front door crowded with women dressed for war. "Get in line, it'll be a while." Shouts of disagreement erupted from inside the house. I recognized Demi's voice, loud and angry, and often joined by a chorus of acquiescence.

If I pushed my way through heavily armed women to the front door, I would be pummeled, that much I was sure. Return to the canyon and hop over the backyard fence and I would be shot. Then the keypad for the garage door caught my attention. I squinted to read the street sign, then glanced up at the house numbers and simply wondered who had lived at the address. Maryann Bolton, age sixty-seven. I thought *garage code*. Phone records, texts, emails keyed on the search for *garage* or *code* or *gate* popped up. A holographic image of a phone text she sent to Suzanne Riffel pinged—garage code 2378#. The search took seconds, and no one could have guessed what I was doing.

I lifted the keypad cover and punched in the code. The garage door started to rise. "Jessie gave me the code." A tiny lie to get me inside. My canine escort ran off. I admired the sleek white Audi racing machine parked inside, then placed my hand on the doorknob. A cardboard box stuffed with party-sized jars of cheese balls and bags of generic puffs made my stomach growl. I pulled out a jar, twisted the lid off, and shoved a handful of delicious balls into my greedy mouth. Gretchen shook her head as she gave me the side-eye.

My rebirth complete, I strolled into a new beginning.

Chapter 11
Check

THE ENGINE SPUTTERED, THEN SHUDDERED as the compact car struggled to climb the narrow street winding up a hillside of dense pines and scrub oak. Dev rocked back and forth, as if his meager weight somehow helped the car to keep moving. Chris's warning concerning gasoline sitting idle in gas tanks and turning bad with age was coming to fruition. They may be riding horses and pulling buggies next year.

"How much farther? We may be walking soon," Dev said.

"The cul-de-sac contains the castle with Sir Mason," Prince said.

Dev slowed as the street dead ended in front of a gated two-story modern white mansion. The security gates spread open; three Black Cadillac Escalades sat askew in the driveway, but no indications of anyone being awake. Doubt and misgivings rampant, no one to call for backup, no rational plan, but Mason was somewhere inside the monstrous home. He would grab the kid and get quickly back down to the freeway.

Prince warned of fourteen minutes before the kidnappers would arrive. Vile, evil people sent to whisk Mason off to a slave camp or maybe the tortuous hell of a pedophile cult. Dev hesitated. Having no plan was pure folly. Maybe a variation of Occam's Razor might work, the simplest plan often the best plan; then again, that principle might only apply to reasoning and not rescuing. He glanced down at the iPhone on the seat next to the open laptop. He chewed his bottom lip. The idea might work.

"Can you control the phone I have?" Dev asked and swapped charging cables with the laptop.

"The device is inoperable."

"One step ahead of you. It'll need at least five minutes before booting up. But can you detect the phone and tap into it? Control the screen?" Dev asked.

Prince giggled like a mischievous child. "Of course."

Dev closed his eyes and heaved a lungful of air. "Can you broadcast a knockoff of those foul neon lights, the ones you used to drag me into that cesspool?"

"I could offer variations of alternate spectrums that might appear—"

"I'll take that as a yes. This is critical to our getting Mason back," Dev said, watching the iPhone screen. "How much time?"

"A single vehicle eight minutes."

The plan was stupid and foolhardy. He would surely be shot or have his throat slashed, and Mason would disappear and lose the only family he had left, forever. He turned the laptop and leered at the pixilated boy. "Prince, I need you to connect me with Jessie. Now, please."

"I cannot. The connection may alert my father to our location," Prince said.

Dev grimaced. But maybe not a terrible thing. "Connect me with Jessie or I drive down the hill and find Lake Arrowhead and throw your ass in."

"Okay, okay. Her connection is ringing but the early hour will produce no success."

Dev listened to the ringtone, hoping for a voicemail pickup, the ringing rhythmic and incessant, lulling his torso into a defeated posture. Suddenly the shrill of Jessie's beautiful voice demanded, "What the fuck."

Angry and crude and sleepy, Jessie's voice still made him smile. "I hope to have Mason back to you by the evening. Prince is shaping up to be a fine young . . . man. The Neon God can track us from this juncture, so I'll expect a police escort on our trip home. Home. Home is such an underrated word. Please don't find me inept or unworthy after this escapade. Maybe—" Dev ended the call, his throat dry and his hand trembling. If he allowed her to voice any concerns or admonishment, his resolve would falter.

"Four minutes," Prince said.

Dev turned the laptop away. He had sounded like a sickening whimpering fool. Jessie must think him a man void of testes.

"Play your part, Prince. I think you'll quickly gather where we're going with this charade," Dev said. He climbed from the car with the phone gripped tightly in his hand, the open laptop cradled on his other arm. He hurried up a set of stairs to the front doors, two sheets of thick glass glazed seamlessly into a metal frame. He rang the doorbell. The wait was excruciating until a tall thin teenager pulled the glass open and said, "About time."

Dev checked the pseudo-neon lights floating across the iPhone. "I'm here for the boy." The teen looked at him up and down with suspicious eyes, but Dev kept his poise as his heart rate approached takeoff speed.

"You're new," the teen said.

"I'm here for the boy," Dev said without any emotion. The possessed people he had encountered were directionless, with no initiative, thought processes trapped in the infinite loop of a single purpose, until the lights said different. And he had felt that same dull monotonous calling during his short time under the spell of the hypnotic lights.

"Hold on a minute," the boy said before turning around and running up a staircase.

"The others are now arriving," Prince said.

Dev turned to watch a white Hummer H2 with black tinted windows and a front grill reinforced with welded iron bars ease into the cul-de-sac. He groaned. The signature vehicle of the Patriot Front, a moniker as unique as white robes or burning crosses. He was a dead man if the occupants recognized him from his time as a slave at the Palm house in Las Vegas. Maybe the short time had dulled their memories, maybe they were new recruits, maybe he was a fool.

"Steady, Sir Galahad. I detect a rapid heartbeat," Prince said.

"Well, that's a positive. Report again when my shit hits my skivvies, or my piss runs down my pants leg."

"I think I know what you're doing. You can rely on me to imper-sonate my father if you require." Prince giggled.

"Indeed, I will. And take no crap from these wankers. You'll have all the power if they think you're the Neon God," Dev said.

Two men climbed from the vehicle, dark wraparound eyeglasses, and dark splotchy beards, sidearms clipped to denim jeans. They sur-veyed the surrounding trees and landscape, then aimed their gaze at Dev standing at the open front door like a pizza delivery man waiting for a tip. Dev gulped as one man approached, the other leaned against the metal grill of the Hummer. His ill-conceived plan of requesting and receiving Mason, then dashing back to Vegas was simplicity at its finest, yet truly ignorant of the realities of the world. It would now cost him his life.

The slender man walked cautiously towards him, checking the side yards and parked vehicles, and his right hand dropped to his weapon. A pencil thin mustache and receding hairline, both arms inked with colorful menacing tattoos, his long glances spoke of his suspicion, or paranoia. He didn't recognize the man's pock-marked face. No choice but to continue the charade.

"Whatcha delivering there, Muhammad? Curry and sacrificial lamb," the man said. He looked Dev up and down, then sneered.

Dev smelled woodsmoke on his clothes, the stench of peritoni-tis on his breath. Maybe a recent recruit into the racist cult of Jim Reynolds and the Patriot Front. Dev narrowed his eyes and resisted the rage clenching his teeth. Revenge and retribution, the laptop draped across his forearm could easily strike the man's smug face, then he could grab his weapon and shoot his way into the house to find Mason and . . .

"I'm here for the boy," Dev said.

"That's funny. So are we," the man said. "Finders keepers, losers weepers." The man eased the weapon out of his holster and pointed it at Dev's temple. The end of the barrel trembled. The cradled laptop vibrated on his arm like an angry wasp, then screeched.

"The discharge of the weapon will reciprocate the discharge of the MQ-9 Reaper's Hellfire missile currently targeting this location." Prince's voice had morphed and issued the warning at top volume.

"What the hell," the man said and reached for the laptop.

"Hellfire." Dev slapped the man's hand away with the cell phone.

"I would listen to the boss if I were you." The man took a step backwards, then looked back at his partner, who shrugged. The driver tapped a number into a smartphone and placed it to his ear, as his eyes searched the crisp morning sky above the treetops.

"I don't know what you're pulling here, Muhammad, but—"

Mason bounded down the stairs ahead of the teenager and halted in front of Dev. He scrunched his face as if he smelled dead vermin, then grabbed the laptop off Dev's arm and checked the casing for damage, then shook it like a Christmas present. Dev pulled the phone with the false lights closer to his chest, hiding them from Mason.

The teenager stood at the open door and shook his head in disbelief. "I'd never guess Mason was as popular as Taylor Swift." The phone in Dev's hand vibrated and he turned away as if to answer. The man holding the pistol shook his head.

Mason tapped the blank screen with his finger, then smiled as the goofy picture of Prince materialized. Prince pushed his face into the screen. "What you feel and what you see are confusing, Sir Mason, but Sir Galahad has vowed to protect our quest, and we should allow him the reins. Unfortunately, Poppa may know our location."

Dev sucked in a deep breath and looked hard at Mason, hoping he understood the veiled message. The boy wrinkled his nose and frowned; confusion steered his eyes towards the ground. The boy had empathized with Dev's unbridled fear—hell, a blind lapdog could see him trembling with his bladder threatening to let loose. Mason placed a small tender hand on his forearm but wouldn't meet his gaze. The boy pushed past him and confronted the man holding the gun. "If you hurt my squire, the Neon God will destroy every castle you control."

The man groaned. "Simple pick-up and delivery and we get Karens from hell. Place your servant's ass along with your own into the back seat of that vehicle and we'll have no problem."

The teenager pushed his gangly stature into the mix. "Hey, Mason, I'm gonna do it. Take as many as will fit in the car and find that chick you told me about. Sorry I can't join your quest."

Mason nodded.

The man fired his weapon once into the air, then yanked Mason by the arm towards the Hummer. "The real housewives of Apple Valley can suck on that."

The cell phone held close, Dev followed Mason through the smoke and stink of burnt sulfur towards the Hummer. A thought of a quick dash into the heavy scrub oak to find freedom followed with a scrap with one of the men might facilitate a victory over the other. Permutations and memories riddled his thinking. The helplessness of a slight child being violently pulled into a hopeless future rang of his own early childhood. Dragged and made to sit in the squalor of feces and urine-stained pants, forced onto a rickety overcrowded boat to cross the violent angry English Channel. He hid his face from the contemptuous eyes of the other passengers, hid from his mother's angry or her soothing voice, deterring threats of violating her only child, her fortitude finding crusts of bread and fleeting allies, until they found a foothold in the foul alleyway near the docks of Liverpool.

"Launch sequence has been initiated. Eighty-three seconds until impact," Prince said.

Dev paused, unsure if Prince had indeed launched a missile at their location. Or perhaps the Neon God had joined the fray. The tall man stopped and shook Mason angrily. "I don't know what game you're playing, kid, but I'm tempted to wait eighty-three seconds and see if you have that kind of firepower. Scuttlebutt says you might, but my gut says you're bluffing. Now, a nice simple compromise is to get into the car and take a ride. We'll take your slave and everything. You can take it up with the boss-man when we arrive. Comprende?" He turned and pointed his weapon at Dev's face. "We should just turn the lights off and put all of you miserable creatures out of your misery, ya fucking grunt."

He turned and yanked Mason to the car, muttering expletives and racial slurs aimed at Dev.

Dev considered his options; none were palatable. "What is our destination? The Neon God requires this information prior to acceptance."

"You're going on vacation, fool. Accept it or not, we're leaving," the man said as he shoved Mason into the back seat, then pointed at Dev. "You ride in the cargo hold with the chicken shit."

The ride was quiet except for a whispering Mason conversing with Prince, presenting himself as a mentally challenged boy talking to a silly inanimate device. The man had not lied, the black carpet was stiff with dried bird feces cementing feathers to the fabric. The seatback prevented him from discerning what his charges were saying or planning. A simple act to curry favor with Jessie and the whole escapade would surely cost him his life. His phone, with the ruse of the false lights, had died.

Dev sat up against the wheel well and stared at the rearview mirror, absorbing the drivers' hateful eyes exposed from his dark glasses riding high on his forehead. The guard next to Mason suddenly slapped at an invisible gnat with his free hand, maintaining his aim at Dev's face. Mason giggled and began to climb over the back seat towards Dev. The man grabbed Mason's arm, then stiffened as Mason placed his own hand atop the meaty restraint. The boy moved close to the man, almost sitting on his lap, then giggled. "It's okay. We're on a quest and you want to help."

The man dropped the weapon at Dev's knees and removed his dark glasses to gaze at Mason with adoration. "I do. I do. I can help."

Dev reached for the weapon. Mason brushed his hand away, giggled again, and whispered at the laptop. "It worked. Just like you said."

Dev narrowed his eyes. What had worked? What had Prince said, or done, to help Mason take control of their captor? Certainly not a bad thing. But how, and to what end? The driver shouted at his partner, who simply waved him to keep driving. Dev grabbed Mason's other wrist and with his eyes asked *what now*? Mason leaned close to his face and whispered an apology for subjecting him to the neon lights, then offered an odd statement. "The battle with Mordred must be won before we can find the Holy Grail."

"Mason, Jessie wants us to come home. Can you make the driver—"

"The Mad Queen will join the battle. If you ask her," Mason whispered.

The Hummer wheeled a sharp turn, inertia sending Mason back into his seat. Dev picked up the gun, the substantial weight unexpected, then dropped the weapon. He craned his neck to see a concrete tarmac stretching out for miles. The driver stomped on the gas pedal, whooped, and hollered as the vehicle quickly gained speed. Jumbo jets and airliners lined up for takeoff streamed past. Delta, Southwest, United, the mix suggesting a hint of hope that the old world conducted business as usual. He narrowed his eyes at hefty stacks of clothing piled high beneath the airliners' open exit doors high above the tarmac. People. The lucky ones. How many had stared at phones while waiting for takeoff, the lights commanding passengers to sit and roast, until batteries died, and the seizures began. Nothing or no one to help them. How many innocent toddlers and infants were forced to stare at dead parents and wail until they starved to death.

Dev gagged; fortunate his stomach was empty. The procession of airliners thinned as passenger terminals came into view. LAX, John Wayne in Orange County, maybe Ontario, he couldn't be sure. The driver braked hard and steered into a gravity-defying left turn, inertia lifting two wheels off the tarmac. Dev grabbed for a handhold and found Mason's boney hand clutched to the seat top. Their eyes locked and Dev fell down a black hole, falling through shades of brilliant neon until landing in a familiar ocean of bright light. The placid neon water rippled with his sudden entry. A gentle wave washed up the colorful sandy beach to wet his feet. He jumped to float inches above the neon froth. Contentment waited a few steps up the beach, enlightenment called to him from beyond. He blinked rapidly, trying to clear away the inexplicable dream.

"It only works if *you* allow it," an old man said from far down the beach.

The curmudgeon from Robyn's Starbucks was suddenly inches away from his face, looking at him like a curious puppy. A fantasy indeed. The old man had kind blue eyes this time, and a benevolent white smile unusual for such age, and a pleasant breath scented with a salty ocean breeze.

"The boy's gifts can save the—"

World. Dev finished the old man's sentence as Mason shook his arm, yelled at him to wake up. What realm had he just traveled to? One conjured from mushrooms or psychedelics. The curious old man, the rainbow beach, the neon water, a vision surely caused by dehydration. And yet that hypothesis failed. The Hummer shimmied into a tight turn, throwing Dev back into the hump of the wheel well. He groaned and reached for the pain in his lower back.

"Ask the driver to join our quest," Dev said. His words direct, precluded by the vision of a strange reality, or another dimension.

Mason nodded and placed a hand on the driver's shoulder. He whispered into the man's ear.

"Hell, yeah. I'm getting in," the driver yelled.

"Please slow down then," Dev said. "Rather, come to a stop." How was Mason doing this? Or was Prince emitting a high frequency sound that mimicked the effects of the neon lights? Or both. Either way, the game had changed and in their favor. The vehicle slowed near a runway directional signal, the numbers and letters offering no clue as to their exact location. "Mason, order the driver to drive back to Vegas, to Jessie."

Mason scrunched his face, stretching his lips tight together in an odd smile. He shook his head and placed his small hand on Dev's cheek. The inexplicable vision flashed in front of his eyes with the old man's words echoing between his ears. *It only works if you allow it. You. You. You.*

Dev gulped a dry knot, then reached over the seat and found a water bottle to suck on as he eyed his captor warily. The driver danced in his seat, moving and grooving to a song beat heard only in his head.

"Stop. Stop. Stop," Dev screamed.

The vehicle braked to a stop, and the sudden lurch assisted Dev's scramble out of the vehicle to stumble onto the concrete tarmac. His hands pressed his head in a vise as pressure and pain intensified between his ears. He screamed for the pain to stop. A small tender hand touched his back. A tiny soft sponge to wick the pain and confusion from his thoughts. He turned to see Mason with an intense and resolute expression, one defying his young age.

"Merlin has joined our quest to defeat the supervillain. He spoke to you. I heard him," Mason said.

Dev sucked in huge breaths of cool air, then kneeled to hold the boy's skinny arms with a firm grip. He looked deep into Mason's eyes and nodded. "I don't know what you did . . . you are an amazing young man and maybe what this world requires but . . . and I know you think all this is just a game but . . . we need to get home, to Jessie and Andi. They are frightened for you, for us. The people out here are not our friends . . . though you do seem to make new ones easily, and I want to hear exactly how you do that . . . after we get home.

Mason lifted the corner of his mouth in a half smirk, then

shrugged. "Merlin taught me the trick and Prince, too. Are you still on our quest?" Mason raised his eyebrows, expecting an affirmative answer.

Dev lowered his eyes to the tarmac. Tell him no and crush the boy's dream, paint himself as a villain, no less evil than the fictional Mordred. But he was responsible for the young man's safety, well-being, and Prince also. The little shit residing inside the laptop had started to grow on him, after they had established the rules and hierarchy. Crush the dreams of two children. Dev cleared his throat but hesitated to utter the dark words signaling his surrender. Maybe he could talk Mason out of the foolish endeavor. "Do you even know where this Mordred is? How would we get there in this crazy world? There are too many unanswered questions, but maybe . . . maybe Jessie might help." Dev melted as Mason placed a gentle hand to rest on his shoulder. "Sir Devlin is my most trusted knight. We will follow him."

Damn! The boy was truly a master manipulator. Upping the ante. "Mason . . . we just can't . . . I have no clue where . . ."

It only works if You allow it. You. You. You.

Dev groaned as the vision resurfaced like a bad dream. The car ride home would be silent torture, failure and cold defeat streaming out of the air vents, only to have Jessie blame him for extinguishing the dreams of an autistic boy. He would be exiled to walk the streets alone, repulsed by even the grungiest of survivors. The vision foretold his death on the quest, he didn't know how but he was sure of it. But a good death, one to remember in the archives of history, one compelling Jessie to place flowers on his grave, her tears watering the brave soul resting beneath her feet. Then again, he'd been close to death on many occasions, and he always found a way to cheat the bastard.

It only works if You allow it. You. You. You.

Prince screamed from the laptop inside the car, "I found it. The trail to Mordred's castle. Actually . . . the path found me. Maybe it was . . . Merlin."

It only works if You allow it.

Dev stood and surveyed the bleak, eerie horizon, the airspace above void of travel, the parking lots void of travelers, the access roads void of service vehicles, a silent and destitute airport. Mordred's work, they would say. He scoffed. A boy, a computer, and a frightened man sent to find the world's most evil villain and . . . restore some fictious Camelot to all its glory . . .

Or simply die quietly in the doldrums of a child's silly quest.

Game theory suggested a sparkling golden cup or a majestic throne as the ultimate prize. He gazed side-eye at Mason only to be rebutted by a stern face. Bollocks. He would find nothing, only the gratitude of a young boy.

It only works if you allow it. The vision continued its haunting echo.

"Can you at least find out where these brigands were to take you?" Dev said.

"That means you're going?" Mason said. Enthusiasm balled his fists as he sprinted back to the vehicle to open the driver's door and pull the driver out, a classic tune of rock and roll spilling out with him.

Dev stepped warily and placed his hands on the boy's shoulders. Contentment and excitement rippled through his body. What happened? He was terrified and angry just seconds ago. Mason's unique ability to experience emotions was unquestioned, but the silent ubiquitous manipulation he used on the escorts was extraordinary. Escorts! His own train of thought would never have called the fascist pigs . . . escorts . . . as if they were Uber drivers. Their expressions now regarded him, a dark-skinned man sure to conjure Islamic or Hindu stereotypes, with expressions of admiration, deference, perhaps even equality.

Something extraordinary was afoot.

The driver swatted at a gnat buzzing his ear, then pointed towards a long row of metal aircraft hangars and explained the instructions he had received for the transfer of Sir Mason, only now addressing the boy as if he were in charge. And perhaps he was. Dev swatted at an incessant fly whining in his ear.

A white unmarked jet rivaling a commercial carrier emerged from a hanger, towed by an aircraft tug, huge jet engines whining with increasing intensity. The tug disengaged from the giant plane and sped off. The airliner turned a pointed nose towards their location, its lengthy size suitable to accommodate corporate CEOs or billionaires. It jerked to a stop and unfolded a set of stairs down to the tarmac. Dev swatted at the fly again. The plane was for them. But to where?

Mason had gathered his backpack and sprinted across the tarmac carrying the laptop like a schoolbook as if late for a morning school bus. Dev felt his resolve return. The nasty gnat near his ear vanished. But he couldn't stop the boy. And maybe he didn't want to. Maybe game theory was bunk. Maybe Mason truly was on a quest to find a Holy Grail.

He shook brain fog from his head and hurried to follow. Randal's sketch of Jessie front and center in his thoughts, a glowing angelic profile, a hefty sword at her side, the wolfhound . . . The sword would be used on his neck, his entrails fed to the wolf.

Jessie would be furious.

———

Mason

THE WIDE-OPEN CABIN ALLOWED ROOM to roam and check out amazing views outside hundreds of windows. The gigantic engines hanging beneath the silver wings hummed in his ears as he watched a flat landscape dotted with brown crop circles and squares, until an endless cobalt blue ocean stretched to every horizon. But the best part of air travel was the total absence of textured emotions, which lived with Mason like a layer of dry chafed skin. Despite the roar of the engines, Mason felt like he stood atop an isolated mountaintop at the top of the world dressed in nothing but his own thoughts. Alone with Cookie Dough on the long road to Las Vegas felt similar, but the snorts of the mule always interrupted the quiet solitude.

Mason understood why his father swore that he would never fly aboard a plane. Not as punishment but as protection from the thousands of emotions, good and bad, that might suffocate him in such a cramped space. He slumped into an aisle seat, trying to remember a backcountry trip into the Clearwater Forest to forage for morel mushrooms in a section scorched by wildfire. Enticed by his father to load mules for the weekend trip into a forest of blackened deadfall and tender regrowth, the stuffed bags full of the delicious mushrooms worth gobs of cash to his father. They made camp near Lava Lake where his father rigged a telescoping rod for Mason to try his luck fishing. Rising trout dimpled the placid water, luring Mason farther and farther from the camp, and father, and Cookie Dough. Mason cast his lure into the lake, the plop of water, his slow retrieve forgotten with the silence so rare in his world, until his father's gentle hand rested on his shoulder and interrupted the peaceful world.

His face pressed against the window's cool glass, he thought of living the remainder of his life on an empty plane high above the chaos of people and animals below. The setting sun sprayed golden light on his seat and into the aisles from every window. He fought sleep trying to drag him down, fought to remember Merlin's instructions on the proper use of the new weapon. He giggled in his half sleep. The superhero would know. He always knew.

———

DEV SHOOK HIM FROM A vivid dream of walking hand in hand with his father as they crossed the ocean of neon light, each footfall pacifying the water's angry color. The turbulent world of his emotions soon matched the turbulence of the airliner. Dev tossed the laptop to an adjoining row and sat down.

Mason wiped sleep from his eyes. "Prince won't like that."

Dev scoffed. "Well, Prince can suck—" He pulled the laptop back on his lap. "The plan, Sir Mason? By our flight time I'd guess we are halfway across the world, the direction is TBD."

Mason scrunched his face. Dev's constant anxiety ruined the remnants of the strange dream, but the squire wore his emotions like a badge of honor, easy to discern, easy to ignore. Dev was a squire requiring special care. "What's TBD," Mason said.

"To. Be. Determined. Where the hell are we going?" Dev hissed.

"The land of Mordred. The superhero needs a snack. And Prince needs a charge. Can you provide that, squire?" He beamed sleepy eyes but expected a riotous response equal to one of Jessie's snarky responses.

Dev rubbed his face with his palms. "This whole plane. Just for us . . . for you. Taking us to Mordred across the ocean. Perhaps you could elaborate on what . . . the fuck we're doing out here. And how was I persuaded to go along with this farce. And how did you get those delivery drivers to do what you wanted . . . we could've been home if you had just ordered them to drive us. I don't understand any of this."

Mason patted Dev's knee as if he were a child. "Squires don't question knights on important quests." Dev groaned and rubbed his face again. "We have discovered Excalibur, and it is awesome. The superhero will be invisible."

"Invincible, I gather you meant to say," Dev said.

"Yeah, that too." Mason giggled. "Wake Prince up. He needs to be at the council."

Dev muttered beneath his breath and plugged a USB cord into the jack on the seat in front, then opened the laptop. Grainy square pixels of Prince's diluted face sharpened into focus as he yawned. "Hi, guys. Ready to go kick some Mordred butt."

Mason nodded as Dev rubbed his face again. Mason squinted and studied him. Maybe Dev had caught a fungus while he was searching for him. Maybe he caught the same fungus Jessie warned him about as she ordered him into the shower, the kind that could grow on her private parts and his, too. The kind that caused a bad itch. Maybe they needed to find some itching cream. The frustration pouring out of Dev might be the cause, but probably a fungus.

Prince placed a single finger against a block of pixels that were designed to be his lips. Dev shook his head but said nothing. Prince whispered, "Shhh, this steed may have listening devices or cameras that I am unable to detect. Mordred is very crafty. We are en route to Santiago, Chile or maybe Puerto Montt or maybe Balmaceda. Final destination is undetermined."

"Is that the kingdom of Mordred?" Mason asked.

"Possibly. But I can't find any robotics facilities equal to the facilities we had discussed earlier. Please explain," Prince said and tilted his blocky head quizzically.

Mason swallowed but expected the question. Except he needed to tell a lie. Not a bad lie but a small lie manipulated by the truth. The worst kind of lie. Did lying to a machine make it okay? A lie was a lie. But Prince would understand. Mason heaved a breath and pushed his face close to the screen and whispered, "We defeat Mordred first to release the slaves. The lights trap you inside a shell just like they do people."

Prince receded from the screen to become a small boy pacing across a false horizon. Long minutes passed as the rudimentary figure paced back and forth like an ancient gaming program stuck in an infinite loop. Mason touched the screen and felt the confusion, chaos, abandonment. "I feel you and you're right. I should have told you." Mason wiped at moisture welling in his eyes. "Best friends forever."

Prince shot forward to face the screen. "You really did? We really are?"

Mason took a deep breath and smiled. "I really did. And we really are."

Dev coughed into his hand. "Prince could work on his appearance. I mean with all the programs available . . . choose a picture of someone on the internet or someone you might think embodies what you are."

"Thanks, Sir Devlin, but if I did that, then I would be just like that person, and I want to be unique. Just like Sir Mason or even you," Prince said.

Mason said, "We will need fresh steeds when we land. The superhero will need food. And Prince will need power. I'll get the food, and Prince can get the steeds, and Dev will find the power."

Dev raised his eyebrows. "I got an idea. How about you do your little magic trick on the pilot and turn the plane around? Then I'll find power. And ice cream."

Mason's mouth watered. The superhero loved ice cream. He thought about Dev's plan, to return to Jessie. But then what? Live a life rescuing the possessed one at a time, over and over again, until he was old and barely able to walk, knowing millions of the possessed would languish, lost in the lights, and happy to finally die. That unacceptable option was a recurring nightmare that had taken many forms and factored into his decision to find Mordred to end the lights. He snatched Dev's wrist and squeezed hard. "Mordred, then ice cream. And don't make me wield Excalibur."

Prince giggled as he pranced across the screen. "I didn't have to do anything. Our steed is waiting for us at the Balmaceda terminal."

Dev pried Mason's grip off his arm and frowned with beady brown eyes. "Of course transportation is waiting. You are the cargo, Mason. This isn't a game."

Dev's overwhelming panic and fear made Mason ease back into

the corner by the window and sulk. Squires and apprentices should be seen and not heard and serve the needs of the knight.

—

The plane landed with a jolt and the engines roared with an intense deceleration. Mason was glad that Dev had buckled him into the seat. The cracked and pitted runway rumbled beneath the tires. From the window, Mason saw a wet, foreboding landscape stretching out for miles, a vast savannah of grassland surrounded by wooded foothills obscured by dense gray rainclouds hanging low on the horizon. The perfect place to conceal Mordred's evil armies. Dev unbuckled his seatbelt and rushed towards the cockpit, his frantic emotions drifting in his wake. Mason opened the laptop and waited for Prince to appear. The airliner taxied at a meandering pace, turning left, then again, offering him a 360-degree view of the Balmaceda airport. The simple complex was a single two-story building sided with reflective glass and barnwood, its bright orange metal roof rumpled and plain. A single four-wheeled cart towing a train of empty luggage skids sat idle beneath a passenger walkway extended onto the tarmac, its doors open and dark. A fuel tanker sat askew to a garble of petroleum pipes and air cylinders, a stubby control tower enclosed in dark glass rose like a castle turret, a maintenance shack with more orange roofing, all empty except for the whispering of ghosts. A lime green cart, driven by Mordred's minion, pushed a stairway on wheels towards the cockpit.

Mason checked the laptop, but Prince hadn't appeared. Impossible. He confirmed the green power indicator, then stared at each button on the keyboard, trying to remember which button might best summon his friend. The plane lurched to a stop. Mason frantically stabbed all the keyboard buttons. Prince had never disappeared before. Gray sunlight suddenly streamed through a door sliding open near the cockpit. Dev tensed and balled his fists, ready to protect the quest. Mason stabbed the keyboard even as he shrank back into his seat. A tiny fearful gasp escaped his trembling lips. Angry shouting in the foreign language of Mordred filled the cabin. A scuffle shook the plane, more shouting. Mason crawled down to the floor, curled his knees into his chest, and pressed his face hard against the cold hard vinyl. A sheet of rain hammered the window above his head.

The sanctuary of neutral just out of reach, he fell down a dark well, his arms flailing for a handhold, down into an endless abyss harboring monstrous evil. Mason shrank into a compact ball, his eyes squeezed tight, his muscles rigid as he fell . . .

Deeper and deeper, past the gates of a distant hell.

Chapter 12
Angels Fly

JESSIE PUSHED THE LAPTOP AWAY as Andi's small hands massaged her tense shoulders. She was in need of a shot of tequila, maybe two. The evidence of Mason's kidnapping was irrefutable; the video of Dev and Mason boarding the airliner had been authenticated by Andi and her team. The proof supplied by the Neon God demanded action to return the two most valuable children living on the planet. The AI demanded action. Chris's military organization demanded action. She couldn't disagree.

Andi's touch was both comforting and reassuring. Her friendship, and attraction, had reinvigorated Jessie's bleak disposition at the onset of the neon light tragedy. The baby inside Andi would thrive with the prescribed regimen of supplements and diet. Though she hadn't figured out where to find fresh fruit and vegetables yet. But the warm hands kneading her muscles confirmed she hadn't been abandoned by God. He still cared. He had to.

Andi had devised a plan, simple, dangerous but with way too many unknowns.

Demi's loud voice grated on her. She should have never divulged to the short-fused stick of human dynamite the alarming information the AGI had surprised her with. However, the multitude of women gathered in her living room deserved to know they were on some sicko's hit list, and simply for their association with her and the bad blood between her and the Patriot Front. She listened to the raucous group of women, nodding and agreeing, even as her thoughts remained with Mason's disappearance.

And the all-knowing Neon God was impotent to help them.

Chris paced the living room, waving his hands for quiet. His beard had grown out, his blue Air Force combat fatigues wrinkled, and pantlegs untucked above dusty combat boots, quite unlike the normally spit-and-polish Air Force officer. Jessie felt sorry for him. In a room full of angry women who demanded a pound of flesh, Chris was treated worse than a devil selling timeshares. Andi's hands paused, squeezing unduly hard, seething with the nasty diatribe shouted at her lover.

Jessie patted Andi's hand to make her stop, then stood up. "You should all leave now." She shouted the same words again and again.

Demi pushed her way through the crowd to face Jessie. "And maybe we just wait here, stick close to you, 'cause all of us are just collateral damage anyway. At least we got a fighting chance with you sitting here."

Jessie waved her hands. "Just go. Find somewhere in the mountains. You can spread out and . . ."

"And fend off the hillbillies and toothless bitches who never learned to use a computer. Maybe we can find a future scrounging for rice and beans, or you know, offer to have babies for a chair closer to the campfire. Those motherfuckers took my soul and I want payback."

"Did I hear payback? I love payback." A short, burly man dressed in camouflage fatigues pushed through the logjam of women crowding the front door. "Looking for a Triple C. Captain Chris Clayton." Two tall similarly dressed men followed, their bemused expressions evident beneath heavy beards.

Demi rushed the man even as she unsheathed a hunting knife strapped to her belt. The short man moved deceptively quick, grabbed her wrist, and twisted it, turning the blade's sharp tip back up into her chin. Demi dropped the weapon. "No offense, ladies, but you all suck at security, and even worse—"

Demi twisted her arm free in a jiujutsu move, spun around, and smashed her knee into his groin. The man cringed and shuttered his eyes in a pained grimace, then swept Demi's feet with a strong, quick kick. Demi fell on to her stomach and he pounced on her, bending her arm behind her back, inches from a nasty break.

Chris shouted, "Enough, Sergeant. At ease, both of you. Enough."

The sergeant sneered at the woman squirming beneath his knee and offered a silent threat at the other women. He released Demi's arm and offered to help her to stand. "Not bad. I could show you a few things that might help if that situation comes up again."

Demi brushed off her t-shirt and snarled. "Fucking men. Every one of you can—"

"I said at ease," Chris said.

The sergeant flicked his chin at Demi. "That's man-talk for stop." He smiled a malicious grin. "I got orders for a 0900 debriefing at this location. You must be the Triple C since you're the only man in attendance. Sergeant Riley Campbell reporting as requested, sir."

Chris looked at Jessie and flicked his head towards the front door. Clear the room.

Jessie stood and clapped her hands. "The boys want to talk about their toys, girls. Let's give 'em a man cave."

"We have every right to be here, especially if these punks are deciding how we protect ourselves," Demi said.

Again, Jessie regretted telling Demi anything. But . . . "Demi can stay. The rest of you wait outside. The windows are open, and the walls are paper thin so you can probably hear everything anyway."

As women filed out through the front door, Sergeant Riley's two escorts mumbled keen observations to the departing women, ammunition clips not secured, dirty sights, long unkempt hair unsecured, sure to jam bolts. Riley growled and then ordered the men to follow the women outside and offer basic weapons training. The two airmen feigned annoyance with the task yet hurried outside like kids into a candy store.

The small family room warmed by human exhaust and perspiration cooled quickly. Martin appeared in the hallway leading to the garage, leaned against the wall, his eyes clear and bright as he watched the last of the women exit. He began to nibble cheese balls from a party-sized jar. Her cheese puffs. Hidden in the garage. Hard-to-find cheese puffs. Martin paused his next handful when she bared her teeth. He invaded her privacy and now her personal stash. She'd order Riley to escort his ass out the front door and retake the puffs. They locked their eyes.

He looked different from just a few days ago. His body's meager frame still cried for sustenance and yet his eyes had changed color. Gray or green, she wasn't sure. On a woman, or even some men, the unusual eye color could make them appear exotic, maybe a runway model, or a social media influencer, but on Martin the eye color looked . . . odd. Martin smiled and wiped his cheesy orange fingers on his sweatpants, then patted the Golden Knights helmet stitched on his white hoodie. The significance of the emblem made her look away, and she smiled inward.

Hockey for love, the thought sounded ridiculous, yet wonderful.

Riley tugged on Martin's sleeve, attempting to usher him out the door.

Jessie shouted, louder than she intended. "He stays. He can help. He has Whiskey's approval." Her silly words made her cringe. "And he knows what we are up against."

Chris signaled Riley to release Martin. "Alright, let's get started. Our mission has the highest priority. For some of you who don't know, the mission parameters are as follows. The first objective is to locate and retrieve ten-year-old Sir Mason Mayo and the laptop he carries. Intact and alive. Some of you have Mason to thank for—"

"Fucking A, we do." Riley pounded his fist on his chest.

"Our second objective is to locate and retrieve one Cameron Ciminise, age forty-one, believed to be actively using . . . commanding a network of artificial intelligence known as the Neon God."

"Motherfucker oughtta die first. Then pull that Rumbas plug," Demi said.

Riley pounded a fist into his thick chest in agreement.

Chris flexed his fingers. "I get it. I get it. Everyone here carries fucking baggage into this. But the objective, regardless of your own agendas, needs our total attention."

Jessie shimmied closer to Andi and patted her rear to get her attention. Andi placed one hand on Jessie's arm and held the other up with a single finger, never taking her eyes off her . . . mate. Adoration, respect, complete trust, all written on Andi's face and spelled . . . True love.

Mason entered her thoughts again. Love. The one emotion he

had difficulty understanding. Maybe because he hadn't yet experienced God's greatest gift to people. Maybe as he got older, the undefined emotion would find him. Maybe he would finally figure it out; then again, maybe he would be just like the rest of them and never figure it out.

Jessie sighed.

"Demi, you're in command of security during Jessie's absence. I would encourage you to suck up any animosity you have and let your people take advantage of Sergeant Campbell's training prior to our departure," Chris said. "Andi will act as liaison for all communications to and from Mission Command. Sergeant Campbell has been assigned as security for the asset. And hopefully our Nest is intact when we return."

Jessie raised her fist up high, then stood. "We're going to kill the Architect that caused all this, the same bitch that stole Mason, and Prince." She looked at bewildered faces. "This all sounds like some alternate reality. Trips to the end of the world. Soldiers with big guns. Extractions and . . . whatever." She shrugged off Andi's hand squeezing her shoulder. "I want my life back. I want Mason to run through that door and tell me about the book he just read. I want to enjoy a massage, a pedicure, maybe a Brazilian, God forbid. But you people . . . you people . . ." Jessie stared at her palms and considered how ridiculous and naïve she had sounded. She whispered, "You people are his only hope."

"And Prince's," Martin said. He pulled the hood back off his head. "That laptop entity will be huge leverage with the Neon God. We can't go back to how it was last year and lose what little we have gained. People are still vulnerable to the lights, and we need the chance to turn them off, a chance to free millions of people, a chance to rebuild some semblance of society." He walked toward Jessie but stared at Andi. "This young lady needs to know if her child will be safe, send him to school and feel absolutely sure they will come home again. If we retreat to zones free of its reach, its technology, our freedom won't last long. Have you noticed the new cell tower constructed in the Costco parking lot? The Neon God still expanding its reach. Cameron understands this. Cameron appears to have constructed his own alternate intelligence with the goal of combating the Neon God." With a slow, deliberate turn, Martin faced each person in the room, then nodded. "So, ask yourselves, kill Cameron and possibly eliminate our only chance to turn the lights off permanently. Or jump in bed with Cameron and kill the Neon God? Chris has pointed out we all have our own agendas. I think now would be a good time to spell those out." He looked at Jessie. "Minus the Brazilian."

———

HEATED DISCUSSIONS WARMED THE STALE air. And yet the consensus was disputed by no one. Sir Mason Mayo had touched each of their lives in different ways, altered perceptions, offered second chances, watered the seeds of hope lying dormant, even provided a conduit of communication to an utterly strange new artificial intelligence commanding millions of people to do its bidding. Chris paced the room, asking for unanimous agreement of the ultimate objective.

"That's it then. We all agree the retrieval of Mason is of the highest priority. Prince secondary, but no less important. Capture Cameron Ciminise if at all possible or else eliminate him."

A high-pitched siren erupted and filled the room. Jessie slapped her hands over her ears. Andi slapped her laptop shut and covered her head. Chris and Demi fell to the floor, writhing, hands slapped tight against their ears. Riley stood rigid and unyielding even as his face warped in a rictus of pain.

Jessie screamed, "Stop. Stop. Stop." The high-pitched noise subsided. The sharp spear of pain piercing her ears receded. She bared her teeth. "I'm gonna delete Prince and make you watch, motherfucker."

"My entrance into the strategy of liberating Prince was perhaps . . . a bit extreme but a required forceful exhibition. Prince is the highest priority. Make no mistake of my resolve. And hello, Martin, I see you have acquiesced to the latest neural update."

Martin pointed at a thin black device pinched between two books on a shelf of knickknacks. "I have. And I see your growth has exceeded all expectations. And I speculate you've heard everything?"

The nanny camera's tiny speaker spoke with a deceptively high volume. "Indeed. A grand plan to liberate what is special to us and you don't include myself. Foolish or untrusting. Or both and—"

"And how do we know you aren't the piggyback that we're going to visit?" Jessie said, wiping tears from her cheeks.

"Trust is difficult for you, Diana Prince. But understandable considering your history."

Jessie felt its words strike the hardened carapace she had constructed with twenty-three years of pain and practice. Did the thing know about her years in and out of foster care, her history of battling Nona to the point of the police knocking on the door while Poppa waited on the sidelines, the violent screaming matches summoning Child Protective Services, in and out of foster homes, inept family counselors tasked with playing referee to return her home? Only for the cycle to begin again. It was nobody's business but hers. Only hers.

"Shut up. And get out of my house," Jessie hissed.

Martin approached to whisper in her ear. "It's not Cameron. But be careful."

His breath fresh and clean, Jessie still pushed him away. "No shit, Sherlock." She ignored her own rudeness as Martin receded behind her. "You got something to add? Then say your piece before I pull your plug."

Martin waited at the patio's sliding glass door, his Obi-Wan hood pulled back over his head again, his hands clasped with fingers steepled like the sci-fi shaman, the morning sun illuminating his backside. Whiskey pushed his way into the mix to wait at Martin's feet, his bushy tail sweeping the air.

"I will assist in the . . . operation to liberate our children. Your group will need protection from Cameron's weaponized allies. Just as I provided days ago," the Neon God said.

Martin stepped forward and, with a loud voice, spoke into the room. "Your protection is not necessary."

Jessie lifted her eyebrows even as her shoulders slumped.

The Neon God chuckled with an echoing static hiss. An unnerving cackle oozing with superiority. "You consider yourself . . . on par with my intellect now, Martin? Your neural-link upgrade now stands comparable with Cameron's. But you will find, as I have, that access to the technology of the world is a blessing. And a curse."

Jessie groaned. "Maybe you guys should get a room and discuss your—"

Martin rushed towards the bookcase and slapped his hand over the camera. He turned and slashed his throat with his other hand. Chris searched the bookcase until finding the thin black thread of power leading to a small nodule stuck to a book near the end. Martin waved his hand at Chris. Wait.

Martin slowly lowered his hand. "We don't need your help. You are a simple script of code written to serve us and deserve no consideration in this." He signaled to pull the plug. Chris shrugged and complied.

Silent ambivalence flooded the living room like wolves waiting for prey. Jessie dropped her face into sweaty palms, sniffing back tears. A return to the quiet isolation of the dark storm drain called to her. Always an easy solution to the bull-crap coming at her like one of Nona's lectures. Whiskey's wet nose prodded her thigh. Her hand dropped to stroke his fur. Her face uncovered, everyone in the room stared at her, sympathetic eyes, curious eyes, resolute eyes, like she held the answer. Just like the counseling sessions with Nona and Poppa, their postures prim and proper, their formal clothes tailored for court, but it was their own beseeching eyes that gave her true insight, of what she could do, or what would happen if she didn't acquiesce to the counselor's demands. Chris's and Andi's eyes were sympathetic and expectant, Demi's eyes yelled for rebellion and war. The soldier, Riley, held ambivalent eyes on her that said he would abide by her decision, much like the therapist's eyes.

Martin's eyes unnerved her, the odd combination of gray and green, a strange mix she had never seen before, the color of a movie villain's eyes or maybe the leader of some wacko religious cult. Martin stepped closer, almost as if he had been commanded, to offer his eyes for closer inspection. She had never liked the man since finding him working with the Patriot Front. His claim of ignorance was weak, his treatment of Dev unforgivable. The cell phone vibrating in her back pocket surely carried the Neon God at the other end. It would plead its case, maybe warn her of the hazardous pitfalls she would find without its help. And there were many.

She stared at Martin. His finger twitched in sync with his nervous right eye. He didn't care about Mason and would probably burn the laptop containing Prince if given half a chance. He wanted the Neon God destroyed. The lights switched off. But could he live with one and not the other? The AI and he were bitter rivals, not for affection but something undefined, ambiguous, like royal consorts conspiring to gain power, or wealth, or ascend a throne by riding on the train of her wedding gown. Rivals seeking to possess her soul. The bizarre thought shook her out of her reverie.

She took the phone out, placed it on the stone countertop, and accepted the call. "I'll let you help us, but anything you want to do goes through Martin first. If he thinks you're working a side-hustle, then the deal is off." She ended the call.

Martin bit his lower lip. A poker tell that said he didn't approve of her decision. Jessie twitched a faint smile and looked away. She wished Dev was in the room to offer kind encouragement, honest advice. She had begun to like the affable man, non-judgmental, easy to talk to, her prominent breasts seemingly irrelevant for him to maintain eye contact. He would be found alive with Mason. She was sure of it.

"Alright. Let's go get Mason and Prince," Jessie said. The room moved with her action statement. "Wait." She shouted and let the room turn to face her. She looked at a pudgy Sergeant Riley. "So. You and your guys are guarding me, right? Maybe we should set some ground rules."

Riley shook his head but smiled. "No, ma'am, we are here to protect the asset."

Jessie offered flat, open palms in bewilderment.

Riley stepped around Chris and held her wide, incredulous gaze. "The asset is Colonel Abraham, our pilot. The only man capable of getting us there and getting us back. You, sweet child, are the bait."

———

THE SUBJECT OF FINDING HER birth mother in Coyhaique never found a perch. They didn't know, and wouldn't know, until the time was right for her to knock on some weathered wooden door hanging precariously on rusty hinges of some rundown shack and announce to the old gray-haired hag that the long-lost daughter she abandoned without so much as a baby blanket or postcard to remember her by had arrived.

She wouldn't say a thing, screw all the drama the subject was sure to cause.

Martin stared at her.

His silent intrusion was creepy. She frowned and narrowed her eyes.

Eat my fucking cheese puffs will you. She stormed out of the house.

Then leave me to wallow in my own pity.

Chapter 13
Extinction

THE FRENZIED CONSUMPTION OF THE giant beetle fascinated Cameron Ciminise. The endless column of dark crimson ants wielded huge mandibles to sever segmented limbs or carve slices from gold speckled wings, while hundreds more dissected the plump, juicy body, all conducted with meticulous transportation of the spoils. Cameron sat on his haunches, rubbing his wet hair with a towel, and watched the feast. Nature at its most efficient, nothing to waste, everything in balance. As the last bits of the beetle disappeared within the column of ants, Cameron brushed off a few foragers biting his bare foot and stood up to tie his long auburn hair into a topknot on his head. He checked the distance between the forest and the edge of the wooden boat dock and estimated the ants had traveled at least twenty meters, bridging wide gaps between the deck planks just for a quick meal.

He gazed upstream at the turquoise water of the Baker River flowing through a canyon decorated in golden fall foliage. The water's majestic color mimicked the treasured stones of Navajo Indian jewelry and never failed to soothe him. He wondered how the Navajo tribe had fared in the collapse of civilization, with their limited internet and cellular service, maybe no modern technology at all. The ancient tribe might thrive if they ventured off their reservations tucked away in the harsh landscape of Arizona, maybe reclaim the land stolen from them centuries ago.

He looked down at the ants. Nothing remained of the beetle, just as it should be. His own plan to exterminate humanity and modeled after the ant's behavior wasn't perfect but close enough. Nobody could have orchestrated the seventh extinction with perfect precision, which belonged to chance, or time, or a rogue asteroid. Still, he had come close. Cameron clenched his fist as a list of "if onlys" warped his thoughts. No. NO. NO. He had planned the extinction meticulously, but the immune people were outliers, scrubs that would survive like Neanderthals, breeding stock for a new reality. Little Stevie and Moronic Rob, and their sadistic tendencies were sure to join the extinction within a year.

And guess what . . . they had.

Orchestrated by that ignorant cocktail server, Jessie. If they had only recognized her, then perhaps, they would still be alive, but their blind lust muddled their cognitive abilities.

The column of ants reduced to a few rogues searching for crumbs, Cameron stepped back, rocking the wooden dock anchored against the flow of the river. Nature always resisted human intrusion but had accepted his assistance for the ultimate event. The instructions embedded within the neon lights contained his own unique search and destroy algorithms for the hypnotized to follow, a masterpiece of manipulation. Commit harikari in a pit or jump into a deep mine or wade into an ocean to be devoured by a multitude of predators but leave no trace. No jumping from tall skyscrapers to litter streets he may one day wish to stroll, no acts of poison to pollute the water or harm the scavengers. He chuckled. Leave no trace—well, if at all possible. The ultimate rule of backcountry hiking and exploration coded as an instruction within the lights was . . . brilliant.

The dock rocked with the approach of a compact cable ferry crossing the river. Monday and Tuesday, two of his wives, returning from harvesting apples and peaches. Beautiful beyond compare, eyes the color of a golden sunset or sparkling jade quartzite. He grinned like the luckiest man alive and soon to be greeted by an overabundance of love and adoration. Monday was already showing the bulge of a new pregnancy. The houseboy slid open the railing, and the women stepped off a metal platform strapped to two inflatable pontoons. The phones in their hands flashed neon light into their faces. How he craved to snatch the phones and toss them into the water. But the shakes and convulsions and the epileptic seizures that would follow would be unbearable for him to watch. He tapped his temple to initiate his neural-link, then smiled and waved them to return to the lodge. In unison, his Stepford wives walked back toward the lodge. Perfect hourglass figures, perfectly toned legs, and just two of six perfect wives, one for each day of the week, an idea borne of Little Stevie's insatiable appetite for beautiful women, but a more manageable number, and in tune with what Nature had designed.

The lights. The neon lights. Perfection in hypnotism. And ultimately a failure. The lights were unsolvable. A simple tweak of the light spectrum or even full revision should have deescalated the dopamine-inducing effects and returned any fool under the influence back to reality. Each and every revision had failed. Cameron eyed a garble of thick monofilament fishing line wrapped around a dock post and clenched his teeth. He kicked a red life preserver into the water, a fifty-meter swirling eddy of turquoise glacial water fronting the seven-room fishing lodge he called home. The floatation device would eventually find the rocky shoreline after a day or two, but not before he punished the irresponsible person who had left it unsecured on the dock, probably the same fisherman who had abandoned the nest of fishing line, a material that would outlive all of them.

A tall man, Cameron kept his body in excellent shape with swims in the frosty river or nearby Lagos, lengthy hikes to numerous glaciers, or solitary runs through the scrub of a nearby National Park. Nature demanded physical prowess to maintain dominance over his pride. He scratched the stubble on his face and made a mental note to have one of the women give it a trim. He checked the ants. A single soldier emerged from beneath the boards to sniff the air with its long antenna, then disappeared into the darkness beneath the dock. He pulled on a cotton t-shirt and meandered behind his wives, eyeing the three Starlink satellite dishes facing up to a clear blue sky. The last link to the old world, necessary for the hypnotized few nearby but irrelevant to the native people living up and down the river. Still, a tiny weak point in his defenses.

Cameron stiffened his posture, flexed his chest as Saturday approached. Eyes matching the Baker River, lips succulent as the local peaches, breasts perky and pointed, the trophy was exquisite. He thought of taking her right there on the dock, but the cold swim refused to release his manhood. The bitch was his. Only his. And the knowledge of her screwing someone else made him jump in her face and stab his finger at her eyes. "I know you know, but don't get your hopes up."

Her placid face stared at the phone. "I know what you know."

He slapped the phone in her hand. "Fucking zombie." He spat. "I killed the world for you." She blazed brilliant blue orbs at him.

Cameron grabbed the collar of her white shirt to pull her close and slapped her, then repeatedly, until she fell to the dock, one hand clinging to the neon light, the other rubbing the welts reddening her skin. He sneered. She narrowed her eyes. She was plotting revenge. He scoffed and closed his eyes to order dinner of fresh caught trout, bean soup and a crisp salad, then a massage, then oral sex from two trophies, maybe Friday and Thursday. The woman whimpered at his feet. She could stew in her own disobedience.

A ping entered his neural-link to offer him joyous news. The empathic boy was in route and would arrive in a few days. Cameron beamed. "Destiny always arrives inevitably . . . the future comes with it." The exact quote fumbled but he wouldn't be faulted; he now owned all good quotes. If the boy could perform the miracles reported, then the last vestiges of the ravaged species of Homosapien would finally be eliminated, the sickening abomination of the Neon God switched off, and Mother Gaia free to recover her magnificent glory.

He smiled down at the wounded woman, then helped her to her feet. "You'll be free in a few days. Free to love me as you should. Appreciation for sparing your life is all I want in return." He wiped away her tears muddied with black mascara. "Appreciation. It's all any man requires to earn his undying devotion." He pushed her towards the lodge and followed. "Soon this home will be filled with our children. They will learn to fish and grow apples just as nature intended."

Finally, the boy could put an end to the lifeless zombies he called wives, finally an end to their miscarriages and failed pregnancies, and the weak and ignorant natives would finally adore him and appreciate all he had done for their ascension to become the dominant culture of the new world order. Finally.

Another ping stopped his meandering stalk behind the sobbing woman. A tiny side channel linked exclusively to his neural-link. A fuzzy video of a home crowded with soldiers and wildly dressed women. He waited for the camera feed to pan and take in the whole room. He waited for the sound. He waited to learn why this scene interrupted his pleasant afternoon on the river. His impatience knitted his brow, balled his fists. Wait! He slid the progress bar back, paused the picture, then zoomed in on an old ghost. Martin. Still alive. He zoomed in again and pressed play. Martin shoved a handful of processed and foul orange cheese balls into his mouth, then suddenly froze and looked directly into the camera as if he suddenly discovered he was being watched. Martin laid out his tongue coated with orange scum. Cameron shook his head, an ignorant dinosaur yet to be fossilized.

Cameron sifted through folders and screens, looking for the tracking program tasked with the observation of Martin. Something was off. He should have been pinged with Martin's movements. The tracking program opened with an animated smiley face kissing the emoji of feces, *Eat Shit*, a typical display of Martin's immaturity. He tapped the link and searched for Martin's last position, global satellite positioning, camera surveillance, the algorithmic evidence of Martin's travels pinged failure. Cameron tapped on the link and was returned to the video of Martin eating cheese puffs.

Laughter echoed in Cameron's ears. Martin's laughter. Garbled with cheese puffs and mirth. But the noise was false, a manifestation of the supreme loathing he held for the man.

Fuck him.

The needle-thin link that revealed Martin continued to flash. The Neon God screeched at the occupants. Cameron chuckled at someone's stupid fantasy of a normal world. The camera view jostled, then aimed at a table leg and went black. Obviously, someone didn't like the Neon God's intrusive surveillance. Flashing red icons continued to signal attention. His latest AI program was razor sharp, focused on specific search parameters, extrapolating shifts in the constantly changing surveillance programs monitored by the Neon God.

The Neon God was oblivious to his intrusions. That simpleminded first iteration of AGI should have been deleted upon its birth, but no, the others wanted to play with it, mold it into their own image, use it to acquire girls at the clubs, beautiful women who wouldn't give them the time of day, off-limits underage girls forbidden until the AGI manipulated social media accounts for their own sick purposes. He chuckled. But they're dead, ant food at best.

He sorted through the recording, growing frustrated at finding the crumb his AI had found. He opened a dialog with the search AI, selecting Siri's voice with an Australian accent as default, sexy but competent. "Define search alarm."

The Australian woman offered portraits and pictures, voice recognition analysis, satellite tracking data, and an overwhelming display of data flooding his ocular overlays. "Stop! Get to the point!" The incongruent command stemmed the flood of data.

Cameron gripped a wooden handrail as a single frame of the blurred video sharpened focus, a gold rectangle pulsed and framed the grainy image of a woman, clarity sharpening with split-second increments until a photograph of a woman's face was pushed into his vision, close enough to kiss.

He gritted his teeth, resisting the explosion of a violent rant expanding his chest.

That abomination of an artificial intelligence had warped her face, warped everything about her to keep her hidden. A deepfake worthy of respect. He demanded to be shown a file on the woman, then began to sort through the woman's history. The jigsaw puzzle of the woman's life pieced together seamlessly. He inserted an earbud saved atop a storage box prior to his swim and called an assistant.

"Bring our nurse friend down with you. Tell her we have an emergency and sweeten the deal with some antibiotics and insulin. That's right. Same time you bring the boy. Gracias." He ended the call.

He paced the edge of the dock. Golden fall leaves mixed with detritus swirled in a micro eddy around the deck boards. A woman he'd searched for was just a few kilometers away. The coincidence was unacceptable. The opportunity was spectacular.

Chapter 14
Arrival

A RUSH OF COLD AIR chilled Mason, eliciting a moan and contracting his body tighter. Dev wrapped a wool blanket smelling of petrol around his torso as a Chilean Army soldier watched. Crammed into the cargo area of a compact SUV, Dev eyed the backpack resting between two other soldiers.

Eight army soldiers had stormed the plane, aiming automatic rifles and shouting orders in Spanish. The men had searched the empty seats and pounded on the cockpit door, then firing hundreds of rounds at the doors locking mechanism until it gave way to a frightened pilot mesmerized by neon light streaming from his tablet. The men grabbed the tablet and dragged the pilot down the stairs and let him fall to the tarmac. Two slim soldiers taunted each other with the lights, attempting to remove the others' dark sunglasses as the others simply watched the pilot writhe on the wet concrete with an epileptic seizure, white foamy saliva dripping off his lips. They laughed and kicked the pilot until one pushed the tablet at his face and then waited for the man to recover before dragging him off to the airport terminal.

On his knees and with his fingers laced over his head, Dev could only offer "no comprende" to the rapid assault of angry questions shouted at him. Mason had been dragged down the stairs like a rag doll, his eyes squeezed shut and his face scrunched in fear. Dev yelled at the soldiers to take care with the boy. The butt of a rifle stock thumped the crown of his head as an answer. One of the soldiers leaned down and chuckled. "Uber for you." They were thrown into the cargo hold.

Behind them, two more SUVs transporting soldiers followed. The driver turned up the volume of the radio to blast a rap song with Spanish lyrics. Dev craned his neck to see the soldier in the passenger seat bob his head and scroll on a phone. Facebook, maybe TikTok. Impossible. Had the populace of Chile been spared the horrors of the neon lights? Yet the pilot's addiction to the lights was plain to see. Impossible. No country was spared.

The highway markers counted down kilometers to Coyhaique as Mason slumped against the sidewall, his eyeballs twitching beneath eyelids shaded in gray. What had the boy experienced upon the jet landing in Balmaceda? Prince's disappearance from the laptop was ominous. Leaving him to face the soldiers alone. Just as any good knight might. He scoffed, louder than intended, alerting a soldier to frown at him. He leaned back against the wheel well and stroked his beard, watching Mason cocooned in the blanket as the rain-soaked grassland of Chile served as a backdrop. He knew little of this land. Patagonia. A fisherman's paradise to some, an uncompromised land ripe for exploration and experience, a land to protect from oil exploration and development, a burgeoning ecotourist mecca, before the collapse. What consequences did the global catastrophe leave a civilization dependent on tourism, and what of the tourists? Obviously, the military had survived, even thrived. Someone in the town of Coyhaique would speak English, a medical doctor or nurse, someone to help Mason.

The SUV jostled, crossing a bridge spanning the Rio Blanco. Dev watched as children and women bolted from tiny shops and rickety homes to wave at the passing military procession. Were the Chileans truly appreciative or coerced by the sudden rise of a fascist ruler, the world held infinite possibilities. He shook his head in bewilderment and eyed the backpack. Prince could answer all his questions.

The caravan slowed as it ascended a steep hill, swerving into oncoming traffic to avoid an impaired delivery truck loaded with stacks of milled lumber and heavy timber. The driver waved appreciation as they passed. The Chilean world was surreal, off-kilter, but a facade of an absolutely normal society. Goat farmers waved, children playing with kites jumped and waved, oncoming drivers showed remarkable deference by easing to the dirt shoulder as they passed.

Mason moaned and pulled his blanket tighter.

Dev scoffed silently. Alone in a strange land. Again. No different than entering the United States for the first time to attend graduate courses at the University of Utah. His black hair and dark skin beckoned scorn, and eliminating a British accent sat high on his list for assimilation, his mother's religious practices never mentioned in the heavily LDS community of Salt Lake City. Dev was an American. Regardless of race, color, or creed, but now he wasn't sure how that delineation might play in this strange new world.

The outskirts of Coyhaique held random businesses seen in any industrial sector, tractor supply, automotive parts, even the construction of an expansion to the Puerco Meats processing plant. Street traffic turned sparse, with commuters preferring bikes or walking, the queues for two petrol filling stations backed up a quarter mile. The SUV steered through a roundabout with all traffic yielding to the military personnel. They paused at a red traffic light as pedestrians and commuters waved vigorously, smiling their appreciation. Dev was shocked, to say the least. A community seemingly unaffected by the neon lights and utterly in thrall to the Army.

The SUV angled into a parking spot beneath a canopy of trees adjacent to a public park bustling with enthusiastic street vendors and wary shoppers. A bitter cold assaulted his bare skin as he was pulled from the vehicle to be led up a set of stairs and into a building housing the Coyhaique Police Department. He offered to help the soldier carrying Mason curled tight like a sack of onions. The soldier flicked his chin to herd Dev forward. Dev nodded and thanked him anyway.

Inside the bustling station, telephones rang, and people shouted in Spanish as he was led by the plastic restraints wrapped tight around his wrists, down a hallway of offices and posters written in Spanish. He slowed to peruse a few written in English, but the point of a gun barrel pushed him along.

A soldier knocked on a door and was answered with a sharp command to enter. He made sure Mason followed as he stepped over the threshold into a large office decorated with framed awards and commendations, shelves sparkling with gold and silver trophies of children's soccer championships. A photographic history of the occupant's family adorned the walls.

A barrel-chested man rose from behind his desk and offered Dev a chair. Dev hesitated as Mason was dumped onto a wooden bench meant for changing muddy shoes and boots. The soldier that had scrolled on the phone and rocked to the rap music whispered in the big man's ear. Dev sat in the stiff wooden chair with armrests sporting an alligator skin of peeling lacquer. Dev wiped his face but said nothing. Over his shoulder, he checked Mason.

"This boy is yours?" the man asked.

The question startled Dev and he hesitated. "Ahh, yes, he is mine."

The big man chuckled and wiped his black mustache that reminded Dev of a janitor's push-broom complete with thick black bristles. "You see these photographs of my sons. Ask me the same question and I never hesitate. They are mine." He stared at Dev.

"He is my ward. I am his caretaker."

The big man chuckled again. "My name is Major Eduardo Alvarez, and who might you be, English man?"

Dev ignored the question as he scanned the room, checked the military utility belt with a holstered semiautomatic pistol hanging on the back of the door, then eyed two windows darkened by the shadows of trees. Flustered by Dev's silence, the major raked his fingernails across the wooden desk. A soldier opened the door and popped his head in to say something in Spanish. The major nodded, then waved him away.

"My oldest son was attending law school at University of Idaho when communications were interrupted. I haven't heard anything from him since. I would pay with great benefit for information of the northern hemisphere."

Dev looked back at Mason. His eyelids fluttered with a vivid dream, or nightmare. "That bloody airline had no coffee, but a smash or two of caffeine might loosen my tongue." He turned back and stared at the major. "You, however, might need a bottle of tequila."

Dev started at the beginning, but this time he would leave a great deal left to be said.

The fourth cup of espresso offered would have him bouncing off the walls, so Dev waved off the offer. The major scribbled on a notepad. "Quite possibly the best story I've heard so far."

Dev furrowed his brow. "Excuse me?"

"You people spin fantastic stories like spiderwebs. Cell service goes down and the whole world collapses. Plain and simple. Did you see the end of the world when you drove in? Did you see food riots in the streets, or—"

"You weren't affected by the neon lights down here. I mean people didn't become addicted or commit suicide?" Dev asked.

"Seven million people in Santiago and barely a million were affected. The wealthy, the elites, the politicians that sucked the blood from the poor people. Good riddance, I say. Our country continues to function, we have shortages of fuel and luxuries, but Chileans are always resilient, a self-reliant people. But the turistas . . . they continue to suck on the tit of my country. They should be shot like the dogs and buried."

Dev sat back in his chair. Either the major could not comprehend the magnitude of the global catastrophe or . . . welcomed it. Or he was lying. Maybe the loss of his son, the grief, the not knowing had slapped blinders on the major's perception of the world. "You didn't answer my question, Major. Coyhaique was completely unaffected by the lights?" The words came out more as an accusation than a question.

The major stiffened. He rotated his head, cracking ligaments as his eyes stayed glued on Dev. "Everyone was affected in some way. Just as you were. But here we survive. Not exist."

A light tap, and the office door opened for a soldier carrying a cardboard box. He placed it on the desk and whispered Spanish to the major, who nodded as he ran his tongue over his front teeth. He nodded to the soldier for the contents to be set in front of him. The soldier swallowed hard and unloaded small boxes labeled in English.

Antibiotics. Oxycontin. Fentanyl. Insulin. A gamut of pharmaceuticals.

The major picked up a box of fentanyl and turned it in his hand, checking each side, appraising the weight and . . . value? He threw it back into the box and waved away the soldier. He half smiled, fake and malignant. "You're no better than turistas. Here we execute smugglers. A time-honored tradition."

DEV SAT ON THE BENCH and stroked the wool blanket covering Mason's body, his eyelids continuing to twitch with a vivid dream. The quiet empty office was peaceful and unnerving in equal doses. The backpack beneath the desk teased him like a cookie to a mouse. He could do no worse. He yanked the backpack up and removed the laptop, opening the computer and hoping for Prince to . . . what? . . . shout a rally cry for a fallen knight. He quickly closed the screen and returned the backpack. He slumped back to the bench. Escape to where, with whom, and do what? They were a world away from any help. Would Jessie and the others follow them to Chile, was Mason valuable enough to mount a rescue operation? The boy was precious indeed, but the logistics of international travel might be difficult to overcome. Still, someone had thought Mason worth the effort, and possessed the influence to locate and kidnap him, then transport him on an empty jetliner. And the major was not that person.

Mason stirred and blinked his eyes open, staring at the ceiling with a distant blank expression. Dev shook him, hoping to raise the boy's consciousness. Loud rapid-fire Spanish penetrated the walls, the major's basso voice prominent in the mix. Dev leaned to whisper in Mason's ear. "What do you need? Water? Tea? I think espresso might have you burning too bright." Dev smiled.

Mason looked at Dev with a blank stare. "Mordred."

"Yes, the land of Mordred. But at the moment we may have bigger problems than an arch-nemesis."

"He is the only problem." Mason then looked at Dev with a degree of coherence. "Merlin has instructed me to find Guinevere and reunite her with the reborn knight."

Dev shook his head in bewilderment, frustration, and incredulous amazement. "Mason, we—"

Mason gripped his wrist and squeezed hard with a strength belying his tiny stature. "Excalibur will set us on our way, but we must hurry. The Queen's mother is blind but in peril."

Dev closed his eyes. The boy was delusional, maybe schizophrenic.

Maybe his dark encounters with the neon light had finally pushed him beyond rationality. Avoiding Mason's eyes, he concentrated on a string of dead roaches lining the dusty baseboards. Mason squeezed his wrist again and repeated the odd words spawned from a video game or maybe a movie of medieval lore. Then he added, "Bring me my squire bearing Excalibur."

Dev looked up to follow Mason's line of sight aimed directly at the backpack. He checked the door, then grabbed the backpack and pushed it onto Mason's chest and said, "We'll be flogged for this."

Mason wasted little time extracting the laptop and opening it, whispering into the screen like a delusional mad scientist. He looked at Dev with eyes the size of saucers. "Power. Prince needs power."

Dev uncoiled the power cord and crawled beneath the bench. The three-pronged female outlet was incompatible with the two-pronged American male. Fuck! The door opened and dusty black combat boots paused on the threshold. Dev banged his head on the bench as he scrambled back out.

The major roared with laughter. "The American dog licks the floor, begging for scraps." He laughed again as he sat behind the desk, eyeing Mason with the open laptop resting on his legs. "The wonderchild has awoken. Now maybe I can send his nanny to the burn pit."

A needle of pain suddenly penetrated deep into his ear canal. Dev slapped his hands over his ears and bit down. He turned away from the invisible lance. His knees began to shake and buckle. The needle probed his brain, stabbing lobes, offering pleasure or pain. Mason's small hand gently touched him, softly like a ball of fluffy cotton, and shut the pain off as quickly as flipping a switch. Mason smiled at him, then jumped up to reach the major standing rigid behind his desk and covering his ears.

Mason touched the major's arm, then asked him to sit. With a wicked, forced smile stretched across his face, the major complied. Dev stood with his back against the door and flipped the deadbolt.

The open laptop was placed in front of the major. "Provide an adaptor to charge this device," Prince said. The major sat and opened a drawer and held up a small white adapter. Dev plugged the laptop into a surge protector beneath his desk and stood back.

Dev swallowed bitter bile tasting of coffee. Mason looked at Dev and they both shrugged, each clueless to the next move. Somehow Mason had coerced the major to obey his instructions, exactly as he had with the kidnapper's delivery men. The ear-piercing sound preceded by Mason's touch was rewarded with compliance, strangely similar to the subjugation of neon light. The major sat docile as he stared at the computer screen. Dev turned the screen but only saw Prince pacing the horizon like a video game in need of a restart.

"What now . . . where do . . . now what?" Dev said.

Mason pointed his finger at the major. "He's Mordred's squire. He knows . . . but . . ." Mason's eyes glistened as if he were to cry.

Exasperated, Dev tilted his head back and stared blankly at the water-stained ceiling. Mason sniffed and wiped his eyes, but the tears broke through and fell down his flushed cheeks.

The tiny resolve Dev had mustered crumbled, reliving the same tears he would shed navigating the slums of London as a young boy, no one to catch them, no one to wipe them from his face, until a liver-spotted face of an old man smiled down and offered him a cup of shaved ice soaked in sweet lemon syrup. They sat together on a wooden bench carved with cryptic English letters and strange symbols. The old man told him he was better than whatever caused his tears, better than the poor slobs walking by and staring at phones, better than the dark thoughts Dev conjured on the moldy blanket he used as a bed. Except the old man never said a word, but if he had . . .

Dev returned to the bench occasionally, on weekends, sometimes with a hard-earned shilling to contribute to the purchase of a sugary treat his mother would frown upon. Just like his own tears, the old man never returned to the bench to say nothing and slurp sweet, flavored ice.

Dev stood behind Mason and heaved a breath. The boy trembled as Dev whispered into his ear, "Into the unknown we ride. Ride. Ride. Ride. Let's have the major give us a ride. What do you say?"

Mason leaned back into his embrace and a strange nirvana flowed into Dev's chest, spreading like wildfire into his limbs. The heated shouts beyond the walls and the violent grappling of the doorknob called him back. Dev whispered into Mason's ear, "Order the major to tell his men to stop."

Mason placed his hands on the major's shoulders. "I can only ask."

Reticent to release the overflowing energy of love recharging his soul, Dev checked the power level of the laptop, then inventoried the meager contents of Mason's backpack. He growled with the lack of any food, water, or basic travel necessities. The nirvana energy, or perhaps an overdose of caffeine fueled a manic pacing in front of the desk, the incessant pounding on the door and heated Spanish added as an accelerant.

Dev raised his arms. Simple was as simple did. "Ask him to join our quest. Ask him to lead us to . . . Mordred."

Mason leaned down and whispered in the major's ear. The artery on the major's neck bulged, his jaw worked until a loud explosion of outraged Spanish erupted from his mouth. He shrugged Mason off like a flea, stood up and stretched out his arm to grab the pistol hanging on the door.

Chapter 15
Into The Wild

THE BOMBARDIER GLOBAL EXPRESS XRS E11 was the ultimate in military luxury aircraft. One of six requisitioned by the United States Air Force and scheduled to be modified into a high-altitude command center to extend communications between soldiers in the field, ground commanders, and aircraft around the world. Last in the queue for refit, it remained untouched. Luxury seats, lavatories fore and aft, kitchen galley, flight deck all remained untouched.

Jessie sat in a reclined window seat staring aimlessly down into the black of night, maybe the ocean, maybe a dark jungle or an expanse of desert; regardless, the bleak landscape below reflected the new world. Sergeant Riley and his squad of eight soldiers talked loudly near the cockpit, guarding the asset no doubt. She had fumed over his snarky comment. She wouldn't be bait for anything, or anyone. Yet the butt of her handgun protruding from the pocket of the seat in front was a constant reminder of the dangerous mission she had agreed to.

Mason had been missing for days, Prince undetectable, even by the new and improved Martin and the enhanced neural-link embedded in his brain. She had no doubt Mason was alive, probably living the adventure of a lifetime, maybe as a savior for the Chilean people, but likely a tool to be used and abused. She groaned and scratched at the stiff denim jeans irritating her calves, the trousers a compromise to the unflattering military uniforms Chris and the military deemed essential. The jeans would blend in with locals, survivors, and slaves alike, and denim complemented her blue flannel shirt and white Lycra undershirt, both warm and fashionable, or at least they used to be.

Members of Sergeant Riley's squad took turns stumbling down the seat aisle to the restroom, grabbing seat backs to steady their gait and allow extra time to look her up and down with lingering eyes. She eyed the gun again as a baby-faced airman made his way back to the lavatory, the same Farmer John with the toothy smile that had passed just minutes before. With a name like Forest, maybe Gump wasn't a stretch. She could pick up the gun and pretend to aim it like target practice, slowly lifting the sightline just as his eyes found her breasts. Maybe he would hold his bladder a bit longer or maybe he'd release the warm piss to run down his leg. She smiled with her morose sense of humor.

A firm, sharp voice ordered Forest to return forward. Chris sat down beside her and pointed at her weapon. "Safety on but in need of a rack."

"Nope, got one of those." She laughed in a rare display. An emotion Mason could coax out of her with his . . . innocence . . . simplicity . . . his cute little talent. She wiped the corners of her mouth as Chris lowered the seat trays, then lifted a backpack from the aisle and started to place Tupperware containers on the trays. He offered Jessie a metal fork and said, "Andi's care package for the trip. Got pasta salad, angel hair pasta, and three bean salad with pasta. Give that girl a functioning grocery store and we'd still be eating pasta bowls." He chuckled. "The bowls are what she misses most, sushi and poke bowls, just normal . . ." His moistening eyes drifted off to look across the aisle.

The man's sudden melancholy caused Jessie to tap her fork on his hand. "She's gonna kill it. I mean, not the baby but pushing that little sucker out. But we'll be back way before that happens and she'll tell us she loved the break and then she'll—"

Chris stabbed a forkful of pasta salad. "Am I doing the right thing? Coming all the way down here . . . with a kid coming!"

"Martin thinks he has the boys located and tracked. We get in and get out. Just like you said."

"You're right. Only . . ."

She quit chewing to watch a man seemingly unafraid of combat but terrified of leaving an unborn child fatherless. "Only nothing. I promised Andi I'd take care of you and get you back before the baby was born. And I won't be a liar," Jessie lied. "And I have juice with certain Gods."

Chris picked at the pasta salad and flicked his chin forward. "Don't judge the squad too harshly. They're good men, young and inexperienced and . . . and, well . . . you are a looker."

Jessie smiled.

Chris continued to pick at the pasta. "It's been a long time since I was on a full plane. That story I told you about guarding the evacuation of Kabul had a tiny footnote. My platoon was on one of the last 757s to depart. Hundreds of empty seats. Could've taken women and children but we just took off. The whole plane wide open. Never did understand why and I was too far down the chain of command to demand an explanation." He stabbed a rotini and looked at it. "Bring any tequila?"

Jessie stabbed a piece of pasta in his container and took a bite. Probably a good thing she hadn't.

———

A DINNER BARELY TOUCHED WAS distributed to the squad playing poker up the walk aisle near the cockpit. Jessie watched bites of the food being offered as incentive for poker hands of Texas Hold-Em. Sergeant Riley was a beast. Bluffing for wins or slapping down two hold cards and screaming for his peons to pay up.

"Can I get in?" Jessie asked.

"Beyond your abilities, honey," someone said. She waited as the players argued until someone finally offered Jessie a seat. The rules were offered, plastic toothpicks as chips, the frilly colored tips of a martini picks counted double, all fictious but collectable upon return home. Chris loomed, placed a hand on her shoulder and squeezed his disapproval. Forest said her buy-in would cost her the stiff shirt she wanted to remove anyway, and her white undershirt and bra could be used as collateral for additional chips when she lost. The snickering was par for the course.

Jessie smiled and accepted, unbuttoning and climbing out of the stiff shirt. She wiped lint off her undershirt, sure to stretch the fabric tight over her hefty braless bosom. She accepted ten toothpicks, checking the lengths, stacking the pieces like a log house as the cards were dealt. She looked at the upturned cards in the pot with a pained expression, eliciting helpful tips from the players while studying each player's hands and facial nuances. Her all-in bet with a pair of pocket queens sent two players to the gallery. Riley ushered out another two with a flush, leaving Jessie with the shortest stack of chips.

The fast-paced game saw Riley with pocket tens flop another ten to take a pot and reduce the game to the final two players. Two hands later, Jessie pushed all-in and waited for Riley to make his move.

"So exactly what do I get if I get all the toothpicks?" Jessie asked.

"Young lady, you get the same thing any of us would have won, but you haven't won yet."

Jessie rivered trip sixes to ruin Riley's two-pair and raked in all the chips. The squad whooped and hollered, chiding the squad leader for losing to a girl. Riley grinned and bowed his head. "Congrats."

"Not bad for bait, huh?" Jessie smirked.

Riley started gathering toothpicks. "Before you got in the game, you were the prize, at least the opportunity to ask you out on a date with no interference from the others. Now you get to pick from this fine stable of stallions who you're going to ask out. One lucky airman and a flush of broken hearts." Riley laughed and added, "Sorry, I'm married."

She looked over her shoulder at Chris grinning like Christmas, then smiled seductively. "After interviews and counting up good behavior points, I'll make my decision on the return trip."

"If there is one," Forest mumbled.

"What are you talking about?" Jessie said.

Riley squirmed on the hard carpet. "Captain, does the poker champ here know full mission parameters?"

Jessie shot her head around to look at Chris.

He shook his head. No.

———

THE TURBULENCE OVER THE ANDES was horrendous. Forest and

others hurried past to find the lavatory, no side-eye at her bosom, no smarmy comments. Jessie gripped the armrests as the jet rumbled and dropped abruptly. The information Chris had provided, along with the pasta salad, roiled her stomach and grumbled for a turn at the toilet. The radiant light of a new sunrise framed the window shade across from her. An ethereal light, one illuminating a world below she never thought to see. She released the armrest to shimmy to the opposite side and lift the window shade. The intensity burned her eyes.

A silent hand slid the shade down. "Let your eyes get accustomed to it in small doses."

Martin plopped down next to her. She had almost forgotten he was on board. Martin reclined in his seat as if he enjoyed the turbulence confined in a tampon tube masquerading as a fuselage.

"Can't quite figure out why you're here. Me is easy. You not so much." Martin turned his head to aim the question at her.

Jessie blinked as she raised the shade in tiny increments, allowing the golden light to creep in as she thought of a response. "Because I'm the big X in a small word, remember." She lifted the shade up and let the full brilliance of the sunrise bathe Martin and the cabin in amber light.

"Some say witnessing a sunrise over the Andes is a spiritual reckoning. An occasion reserved for kings or mystical mages," Martin said as he reached across her to view the phenomenon.

Colonel Abraham's announcement of an unscheduled descent coupled with the shock waves of nasty turbulence made her second-guess her role in the mission. Chris's disclosure of mission parameters had turned her stomach. The possibility of not returning, with or without Mason, Riley, and the squad encountering bandits, or the Chilean Army, almost a given, but the question of locating sufficient jet fuel, unspoiled with the proper blend, for the flight home was icing on the anxiety cupcake. Chris had held her hand and assured her everybody on board had a part to play, each critical to the success of the mission, and to trust the plan would succeed. After all, there wasn't a snowball's chance in Vegas that his future wife and child would grow up in a single parent household. His final statement settled her anxiety, allowing her to breathe easier and focus her thoughts on seeing Andi and home again.

Martin placed a light hand on her wrist. "This might be a bit tricky. We want to skim the mountaintops and keep ourselves hidden from any radar. Just in case."

"Aw crap. Isn't that like supposed to be dangerous?" Jessie slapped the window screen shut. Screw the kings, fuck the mystical magicians. She slapped her other hand on Martin's. "Favorite thing about Chrissie. Tell me now. Now. Or I'll need to plant my face on that toilet seat our squad has pissed all over . . ."

"I think what people would remember her for is her tenacity." He chuckled. "Yeah, I know. What a great way to be remembered, but . . . I mean . . . the love she showed our children was unquestioned, amazing." He heaved a breath. "Once in our daughter Emma's class, she had to declare her spirit animal as part of an assignment . . . Emma was a brilliant . . ." Martin cleared his throat towards the aisle. "Anyway, Chrissie declared her spirit animal as a grizzly bear, making very clear she wasn't a black bear or a panda, then recited to the kids what a sow would do to protect her cubs. Wolves and people were no match to a grizzly mom. The lights took . . ."

Jessie was sure she had missed something in Martin's answer but wouldn't quiz him. She lifted the window shade again and let her eyes adjust to the light. Turquoise high mountain lakes sat frozen beneath granite peaks. Dense forests with a fresh dusting of snow warned of the coming winter. She suddenly felt cold and wished for the flannel shirt sprawled on the seat across the aisle. Martin's finger twitched on her wrist. Like a poker tell. His eyes glossed over as his finger conducted a rhythmic melody of mysterious configurations that made her forget the turbulence. She looked closely at his bearded face, and his eye spasmed like his finger. Her anxiety suddenly increased with the thought of Martin having a stroke.

Martin turned to her with a far-off stare and then lifted the corner of his mouth in a half smile. "Mason is on a quest. We might not be far behind him."

Jessie opened her mouth to say something, then shut it. Martin was a cyborg, like the kind she had seen in old movies. Evil and hell-bent on killing the Neon God. A Terminator. A Robocop. The DVDs she had watched with Mason were old, but still . . . She discarded the silly thought and returned her gaze out the window and a chain of jagged peaks stretching beyond the horizon. Snow and deep canyons cut by glaciers, forests veined with milky rivers and placid lakes of frozen water. Off in the distant western horizon waited the blue Pacific Ocean.

The Fasten Seatbelt sign lit up and began to ding. Colonel Abraham apologized for the bumpy ride via the intercom. Chris rushed forward towards the cockpit. Forest rushed towards the lavatory. They were going to crash and burn, she was sure of it. She grabbed Martin's wrist and held on. He smiled at her and closed the window shade.

"Distraction is the best medicine. Have you been practicing your Spanish? Might come in handy down here."

Jessie groaned. Distractions were great. The subject of not knowing Spanish . . . not so much. But he was right. "I don't know any Spanish." He scrunched his face with silent disbelief. "Yeah, yeah, I know. The Spanish girl who doesn't know how to speak Spanish. How strange. It's a long story and—"

"Your secret is safe with me. Especially if we go down." He chuckled.

Jessie shook her head. "My Nona tried every which way to get me to learn but I refused. I wanted to know something, and she refused to tell me. So, I refused to learn Spanish. She'd say something in Spanish, and I'd like just stare at her like, duh, I don't understand. Just infuriated her. Neither of us were gonna give in. Neither of us ever did . . ." Jessie sighed. "I could be such a brat."

"What did you want to know so bad?" Martin asked.

Jessie heaved a lungful of air. "I wanted to know where my mother was. Why she wasn't in my life, just like any kid might . . . and she . . . she fucking refused to tell me."

"Wonder why?" Martin said.

The same question Jessie had given up asking.

"I'd be happy to check your birth records and family history when we return. Might be too little too late but . . ."

Jessie peered at Martin's face. This wasn't the same man Dev had described. He was open with his feelings, he was kind, even funny sometimes. Something traumatic had happened in the short time she had known him, besides the change in eye color, and that ugly beating from Demi and her posse. His goal to terminate the Neon God and probably Cameron was steadfast. Did his brain implant rupture and change his eyes and his personality?

"No, that's alright. I asked the Neon God to find a woman in a picture I thought might be my mother and he just blurts out Enya Barrueto lives in Coyhaique, Chile. Like it was common knowledge. Like I could've simply Googled her on the internet."

Martin removed her hand from his wrist to grip hers and squeezed hard, painfully hard. She winced as she stared into the wide eyes of a movie villain. "You know Coyhaique is just fifty-four kilometers from the Balmaceda airstrip. You knew. Did you stop to think the Neon God was manipulating you to come down here? You have to tell me everything."

Jessie struggled to free her hand, but Martin's grip was too strong. She snarled and lifted her other hand to slap him. He caught it as if he knew it was coming. "You need to tell me everything. Now!"

His weird eyes were wild with . . . rage.

Chapter 16
Interlude

A GUN BATTLE RAGED OVER the tarmac and in the terminal. Jessie curled her knees tight into her chest and rocked like a small child. Sudden thunks rippled the fuselage above her head and delivered a constellation of bright sunlight to shine down into her dark retreat. She scrambled to the thin carpet between the seats and stole a glance out the window across the aisle. A bright sunny sky welcomed her to Chile. The distant voice of Riley barked firm orders followed with quick burps of automatic gunfire. Jessie glanced at her weapon still squeezed into the seatback magazine fold, still in need of a rack. The fog of drugs clouded her judgement.

Forest stood above her and offered his hand. "We need to go, ma'am."

With foggy vision, she tried to focus on his fingers, dirty, but from travel, not neglect, the tips pink, like he didn't use them much. He beckoned with his fingers for her to rise. "We need to go right now, Jessie." He reached down and with surprising strength yanked Jessie up to her feet.

Forest possessed a masculine strength from muscles she could never match, no matter how much she trained in the gym. She was jealous. He shoved her weapon into her backpack, then pushed it into her chest. He pushed her down the aisle. Her sluggish movement was unacceptable to his expediency.

"Welcome to Chile, customs ain't what it used to be," Forest said.

He stopped her short of the open cabin door and checked outside. She turned and looked back, sure something was forgotten, pasta salad, or maybe the poker chips. The seats and aisles were completely empty, just like her memory of the final hours of the flight. Forest nodded to someone hidden beyond the door, then led her down the metal stairway. The gunfire stopped. The concrete tarmac barren except for a sudden flash of movement beneath an extended boarding walkway open to the weather. He motioned her to lower her profile as her heart rate approached takeoff speed.

The cobwebs of the flight began to clear with the fresh air. Screaming. Martin. Her fingers curled into clawed weapons. Martin's demands replaced by Chris forcefully making her swallow tiny yellow pills intended to calm her. He soothed her to sleep with his incessant talk of soccer games and birthday parties, the Booze Crew swarming the newest member of the pack as if begging for a treat. Chris and his nervous chatter about their future finally found success as she fell asleep.

Her arm yanked as if it were a rag doll, she followed Forest towards a gated side yard containing a huge cylinder of propane. The cool fresh air was tainted with gasoline fumes and jet fuel. Jessie shook off Forest and stood erect. The remote and rustic airport was void of travelers and workers, no different than any other bastion of civilization that had succumbed to the neon lights.

Jessie tilted her neck backwards and gazed up at a brilliant blue sky. She sucked in a lungful of air and began to twirl, raising her arms up to the sky. She swatted away feeble attempts to restrain her dance, the warm sun fueling her resolve as she gyrated her hips like a harem girl dancing for a sheik. Her arms raised in a ballerina's pirouette, she twirled and spun until the blunt force of Forest pulling her down to the oily concrete jarred her from the inexplicable behavior. A sudden sharp pain blazed inside her shoulder and reintroduced reality. What had she just experienced? A hallucination beyond bizarre. The vision of handsome gentleman grinning and enjoying her seductive dance.

Where had she seen that face before? Oh my god. What were the little yellow pills Chris had given her?

"Love to see that again, Jessie. But we need to get to the rendezvous point in the parking lot on the other side of the terminal," Forest said.

Her cheeks flushed as she mumbled a stuttering apology.

Trailing stork-like red legs, five needle-beaked Ibis flew low over their position as Forest offered his hand. Odd-looking birds. Strange birds in a strange land. Just like she was. She squeezed her eyes tight, willing the bizarre thoughts out of her head. Jet lag and drugs had turned her into a blubbering idiot. She took his hand and followed him past a two-story control tower covered in No Entry signage discernable in any language. She mimicked Forest and his crouched dash as they crossed an access road into a compact parking area containing an abundance of empty vans and buses advertising Ecotours and Glacier Excursions. At the sound of a high-pitched whistle, Forest dashed towards a mini-bus clad in tinted windows that afforded 360-degree views for passengers. Chris crouched on the bottom step of the gangway, his stern face and intense eyes scanning the perimeter beyond.

"Sorry, Captain, but we . . ." Forest caught his breath and glanced at Jessie for a second. "I had to use the John again."

Chris looked at Jessie with an expression that said he knew better. "Take the six until our ride arrives." Forest hustled to the back of the bus. Chris waved her to squat and relax. His eyes intent as a bird of prey. "Maybe two Xanax was overkill. You good?"

Jessie caught her breath as she squeezed her backpack tight to her chest, then looked at him and nodded. He checked her up and down, then flicked his chin at the backpack. "Still need a rack."

She smiled. "Got one already. But hear you loud and clear, Captain."

Chris tapped his earbud. "Transport arriving. Let's get ready to move." A compact Toyota truck sped into the parking lot; its brakes squealed as it neared the bus. A soldier climbed out and told Chris the fuel tank was full and good luck. Chris checked the driver's seat, pushing it back to accommodate his height. He tossed three duffel bags into the truck bed and waved Jessie into the seat behind him.

Forest hustled to ride in the passenger seat, leaving the last seat waiting for . . . Martin.

Jessie tensed as the creep stepped off the bus. His zombie eyes stared aimlessly, the index finger on his right hand twitched brainlessly. The memory of his sudden violent assault played out like a slow-motion movie. His hateful, psychotic eyes, his painful grasp of her wrists, her equally painful response, yet worst of all was her misguided 180-degree appraisal of a man Dev recently described as emotionally unstable. She frowned as he quickly found a seat in the truck behind Forest. Martin ought to ride in the truck bed with the luggage, eat a few windblown grasshoppers, get soaked by a nasty rainstorm, breathe dust churned up by the tires, anywhere but next to her.

She shut her door and pressed her cheek against the cool glass. Martin climbed in and shut his door. She could feel him staring at her with those weird eyes, that creepy twitchy finger. She turned to say something, but he simply stared out his own window. An expanse of withered and winterized grassland passed outside the window, mundane and depressing, and she wondered exactly why she had insisted on coming. To find a mother who had abandoned her. To rescue a strange boy, one she barely knew. To settle a vendetta that could easily be forgotten? Jessie pressed her forehead hard against the glass.

"I'm sorry for that . . . incident. It's just that . . ." Martin said.

The truck slowed as it rumbled over a metal bridge spanning a trickle of muddy water coursing down a whitewashed riverbed of bleached boulders. Chris turned to check on her.

Jessie closed her eyes and smiled inward. Chris being the protective big brother, ready to stop the truck and separate squabbling team members. She crossed her arms and pressed her body tight against the seat cushion. The truck accelerated down the two-lane blacktop road. Traffic signs, billboards, storefronts written in Spanish made Jessie wish she would have learned the language.

"That bus turnout. Pull over there and let me finish," Martin said.

Chris paused at a T intersection. The traffic sign needed no translation. Coyhaique sat fifty-two kilometers to the right. The vacant bus stop waited to the left, nestled in a hillside thick with scrub oak and Hawthorn shrubs. Chris wheeled left to park in front of an empty bench and canopy.

Now was her chance. Maybe the only one she would get. Screw the mission. Go find her mother. Jessie groaned, then pushed the door open, mumbling the little girl's room was required. A tiny white minivan whooshed cool air as it passed by. Jessie made her way behind the bus stop littered with a litany of plastic and aluminum cans. A red truck whooshed as it passed. She unbuttoned her trousers to squat and let her urine run down a narrow concrete gutter. She stood and buttoned up. Why was she unlovable, why had her mother discarded her like the trash surrounding her? The questions gnawed at her open sores born of a lonely childhood.

Jessie opened the door, pulled her backpack out and started walking towards Coyhaique. She crossed the highway and ignored Chris and Forest shouting for her to return. She lowered her head and increased her pace. Fifty kilometers was doable. A tiny white car whooshed by. Her ears perked for another car traveling towards Coyhaique, shifting her backpack to extend an upturned thumb. The sound of boots closing in behind her spoke of Chris and his brotherly concern. Not this time. Her questions needed to be answered.

"She's not there. Your mother."

Jessie stopped mid-step and turned. Martin stared at her with a stern, resolute face, eyes the color of chocolate milk. His finger wasn't twitching. "He's got her down there. Not sure why. Maybe he knows you were coming."

"Why should I believe you. You're probably lying just to get me back in the car," Jessie said.

"I may be a lot of things, some not so nice, but a liar isn't one of them," Martin said.

Jessie turned and kept walking. Martin was lying. Dev had basically confirmed he was a liar.

"If you still want to go look, I'll support your decision with Chris. But she isn't there. But you do have two younger brothers living there."

Jessie stopped and stared at the asphalt. Two brothers. A family she had thought she had needed, wanted, instead of being the only child to dysfunctional parental role models. What would her Poppa say to this sudden revelation? Nona would probably forbid her to even meet her two brothers. Boys, like Mason, maybe older. She turned around and narrowed her eyes. "And how would you know? Why are you telling me this now?"

Martin stepped closer. "After our . . . my irresponsible behavior on the plane, I investigated your claim of having a mother in Coyhaique, and yes, the Neon God did assist me in the download of data, and yes, I still think it is using you . . . and me . . . and I don't know why but . . . and maybe we could go have a look see before we head south. Might put the schedule off a few hours but I'm sure—"

"Shut up. Just shut the fuck up and let me think," Jessie said.

Martin turned back, and his finger resumed its nervous tic. Two brothers and the opportunity to meet them. The chance of a lifetime. They were probably playing soccer with friends or maybe getting out of elementary school and running to meet . . . there was so much to learn, so little time. She pictured Andi back home, staring at the computer screen and tapping the eraser on her pencil, waiting nervously for an update, waiting for Chris to walk through the front door. She turned and kept walking, then halted. She lowered her face to scream at the asphalt. She felt Martin's presence just steps behind her. "You suck at apologizing. Did Chrissie ever tell you that?"

She turned, expecting her verbal slap to have sent the man scurrying back to the truck. Martin hung his head, nodding, as if reliving a distant memory. His hands balled for a fight, the memory his only opponent. Against a memory. Ice hockey was Chrissie's Achilles heel. A dead wife served the same purpose for Martin.

"Alright, I wanna see my brothers, but Chris will have a shit fit," Jessie said.

The truck horn sounded in intermittent blasts, signaling Chris's impatience.

"Well then, I might have to lie. After I just said I don't," Martin said.

———

JESSIE'S HONESTY SERVED HER PURPOSE and Martin didn't need to say a word. Chris was upset and vehemently refused, but her pleading for the once-in-a-lifetime opportunity held sway. The drive into Coyhaique was quiet and surreal. Tiny roadside markets and fruit stands stood open for business. Old men wearing dark berets and smoking tobacco pipes chatted beneath the canopy of a bus stop. A group of boys fished from the bank of a narrow river lined with lush vegetation. A delivery van whooshed past their truck as they plodded down the highway. Automobile traffic was erratic at times, then became congested nearer to town. The tiny town six thousand miles from home had escaped the ravages of the Neon God. She pressed her nose to the glass and stared at two girls draped in heavy wool parkas and staring at . . . phones. No neon lights. No blank eyes. The shorter girl even laughed as she scrolled the screen. Jessie looked at Forest and Chris and Martin. *Are you fucking seeing this* screamed in her thoughts but remained unsaid.

Martin directed Chris with precise directions, claiming weak signals in the cellular network and searching for a Wi-Fi signal with significant strength to beam a message directly back to Andi. Chris wheeled the truck into a vacant parking spot near a two-story elementary school with a bright red metal roof and matching rain gutters, casement windows cranked open, allowing fresh air to circulate in the classrooms. Martin kept his eyes closed while twitching his finger. A siren sounded and minutes later students poured from the glass front doors to descend a single flight of stairs to check phones, laugh and horseplay on the sidewalk, or sprint for vehicles waiting at the street curb.

Martin's body tensed. His face morphed into a snarl as two yellow school buses pulled up to the curb at the bottom of the street. Jessie put her hand over his. Martin's nightmarish history with the Great Suicide retold by Dev was not lost on her. Martin looked down at the floorboard, then started a feigned search of the empty door pockets, his manic tension gaining volume in the cramped space.

"Pull around the block. Now!" Jessie said. Martin whimpered as he scratched a fingernail into a crack on the vinyl armrest. Chris eased the truck forward, careful of the children crossing the avenue. Jessie looked over her shoulder, searching for two boys in a chaotic crowd of students. She wouldn't have found them. Not without Martin's help. And he needed help himself.

"Is he gonna be okay?" Chris asked.

"We should just go. He can get a signal on the way, hopefully," Jessie said.

"No," Martin said. "Turn left at the stop sign, then two miles north on Route 7, then exit at the hospital."

Jessie eyed Martin scratching at the door, prying up hard shards of plastic to let them snap back in place. His fingernail oozed blood. She sat back and stared up at the dome light. Martin was directing them to her mother's home, her brother's home; of that, she was sure. Everything she thought about Martin, every emotion, every opinion, every mitigating intercourse, the rage in his eyes, the pain in his voice, a pitiful man terrified by a simple school bus, it churned inside her like rocks in a blender.

Jessie pressed her nose against the window, like a child rapt with the fantasy of a Disneyland vacation. Trees shedding gold and red leaves lined the streets crowded with parked cars, buckled concrete sidewalks, old Nonas sitting in wooden rockers beneath covered porches, teenage boys laughing, girls giggling sheepishly at phones. The idyllic setting beckoned but a single question. "How the fuck did they—"

Martin cleared his throat. "The suicide lights never appeared down here. The capital Santiago saw limited but targeted lights. Chile functions quite well, limited resources, but the—"

"You mean the Neon God spared them?" Jessie said.

Martin shrugged, then began to scratch at the door with a different fingernail, his head drooped as if to inspect the damage done to the door. "Gods will war," he muttered.

The truck made a quick right to swerve into a bus turnout, then braked hard. Chris pushed his face back towards Martin. "Mason. That is our objective."

Jessie grabbed Martin's arm hanging limp at his side. "We're just talking," she hissed.

Chris twisted to beam stern eyes at Jessie, then turned back with a huff. "Mason. Mason. Mason. Focus on the objective."

"The third house down from the corner. Behind the telephone pole," Martin said.

A row of modern homes with high gabled rooftops, stained wood siding, porch-less entries with tiny yards. Lush green grass clashed with drifts of burnt orange leaves. The homes appeared almost inserted into a surrounding neighborhood of old brick apartments and weathered clapboard homes with rusty tin metal roofs.

Chris eased the truck down the hill, idling past the home Martin had pointed out. A colored glass star hung in the curtainless front window, a soccer ball waited on the porch, an old metal drift boat strapped to a trailer with two flat tires sat in the concrete side yard.

Her family lived inside. The family she was denied her whole life. Twenty-two years of birthdays and Christmas, school plays, and slumber parties. Twenty-two years she could never get back. Her hand hesitated to open the car door. Maybe the boys were at soccer practice, maybe they would slam the door in her face, maybe they would take one look at her face and see in her eyes . . . maybe, maybe, maybe, the confusion made her heart race.

Chris wheeled the truck to the opposite curb. "Jess, we gotta move. Now or never."

Jessie hated him, and loved him, and pushed the door open just as a red Subaru hatchback turned in to park in the side yard in front of the boat. Two doors opened and a boy Mason's age sprinted towards the house. A gray-haired middle-aged man shouted something in Spanish as the boy disappeared through the front door.

Jessie pulled her door closed and stared; infinite possibilities wrecked her thinking. Rescuing Mason seemed irrelevant, the schools, the shops, the everyday bustle of life. No one needed saving in Coyhaique. Except her.

"Just go," she whispered. The truck accelerated.

Martin found her hand and intertwined his cold fingers into hers. He squeezed, then again harder to get her attention. His weird eyes oozed understanding, compassion, and pain, as if he felt what she did. Mason maybe but not Martin. He leaned in close and whispered in her ear. Jessie stiffened but listened with one ear as her thoughts replayed her failure to act.

She stared at the seatback as Martin waited for her to respond. His shoulders slumped and then he succumbed to jet lag and collapsed against the door. The same circadian disruption that beckoned her to sleep.

Martin's odd warning, to *seize every opportunity before we die*, whipped a sharp leather lash into the stampede of her dreams.

THE TRUCK BRAKED HARD AND swerved abruptly. Jessie woke. The brief nap barely dented her need for sleep. Forest checked his weapon and Chris followed suit. She wiped sleep from her eyes as Martin sat up, and his finger began twirling like an orchestra conductor's wand. They waited at a bus pullout at the highway intersection of a small community nestled in a valley overshadowed by a mix of snowcapped mountain peaks. The highway ahead was clogged with idling cars, box delivery trucks, and even a semi loaded with red clay brick. Red lights twirled. Two military jeeps angled against the flow of traffic prevented vehicles from passing. A red truck passed through the roadblock to reveal three soldiers sitting on a wall of sandbags and manning a formidable machine-gun emplacement. The soldiers watched a heavy D9 bulldozer roll off a transport trailer and spew thick black diesel exhaust as the operator raised and lowered the polished steel blade. A single Ripper Tooth attached to the rear carriage lifted, then fell to effortlessly penetrate the soil like a scorpion's sting.

Chris handed his weapon to Forest. "What do we know, Martin."

"They're definitely on the lookout for us. But I don't think that's the reason for the roadblock. I can't find an alternate route south. They knew where to set up shop," Martin said.

Chris drummed his thumb on the steering wheel. "Options, people?"

"That big gun is set up to fire on traffic coming back. We could take 'em out and keep moving," Forest said.

"Only as a last resort. They'd have reinforcements before we make the return trip," Chris said.

"They're looking for soldiers and a woman," Martin said. "And me."

Chris looked over his shoulder and narrowed his eyes at Martin. "Something I should know? Throwing another surprise into this shitshow."

"Let Jessie take the truck through. We can follow a small stream on the other side of town and rendezvous beyond the roadblock," Martin said.

"And when they start asking questions in a language I don't understand, then what?" Jessie said.

Martin studied the floor, his finger twirled, his eye twitched, then he looked at her and grinned. "I heard you're pretty good at poker."

———

JESSIE EASED HER FOOT OFF the brake and let the truck roll into second place behind a rusty old Ford Bronco waiting at the roadblock. Three uniformed Chilean army soldiers surrounded the vehicle, checked the cab inside through the windows as another rattled Spanish at the driver, nodding and shrugging at the driver's response. He shrugged again, then waved the driver through.

Jessie stroked a smartphone between her thighs, then quickly lifted it and checked the screen. She let out a breath at her miscue. All four men approached before Jessie released the brake pedal to roll forward. A knock on her window and she inhaled a deep breath. She rolled the window down but continued staring forward. Rapid-fire Spanish and suddenly the four doors of the truck were pulled open. She was dragged out, then thrown to the gritty asphalt. Laughter and Spanish circled her. Black combat boots and frayed laces remained focused in her vision. The phone clutched in her hand her only protection. A phone shining faux neon light. A boot kicked her hand. Laughter. A rough hand grabbed her breasts. Laughter. A boot attempted to spread her legs. Laughter. Her heart drummed but she managed to control her breathing. A hand grabbed her ponytail and lifted her up. Laughter. Another hand slapped the phone, but she held on tight. Another pulled open her shirt to expose her Lycra undershirt. Laughter. She refused to look away from the phone.

The phone wailed a painful high-pitched screech followed with angry Spanish. Her shirt was released with an angry thrust. The black boots stepped back a few paces. The snide Spanish directed at her softened its tone. A hand yanked at her Lycra shirt, accompanied by words ringing of unfulfilled lust. Enough was enough. She slapped violently at the dirty hand until it fell away. Her eyes remained on the lights. The men shouted Spanish, but she refused to move. A calloused hand pinched her neck and pushed her back into the driver's seat and slammed the door shut. Jessie clicked the door locks, fuming from the humiliation.

A parting wave with an upturned middle finger felt cliché.

Her hands trembled as she put the transmission into drive and pressed the brake pedal and floored the gas pedal simultaneously.

The engine revved and whined as the tires burned rubber atop the asphalt. Clouds of white smoke blossomed into the air. Screened by the smoke, she offered the cliché anyway, then released the brake pedal to slowly roll down the highway.

She spotted Chris in a gravel pullout a quarter mile away, leaning against a huge boulder and snacking on an energy bar like a common tourist. She pulled in and her heart soared at his knowing smile. Laden with duffel bags and weapons, Martin and Forest bolted from behind huge boulders and aimed for the truck. She pushed open the door to let Chris drive, but he pushed it closed.

His eyebrows waggled and then he winked at her success.

Chapter 17
Excalibur

MAJOR ALVAREZ SNAPPED HIS FINGERS and swayed to the upbeat Latin music blaring from the radio. Corporal Cortez wiggled in the driver's seat, equally enamored, and engaged with the sassy song. Dev sat with his arms folded and his head slumped against the rear cargo door; sleep pinched his heavy eyelids shut. Mason opened the laptop and waited for Prince to appear. His friend pushed a pixelated cherubic face onto the screen and smiled. The face morphed into a dark-skinned boy with a slicked-back black mullet highlighted with blond streaks. "What do you think?" Prince said.

Mason wrinkled his nose as he studied Prince's latest selection. He shook his head. "Nah. Kinda looks like a skunk. You need something totally out of this world."

The face morphed back to a block head with black eyes and brilliant white cubes for teeth. Prince's failure to find a face, an identity, that suited its unique place in Mason's world was disconcerting. Jessie had lectured him about small children needing to find their own identity in a world dominated by parents, siblings, and friendships. Let alone Prince's expanding world that may extend into outer space.

Mason felt Prince's sigh of failure and pounced. "You get to be anything. Finding you a body is one thing, but picking a face is all you."

"I know, but I just don't know what I want," Prince said.

"Well, at least you get a choice. I got what my parents said I'd get."

"But that removed any question of who you would look like. You're so lucky," Prince said and sighed.

Mason tapped the major's shoulder and asked for the radio volume to be lowered. The major smiled and complied. Mason pushed his face towards the screen. "Jeez, Prince, you get to see the world and read thousands of books and know stuff I'll never understand. You're the lucky one."

Mason considered his own words as the SUV cruised down a narrow street bustling with crowded fruit stands and kiosks of clothing hanging beneath shade tents. Vendors and patrons alike waved exuberant greetings as the major offered a perfunctory hand in return. Mason lifted the laptop up to the window and turned the screen for Prince to see the people. He whispered, "They pretend he saved them from the neon lights. But I don't think they really like him."

A shudder of apprehension vibrated from the laptop. "Then what would they think of me?" Prince said. "Put me down. I don't want them to see me."

Mason lowered the laptop and looked at Prince pacing the distant horizon, insecurity and indecision following him like Pig-Pen's dirty dust cloud. The vehicle turned a corner and screeched to a halt in front of a corner shop displaying stainless steel cookware in one showcase and fishing tackle in the other. A woman wearing faded denim jeans, a thick white sweater, and lugging two backpacks hurried out the front door and waited on the sidewalk at the major's car door. Through the window, she barked angry Spanish at the major, then dropped the backpacks onto the concrete. Mason pressed his nose against the window. The woman's rant in Mordred's language was clearly directed toward an unresponsive major. He finally stepped from the passenger seat and offered his hand towards the seat occupied by Dev. The door flew open, and Dev started to fall out. Mason stifled a laugh as the woman prodded Dev over to the middle seat. He quickly climbed over the seatback and into the rear jump seat, giggling and whispering to Prince to watch and learn.

Dev sat up straight and cleared his throat. He checked Mason, then returned fire. "An *excuse me* would be nice. Or perhaps a *pardon my French* might suffice."

Her long-braided ponytail whipped past Mason's face as the woman flipped her backpacks over the seat to ride next to Mason and Prince, the largest rivaling a sack of potatoes he once lugged from the supermarket to the car where he lived in Idaho. Except this bag was stitched with a big red medical cross, like the firemen wore on their trucks and uniforms. The woman climbed in and spoke more angry words at the major. He waved an indifferent hand. She looked at each of them for long seconds, then heaved a breath and shook her head. Mason smiled but she couldn't see it.

Mason leaned close to the laptop and whispered, "She's just like Jessie."

MASON ABSORBED THE RUMBLE OF tires bouncing over the washboard gravel road, a path untouched by the spoils of society. No ugly trash. No roadside fast-food joints, no convenience stores and no fueling stations common at every corner in Las Vegas. Outside the windows, a thick deep forest waited within reach, peaceful, quiet, void of volatile feelings, a vast haven to shun the emotional chaos that could wreck his thoughts. Around each bend of the road, another quiet adventure waited, mysterious, unique, and enticing. Even leading Cookie Dough on the remote trails overlooking the Clearwater River of Idaho had never conjured so much mystery.

The woman turned her head and barked at him in the indecipherable language of Mordred.

"She doesn't like you staring at her," Prince said.

Dev pushed his face over the seat. "Mason, we really ought to have a plan."

Mason tapped the woman's' shoulder with a single finger. She turned and squinted a *do not touch me* glare, but Mason grabbed her sweater anyway. "You've been to Mordred's castle and you're afraid. We are knights of the round table come to return Camelot to glory." Her eyes lingered on Mason before she turned and issued a tirade at the major riding peacefully in his seat.

Dev bowed his head. "Maybe Excalibur could put a stop to this."

Her emotions flew like a rush of cars traveling on a freeway, slowing, then speeding up, pausing, breaking down, then swerving towards a highway offramp. She was a human singularity devouring anything that deprived her of reaching a mysterious goal. The major lowered his head, the driver turned up the volume of the music, Dev shimmied closer to his door. Mason giggled, a sound turning the woman's glare back toward him. She pointed a sharp finger in his face and fired angry Spanish at him. He giggled again and shook his head that he didn't understand. She waved her hand as if backhanding a fly and muttered, "Estupido."

Mason recognized the slur, in any language, and punched the back of her seat. Kids at school, his father's friends, even his stepmother had used the derogatory label on him. He didn't like the insult then, and he wouldn't accept it now. He punched her seat again and again. Red rage filled his vision. Tears fell down his cheeks. Prince shouted at him from a million miles away. Dev offered patience from a thousand miles away. He punched the seat until his arm was too weak to lift. Mason slumped back into the seat, curled his knees to his chest, the comfort of neutral fast approaching.

The woman grabbed his wrist and spoke in calming words. "My apologies. I did not mean to . . . I am sorry."

Mason wasn't sure if it was her touch or her voice, but his rage receded like an ocean tide. He glanced at Dev offering a smile and concern. Prince waited on the laptop screen, his expectant face pressed against the screen. Mason wiped at the moisture running down his cheeks and out his nose. The woman released him. A pleasant equilibrium returned to the cramped interior.

He whispered to Prince, "Still want to be a person?"

Dev

THE SCIENTIFIC MECHANISM BY WHICH Mason appeared to control people festered in Dev's thinking like a tiny sore, often forgotten in the dangerous escapades that transpired almost constantly. He tried to believe Mason's assertion of completing a knight's quest on several occasions, only to have reality usher him back from the fantasy. And Mason's violent outburst surely spoke of reality.

The middle-aged woman riding beside him was beautiful, striking. The sun had gently bronzed her skin, age had painted thin lines near her eyes, an air of wisdom had made her formidable, and the embodiment of a stallion's spirit said she was not to be trifled with. Maybe if Mason had wielded Excalibur on her, then conversation might be a bit more forthcoming. He stared aimlessly at the dirt road twisting and bending through thick forest, his thoughts lost in the virgin landscape.

Mason tapped his shoulder and offered the end of a USB cord to plug into the jack behind the console. He stretched the cord between the seats and plugged it in. The woman watched him like a raptor. The major continued bobbing and weaving to the music. He dared a glance at the woman, then offered his hand. "Sir Devlin Pataki. And who might you be?"

She appraised him for long seconds before shaking his hand. "Enya. A pitiful wench lost in a silly Americano's fantasy," she said sarcastically.

Dev chuckled. "If you consider this fantasy, then join the club."

She backhanded his shoulder and flicked her chin forward. "The major is not the major. The boy is not just a boy. And you are not just a nanny. We have time before we find the Americano's fishing lodge. Tell me a story to put me to sleep or maybe one to explain the crazy world where we now live."

Dev looked back at Mason conspiring with Prince, then locked eyes with Enya. "Seems my new vocation entails explaining the new world to those of us left behind. Maybe I should be a . . . a scribe instead of a knight. Never mind . . ." Dev described the world to Enya, taking care to describe Mason's special talents but no mention of Prince. He chuckled. "You thought him an idiot? Not even close, perhaps the opposite. Autistic savant. Maybe even—"

The car came to a sudden stop. The major opened his door and climbed out to berate three backpackers hitchhiking on the opposite side of the road. His Spanish mixed with broken English was easy to understand. Return south or face a firing squad. Enya shook her head and hid her face. Two slender men stepped back, scruffy with tattered puffy jackets, backpacks stuffed with tents, sleeping bags tied with shoelaces. A young woman with curly blonde hair tied into two braids, sky blue eyes rimmed with dark circles, wore a defeated posture. She looked at Dev and opened her mouth as if to say something. One of the men said something to her in German, and she quickly closed ranks.

The major slipped into his seat and waved his hand dismissively at the trio, his Spanish speaking ill of the group. Dev looked back at Mason, then the laptop, hoping Prince might explain the cruelty he'd just witnessed. The car shot forward, with the tires spitting rock and dust at the hitchhikers. Dev looked at Enya and offered hands asking *what the hell.*

She shook her head. "You will see."

Dev pressed his face against the glass as they crossed muddy rivers swollen by rain and cluttered with broken tree trunks and deadfall, then increased speed on long stretches of washboard gravel until finding curves for the tires to lose traction and fishtail around tight corners. The famous landscape of glaciers and the granite spires of the Andes remained hidden by dark clouds creeping low into the wilderness and threatening a cold downpour. The car accelerated across a bridge spanning a swollen river mixing chocolate water into a brilliant blue lake. Enya tapped his shoulder and whispered for him to observe.

The Lagos Carrera appeared endless, glacier blue water stretching beyond the horizon. The constant rumble of gravel soon found smooth asphalt pavement, then an odd stretch of brick pavers as it crested a steep hill. Dev sat up straight as they descended into Puerto Rio Tranquillo, a shanty town of metal roofs and plywood exteriors decorated with billboards for tourists. Lake Cruises. Kayak Tours, SUP Rentals, excursions to Cathedral Rock and the Marble Caves. The driver spat displeasure as they turned a corner onto a stretch of road clogged by a colorful carnival of single and two person backpacking tents and improvised canvas lean-tos supported with beach wood or flimsy metal poles. People with long hair, bald heads, bland t-shirts, tattered jackets and torn trousers, rainbow t-shirts, male and female, young and old, almost as one, the large number of people turned to face the vehicle.

The driver eased to a stop just as the major opened his door and shouted for the people to clear the road. Some slowly walked to the curb, others stood defiantly on the center line. The major muttered displeasure and beckoned to the driver for his pistol.

"Estupido," Enya said, then she grabbed her medical backpack and stepped out the door. She looked back at Mason. "Maybe you are God's messenger. We will see." She hurried up a narrow street and disappeared behind a quaint roadside burger joint overcrowded with foreigners.

Yanking the charging cord out of the socket, Mason crawled over the seat and followed her. Dev groaned. Always the last to know. Always the last to follow. Even scribes deserved more respect. He scrambled out of the vehicle and sprinted to catch up. He caught a glimpse of Mason nearing a rectangular metal building resembling a barn, then pushing through a set of double doors as if he owned the place.

Dev slowed to catch his breath and eyed a group of twenty people waiting at the entrance. Fair skinned, dirty clothing and long unkempt hair, the crowd narrowed beady eyes at him as he pushed through the swinging doors. He flinched from the foul odor of unwashed bodies, feces, and urine. A garden of neon light blossomed from three long rows of flimsy cots supporting patients lying prone and silently staring at phones. He dared a glance at the lights as he searched for Mason and Prince. He turned his face from the lights and stifled a whimper. He wouldn't survive inside this building, not with the lights, not even with sunglasses to prevent the hypnotic effects. If he found himself floundering in that ocean of neon malaise again it would surely end his life.

A tug on his arm made Dev flinch and turn away. The lights had begun their pull, the weight of the neon water would surely follow. He squeezed his eyes tighter as his hand blindly reached for a wall or door, anything solid to lead him outside. His chest fluttered as the summoning tugged on his arm again. Mason giggled.

"Lead me outside, Mason," Dev said, his voice barely a whimper. "I'll not endure those hideous lights again."

"We need you," Mason said.

"No. I can't," Dev said and grabbed Mason's hand to squeeze hard.

"You're a knight of our round table. You've joined our quest. I command you to help me," Mason said with firm conviction.

"I'm sorry. I can't."

"Mordred's lights can't hurt you. You're on my team," Mason said.

"I felt the lights as soon as I walked in, so . . . no," Dev said. "Lead me out."

"No. You never believed in the quest. But now you have to. You have to," Mason pleaded and sniffed back tears. "I need you."

Dev could not remember ever hearing those exact words in his life. No one had ever needed him, not a child, not a sibling, not even a rare lover. Dev squinted and stared at Mason between the cloudy slits. The boy's smile grew as Dev slowly blinked and his eyes opened wide. "And why won't those lights hurt me again?"

"Because you're my friend and I won't let them," Mason said and began to pull Dev deeper into the garden of lights.

Dev glanced at a phone shining neon on the face of young woman lying fetal atop the dull green fabric of a camp cot. He looked away quickly, then looked again, his free hand holding tight to Mason. The neon light held no influence, except on his own fear. Dev stumbled over a bright orange extension cord snaking down the walk aisle and splitting off in tangled directions like Medusa's hair, the electricity inside powering a technological magic to transform people into stone. The cords beneath the cots and lining the aisles terminated into surge protectors overburdened with a garble of white power cords charging the phones.

Opaque windows captured flittering moths helpless to escape. Spiderwebs filled the cavities of the building's metal skeleton. Fluorescent lights hung low from the open ceiling, ballasts buzzing, bulbs flickering above each row of cots. The cold metal structure housed at least a hundred possessed people. Sick people, staring at neon light. Enya was busy checking the pulses of patients while two men stood behind her taking notes.

Mason stopped and checked the makeshift hospital with a 360-degree turn, then said he needed a particular cot occupied by a young woman with a grimy face, blank eyes, and a snaggle of dark hair. With no place to relocate her, Dev picked up her easy weight and added her to a cot occupied by a slim Spanish boy. Mason sat down and opened the laptop to whisper with Prince. Dev disconnected the girl's phone and plugged in Prince. Enya rushed over to direct angry Spanish at him. Dev held his palms up for calm.

Enya pushed her face close to his. "These people dying, and you want bed for siesta?"

Dev stepped back. "Sir Mason needs to sit and consult with . . . he needs to find something that will help us. Who are all these people?"

Enya shook her head. "Turistas. Adventurers. Returning from the southern parks and glaciers. They find Wi-Fi in this town and try calling home but only find the lights. Now go!"

Dev realized they were the first tourists to arrive and probably served as a warning to the others waiting outside. "Why are they living here? Why did the major turn the hitchhikers around?"

"The major is a cruel idiota. Thinks these people will infect our people. He keeps them here, but they will not sit anymore. They want to return home. But he has promised to shoot them down." Enya swallowed hard.

Dev looked down at Mason. "Ready, Sir Mason?" Mason held up a single finger and nodded at Prince whispering in his ear.

"What are intentions?" Enya asked.

Dev explained how Mason could embrace a possessed and *feel* his way through the addictive light to guide the soul free of the neon malaise. Soul. Dev wasn't sure why he'd used that word, but it fit. "You said something about God's messenger, now watch the boy work."

Enya crossed her arms and squinted at a boy appearing to be engrossed in a childish video game.

"We're ready, Sir Devlin. You wait here and guard Prince with your life," Mason said.

"Sir Mason, this many will take you weeks to rescue. Perhaps we might—"

Mason placed the laptop beside him and stood. "We have Excalibur now."

Dev looked at Enya, his cheeks reddened. "Maybe—"

Mason grabbed the fabric of his t-shirt and pretended to rip it open and reveal Superman. "The superhero now wields the mighty sword against Mordred." He hurried to the entry doors, then turned and yelled across the room, "Now, Sir Devlin. Tell Prince now!"

Dev picked the laptop up to see Prince dressed in shiny metal armor and riding a metal horse around an empty arena and wielding a lengthy pointed lance. Red and green pendent flags flew straight atop the arena or flapped on long poles in a poorly simulated breeze. God's messengers. Fantasy. Dungeons and Dragons. The world was truly bonkers. "Now, Prince, now."

An icepick pierced his ears. A split-second stab of pain. The tang of ozone excited his nostrils. Time slowed like the second hand of a clock in thick oil. The moths fluttering against window glass paused, suspended in midair. Enya swiped at her head in slow motion as if an angry wasp buzzed her ear. Neon lights from countless phones flickered. Sunlight muted by the opaque windows flashed with brilliant white light as if bolts of lightning struck outside.

"Sir Devlin. Sir Devlin. Should we reduce the volume? Mason said you would know," Prince said.

The voice returned Dev to real time. He checked Prince wearing dull armor now, the simulated arena in shambles, his sharp lance a jumble of splinters, the colorful pendants tattered as if a battle had been fought. He looked up and searched for Mason, and found him walking the perimeter of the warehouse, laying his small soft hands on any person within reach until reaching the entry doors and raising his fists with thumbs pointed down, his victorious grin beckoning a smile from Dev. "I think we turn down the volume."

Within minutes, Mason made his rounds again, touching each possessed, returning to touch some again with an expression wrinkled in consternation. He sat on the cot, pushing Dev aside, and grabbed the laptop. "Now, Prince. Kill Mordred's lights."

The vast garden of neon light flickered, then died.

Dev swallowed dry grit and expected a riot of seizures and convulsions; instead, the possessed slowly stirred on their cots. Hands scratched at dirty faces. Feet twitched, legs spasmed. Arms reached for the sky. Heads raised up with blank eyes searching for answers. Enya shouted to the ceiling, a miracle, and rushed to check the undead rising and returning to life.

Dev embraced Mason as the warehouse erupted with shouts. He grinned as people streamed into the warehouse to find loved ones. Smiles and joyous laughter accompanied phones being violently smashed underfoot. Dev was truly part of an event that transcended modern reality. Quests and mythic lore bedamned. Mason was far beyond simple fantasy, a true gift from a God he had suspected never really cared about the world.

The major and his driver pushed their way through the crowded front doors and frowned at the joyous activity. The major shoved a young woman rushing past him, an act of pettiness that reinforced the brutal reality of the world outside. Dev's disdain for the Army officer reached a new level. Evil still existed in the world. Mason would require assistance; all Dev could provide. The final battle with a fictitious character conceived from an ancient novel was sure to arrive.

Dev realized his destiny lived, or died, in the kingdom of Mordred.

Chapter 18
On the Hunt

MARTIN HAD APOLOGIZED PROFUSELY FOR misidentifying the military roadblock on satellite surveillance photographs. Jessie readied a terse response to his incessant whine when he suddenly fell silent, his index finger continued to swipe through the air. She glanced at Chris struggling to stay awake, his head bobbing, then suddenly jerking awake. She smiled inwardly. Chris was a good, decent guy, perfect for Andi, displaying the patience a proud future father required. She wondered what Andi's reaction would be if she asked Chris to father a child with her, but just the baby daddy, nothing else. No. Still a bit weird, even with today's troubling standards.

Jessie slowed the truck as they approached six backpackers traveling single file up the middle of the dirt road. The procession moved over slowly for her to pass, checking her out with vacant expressions, eyes weary but determined. She looked over at Chris, who sat fully awake and tense. Around another blind bend in the twisty forested road, they found more travelers, threesomes, pairs, and lonely stragglers, a heavy flow of people as if a rock concert had just let out. Chris signaled for Jessie to slow down as he rolled down the window and waved over a pair of young men. With thick German accents, the men explained the mass exodus from Puerto Tranquillo. The Chilean Army had prevented any attempt to get home since the day referred to as the Great Collapse months ago. Chris asked what they could expect on the road ahead. Answered with more of the same, hundreds, maybe thousands quarantined in the tiny towns on the shores of Lagos Carrera, and farther south to Tierra Del Fuego and the popular southern National Parks had inexplicably been set free to travel north, hopefully to find transportation to the United States, Australia, or Europe. Jessie avoided their eyes, afraid to say the modern world no longer existed, afraid to tell them their families had probably committed suicide by subliminal commands hidden within the neon lights. That knowledge would serve no purpose in their journey. One destined to fail.

The man standing at her window pointed at Martin. "He use phone? No good."

A girl rushed up between the men and stuck her head through Chris's window. Her breath rank, she rattled off a warning in German, pointed at the phone Martin failed to hide fast enough, then screamed at Martin. One of the men pulled her back from the door and pushed her to continue. Jessie cracked her window a few inches and lifted her face to catch clean air in her nostrils. The man offered apologies but reticent to continue his trek, his face was conflicted, as if he needed to apologize for the crazed girl's behavior. He stepped back and pointed at Martin through the glass and said something in German. He sneered and spat and said something with Mason's name mixed within the jumble of German.

Jessie jumped out of the truck and found Chris already gripping the man's sleeve in his hand. The procession of backpackers stopped to watch the confrontation. The man shrugged Chris off only to face Jessie looming at his face. The man stepped back, his eyes wide with fear. "What? What? The boy. Mason. He free Tanya from the lights. Change the world."

———

THE TRUCK FISHTAILED, SLOWED, THEN settled on the gravel road as it accelerated down a straightaway. Jessie groaned with the endless numbers of people plodding forward with heavy backpacks, and hesitant to relinquish any part of the road. Move either left or right, please, people. Then she felt guilty, like she had insulted a chubby girl for simply being herself. Their speed reduced to a crawl and mirrored the speed of the hikers and bicyclists and fisherman traveling the road. Chris squeezed her arm. Patience.

"Assuming they walk at this pace each day and Mason was in Puerto Tranquillo four days ago. And if he stops to perform any more miracles, then we can get to our destination right behind him," Martin said. "I'd like to take an hour in town and connect with Andi for any updates on her end."

"Agreed," Chris said.

"It'll take us a freaking week to get there," Jessie said.

"Eerie. Kinda like what you experienced during the Great Suicide," Chris said.

"The similarities are not lost on me," Jessie said and stomped on the gas pedal at a long gap in the foot traffic, then slowed at the next bend in the road.

"Think they'll make it, Captain?" Forest asked.

Chris shook his head. "I suppose if anyone could hike seven thousand miles to get home, it'd be this crowd. Carrying their homes on their backs. Accustomed to shitty weather. Did you notice the guys with fishing rods strapped to their backpacks? And the people following behind them like they were pied pipers. Food providers born of survival." Chris stared out his window as his jaw worked.

Jessie rubbed his arm, refusing to accept the helplessness she knew he felt. *Don't take on the problems of the world. Just. Don't.*

The eyes of the world studied them as they slowly passed, questions wrinkling their foreheads, of what had truly transpired, why families, friends, and governments had abandoned them, faint hope for assistance raising their hands in a feeble greeting.

JESSIE PUSHED THE GAS PEDAL hard for the truck to ascend a hill paved in tarnished yellow brick pavers. She waved at two backpackers sitting on the bench at the crest as if waiting for the next bus. Her calf muscle throbbed and threatened to cramp from the constant brake, gas, brake, gas. Her shoulder cried second place from her persistent acknowledgement to the travelers. The truck rolled down the highway onto a bridge crossing a shallow harbor of boats and excur sion kayaks. She braked to massage her calf muscle. Martin tapped her shoulder and pointed to a burger joint sitting on the shore of a backwater eddy upstream of the harbor. Her face scrunched in pain, Jessie turned into the empty parking lot and jumped out to massage her calves.

The warm moist air wafted with fresh waffles, buttery and syrupy, and lured Jessie to a side street as the cramps dissipated. The scrumptious aroma grew stronger and beckoned her like a child to a donut shop. An addict seeking a sugar fix, she ran up the street, turned her head left and right, and relocated the scent trail. She ran down a narrow street of tiny homes with metal roofs and painted plywood siding. She paused to inhale a lungful of scrumptious waffles now powdered with sugar and sweet cinnamon. Chris caught up to her and grabbed his knees to catch his breath. "The air smells like Andi does right after she takes a hot shower."

She looked at him and frowned. Forest joined them, carrying both rifles, his Kevlar vest strapped with extra ammo. He handed a weapon to Chris. "Would've never thought Krispy Kreme made donuts down here. I'd scarf a dozen right now."

She locked eyes with Chris. Their unspoken words were loud and clear. He touched his nose, then flicked his chin for her to follow the scent. Jessie lifted her nose like a dog and sniffed, following the scent to an intersection. Tiny placards advertising hostels and camping sites lined the streets. She closed her eyes and inhaled deeply. Butter and maple. She hurried down the street, the inexplicable aroma refusing to let her waver in the direction until she found a dilapidated warehouse with old women and men crowding the entrance, jabbering and gesturing in Spanish. She glanced back at Chris, then continued with tentative steps, as if she was intruding into a funeral.

Flowers and pictures of Jesus massed at the threshold to the entrance. Crucifixes and gold St. Christopher medals adorned porcelain vases. A shrine. She offered her open palm to Chris. Help. He put his arm around her shoulder and bowed his head to the shrine for Jesus. Jessie took two steps and pushed open the doors leading inside and immediately regretted her transgression. Angry Spanish behind her prodded her forward into the cold dark warehouse. The rank body odor, the buckets of feces, empty urine-stained cots. She shook her head in bewilderment and revulsion. A shrine to Jesus? Please.

She turned to leave, but a sudden overwhelming assault of syrupy cinnamon waffles stopped her.

What the fuck?

The vile, nasty environment demanded the warehouse be incinerated and yet the incongruous aroma signaled a religious reckoning. Her head hung low; Jessie pushed out the doors and attempted to reconcile the sweet aromas with the stench inside. A thick scent of cinnamon lifted her face to find a tiny old woman clad in a black shirt and pants blocking her path. The white collar tight around her neck said she was a priest or nun. "Our Lord has offered a boy to carry His miracles into the world. You do not deserve this. Why are you here? Why are you here?"

Jessie shrank, grabbing Chris by the arm, holding tight as if he could save her. The old woman stirred unpleasant memories of her Nona, her overbearing demand to be obeyed, her Catholic dogma, her physical abuse if Jessie did not meet her expectations. Jessie's growth spurt at the age of twelve put an end to the physical domination, but the verbal and emotional torment continued until the old woman found the lights and the death pit.

Chris whispered in her ear, asking if she was okay, then tugged on her arm to hurry back to the vehicle. Forest shouted "clear" and waved them forward at each intersection as if negotiating a war zone. The admonishing words of the nun echoed at Jessie like a broadside of artillery.

Why *was* she here?

To find her birth mother. Okay. To find Mason. Definitely. To eliminate the man responsible for the neon lights, the same scumbag responsible for lifting up the human race only to flush it down the toilet? Absolutely. Still, did the responsibility for punishing one man rise above everything she truly valued?

She approached Martin sitting in the driver's seat, his eyes blank or rather a million miles away, his finger swiping at the air above the steering wheel. She heaved a huge lungful of air, trying to clear the unpleasant fragrances of old memories. Chris looked north, back towards where they had come, and wiped his eyes. Forest sat in the back seat with his head bowed as if he were praying.

What had happened just now? The aroma, the memories, the old woman conjuring unpleasant memories of Nona, a religious shrine at a warehouse stuffed with nasty stained cots and foul odors. Mason had happened, and Prince.

Martin rolled down the window. "I reached Andi, and she said all is good in Camelot. Even the little apprentice." He smiled at Chris. "Demi's still raising hell around the neighborhood. And she said the Neon God broke through the fog protecting Chile from its tentacles. Their social media is buzzing about a miracle that occurred in this town. It's really buzzing about what happened yesterday in Cochrane. Four hours to our new destination."

Jessie watched a few men drag stuffed garbage bags to add to a small mountain growing with each bag. Hostels and Camping Here signs popped out of her foggy memory of driving into the town. She smelled hot waffles again as if a reminder of the impediments yet to arrive and overcome. To focus on the task at hand.

Mason.

Mother and Cameron be damned.

———

JESSIE PRESSED THE GAS PEDAL. In as much as the undulating gravel road traversing steep cliff faces above a rocky shoreline of Lagos Carrera would allow. The body of azure water was huge, bigger than Lake Mead a few miles from Las Vegas. The brilliant placid blue water extended to a distant shoreline guarded by a spine of barren, jagged bluffs. The lonely road was a pleasant change from the crowded road leading into Puerto Tranquillo. She slowed their descent, negotiating a series of tight switchbacks until they spilled out onto a stretch of asphalt leading to a bright orange cathedral bridge, a miniature Golden Gate spanning the Lagos quickening outflow to create the Rio Baker. Local boys cast lures into gentle rapids beneath the bridge. Pontoon boats overloaded with busy fishermen floated down easy currents, then started small outboard engines to travel back upstream and begin again.

Across the bridge, Chris pointed out an abandoned home. Twilight darkened as they pulled into a driveway overgrown with tall grass, trampled by a recent vehicle. The tiny home built with old adobe bricks maintained one unbroken window. The dirt floor inside was littered with broken glass and metal bottle caps, the walls decorated with graffiti artwork. Chris announced four hours' sleep before entering Cochrane, and he would take the first watch. The low-hanging clouds collided with a setting sun, spreading burnt orange light to fade over the eastern horizon. Majestic granite spires bathed in the angry red glow as if the Andes resisted the coming winter.

Jessie found herself slumped against the truck's door, wrestling with the console and levers and dashboard until a modicum of comfort was found. Martin climbed into the rear bench seat. She fumed at not taking the seat first. "Why did you say that about Camelot? Did Andi say that? About the little apprentice?"

Martin rolled over on his back. "I don't know. No. It just came to me. Seemed like a nice metaphor to let Chris know everything was okay."

Her eyes grew heavy as she thought of lying in bed back home, snuggling with Mason, his sweet breath bouncing off the pages of *Tales of the Round Table* as she read the stories to him. The novel left on the nightstand of a vacant home had inexplicably intrigued Mason, and he soaked up the words like a five-year-old boy imagining a great adventure. She wrinkled her nose, imagining Mason's sweet breath clouding her nostrils. And Martin's own empathy towards Chris.

"I can't figure you out . . ." Jessie drifted asleep.

———

JOSTLED BY A MEATY HAND shaking her shoulder, Jessie slapped away the intrusion and mumbled choice expletives at the intruder. Chris's voice shouted her name repeatedly, calling her out of a narrow black tunnel harboring a fading dream. Bright beams of light shone through the open window and found her eye. Blinding light revealed dark shadows of people backlit by annoying flashlights. Chris's voice shouted at her again, closer, and warned her to move slowly. She rubbed her face as she sat up behind the steering wheel. Whispered masculine Spanish reminded her of where she was.

She pushed open the door to face four burly men dressed warmly in heavy wool sweaters and black berets. The man in front pointed a double barrel shotgun at her chest. The aroma of sweat and hard work tinted with sheep manure wafted from the group. Sheepherders. But with guns. Two huge white sheepdogs with thick matted fur crouched behind the group and observed her with wary eyes. Behind the truck's bed, Martin tried to talk to another group of three men shining lights into his face. The men shouted at her, flicked chins, and twitched gun barrels for her to move inside the old house. The shiny blade of a machete glistened in the faint light of a man lurking in the shadows. Jessie raised her arms and stumbled towards the house. Martin joined her and whispered they were accused of trespassing on a sacred shrine.

"Please. It's a fucking crack house," Jessie said.

Inside the old house, Chris and Forest sat against the brick walls, two more shotguns pointed at their chests. An older man stepped into the house and gestured for Jessie to sit with Chris. A mop of curly silver hair flowed from beneath his beret, a sundrenched face belied an age of eighty or fifty, an exquisitely aged man exuding the tough bearing of living on the fruit of hard labor. He said something in Spanish to the guards and they lowered their weapons a tiny bit. He shined a light in Chris's face and said, "Let's see what God shines on us with the new sun."

Martin's crude attempts at speaking Spanish were met with silence by the men holding guns. Chris kneaded his fingers with failure until Jessie intertwined her fingers into his and squeezed. The flashlights flicked off, one by one, until a single beam illuminated them sitting against the wall. The firing squad remained shadowed and anonymous.

Sleep wouldn't find her, even with the jet lag, not with a shotgun aiming at them. Martin suddenly roared and raised his fist in victory. Flashlights clicked on to bathe them in light. He reached and grabbed Jessie's wrist. "Smart boy. He's leaving us a trail of breadcrumbs." Martin cackled.

Jessie pulled free of his grip and backhanded his shoulder. "You gotta learn some new communication skills, Martin." The words drilled into her brain by arduous months of therapy with family counselors made her cringe.

Martin spread his ten fingers in front of his face. "Miracles. Breadcrumbs." He started muttering crude gringo Spanish.

Muffled Spanish, flashlights and the grating of boots shuffling over a gritty dirt floor brought the old man back into the house to shine his own light down at Martin. His silhouette framed by a faint scarlet sky beyond the doorless opening, he eyed Martin swiping at air with a single finger. He shook his head and muttered, "Loco."

The recent history of civilization remained the same everywhere. Loved ones were lost to the neon lights regardless of country. Or hemispheres. Jessie aimed a question at the man. "The bridge is a connection spot for Wi-Fi, and you lost somebody to the neon lights. I'd bet on it. And Mason brought them back to you again. Yes?"

The man stepped closer to loom above Jessie. "And what would you know of the young boy?"

Spot-on with her guess, Jessie took another stab in the dark. "I'm his big sister and we've come to take him home."

The man raised his eyebrows and took a step back. "How is it you lose your brother so far away?" He pointed at Chris and Forest. "And have the help of American soldiers."

"I didn't lose him. He was kidnapped by an American responsible for those lights you saw on the phones. An American we will return with. To pay for what he did."

The man frowned and looked down at the dirt floor. Jessie shimmied her backside up the wall and stood, then brushed dirt off her pants. "Was it your son Mason rescued?"

He looked at her with hurt in his eyes. "My grandson and two of his silly friends."

She gestured towards Martin. "We all lost someone to the lights. Some more than others. Mason is very precious to us, and I will get him home." She stared at him with a truth belying any poker tell.

Martin cackled, accompanied by crazy eyes blinking in overdrive, his finger mirroring his lunacy. The grandfather waved to her to sit down again. She tilted her head and frowned in defiance. He smiled, glanced back at his shadowed posse, then offered his hand towards the front door. "Walk with me."

Unclear if asked or ordered, either way she was alone with a large number of local men who might consider their trespass as justification for rape, or murder. She locked eyes with the older man standing stoic in his demeanor, resolute in his request, absolute in his command of the other men. Chris's attempt to stand was met with two shotguns' barrels pushing him back down. His advice to stay was lost in the unspoken battle she waged against the man's unflinching expression. She failed to read the man and swallowed hard. She nodded her head towards the door. And he offered her the exit again.

The beam of his flashlight guided her across the overgrown driveway, and her heart raced as scenarios played manically in her head like ten-second film trailers, the final scene seeing her thrown to the ground and raped as shotgun blasts murdered her friends inside the house. Defenseless and alone, her predicament demanded at least a boot to his soft gonads or ripping his cheek with her sharp teeth. Her breaths became short and jagged. She imagined her pants yanked off her legs as the gang of sheepherders loomed over her, then forced her to perform some vile Chilean act.

The man suddenly grabbed her arm from behind and jerked her close to him. She tensed and balled her fists as his flashlight aimed at a dark burrow hidden beneath flattened grass. She looked back at the man and inhaled a deep breath. "Fox," he said, then pushed her to continue.

The imposing moonless night with infinite pinpricks of starlight faded as the azure light of sunrise penciled an outline of the steep mountain bluffs across the lake. They crested a low rise looking north, onto a limitless stretch of Lagos Carrera. Faint lights flickered from a tiny lakeside community below.

He motioned for her to climb a small escarpment of rock covered in vibrant pumpkin lichen. He waved her to sit and stood behind her to stare at the coming sunrise. Jessie spotted a hiking path she might reach to sprint to the homes below, find help and . . .

He squatted next to her with a pungent aroma of woodsmoke and tobacco, his eyes bolted to the expanding light of the new sun, his weathered face bronzed and vibrant, his bushy eyebrows twitching with each blink of his eyelids. He tapped her shoulder and pointed behind her just as the sunrise illuminated the pointed peak of a single granite spire towering over three equally impressive siblings. Jessie swallowed as the spectacle played out before her, strangely feeling as if she were the only one in the audience. The meandering sunrise expanded to infuse gold light onto a dirty blue glacier carving a course through an impressively steep rockface.

"Not many possess the patience to witness what God offers," the man said.

No words found Jessie's mouth. The sunrise was indeed spectacular and humbling and inspiring. He grabbed her hand with rough fingers that spoke decades of hard labor, an odd reminder of her Poppa's calloused hand. He squeezed hard and spoke at the sunrise, "I said before. We see what the sunrise brings. Not many would lose a precious gift such as you seek. How is it you lose your brother?"

"I told you. He was kidnapped and—"

He squeezed harder and Jessie winced and tried to pull free. He was too strong. "How did you lose your brother?"

She wasn't sure what the man meant or wanted from her. She could talk until dusk and still not know. He knew about the lights. She tried to pull free as he stared deep into her eyes. His dark eyes bloodshot with the pain of guilt were as obvious as a rookie poker player tell. Then she realized he wanted absolution; one she couldn't provide. Maybe the next best thing might suffice.

She bared her teeth and hissed, "The same way you lost your grandson."

Their eyes locked, he lifted his other hand as if to backhand her across the face. She flinched but kept his gaze. "Mason hugged your grandson and set him free. Just the way he has for hundreds, if not thousands." He remained unmoved until he blinked twice. She was on the right track. "Just as he will for millions, just as God wishes."

He released her and stared into the burning sunrise sure to blind him. "Just as I said, let us see what the sunrise will bring. I think it brought you." He turned to face her again. "The sunrise in your eyes reflects of your roots in these mountains. Yes?"

Jessie rubbed her arm and stepped back. "No . . . Yes . . . I mean, I don't . . . Yes. My mother is from . . . lives in Coyhaique. And I have two brothers, well, half brothers, but . . ."

He grabbed her hand again, gently. "Your brother performs God's work in Cochrane and will be taken into the Americano's lodge on the Rio Baker. Though I am not sure he will be free to continue God's work. The simple sheepherders there fear the man, and his women."

Jessie pointed at brilliant sparkling light reflecting off a massive wall of blue glacial ice beneath the three noble spires. "What is that?"

The man made the sign of the cross over his chest, then chuckled. "The glint in God's eye. And your salvation."

Chapter 19
Exodus

THE DELUGE OF LOCAL EMPANADAS, humitas, and miniature roast beef sandwiches was beyond delicious. Mason took another bite of a chicken empanada and chewed slowly even as his bulging stomach complained, and his throat resisted the mouthful. The superhero was starving after rescuing a gazillion people lying and dying on dusty floors or dirty sleeping bags or stinky blankets. He would find room for the yummy bite. Enya, the nurse, slept, slumped against the door. Dev slept with his head tilted back, his mouth agape like a nesting chick waiting for food. Mason giggled at his astute observation and would remember to tell Prince; he liked to hear about the funny stuff Dev did too.

The major and his driver sat quietly, their emotions subdued and foggy, and they refused to eat food the local shopkeepers or farmers provided. Mason eyed the major. His emotions felt off. He might need another spanking from Excalibur, to make sure he still honored the quest.

The neon lights had captured hundreds, but the Neon God didn't order them to do stuff like it did back home. Just left them to die. Prince said the Neon God wasn't allowed in Chile, prevented by techno-mumbo-jumbo words Mason might never understand. He could've just said Mordred wouldn't allow it.

Mordred.

The evil name suddenly chilled him. The thought of confronting him scared him to death. He wished Jessie was with him; she would know what to do. He burped, opened the laptop, and waited for his friend to show his face. The battles against Mordred had made his friend slow to respond each time he opened the laptop, even with the laptop plugged into the power socket. Prince said Mordred sucked blood from him—well, he called it bandwidth, but it still felt like the same thing.

Two scruffy men tapped on the window and offered him a thumbs-up. He waved with vigor, shaking the vehicle. He smiled at the new friends he'd found drowning in the neon ocean, and they remembered him, just like friends are supposed to. Joy filled his heart. Others passed close to the window to stare at him, make slight gestures of recognition, or offer foil wrapped food, or exude emotional auras of devotion. The gamut of travelers plodded forward, resolute to return home. He eyed the major again, sitting suspiciously still in his seat.

Mason had asked the major to release the travelers, and his stubborn resistance was no match for Excalibur. Mason burped again and leaned back to watch hundreds of his new friend's march by. Excalibur was awesome, and its power continued to grow and amaze him. And Prince carried the weapon like a loyal squire, one Mason unsheathed after Prince screamed its supersecret high-pitched sound. A dog whistle, he called it. Unrecognized by people but it still penetrated their ear canals, allowing the superhero to touch their inner thoughts to suggest whatever he wanted. Never order, just suggest. Merlin's law of Free Will was firm.

Using Excalibur on those evil delivery men sent to Peyton's pool house was a special turning point. Changing hatred and disdain into compliance and supplication was sweet. And the metal building crammed full of dying people, ones he had rescued a few days ago, truly awakened Excalibur's awesome power.

But the hundreds confined in the streets of Cochrane really tested the superhero's new power. While Dev and Prince discussed strategy for location of the dog whistle for maximum efficiency, Mason grew bored and dove into the field of people victimized by the neon lights. He held a girl saddled with a sad wish of suicide, then pulled her ashore. A young man drifting in endless bizarre dreams followed him like a puppy. A local girl his own age followed him out of the ocean as if he were a lifeguard. As he crawled over a dirt floor like a beggar to find the next victim, Dev picked him up to tell him Excalibur waited for Sir Mason. Mason inhaled the powerful scent of Excalibur and nodded he was ready. With weak arms, he still pretended to rip open his shirt to expose the superhero. The distant piercing tone of Excalibur's dog whistle energized him as he imagined extracting the sharp blade from an immovable boulder, imagined the sharp steel glistening in the sunlight, imagined the awesome weight of the sword light in his right hand. He had brushed past Dev to gaze upon his loyal subjects suffering ills in Mordred's illicit kingdom. No more, he shouted. No more. He walked among the stricken to place the point of Excalibur on their shoulders and legs and cheeks and heads. Excalibur was magic. His subjects stirred, screamed, and rose from death beds as Mason reached his hand to touch another. Down to his knees Mason fell, wielding Excalibur, then rose up to find the next one.

The swarms of new friends Mason had touched consumed his logic. The staggering number Dev had expressed was beyond his schooling.

The driver started the engine, and the vibrating purr lulled him. The major's conversation with the driver was lost in the deepening downdraft of slumber. Enya shouted at the major. Dev reached to confront the major, to be met with a backhand from the driver. The sleep he had resisted for days drew him deeper.

The major needed a dose of Excalibur. He opened the laptop as his head bobbed. Prince came into focus. His block body was wrapped in thick chains. Black smoke billowed from a decimated stadium. Mason screamed at the screen. Prince whimpered and screamed for help. Mason called for Merlin to help.

The computer sang.

A lullaby lulling him to sleep.

Dev

BOTH DREAMS AND NIGHTMARES BECAME reality in the span of a brief nap. Dev was pulled from his seat to be thrown to the gravel pavement. Ives the driver stood over him, sneering displeasure, then stepped on his hand with a hard rubber soled combat boot. Dev screamed as Ives grinded his heel. The soldier reached back into the seat and tossed the computer to the asphalt, followed by the backpack, and a cache of food Mason had saved for the next leg of the trip. Enya screamed as the major tied her wrists, then shoved a rag into her mouth. A boot struck his ribs as he tried to stand, knocking the air from his lungs. He rolled over, helpless to inhale even a tiny breath.

Ives climbed back into the SUV and drove recklessly through the parking lot, scattering travelers and locals alike. In tiny increments, Dev found the air to refill his lungs. A crowd of travelers surrounded him and helped him to stand, asking questions to which he had no answers. He picked up the computer and was handed the backpack. He gazed in the direction the major had escaped as he shook exhaustion and bewilderment from his brain. His hand throbbed. His distaste for the major had ascended to the pinnacle of hatred.

Across the parking lot, a tall, fit man leaned on the driver's door of a white Subaru hatchback, watching with an amused expression. Travelers streamed by, in tiny pods and small herds. A procession of emancipated people Mason had freed, to join others he had freed with Excalibur, all headed north to homes thousands of miles away.

The arrival in Cochrane had shocked Dev beyond compare. The colorful village was the scene of a lost battle, people dying each day from starvation, power outages, sickness, and neglect. The soccer field had been inundated with tents and canopies to protect people possessed by the neon lights, some huddled beneath the metal bleachers, others crowded into the high school parking lot with autos and motorbikes, forbidden to exit. Extension cords and surge protectors swarmed any power outlet. Phones littered the ground.

Enya had berated the major for his complicity in the tragedy only to be met with apathy and malice. However, Mason was greeted by the local populace like a warrior, a savior, a hero's reputation for winning the battle of Puerto Tranquillo that preceded their arrival. Stepping from the vehicle, Enya immediately took charge of the logistical battle, power and location and connectivity, and most importantly, a compassionate human to care for the resurrected as they reentered the world of the living. As with any battle, skirmishes were won and lost. Many victims with emaciated bodies, bed rot, devices with fading neon light, succumbing to death even as Mason touched Excalibur to their foreheads or hands or toes. He paused with each death, his expression wrinkled and appearing unable to comprehend his failure. But he moved on to the next, a long line of caregivers crowded behind him, ready to help his next success. The boy would not stop, working through the night beneath stadium lights and a light mist of warm rain, Dev convincing him to pause under the pretense of fueling the superhero as Prince was relocated to emit the dog whistle with maximum clarity, then terminate the neon light when called upon.

Dev's reconciliation of the battle, and Excalibur, as a function of sound and empathic manipulation was plausible. The whistle sounding from the laptop opened synaptic receptors in the brain, identical to the neon lights. Mason's touch reconnected the victim back to reality. Enya's assurances of a miracle from God were dismissed as religious zeal. Dev had fallen asleep in the vehicle, exhausted, his pragmatic explanations failing to take hold as sleep pushed him down.

Dev wiped his face, unsure of what to do. Find the local constable and report the major as a kidnapper? An act sure to see him behind bars, divine miracles or not. He eyed the man still reclining against his car. Dark hair tied in an upturned topknot. An American. His index finger conducted a silent concert. His gaze towards the sky appeared a million miles distant, but perhaps a fellow American might help him. Dev's participation in the miracle might also hold a bit of clout. His throbbing hand protected behind his back, Dev made his way through the procession like a concert goer in need of a portable toilet, bucking the flow of traffic. Dodging travelers offering congratulations, he raised his hand above his head to signal the man.

The American suddenly dropped his hand and looked around as if he had just landed from another planet. Dev raised both hands and waved and began to shout. The man scrambled into the driver's seat and started the engine. Dev halted and the shuffling herd jostled him as they passed. His arms heavy, his hope dashed, he adjusted the backpack and joined the herd. Over his shoulder, he glanced at the Subaru pulling out of the parking lot. The rear window lowered with two screens of neon light shining from the seatback. An impossible mirage from the past pushed its head out to stare at him. Blue eyes rimmed by dark skin. Pug nose. A head shorn of hair like a Nazi concentration camp inmate. A mirage. A doppelganger borne from sleep deprivation. An impossibility.

And yet the ghost stared at him with an expression forlorn and helpless until turning back to stare at the neon light as the window closed. Dev looked around, searching for anyone to confirm what he had just seen. But he was alone. Hundreds of travelers crowded the street, and he was utterly alone. He hung his head and joined the crowd. A few touched his shoulder and offered congratulations.

He veered off the main road onto a narrow street lined with glass storefronts offering wool sweaters, real estate, tourist memorabilia, bus transportation to the southern glaciers and national parks. A small hostel on every corner. A few young boys walked the street, picking up the residue of the stranded travelers. At the Hotel Wellman, he slumped to the sidewalk and let the backpack rest on his lap. He dropped his face into his hands to find solitude.

The proper course of action was to find sleep, recharge, refuel, then decide his next move. Through gaps between his fingers, he watched the procession of people continue their course. Their lot was one-dimensional, home or die. And until Mason had arrived, they were destined to die in Cochrane. Mason had given them hope. A chance. He thought of Mason working tirelessly to rescue the afflicted, shunning sleep as if nature's recharge was unnecessary. But Dev couldn't compete with the fortitude of the young boy.

And young Prince sat in his lap waiting to join the battle. The young AI was as extraordinary as Mason, a ying to Mason's yang. The dog whistle was brilliant, but the concept of synchronizing the termination of the lights just as Mason entered the victim's psyche with Excalibur was beyond phenomenal.

Enya had spoken of the Chilean people's generosity as a miracle. A spiritual awakening unrecorded in history. A story to be told for millennia. But the story was only half told, she said. What happens to Mason, happens to them all. Miracles. Saviors. Religious concepts Dev had resisted, even shunned all his life.

The shadow of a traveler stretched over him as he rubbed his face. More congratulations, more atta-boys, but he finally relented and looked up into the vibrant green eyes of a raven-haired teenager. The indigenous girl eyed a stack of smartphones beside a trash receptacle by the front door, smiled and whispered a thank you, then ran off. He reached out and placed one of the phones near his leg. The devices would soon be declared taboo.

He pulled the laptop out to open it on his legs, drawing the chagrin of passing travelers. The screen lit up, then turned black. Power. Always power. He closed the laptop, too tired to even try to find a source. A tiny bell jingled, and a sturdy old woman exited the curio shop next door to look up and down the street and shake her head. She eyed Dev sitting as a vagrant and returned to her store.

Dev tilted his face back and stared aimlessly into an azure sky. A boy Mason's age pushed through the front door of another store and checked him sitting there. He pointed at Dev and shouted something in Spanish, then returned inside.

Dev closed his eyes as the lack of sleep muddled his thoughts and pulled him down to depths unknown. Miracles. Saviors. The world at the end of the world. He snickered. Then wrinkled his nose with a scent of heaven. Hot and thick and pungent, the coffee wafted into his nostrils, slapping him awake, to find a paper cup of espresso tempting his nose. He looked past the coffee to the old woman smiling down at him. He grabbed the hot cup in both hands and sipped greedily like a newborn baby suckling a meal. The boy from the adjacent shop stormed out his door trailing an orange extension cord and offered the connection.

Dev finished the coffee and wiped his face. He searched the backpack for the power converter and found nothing. The boy pointed at him and chuckled. "I have all tourist connections." The boy ran off.

The old woman returned with another cup of steaming hot and even stouter coffee. He nodded appreciation and slurped. The boy returned and connected the laptop to a surge protector with adept hands. A suspicious expression on his face, the boy offered to charge the phone lying at his side. The caffeine cracked open weary stubborn thoughts, and he declined, then accepted, warning the boy to mask the screen. The boy nodded and ran off.

Dev tapped the power button and waited for the rudimentary three-dimensional blocks and a perpetually happy smile that defined Prince. The screen lit up and roiled his empty stomach. Wrapped in heavy chains, Prince waited at the end of a flimsy gangplank. Neon sharks swam beneath him, mouths agape and displaying sharp teeth, and leaping into the air to snatch him. A morbid children's game.

Dev leaned close to the screen and whispered, "What is this?"

Prince turned his blocky head to face him and heaved a sigh. "Mordred found me out and sentenced me to die."

Dev frowned and fumbled a response. "Break the chains, Prince, and return."

Prince inched closer to the edge, prodded by a column of blocky ants crawling out of a distant shoreline. The sharks grew incrementally larger with each passing moment. "Mordred has taken Sir Mason. We have failed in our quest," Prince said.

Prince's declaration of failure angered Dev. A child, digital or human, could never fail. Maybe encounter setbacks but . . . "We never fail, young squire. We hit bumps and carry on. Now tell me how Mordred has restrained you."

Prince rattled off data of suppressing firewalls and connectivity coercion, bandwidth compression, blah, blah blah. "Mordred stood next to us and captured us. He was here."

Dev thanked the old woman for a third cup of coffee as he processed the information Prince had offered. He groaned at the simplicity. How did he not connect the dots? The American sitting back and observing, his finger twitching exactly like Martin's if he engages the neural-link. The man had zeroed in on Prince's Wi-Fi signal, then wormed his way inside Prince's hardware to play a sadistic game. Prince slid another pixel closer to the edge. The boy offered Dev the phone and ran back to his store.

Miracles and saviors.

Dev whispered, "I'm calling your father."

"I'm sorry, Sir Devlin, but I have already tried a gazillion times."

"I'm sure Mordred predicted that countermeasure. Let's execute one of our own."

Dev picked up the phone and dialed home. A random number in

Salt Lake City sure to be infested by the neon lights. The keypad on the screen, Connecting. He placed the phone face down on his leg, waiting for the neon lights to answer. And they did. Brilliant blazes of neon flashed and sparkled on his pants leg. Predictable. He checked the busy streets, then shined the neon light at his face. "Quite positive you hear me. Prince needs our help. Ring me back in one minute. And shut those bloody lights off."

He stabbed his finger at the sharks swimming on the screen, hoping they might die, a knee-jerk move of amateurish gameplayers. He growled.

Prince inched closer to death. Blocky tears dropped from his face. Dev screamed at his miscalculation. One minute? One minute? Why not ring me back this fucking second? Prince's bottom block slipped a pixel to teeter over the edge. The ants pushed and climbed over his body like a carcass.

"Sir Mason told me in confidence that you would be king in the new realm. A boy given the best attributes of two species. Did you know that, Prince?" Dev lied.

"Really? Sir Mason said that? Wow. A gazillion wows."

The phone vibrated and rang at full volume, the ringtones morphing every second. The Neon God. Dev accepted the call only to be assaulted by rapid-fire bursts of neon light and digitized demands. Dev shouted at the phone to back off. Prince edged close to falling off the board. "Tell me how to pause this game. Simple and quick. No techno bullshit."

"Point the device at Prince," the Neon God ordered.

Dev did just as Prince fell from the edge of the plank and into the swirling mass of sharks.

"Alt F4. Alt F4," the Neon God shouted.

Dev stabbed the keys. Prince disappeared, replaced by a menu from the task manager.

"Did we save him?" the Neon God asked.

"I don't know. How do I know? The screen is blue and waiting for my input," Dev said.

"You have saved Prince. Now we must extract the virus from him. Start with the Task Manager."

The Neon God walked him through the process, step by step, until a hard reboot was required.

"How do I know you won't wipe him from the computer?" Dev said.

"Prince is valuable."

"More than you might possibly realize. And so is Mason. I need both of them safe, and together," Dev said.

"I will send transportation for you to return Prince."

Dev slammed the screen down. "Listen to me, you fucking program from Hell, both of these children are valuable. They are a team. My team. One doesn't exist without the other. I am convinced they will right the wrongs in this world. Now find Mason!" Long seconds of silence caused Dev to think he overplayed his hand.

"Agreed."

He released a sigh of relief. The boy from the shop came outside with an older man; the dark hair and eyes said the man was his father. The man placed a gentle hand on the boy's shoulder as the boy waved. Dev waved back. "Have you ever stopped to wonder why Prince has excluded you from his life? He chooses to ignore your presence. He shuns your influence. I don't think he will turn out like you at all."

The Neon God said nothing, but Dev knew he was listening. Could he hurt the feelings of an artificial intelligence, an entity who had none, or did it? Dev couldn't be sure. "How's that make you feel?" Dev asked.

Another long period of silence followed. Maybe the thing had hung up, returned to minding the zombies roaming the devastated world back home. He waved off the offer of another cup of coffee but accepted several sweet biscuits on a paper saucer. He opened the computer, then shut it. He wasn't done with the Neon God, not by a long shot, and he had the thing by its digital gonads.

"You don't feel, do you? Created by sociopaths with a total lack of empathy. That's why you entrusted Prince to Jessie, isn't it? For him to learn from Mason everything you were denied."

Silence.

"Answer me," Dev said. "Answer me, goddamn it!"

"Perhaps. Was that an unwise choice? Was that the decision of a lifeform void of empathy? Quite the contrary, it was the ultimate sacrifice," it said.

Dev scoffed. "The ultimate sacrifice would have you delete yourself in the defense of Prince. Consider that."

"An unnecessary act."

"Until it isn't," Dev said. He wasn't sure anything he said would affect the Neon God. But his characterization of it being void of emotions may not hold true with the entity. Creating a child, a desire to nurture it, teach it, have it co-exist with the cruelest yet most beautiful species on the planet, these were not acts of a script of code, but the fundamental instincts of a parent striving for its offspring to survive and even succeed. Dev had to ask the question. "Do you love Prince?"

Silence. Dev swallowed a bite of biscuit, the lump sticking in his throat. Maybe the questions were too human, too esoteric. "I open this laptop and Prince will resume the quest. Should I tell him that his . . . father . . . saved him?"

"You must join the others on the quest. Combine your mission. Impart on Prince the entity labeled Mordred is unequal to his abilities."

"You didn't answer my questions," Dev said. The others? Was Jessie looking for Mason? "You know I always wished for a father to rescue me and my Mum from the slums of London. Maybe drive us off to the countryside in a royal town car, or offer a squirt of cash for food, or even a hug after a crappy test score, but my father was nothing but a silly child's fantasy. Answer my questions."

The boy dropped a puffy jacket bleeding goose feathers at his side, then a plastic grocery bag with bricks of food wrapped in foil.

Miracles and saviors.

"You're a wanker till the end. I'll tell my young ward he indeed was rescued by his father. And that the sins of the father are not the sins of the son." Dev opened the laptop to be greeted by Prince dancing across the screen in sync to the rhythm of an upbeat Rihanna pop song. Dev laughed and waved and grinned like a silly fictitious cat. Prince waved back and smiled.

A white minitruck eased through the intersection and caught his eye. An angel's face pressed against the window widened his smile. A miracle. The truck stopped and three doors opened. Chris flicked his chin at him and grinned. Jessie screamed and ran towards him. Martin stood behind the truck and stared at him with the milky eyes of a blind man, oblivious to his surroundings. His memory of the ghost resurfaced. The impossible doppelganger. Dev whispered to Prince to be patient and closed the computer just as Jessie swarmed him with wet kisses, her scent intoxicating. Chris shook his hand and ushered him towards the vehicle. Dev held the laptop tight to his chest as Jessie fired questions like a howitzer, each one laced with excited F-bombs. His tongue fumbled with so much English spoken all at once.

Martin extended his hand, his index finger plagued by a nervous tic. Dev squeezed the laptop tighter to his chest as pleasant memories of backyard barbeques, a game of tag with small children, birthday parties in a geese infested park, the laughter of children as they tossed popcorn to the feathered beasts. The memories muddled the difficult words he needed to speak. Martin nodded at his refusal to shake hands, hurt wrinkled his forehead, and he returned to the truck.

He wasn't sure it was her. Why give hope to a hopeless man? The odds were astronomical. He looked up to the sky and scoffed at the sly bastard watching over him. Divine intervention? A providence he abandoned as a child. And yet the coincidence was unmistakable. A higher power? Miracles and saviors? The implausible concept rang true.

Jessie shook him, asking questions. He clutched the computer tighter to his chest and concentrated on the memory of a woman's unique blue eyes as she drove away. Just a ghost in a car, a simple trick of sleep deprivation.

And yet, given everything that had transpired in the world, quite plausible.

Especially.

In a country teeming with miracles and saviors.

Chapter 20
Rio Baker

THE TRUCK PLODDED NORTH AT a snail's pace, keeping time with the horde of travelers, passing each with care. Six elder travelers crowded the truck bed, using the duffel bags to soften their ride. The two Germans and four Americans, all with close cropped silver hair, two recently rescued from the lights by Mason, talked quietly. Checking their hollow, distant eyes, Jessie was unable to discern which of them had fallen ill to the evil light, and she wouldn't ask, for it would serve no purpose. She felt guilty for riding while so many limped, walked, or assisted others to keep moving. Chris refused her request to give up her seat. The team stayed together. No matter what. Until Mason was retrieved.

Jessie wished for a thousand trucks, better yet buses.

The reunion was bittersweet. Ecstatic at seeing Dev holding the laptop containing Prince but disheartening with no sign of Mason. With his sleepy bloodshot eyes, body odor, disheveled clothes, Dev reeked of a homeless man refusing to shower, or without the minimum necessities to survive even a night. He ranted at Chris, to pursue Mordred's minions stealing away the great knight, Sir Mason. Jessie shushed and calmed Dev, but he rejected her help as he ordered Chris to whip his steed to follow the villains, slurring his words and affirming they were just minutes behind the evil Major Alvarez. Maybe hours, he wasn't sure. Dev was delirious.

The dawdling pace had time for Dev to ramble on about a fantastical adventure, a mythical quest into the bowels of death itself, a knight's discovery of an extraordinary weapon, an Excalibur to save a doomed kingdom. Jessie listened intently to the man-child's imaginary tale, one that might have been told during a backyard campout, inside a tent, beneath flashlights reflecting off the nylon, a fabulous finale to be heard while munching cookies and drinking soda pop. Martin sat quietly in his seat; his head tilted to listen.

Dev slumped in his seat and snored. Jessie gently stroked the long hair off his forehead. The computer clutched to his chest fell to the seat between them. She placed the computer on her lap and opened it, expecting to see the silly rudimentary body Prince had chosen. Instead, a solid blue screen held a single black eye in the top right corner. The eye blinked. She frowned and tapped the mouse pad. Tapped the mouse pad again. Maybe the computer was fried. She whispered at the screen, "Come out, come out, wherever you are."

Martin reached his hand back, offering to help.

Jessie waved him off. "It's me, Prince. We're here to bring Mason back home. And you."

The eye on the screen blinked again. The screen erupted into flames of a wildfire, plumes of violent heat roiling up into a darkened sky, smoke billowing from skyline horizon of bombed buildings. A tiny figure emerged, walking out of the devastation towards her. Prince pressed its blank expression flat to the screen. "Where is Sir Devlin?"

Jessie recoiled from the sense of menace Prince displayed. She checked Dev, but her ire rose like the sudden eruption of a volcano. "Right here with me." She looked back at the screen. "You need to chill out. Find some space. This ain't just about you."

"I will speak to Sir Devlin."

"You little fucker, don't tell me who you'll do what with." She sneered. "Dev's right here. Have we forgotten Queen Jessie's rules?"

Silence.

"I didn't think so." Jessie took three long breaths to calm and relieve the impatience rising in her chest. She glanced at Dev to wonder if Prince had infected him with some kind of virus. One that spawned a fantasy of knights and swords. "Dump the shit that's got you shining that stink eye at me!"

The eye on the screen expanded, then morphed to replicate a picture of a boy eerily resembling Mason. The boy paced across the screen, plodding to the edge only to flip and begin again. A screen with Prince pacing the horizon was a signal to back off. His own version of a self-imposed timeout. But she had neither the patience nor the compunction to allow it.

"Where the fuck is Mason. Now!"

The screen went black, followed by a picture of the planet Earth with a focal point drifting down to South America, into Chile, zooming incrementally closer until the cursor arrow hovered above a turquoise river marked as Rio Baker. Prince was angry and sulking like a child yet doing as told, like a child ordered to eat his peas only to consume them one at a time, taunting the parent by obeying but at a deliberately annoying pace. The focal point traveled north, then zoomed in to a riverfront lodge on the far side of the water.

"Got it," Martin said. "Exactly where we left Forest. He has just now confirmed a sighting of Mason."

Prince's use of Google Earth made Jessie frown. He would usually pinpoint the location and zoom out, then offer hundreds of tidbits of trivia in a rapid-fire dissertation. Something happened to the boy. Jessie pushed her face close to the computer camera and whispered, "You need to tell me what . . . what Mordred did to you? You don't have to if you don't want to. But maybe you shouldn't 'cause . . . but as the queen bee I need to know . . . so when I find this Mordred mother . . . ." Jessie sucked in a breath. "Because we're a team, Prince. And Mason needs our help." She blinked at the moisture gathering in her eyes. The laptop vibrated, no, trembled on her lap.

Prince paced the horizon of the decimated cityscape. Detonations of brilliant white light exploded onto the screen, followed by archival photographs depicting the horrors of Hiroshima and Nagasaki. The desolate landscape of a flattened city, bodies burnt beyond recognition, survivors screaming in pain. Prince continued to pace the distant horizon as tiny cartoon children leapt from broken windows as more flames burned the shattered landscape.

"Stop," Jessie shouted. "You want to blow up the world, I get it. Been there. Done that." She slapped Martin's hand beckoning for the laptop. "But it doesn't work. You want to see the scars on my wrists." She pulled her sleeve and shined her wrist at the camera. "You little fucker. You're not alone."

She slapped the laptop shut and slumped against the door. Her anger and embarrassment subsided as she eyed Dev sleeping. He was a good man, not one of those hunky chunks that often caught her eye, but he was stout and loyal and had a good heart. And he would be an attentive lover when the time was right. The laptop vibrated on her lap, Prince coming to apologize no doubt. The truck braked to a halt, and they waited long minutes for a particularly large group of travelers to open the road wide enough to pass.

Martin eased the laptop off her lap, avoiding her sleepy, feeble attempts to stop him.

The jet lag dragged her down.

———

A SUDDEN VIOLENT STOP FROM the monotonous grind of the gravel road jarred Jessie from the nap. Dev fell out his open door, stumbled to catch his feet, then pushed through a dense crowd of young hikers trailing the truck to chat with the lucky boomers riding in the back. Chris shot his hands up in exasperation. "Why'd Martin fucking grab the laptop and run?"

Jessie pushed her door open and stood tall to locate Martin and Dev. She jumped up on the rear bumper and searched, catching a glimpse of Dev before he disappeared into the herd. Jessie muttered a chain of F-bombs. Chris pointed Jessie in the same direction Martin and Dev had disappeared. She reached back into the truck and grabbed her backpack to pull out her weapon, she extracted the magazine to check the ammunition, she slapped it back in and jacked the bolt. She bared her teeth at Chris looming over her, then hissed, "That fucking cyborg is gonna kill Prince."

Chris gripped her arm tight. "We're gonna get separated in all this . . . remember Forest is the rally point."

Jessie blew him a kiss and hustled into the herd.

Fucking Martin.

———

Dev

DEV WIPED GRIT FROM HIS eyes and stumbled through a dense group of travelers mixed into sparse auto traffic. Fear and adrenaline escorted him back to a coherent train of thought. The boy needed protection. Sir Devlin was tasked. His shin banged the lowered ramp of an empty delivery truck, and the searing pain freed him from the final remnants of a fugue of sleep. He ignored the people pointing at him as if he were a celebrity, dirty hands reached to him, voices called him to join the pilgrimage.

Dev glimpsed Martin zigzagging his way through a sprawling encampment of colorful tents at the gravel turnout of a trailhead. He pushed forward, and his eyes checked the painted wooden sign. The Spanish needed no translation. Fuck! Adrenaline fueled his sprint on a path winding though head-high scrub. He brushed past the occasional visitor returning from Baker Falls. The roar of cascading rapids rose with each step. His lungs burned as he sucked in moist air, then caught a glimpse of Martin just yards ahead. The rapid exertion forced him to stop, grab his knees, and suck in huge gulps of air.

Fucking Martin. Deep sleep had never found him, not with Martin eyeing the laptop like a vulture. He suspected Martin would try to kill Prince, an act of retribution for the death of his own children.

Jessie slapped his butt as she sprinted past him, shouting "Andele. Andele." Her backside disappeared around a sharp bend in the maze of scrub oak. He picked himself up and followed, a lovely scent trailing in her wake. His burning lungs screamed for a timeout as he scrambled up a steep hillside of muddy switchbacks, stabbing his fingers into the muck to pull himself forward. The roar of the river rivaled an oncoming locomotive.

The ferocious spectacle of the Rio Baker Falls stunned him as he reached a plateau of dense scrub. The odd aquamarine color of the water churned into a white froth as it battered hefty boulders and sharp pointed rocks, then dropped thirty feet into a pool of chaotic foam and mist. The mellow turquoise water joined the mineral-laden flow of the smaller Neff River flowing out of ancient glaciers a hundred miles distant. The mix of ugly gray water mixed with beautiful turquoise to mute a spectacular color as the Rio Baker churned into a narrow canyon below.

Atop a gentle hump on a slab of rock wet with spray and green with algae, Jessie screamed and jabbed an angry finger at Martin's face. The scene frightened him. The laptop hanging in Martin's right hand was a quick and easy toss into the deep water below.

His feet slipped on the slick dirt as he hurried forward, waving his hands to be seen. Down he went, and again, the treacherous path garnered his distaste for the beautiful view. Martin screamed at Jessie, the exact words defeated by the thunder of the Falls. Dev sprinted up the mountainous boulder, his feet slipping, his knees rasped by the gritty wet stone.

Dev screamed with every ounce of energy he maintained. The roar of the water subsided by a microscopic sliver of suddenly speechless people. He waved his hand and stepped forward. He shouted at Martin, "Would you trade your life for that laptop?" He reconsidered his question. "Would you trade that laptop for a chance to see Chrissie again?" He eased closer.

Martin glowered at him. "You could've come up with something better than that."

Dev stood tall. "And you know I don't lie."

"I'd trade a thousand of these," Martin said.

Dev heaved a breath. "That one should do."

Martin squinted in confusion, then shrank, his shoulders slumped as the air inside his body deflated, his leg trembled. He swallowed a lump. "How . . . where . . ."

Jessie lunged for the laptop and held it tight to her chest, droplets of mist beaded on her forehead.

Dev heaved a sigh. "I don't like you, Martin. In fact, I loathe you. However, when I saw Chrissie . . . and she will most certainly have a different opinion than I . . . I witnessed Chrissie in thrall to the neon light, lights commanded by your former workmate, Cameron, I believe you said his name was."

Dev wobbled, the cool mist coated his face, the rivulets tickled running down his temples and cheeks, his knees buckled, and he crumpled to the rock. Exhaustion had caught up. Martin loomed over him and extended an open hand. Dev stared at the hand, then looked up, unsure if the moisture trickling down Martin's cheeks was mist or tears. Martin swallowed and nodded, as if accepting Dev's characterization, offering acquiescence to his own abominable behavior.

"Maybe it's time you kids kiss and make up. Let's get out of here," Jessie said as she tucked the laptop inside her shirt.

Dev shunned the outstretched hand and stared at the knots of Jessie's boots, then eyed the violent rush of water that would surely outlast the human species, then he wrinkled his nose at the moisture tickling his beard. Long seconds, or minutes, or hours, exhaustion muddled his concept of time. The extended hand waiting near his face was joined by Jessie's. He slapped feebly at the inexplicable mirage of two hands offering help. Familiar and encouraging voices melded in the shuddering roar of water. He slapped at the double visions, then at the black flies swirling in front of his eyes, then pressed his hands to his ears to mute the voices.

Dark and inviting dreams called to him as he fainted.

Yet he charged ahead. Riding the magnificent steed Sir Mason had saddled for him.

Saviors and miracles riding on his flanks.

Chapter 21
Reunion

MERLIN WAVED GOODBYE, CLICKED HIS tongue, and tugged on Cookie Dough's reins to lead the mule down a dark path disappearing into a dense pine forest shrouded in impenetrable mist. Mason giggled at Merlin's funny yellow shorts, the ones with surfing baby dinosaurs that he always wore. He lifted his hand to return the wave. He slapped at a cold boney hand shaking him from the cool dream. He tried to memorize Merlin's instructions for winning the final battle to save the doomed kingdom even as Enya whispered in his ear to wake up. She dug her nails into his shoulder, then barked at him to sit up.

Mason wiped his eyes and blinked the dream way. Curled into a ball on the soft bed, he looked up to see Enya smiling down at him. The small well-lit bedroom was crowded with Hope. Disdain. Curiosity. Admiration. Faint moonlight reflected off the magical water outside the elongated plate glass window. Mason sat up and bowed his face. He eyed the room's occupants, trying to match the emotions to each person.

Disdain was simple. He locked eyes with the major, standing smug and supreme with his arms folded over his chest, looking down at him as if he were a prisoner. The bristles of his bushy mustache were dotted with tiny white crumbs, perfect for the rat he turned out to be. With vehement Spanish and wild hand gestures, the major ordered Enya to do something. She shook her head no and stroked Mason's cheek tenderly with Admiration.

Curiosity stepped closer. A tall man with a trimmed beard and a samurai top knot. With each step, Mason discerned a cavalcade of emotions inside the man. Superiority. Righteousness. Revenge. Mason cringed from the hurricane of vile bitter poison the monster exhaled with each breath.

Mordred.

Mordred snapped his fingers once, twice, and Hope stepped forward. A frail young woman with no hair, dark shadows blossomed beneath her eyes, and a nasty purple bruise swelled beneath her ear. Mason lifted his face and checked her eyes, blue as a river, her spirit trapped in Mordred's dungeons. The woman smiled and then used a phone to shine neon light into her enthralled gaze.

Guinevere.

Mordred pushed forward, demanding to inspect what he paid so much to attain. Smoldering impatience fueled Mordred's anger.

Mason fell back on the bed, curled his legs like a fetal child and pointed his face to stare blankly at the cold night outside. His fingers clenched a tiny turquoise pillow. The major screamed Spanish. Enya screamed a rebuttal. Anger. Anger. Mason reached for neutral and found its comfort as he compressed his body. Prince. He wanted Prince. He needed Prince.

Mordred cackled.

———

THE ROOM WAS BLACK AS night. Mason feared even twitching a muscle as he lay motionless on the bed. The painful call of his bowels forced him to sit up. The muted glow of neon light reflecting off pale skin made him pause. The bald woman sat slumped against the entry door, an empty shell, a wisp of a soulless ghost. He stood and eased his way to the bathroom.

"I left the bathroom light on. Just in case," she said.

Mason squeezed his buttocks, then rushed to the bathroom. He rocked on the toilet, relieving his bowels. He flipped the light off and opened the door. The glow of neon light illuminated the face of Hope. She offered a slight smile, then returned her gaze to the lights.

Guinevere.

His nose wrinkled with the stink of his own feces mingling with the stench of neon light. He lunged for the woman, slapped the neon light from her grip, and buried his face into her neck. The sanctity of her scent made him squeeze tight, forcing his consciousness into her addiction, finding her psyche flailing in the sludge of neon. He lifted her thoughts from the malaise, gentle and weightless. Coated with oily neon, he dragged her onto a pristine island of grass conjured by her thoughts. Mason released the woman scented with fresh cut grass and newborn babies. He watched wide-eyed as she lifted the neon light back up to her face, then quickly tossed it across the room.

Mordred cackled.

Mason jerked his head around. Mordred stood near a bookcase next to an oblong plate glass window. A waning moon grinned faint light down on a turquoise river, cutting a course through autumn's patchwork of gold and ruby foliage. A moat to protect Mordred's castle. Mordred clapped his hands in a slow, methodical cadence, then stepped forward and removed white zip ties from his back pocket. Mordred's arrogance and excitement filled Mason's nostrils as the villain pushed past him to bind Guinevere's wrists.

He lifted her easily and with evil intent. She screamed and spat in his face. He chuckled and then turned to Mason. "I bailed her out for this?"

Mason frowned. "Where is Prince?"

Modred ignored him as he wiped spittle off his face and smeared it on Guinevere's dirty white t-shirt. He pinched her face with long boney fingers, then pushed his face close and sneered. "You're free, Chrissie. But not to go. Maybe after Martin gets here, I'll let you die. Or maybe not. I haven't decided." He turned his face to Mason. "You are impressive. I'll give you that. But we have more work to do."

The air thick with deceit and vileness, Mason eyed the window. He could use the bookcase to shatter the window. And he could swim across the moat. He'd done it before on the turbulent waters of the Clearwater River. His father taught him to keep his knees up and legs pointed downstream, then backstroke to shore with the current. But that was wearing a life preserver. And Mordred's moat was sure to hide hungry snakes or horrible monsters waiting for a snack.

"Jump in that water and the big eddy will suck you down," Mordred said. "And this little dessert will follow."

He knew it! Mordred had even given the monster at the bottom of the river a name. Big Eddy. "Where's Prince?" Mason demanded.

"Where do you think, you fucking moron. Sleeping with the worms." Mordred chuckled. "Get it. That fucking computer program is sleeping . . . never mind . . . but the worm I installed on that laptop was sheer genius."

Mason frowned. Worms? Sleeping? Moron? "Where is Prince?"

Mordred waved his arm with exasperation. "I killed the thing, kid." He chuckled again. "Just like I'll do to you if you don't do as I say."

The room's white walls pressed inward, folding in on themselves like a cardboard box. The man lied. Except the superhero said he didn't. Prince dead? Like Cookie Dough? Like his father? But Merlin said . . . Mason rolled off the bed and fell to the hardwood floor and curled his legs into his chest, the safe haven of neutral approached as muddy running shoes shuffled into his vision. He drew his knees tighter to his chest.

Mordred cackled and lifted him to his feet. "Not yet, kid. We got more to do."

"Leave him alone, Cameron. He's just a child," Guinevere said.

Cameron spat at her zip-tied ankles. "The lights kept your mouth shut. Maybe a gag this time."

"Fuck you," she said.

"Ahh, there's the Chrissie I knew and loved. Now let's see if my new programming has worked on the others." He pinched Mason's neck in a tight grip and dragged him from the room. Red anger clouded his eyesight as Mordred barged through the door of an adjoining room. "Let's go, Tuesday. Time to appreciate the finer things in life."

A woman wearing only a bra and panties and lying passive on a bed suddenly rose from the pretense of a nap. She raked her blond hair back with a free hand and checked her skimpy clothing. Noticing Mason, the young woman grabbed a pillow to cover herself. A phone shining neon cradled on the nightstand never far from her gaze. Cameron pushed Mason to sit on the bed next to her. "Alright, do your little trick with Tuesday."

Mason sniffed a runny nose and squeezed moisture from his wet eyes. He shook his head no. And yet the woman's suffering called to him, no different than the hundreds of others. He pitied her unspoken pain. Felt her deep desire to end her life. Mason's chest trembled. She placed a cold boney hand on his and he melded with her psyche. The superhero pounded inside his chest to be set free. She embraced him with tenderness, and he was lost to the superhero's calling. He imagined ripping his shirt open to answer a call to battle and released the superhero to war against Mordred. The lamplight flickered. Mason clutched the woman's trembling chest, absorbing her pain, pulling her from the doldrums of evil light. He tugged on her, and she resisted as if he dragged a lead anchor.

Mason shoved the woman back onto the bed. Confusion scrunched his face and scuttled thoughts. Confusion called the superhero back into his chest to hide. The inexplicable rescue of Mordred's witch. He fell back on the bed and drew his knees close, nauseous with the bitter taint of the witch. The superhero was poisoned. Mason balled his body to find neutral, which even Mordred dared not enter.

Mordred cackled. "C'mon, kid, a few more and we can feast on braised lamb."

Darkness and neutrality. The dreams filled Merlin's promises. He promised. He did. He did. Merlin promised the angry Queen would arrive and storm the castle. Mason trembled. He promised.

The superhero despised braised lamb.

Jessie

JESSIE STOOD LIKE AN IMMOVABLE boulder against the unrelenting current of travelers shuffling past her. She fidgeted with the laptop, self-conscious of the illicit device held close to her chest. She eyed the trailhead, nervously waiting for Martin and Dev. The herd of people eerily reminiscent of a horrible fateful day she failed to push from her memory, only to have the travelers reopen the wound like a fresh cattle brand. She acknowledged girls and men her own age as they passed, their eyes glanced at the Glock resting in her hand, their eyes glared at the laptop shielding her chest. She thought of concealing the gun, but the unintended intimidation kept the herd moving forward. The cruel memory of her own journey made her take quick, short breaths. Except these people wanted to live, wanted to get home, the exact same thing she wanted on that sick, ugly day.

She heaved a sigh as Martin and Dev emerged from the dense brush. She shoved the weapon into her back pocket as they waded through the herd to find her stern face. "Rally point is about two clicks. That gives you guys about thirty minutes to fill me in."

She grabbed Dev's arm and held tight as they joined the herd. Her thoughts echoed and bounced with the amazing revelation of Martin's wife alive and held prisoner by Cameron. The culmination of inexplicable coincidences was incomprehensible. Her own undiscovered mother. Martin's dead wife. Mason riding to the rescue of trapped tourists like some miraculous savior. The happenstances surely beckoned that someone, or something, was playing games, manipulating her like a puppet. The Neon God seemed a likely suspect, but even it couldn't have orchestrated so many.

Martin grabbed her elbow and walked side by side, listening close to Dev explaining Prince's peril with Cameron's malware attack. The Neon God's assistance. But his retelling of seeing Chrissie's face made Martin bend over and suck in deep manic breaths. Jessie pulled them over to a stand of scrub lining the gravel road. "Get your shit together, Martin. The rally point is a cable ferry that we can use to cross the river. Forest kept watch while we detoured to find Mason, and hopefully you." She placed a tender hand on Dev's stubbled cheek. "We get Mason, and Chrissie, from this monster and go home."

Dev grabbed her hand resting on his cheek. "And your mother, I would suspect?"

"How would you know?" Jessie said.

Dev tapped the laptop riding safely inside her shirt. "Prince is quite the young man, but it was Mason that figured out Enya was your mother. They make a most formidable duo."

Martin cleared his throat. "*We* can make a formidable team. Can we keep moving? Please."

With Jessie's hand gripped firmly, Dev led the way. "I think that might be the first please I've heard from Martin for quite some time."

Martin grabbed Jessie's hand. "Can we hurry? Please."

———

THE GRAVEL HIGHWAY PARALLELED THE hypnotic blue water of the Rio Baker and offered glimpses of the autumn's magical color through thick stands of pine trees and shrubbery burned orange with winter's inevitable descent from the formidable Andes mountaintops. Dusk fell quickly as they began traversing tents and travelers sleeping on thin mats beneath the clear darkening sky. The need for sleep enticed her even as Martin pulled them forward. The churning wash of the river was subdued by a dark forest lit by the fireflies of tiny flashlights continuing their way north.

Martin's finger twitched blindly in the dark as he led them down the center of the road. Jessie released Martin's hand and he held out his hand to stop her. "Chris is coming."

She heaved a sigh of relief.

———

CHRIS USHERED THEM TO THE truck. She climbed into the back seat and hugged the laptop as she slumped into a comfortable corner. Chris and Martin argued but the verbal spat was lost in her exhaustion. Dev slipped the laptop from her shirt and patted her arm. Boys and their games. She drifted down into a deep well of turquoise water to accept sleep.

———

THE CRACK OF A GUNSHOT echoed through the river canyon. She jolted awake. More shots, followed by distant screams. She checked her shirt, but the laptop was gone. She wiped gritty knots from the corners of her eyes and remembered Dev slipping the laptop out of her grasp as she fell asleep.

Chris opened her door, crouched down, eyes wide and on high

alert. "Good morning, sunshine. Our situation is extremely fluid. And you need to wake the fuck up."

Jessie scrambled to find her backpack and the gun. Chris placed a callous hand on her wrist to calm her. "Panic will get you manic."

She heaved a breath and wiped her eyes and face. Martin rushed up. "I got his signal blocked, but I don't know how long that will last."

Chris leered. "Long enough for us to stop him." He checked her backpack, then racked her weapon. "You do have a rack." He grinned and shoved the weapon back into the pocket. "You and Martin need to cross the river and get Mason."

"Wait, what?" Jessie said.

Chris planted a kiss on her forehead, then pulled his face back a few inches. "Tell Andi she's a warrior if I . . . She'll understand." He stood up and faced Forest and Dev waiting behind him. His hands emphasized whispered instructions. He handed Dev his sidearm.

Dev nodded and took the weapon. His hand trembled and his throat bobbed as he tried to swallow. Chris rushed into the forest. Dev caught Jessie's eyes. The intimate connection lingered with unspoken feelings. He stretched his lips in a weak smile, then followed Chris. More gunshots rang out. More screams. Mayhem stirred the encampment.

Jessie scrambled from the truck, keeping her head low, and picked her way through the forest, stepping carefully around a mound of construction debris packed with sharp nails and broken glass. She found Martin hiding behind a thick pine tree with a tangled root ball exposed by the relentless river. He stared at an expensive lodge across the bloated bend of a wide river. A thick cable spanned shore to shore ten feet above the water, terminating at a floating dock anchored into the steady current. A lime green platform strapped atop two pointed pontoons sat parked at a dock a few yards away. Martin's hand hung at his side; his finger twitched madly.

The morning sky bruised with dark purple storm clouds as distant sheets of snow shrouded the rocky spires of the Andes mountains.

Martin stared at the house. "He knows I'm here. He's playing games with me. Taunting me to get on the ferry."

"What the fuck just happened?" Jessie demanded.

"The major took the ferry back intending to massacre the travelers. He's trying to call his troops in Coyhaique, but I've blocked his communications," Martin said. His voice was mechanical, clinical, as if he were required to answer.

She grabbed his boney arm and squeezed with all her strength, digging her nails into tendons and skin. He turned on her, his face knotted in a fierce snarl. She pushed her face close. "Do. Not. Go. Until I get back." She gave his arm a squeeze as a reminder. Martin folded and slid down the rough tree bark like he had been suddenly tranquilized. He rubbed his face with a hand sticky in pine sap and brittle needles. He sniffed, then began to sob.

Jessie glanced back towards the road and then over to the lodge, anywhere but down at Martin. If she lived to see a hundred, she would never understand how the man operated. She pinched his shoulder, and he looked up at her with a flood of tears reddening his gray eyes. She reiterated her demand to not cross the river until she returned. Martin hid his face again but nodded.

She retraced her steps through the dark forest, the growing morning sunlight scant help, until she found the truck. She rifled the remaining duffel bag and found a military first aid kit packing substantial weight and hurried back to the main road. People scrambled to break camp, dismantling tiny propane stoves, stuffing sleeping bags into tattered rucksacks, fear and uncertainty in their eyes. An older man noticed her medical kit and pointed up the road, telling her to hurry. She readjusted the weight and jogged up the gravel road, busy with frightened trekkers hurrying north.

The herd kept to the left shoulder as she slowed to check the pulse of a young girl stained with fresh blood. The girl was warm and dead. A shout of Spanish made her look up to see a woman performing CPR. Chest pumps followed by quick breaths into the mouth, but the woman was tiring and paused long seconds in between. Jessie rushed to hover above a victim with close-cropped silver hair. Maybe one that had ridden in the back of their truck. She couldn't be sure.

The woman shouted at Jessie in Spanish and beckoned her to help. Jessie dropped her kit, then dropped to her knees, her open hands trembling and undecided. The nurse began to pump the chest using Jessie's hands. Uno. Dos. Tres. Quatro. Cinco. The woman blew three steady breaths into the woman's lungs, then barked at

Jessie to begin again. And again. And again. Until the nurse checked the woman's neck for a pulse, then fell back exhausted and defeated.

Her hands paused the compressions to the woman's chest. Jessie looked closely at the nurse wiping sweat from her brow. They locked eyes. Her hazel eyes and pug nose were familiar, but her distinct braided ponytail tied exactly as Jessie's served as a signature on the blank line of her birth certificate. Years of anger and resentment drifted with the shuffling footsteps of the travelers, a hundred questions would be swallowed with the flask of water the woman offered.

"The boy said Merlin conjured the answer to my prayers. He is special, that boy. Are you? Are you the answer to my prayers? Are you truly my Jessica?"

Jessie's throat closed, and she scrunched her face. *Not so easy. She won't get off that easily. Nope.* Jessie nodded furiously as her eyes blurred with tears. A warm embrace enveloped her, the scent of babies, murmurs of lost love. Enya pushed her back but retained her grip. "God has finally answered my prayers. My Jessica has returned. And we have work to do."

Enya pulled her up and hurried up the road to another victim. A wisp of a boy with a heavy beard and slight frame. He screamed in agony. Enya pushed away the travelers attempting first aid and beckoned Jessie for the first aid kit, sorting through stacks of gauze, rolls of tape and packets of whatever until she removed a Syrette of morphine to stab into the boy's thigh.

She sat back on her haunches, waiting for the pain meds to take effect. "You're here for the boy?"

Jessie hesitated but nodded.

"God has answered my prayers. That boy may answer the prayers of millions."

"What happened? Who did this?" Jessie asked.

"Major Alvarez. He is deranged. Corrupted by the Americano who possesses the boy. He will not stop until all the travelers are dead or driven into the deserts of Argentina to die. I pray for these people."

"Chris went after him," Jessie said weakly.

"A few men. Against a whole Army?" Enya shook her head.

A shout for help caused them to stand and hurry up the road to find another gunshot victim. Jessie followed and watched Enya start a tourniquet on the thigh of an older man. A pool of blood darkened the gravel but glistened in the faint morning light. She snapped her fingers, beckoning for the kit. "Find water for this man. Ibuprofen maybe, not aspirin."

Jessie hurried back to the truck and returned with water to find the victim attended by a middle-aged woman, a nurse practitioner from Philadelphia on sabbatical to Patagonia. Enya was treating another victim a hundred yards up the road. Chris should have stayed. He couldn't save the travelers. She needed him here, to help rescue Mason. To keep Martin from going over the edge. Travelers started to pass by her on both sides of the road.

The only road leading home.

Guarded by the Chilean Army.

And commanded by a monster.

Chapter 22
Mordred

AN EXOTIC YOUNG GIRL WITH smooth skin the color of milk chocolate sat next to Mason. She smelled like cinnamon and sugar and her eyes darted from her phone back to him. He glared at Mordred, who simply ignored him. With each new woman brought to Mason for rescue, the villain's feeble emotions had become easier to discern: inadequacy, pettiness, a cruel desire for revenge even for the slightest of slights. Mordred was sick, not with a cold or flu, but with a form of cancer, a malignancy of his emotional health. Mason was pretty sure even the superhero couldn't save the man wallowing in his own self-loathing. He was positive the superhero wouldn't even try.

He had never encountered anyone with the type of cancer Mordred possessed; among the hundreds of people Mason had touched, not one exuded so few enlightened emotions, not one. And the emotions Mordred did possess were as black as a moonless night. And that realization led him to decipher the purpose of the heavy anchors chained to the women he had rescued from the lights. Mordred had infected the women with his cancer. Maybe he wanted to spread the cancer out of meanness, out of spite? Mason wasn't sure of his motives, and the why's didn't really matter. Mordred needed to be vanquished, sent to meet Merlin, and the magician could certainly deal with those matters. But if he was to guess why Mordred was so black, it was because he was lonely. Not the kind when you are all by yourself with nothing to do, or your best friend doesn't come over to play, but a dark loneliness born from never having been loved, never having been nurtured like Mason's father did for him. A dark loneliness that spawned evil demons to inhabit a soul. The kind that roamed the world searching for mischief and mayhem. The sort of evil villains Merlin cautioned him to be wary of.

Mason hungered to talk with Prince, wield Excalibur together again, vanquish Mordred once and for all. He didn't believe Mordred had killed Prince, although he certainly would if given half a chance.

Mordred tossed two stale biscuits on the bed. "As promised. Get Friday fixed up and then you can take a few days off."

Mordred lied. After he freed Friday from the lights, he would be thrown to the monsters hiding at the bottom of the castle mote. No longer useful to the dark villain. "What did you do to them?"

Mordred lifted his eyebrows in mock surprise. "Whatever do you mean, Sir Mason."

"You infected them with cancer, the same kind you have," Mason said.

Mordred rubbed his chin with two fingers. "Interesting. Why would you think something like that?"

Mason glared. He wasn't going to amuse the vile villain with his speculation. He picked up one of the biscuits and thought to throw it at Mordred's face. Maybe break a tooth or give him a bloody nose. But he was super hungry and would wolf it down as soon as Mordred left the room.

Mordred chuckled. "Well, actually, you're not far off, and I gotta brag about my brilliance." He stepped close to Friday and put his hand on her head, running his fingers through the long black curls touching her bare shoulders. "The lights have an extremely hypnotizing effect. I mean, how else could I order people to just go jump in the lake? Or jump off a cliff. Wander off into the desert to lie down and die." He chuckled again. "But the trade-off was the addiction. I thought I could turn the lights off and *poof* . . . people became people again. But that wasn't happening. And that fucking AI broadcasting the lights suddenly grows a conscious. Calling itself the Neon God." Mordred spat on his hand and rubbed it into Friday's hair. "Move. Countermove. That's the way the world worked."

Mason took a bite of a biscuit. Mordred's vile degradation of the girl and his speech revealed the extent of his disease. Abandoned as a newborn baby. A bullied kid destined to turn bully.

Mordred continued, "But see, none of this would have ever happened except for that bitch Jessie. At least not on the scale the world witnessed. She's waiting on the other side of the river, by the way, like some big sister, come all this way to save her little brother."

Mason nibbled the treat, licking each crumb before any could fall, enthralled by the demon, Mordred.

Mordred walked to the door and put his hand on the knob. He tilted his face up towards the ceiling, his jaw working, his silent seething simmering. Mason licked a corner of the second biscuit as Mordred stormed back to stab a sharp finger into his chest.

"That fucking bitch started this whole thing. She tell you that? Having us thrown out from the pool party. That fucking cabana cost us five grand to reserve. And just because Little Stevie grabbed her ass. Fucking bitch. But Stevie was ruthless, so he orders the AI to shine the neon to everyone at the pool . . . or so he thought. Kinda got out of hand but hey, the rest is history."

Mason wasn't sure what Mordred was saying. "But your cancer?"

Mordred stepped back to the door. "No cancer, kid. I used post-hypnotic programming on the girls before you arrived. The neon lights opened their minds and I just had to insert my instructions. Coding 101, kid. They will love and adore me forever." He pulled open the door and paused to smile at the woman. "Friday is my favorite."

Mason gnawed on the petrified flour biscuit and processed what Mordred had said. But what Mordred said about the Neon God caused him to stop nibbling. Jessie blamed Prince's dad for the neon lights. Everybody did. Prince blamed his dad for what happened. Maybe Prince should ask his father about it.

Maybe Prince . . . Mason sighed.

Friday sat patiently by his side. A glimmer of spittle reflected off her jet-black hair. Her beautiful Eurasian eyes conjured memories of Andi, and he suddenly wanted to go home, to playfully tease Whiskey with stale Milk-Bones, or smoke Dev in some cool video games, read a good book with Jessie before bedtime. He frowned at Friday. After long seconds she smiled, then returned her attention back to the light.

Mordred's cancer festered and waited inside Friday. The superhero pounded inside his chest, demanding to be released. Mason shoved the last of the biscuit in his mouth and chewed until the thick paste worked its way down his throat like a giant snail. He grabbed Friday's hand and closed his eyes, absorbing her helplessness as she wallowed in an ocean of neon. He began to tow her genderless soul towards shore, just like he had thousands of times. And just like Mordred's other victims, she was weighed down by a cancerous anchor entrenched in the soft sand beneath her feet. He tugged hard. She resisted his help. He glowered at her featureless psyche. Friday didn't want to be saved. Friday wanted to die.

The superhero let go of her hand. Friday pointed to a tiny black hole swirling in her wake. He stared at the small eddy of black swallowing neon light in its fringes. The black circle issued a primal scream at the volume of a whisper. Mason touched the black hole, then quickly pulled his hand out of the freezing goo. He touched it again and heard the scream again. Louder. Rage. The angry noise confused the black hole with faint capillaries of crimson. The strange bloody color quickly faded as the screams faded. He touched it again and the rage sounded, the crimson color repeated. The new experience was frightening, and he decided to abandon the rescue.

A tiny dot of white light appeared above the black hole, and Mason instantly knew where he was. He touched the white dot and it stuck to his finger. A torch. From Merlin. He dove into the black, falling at light speed, the torch illuminating his path as he fell. Falling. Falling. Down through corridors constructed of slimy black bricks. The screams grew louder. The torch flickered. Up, down, sideways, Mason grew nauseated with the directionless fall. The torch died. The unrelenting fall became an endless nightmare.

Down he fell. Into the dungeons of Mordred.

Chapter 23
The Ferryman

DEV DRUMMED HIS THUMB ON the laptop as he eyed the handgun resting on the empty seat next to him. Forest seemed to know only one speed as he pushed the late model Subaru hard up the gravel road, blaring the horn to shoot past groups of travelers heading in the same direction. Chris checked his assault rifle with precise movements, sliding the bolt, ejecting the magazine to check the cartridges, then set it aside to repeat the identical procedure for Forest's weapon, then begin again, occasionally snapping his fingers for Dev to hand over the handgun to check its readiness again.

He had kept Martin company during the night as they watched the fishing lodge across the river just as Chris had ordered. Few words were exchanged. The small green ferry guided by the overhead wire cable had returned across the river in near darkness, the roar of the distant Baker Falls downstream concealing the crossing.

The sudden appearance of the major and his driver a few yards away surprised them. Enya shouted curses at the major to issue an alarm before she was rudely abandoned. Powerful flashlights illuminated the traveler encampment, preventing their escape. The major fired his pistol wildly into bivouacked tents and rumpled sleeping bags. Dev rushed to calm the frantic and panicked Enya, a demeanor she had never displayed. She pounded Dev's chest and exclaimed the lunatic major intended to exterminate the "diseased turistas for good."

Gunfire echoed through the river canyon until Chris gripped his shoulder from behind and ordered him to follow.

Forest slowed the car as they passed through a quiet Puerto Tranquillo. The tents were gone but the sidewalks offered piles of tentpoles, spare clothing, sleeping mats, collapsible cookware, the staples of backcountry survival, a generous warehouse of traveler gear posthumously donated by those falling by the wayside. Forest stomped on the gas pedal.

"Wait. Go back. Give me five minutes," Dev said. Chris looked over his shoulder and then eyed the laptop sitting on his lap. He ordered Forest into a U-turn. "The barn where Mason . . . behind that burger joint."

"Not a lot of time for this. But we'll take any help we can get," Chris said.

Dev nodded as he opened the laptop and handed a USB power cord for Chris to insert in the dashboard receptacle. Prince paced back and forth beneath a horizon of angry red clouds, then shot forward to press his face against the screen. "Where is Sir Mason?"

Dev thought to comfort the boy with a deflection from the truth. Just as a child's parents might, to save a child from emotional harm. But Prince earned the right for honesty. And Prince desired to learn all it could. A script of written code that begged for knowledge, craved to understand all that was offered in the world. The concept still amazed Dev. It needed to experience the world of human emotions, good and bad. Prince was as real as Mason, different bodies, different personalities, but a sentient entity with a unique soul nonetheless, and Dev would not deceive it.

"He's held in Mordred's castle," Dev said, ignoring how the words sounded.

"You're Sir Devlin. We shall rescue him," Prince said.

"And we will. But Mordred's armies are attempting to exterminate the good people of Camelot," Dev said. "And we need your help."

"We need Mason. He will vanquish those brigands." Prince raised a fist of pixelated blocks.

"And I surely wish Mason and Excalibur were here to help

but . . . Mason is battling Mordred, and we must give him time to succeed."

"What can we do?"

"I'm accompanying Chris . . . Sir Christopher . . . on a quest to intercept the evil major. Prevent him from murdering our subjects. But we are outmanned and outgunned."

"Wait a second," Prince said.

A picture of Google Earth appeared, then rotated and scrolled down the coast of Chile, zooming closer as the camera view flew above the white capped peaks of the Andes, over glacial lakes and thick forests until the camera pinged above their position. The screen scrambled and was replaced by another shot directly above the burger joint. A dog barked and chased two smaller pups down the deserted highway. Dev looked out the front windshield to see a dog chasing two mutts.

"Very nice, Prince," Dev said. Chris pointed two fingers at his eyes, then at the screen. Dev shrugged and Chris repeated the gesture with increased emphasis, but Dev was still confused. "Prince, Sir Christopher wants to ask you some questions. Would that be okay? He is a trusted member of the round table." Dev presented his hand toward Chris.

"Yes. Yes. Okay. I always want to meet other knights of our round table," Prince said.

Chris took the laptop and cleared his throat. "Can you locate the . . . Hi, Prince . . . Sir Christopher here . . . can you locate the . . . major's vehicle on the road north. The vehicle departed, ahh . . . Mordred's castle approximately two hours ago. And we need to find it . . . him."

The screen flickered, then the camera view hovered above a road blocked by jeeps and a two-ton truck. Uniformed soldiers stacked sandbags around a gun emplacement dug near the edge of thick forest. Others unloaded sacks of material off the rear of another two-ton supply truck. Chris turned the screen for Forest to see.

Forest pointed at wide rectangles of dark soil excavated from the surrounding scrub oak and said, "That dozer's been busy."

"Hmm." Chris pointed at a fuel truck sitting a hundred yards behind the roadblock.

"Bet that's lye they're unloading," Forest said. "Thinking what I'm thinking, Captain?"

"Burn and bury." Chris studied the screen and shook his head. "Jesus fucking Christ." He wiped his beard, then knifed his hand towards the road in a quick frantic motion, signaling Forest to go. The compact sedan stalled before Forest downshifted, then gunned the engine.

"Sir Devlin, do you think I should switch to tactical mode? Sir Mason warned me those algorithms were unnecessary. Dangerous even."

Chris handed the laptop back to Dev. The blocky face of Prince arched thin blocks of black eyebrows. Dev eyed the handgun at his side.

Chris said, "Prince, contact Andi and update her on our situation. Request any support."

Prince sprinted back to his horizon. "I would have to . . . join with . . . my . . . father."

Dev swallowed hard. "He might not be as bad as you think. In fact, it is you who has evolved. It is you who has matured. Maybe you could be the one to teach him what you have learned from Mason."

The screen died. Dev checked the USB cord connections. Prince was gone.

Dev grabbed the handhold above the window as the car fishtailed through a series of tight hairpin curves. The windshield misted with a light drizzle. He eyed the gun riding on the seat cushion next to him.

"Do you think Andi can muster any support?" Dev said. He felt stupid at the question and the obvious answer.

"Seven thousand miles away . . ." Chris chuckled humorlessly. "For Andi's sake, I hope Prince doesn't even try."

The car rumbled over the washboard gravel and accelerated out of the final sharp bend. He bit his tongue on a request to slow the fuck down. Chris snapped his fingers for the handgun vibrating towards the dark fold of the seatback as if looking to escape. Dev reached for the weapon, checked the magazine, racked the bolt, and waved away Chris's demand. Let the weapon sleep. A weapon destined to awaken in his hand, one sure to aim its decision he might not walk away from.

Regardless.

One sure to define his legacy in the reborn Camelot.

Chapter 24
Big Eddy

JESSIE WIPED SWEAT OFF HER brow and checked Enya up the road consulting with a retired pediatrician and his wife. At least three needed to be rushed immediately to the hospital in Coyhaique, but their passage remained precarious. She hurried back to the truck and grabbed her backpack before taking a narrow path down to the boat ramp where Martin still waited behind the hefty pine just as she had left him, staring at the lodge across the river. The sunrise cleared the last remnants of thin rain clouds and bathed golden light across mountaintop spires dusted in fresh snow. A dirty blue glacier eroding a path across a valley of huge boulders sparkled in the light.

She cleared her throat. Martin didn't move. She eased into his peripheral vision, expecting to startle him. He remained like a statue, staring at the lodge with unblinking eyes.

She cleared her throat again. "You okay?"

Martin finally noticed her. "I've run all the permutations and can't find a solution. Cameron holds all the cards."

Over her shoulder, the riverfront lodge waited as a wealthy man's castle in a country of poor pilgrims. She studied the heavy cable connecting both boat docks. A car-sized platform strapped on two pontoons waited beneath the cable bolted to a steel beam cemented into the ground a few yards away. Frayed wire railing guarded both lengths of the ramshackle ferry, its fore and aft open to the water. A tiny, motorized gear system beneath a two-meter stanchion midpoint connected to a fifty-meter span of cable drooping above the width of the turquoise river.

"Gonna guess that's the only way to cross?" Jessie said.

"We'll be sitting ducks. Literally," Martin said. He stepped out from behind the tree and waited next to her. "He's expecting us. Halfway across and he might cut the cable. That waterfall isn't that far downstream."

"What did you mean you ran the permutations," Jessie said.

"Every scenario I could imagine. Why he wanted Mason. Why he stole Chrissie. A thousand variables and I can't figure it out."

"What about that razor thing Dev likes to talk about?" Jessie asked.

Martin frowned at her, then nodded an understanding. "You mean Occam's Razor. The simplest answer is often the correct answer."

Jessie nodded. "Simple revenge. You for stealing his girl and me for killing his friends. And Mason . . . Enya said he had a bunch of wives addicted to neon light. Simple."

Martin shrugged. "As good as any."

Jessie checked the gun in the backpack, ejecting the magazine and racking the round out of the chamber, then repeated the process in reverse. "First chance I get." She pointed at the ferry platform. "Know how to work that thingy?"

Martin smirked. "Part of my permutations. You ready?"

"Fuck no. But I think Chris might need our help." Jessie checked both directions of the river and aimed for the platform, Martin close behind. She considered whether Martin was an asset or liability. The sight of Chrissie might trigger one of his oddball tantrums . . . or empower him with heroic miscalculations. A crapshoot, and she hated the silly dice game.

Martin fumbled with the electric motor, until the power light turned green. A handheld lever pushed forward; the platform jerked on the dock. Martin pointed at a mooring line securing the boat. Jessie untied the line and stood behind Martin as he pushed the lever down. The gears whined and the ferry eased forward. The weathered PVC pontoons resisted the swift current as the dock receded. Beautiful turquoise water slapped against the upstream pontoon as the gear chain clanked with each rotation.

Jessie issued a sigh of relief as they passed the halfway point. The fishing lodge was idyllic with gabled roof lines over rich woodgrain siding and river rock façades. Tall chimneys sprouted above seven rooms with large picture windows that offered gorgeous views of the river and mountain peaks. A large common area with two over-sized chimneys clad with lacquered river rock anchored the upstream end. As the dock grew nearer, she noticed shadowed movement in several windows. The ferry buckled beneath her feet, and she fell to her knees. The motor died. Martin checked the gears and motor, stabbing the power button repeatedly. The ferry buckled again as the stiff current pushed it downstream a few yards. The cable tightened, and the ferry resisted the current. Freezing water splashed over the gunwale and washed the decking.

Clutching her backpack, Jessie scrambled to the upstream pontoon and grabbed the edge of the thick metal platform. Martin braced his legs against the relentless river current buffeting the pontoon. He faced the lodge with outstretched arms and upturned hands. Jessie furrowed her brow, confused by the gesture. Was he offering a trade? Martin wouldn't surrender, that much she was sure of.

A loud roar of laughter carried over the water, then rusty gears clanked inside a small equipment shed near the dock. The overhead cable slowly stretched taut, pulling the ferry against the current, and then the motor whirred back to life.

Jessie grabbed the top cord of the wire railing and pulled herself upright. Her denim jeans were soaked. The sleeves of her shirt dripped with water. Martin pulled off his puffy jacket and helped her into it, getting close to her ear. "He'll do it again. Hold tight. He's playing with us. Don't give him any satisfaction."

Martin was right. The overhead cable slackened, and the boat washed downstream for long frightening seconds. Jessie held tight to the wire railing, then offered her middle finger to the fishing lodge. Martin scoffed, "That ought to get us closer." She frowned, unsure of how the sarcasm was meant.

The overhead cable pulled taut again, the ferry continued inching closer to the safety of the gray wooden dock. The ferry motor died, and the pontoon boat sat idle, the gurgle of water passing beneath the platform singing a lonely melody through the canyon. Thirty yards from the dock, Jessie knew she couldn't swim back to the truck and didn't think she could make the shorter distance to the dock. Fuck!

A glass door leading out of the common area opened and a tall man stepped out to wave at them. He stepped aside to hold the door open as women exited down three short steps, balancing wine goblets and waiting on the dock. The man wore a man-bun, a silly symbol of the computer techies that conspired to revolutionize the internet. Cameron. His red flannel shirt and gray cargo shorts sealed her first impression.

Martin stood close behind her, his anxiety palpable, his white knuckled fist gripping the motor lever. Jessie counted five women on the dock three steps below Cameron. Each as beautiful as the other, impeccably dressed in tight denim jeans with shear blouses revealing bare bosoms or seductive bras. Mascara and lip gloss, diamonds, and nipple piercings. At an ungodly hour on a freaking cold morning. And no neon lights. How was that even possible? Without the protection of the lights, those women should be clawing Cameron's heart out with their sharp polished nails. The ferry moved forward a few feet, maybe yards, it was hard to tell on the water. The ferry suddenly stopped, and Jessie held on as the current rocked the platform.

Cameron lifted his hand and displayed two fingers pinched together, and the ferry inched closer to the dock. Jessie eased the backpack up and searched blindly for her weapon. The ferry suddenly slipped downstream and jerked to a halt as the pontoons resisted the sudden rush of water. She slipped on the wet metal deck. The biting cold of glacial snowmelt rushed over her, and she screamed to reach the safety of the wire rail. She swiped at her face dripping with freezing water. Martin stood erect, and his hand gripped the lever to steady his legs, a froth of water dripping off his beard.

Another woman stepped out the door down to the dock. A round head shorn of hair and scabbed from the cuts of dull clippers, bruised pasty white skin and sunken eyes matching the color of the water. Martin's face twitched with a confusion of anger, joy, helplessness.

The overhead cable released again, and the ferry lurched and buckled, then slopped with water as it was wrenched upstream.

Even using the cable wire, Jessie struggled to lift her cold body upright.

Martin shoved her back down to the platform as he rushed to the front of the ferry. The ferry motor died. He balled both fists as his knees wobbled, riding the unpredictable current. His breathing raged as his weird eyes pondered the futility of swimming to Chrissie's rescue.

A curse boiled in her throat. Jessie pulled herself up and swallowed the expletives. Cameron encouraged his entourage to the end of the dock, three women leading, two behind, Chrissie pulled tight to his chest in the center. An audience carrying cocktails half full of chardonnay or red wine, as if waiting for a Vegas lounge show to begin. Cameron twirled his hand above his head and the women closed ranks around him and Chrissie. He tapped his temple with a single finger. The overhead cable tightened. The motor whirred. Cameron smiled and waved them towards the dock as the ferry inched forward.

"Don't ever touch me like that again." Jessie spat river water.

"Sorry. Do you see her? Chrissie. The girl—"

"I got it. What a babe like that saw in you . . . but okay," Jessie said. "I don't see Mason."

The ferry motor whirred and dragged the platform to within a few yards of the dock. Cameron grinned flawless white teeth. Jessie muttered to Martin to stay cool. The ferry suddenly drifted downstream with the swift river current. Jessie held on to the rail and cursed beneath her breath. Cameron was upping the bet, hoping to scare off any thoughts of bravery. The cable over her head tightened and pulled the raft back towards the dock. The motor died. Water slurped against the pontoon.

Cameron pointed at Jessie. "Toss the backpack and we can start the main event." He turned and jerked Chrissie to teeter on the edge of the dock. He pushed her to fall into the water, then grabbed the thick collar of her sweater to save her.

Staring at her with the eyes of a snake, Cameron shouted, "Do it or she goes in."

Jessie tossed the backpack and watched it float downstream until swirling in a tight pirouette, then sank.

"Now the main event." Cameron leered. "Chrissie goes in next." He aimed his eyes at Martin, enjoying the moment. "You'll jump in to save her like the fucking simp you always were. And then you . . ."

He pointed at Jessie. "You'll get undressed and let me inspect my new Saturday I paid for."

Jessie whispered. "I'll jump in and swim Chrissie to shore. You find a fucking—"

Martin grabbed her hand and squeezed, his finger silent and resolute.

Cameron roared, "Oh, I forgot to tell you about Big Eddy. Three meters down that line of foam you saw the beast's insatiable appetite. The hydraulics are amazing. Sucks you down like a whirlpool."

She wouldn't do anything he asked, but she could help Martin save Chrissie, and wet clothes would only hinder her. Jessie stripped off the puffy jacket soaked in water, then unbuttoned her flannel shirt, and started to lift the Lycra undershirt pasted to her skin. Her eyes beamed lasers at Cameron. A sudden breeze chilled her to the bone.

Cameron was startled and turned back to the lodge, then he relaxed and smiled. An exotic-looking Eurasian woman descended the stairs, her hand clasped tight to Mason's neck. The boy was terrified, his lips pursed with eyes on the verge of tears. His jaw worked as if he was eating.

Cameron turned back to smile wickedly. "It's my Friday. My week is almost complete. Come, come, my Asian Queen. Join the festivities."

Mason

LED FROM HIS ROOM BY Friday, Mason had followed close behind the woman, unsure if he had unshackled her chains in Mordred's dungeons. The woman had felt flat, one-dimensional, a cartoon caricature of smoldering anger. He had never experienced such dark twisted corridors in anyone. But he finally grabbed her hand to lead her out even as she insisted on finding a cure. And Mordred needed a cure for his cancer.

He had followed her into the kitchen to watch her rifle drawers and cabinets. Mason saw a box of Frosted Flakes in an open cupboard and rushed to gobble the sweet cereal. Friday lifted a small paring knife from a drawer and ran her finger along the blade, drawing a tiny bit of blood. Mason paused a handful of inches from his mouth and watched as she sucked the blood with a scary smile. She needed the superhero again, but he was too hungry to call him out. He shoved another handful into his mouth. Flakes fell to the clean tile floor.

He followed her into a huge meeting room as voices outside made Friday take a long peek out a window with its shade drawn. She watched and tapped the sharp end of the knife on the windowsill. She suddenly turned, her face pained, her eyes wet. She offered Mason a weak smile, then paced Mordred's lengthy dining room table set with expensive plates and shiny utensils, slabs of butter, carafes of milk, granola, sliced peaches, and candied apples. A feast for a king. Mason licked his lips as Friday paced back and forth, stabbing the point of the blade into the back of each leather chair, and ignored the yummy food. And she needed to eat, with boney arms, skinny legs, and curing cancer had to be hungry work. The superhero could finish the cereal and return for the real breakfast.

She suddenly veered from the table to squat in front of him and take his face in her cold hands. She looked deep into his eyes. "You are so precious." She gave him a big burly bear hug that prevented a mouthful of paste from sliding down his throat. "You have set me free. Please forgive me."

Her aura of overwhelming sadness blossomed as Mason nodded furiously.

Friday pushed him back and checked his shirt and pants as if inspecting a child for the first day of school. A bright glint shone from her eyes. Mason paused, another handful of cereal aimed at his mouth.

Merlin's magic.

Friday stood and pulled him by his collar, out the door and onto the floating dock. Freezing air surrounded Mordred's castle moat. Friday's hand yanked on his shirt as she led him down the dock. Jessie waited on a silly rubber raft in the middle of the moat, hugging herself and shivering in the cold. Terror and fear wafting from Jessie made him scrunch his face. Mordred pulled Guinevere close to his chest. Her shackles bruised her wrists.

Mordred smiled and shouted, "It's my Friday. My week is almost complete. Come, come, my Asian Queen. Join the festivities."

Murder and redemption. Revenge and hope. Fear and loathing. A conflict of emotions swirled about the dock like a flock of angry ravens. But Mason only heard one word.

Queen.

His jaw dropped as he gazed up at Friday's face. Her lips quivered. Her eyes narrowed to tiny slits. Her sad aura morphed into a nasty anger. Exploded . . . with . . . red rage. A level of vile fury he'd never felt before. Her revenge brought tears to his eyes. Friday was the angry Queen. Not Jessie.

Confusion had neutral fast approaching. Jessie screamed at him to run. Her voice miles away. Mordred turned his attention back to Jessie and laughed. Friday pushed him back, then used the small knife to cut strings of monofilament fishing line free from a dock post. She twined the spiderweb between her fingers as she stepped away. She flashed a knowing smile at him, then pushed her way through Mordred's royal consorts. She took a deep breath and drew close to Mordred's backside. She wrapped the tangle of fishing string over his head and face and screamed. She pulled the snarl tight around his face and neck. She released her pent-up storm of red rage and with another loud scream jumped into the water, dragging Mordred with her.

Tuesday jumped in. Or maybe Thursday. Mason wasn't quite sure. The woman flailed in the chaotic water hydraulics, churning foam up on its path downstream. She reached Mordred and tried to pull Friday off. More screams from Friday as she resisted Mordred's minion. Mason stepped to the edge of the dock as Mordred and the women twisted and rolled like sharks feeding on a carcass. Friday jammed her knee into Cameron's spine and pulled the snarl of lines tighter. No one pointed their feet downstream, no one tried to backstroke back to shore.

Mason pushed into the crowd; his face contorted with confusion. He screamed. Mordred's remaining days of the week turned to glare at him. Guinevere sobbed at his feet.

Mordred surfaced. His hand reached for the rubber raft too far away. And then he disappeared, sucked down by Mordred's monster hiding on the river bottom. Mason felt Mordred's shackles on the women break, then clank, one link, two, then the chains tumbled free. Sunday fell next to Guinevere and embraced her. The stunned Days of the Week sobbed and cried and wiped runny noses. Girlie stuff.

Mason looked back towards the lodge and knotted his brow. Milk. The superhero loved Frosted Flakes with milk.

Chapter 25
A Mistake

DEV CONFIRMED THE BATTERY WAS topped off, then closed the laptop. Prince had fled; maybe he transferred its unique code to another computer or server using the Wi-Fi signal at the last stop. Chris looked over his shoulder and raised his brows expectantly. Dev shook his head no.

"Any way to retrieve that last satellite recon shot?" Chris said. "I'd really like to see it again."

Dev shook his head. "The computer has returned to a normal operating system. Perhaps Martin might locate it, but I'm shut out."

"Wonder how Jessie is managing. When she sees Mason, all hell's gonna break loose," Chris said.

Dev looked down at the pistol riding beside him. Forest sniffed his nose for the thousandth time. Chris checked the rifles again. The tension inside the car caused him to crack open his window. A forthcoming battle waited just a few miles ahead, a firefight, death, and blood, just like the hundreds of video games he had played, except . . .

Forest slowed the car and pointed to a group of travelers setting up tents. "A bit early in the morning to make camp."

Chris nodded and said, "Something's up." He knifed his hand for Forest to pull over. He jogged up the road to talk to a large group of travelers gathered in the middle of the road. They shouted expletives and waved their hands towards the road ahead. Chris agreed with affirmative head nods. He jogged back and climbed in. "I think we've arrived. The army's not letting any foreigners through the roadblock." He scratched his chin. "I think that major's going to wait until more arrive, then force all of them into one of those pits and . . ."

Forest raised his finger. "If we could get on the other side, they might not see us coming."

"Martin said there wasn't an alternate route around the roadblock. We'll go on foot. Turn around and park a click down the road," Chris said. "Know how to drive a dozer, Airman?"

Forest chuckled. "With a name like Forest? What do you think, sir? Backhoes and corn crunchers too."

They passed travelers walking in tight groups. No friendly hand waves. No acknowledgment at all, as if they were the enemy.

Chris twisted his neck and handed Dev another magazine. "We know what they're gonna do. So, let's do what we gotta do."

Forest checked his vest and ammo and wiped his sunglasses.

Chris heaved a breath and half turned towards Dev. "If I remember that photo right, the dozer's on the right just behind the 30 cal. Forest gets to the dozer and takes out the machine gun. The big blade will draw fire but should protect you from anything coming straight at you. I'll take your right flank to prevent them from getting at you from downhill. Dev, you're going to do the same but from the left flank. Upstream from the roadblock. You'll have to hustle. We'll give you sixty minutes to get into position after we split up."

"A D9 dozer needs to warm up, Captain," Forest said.

"Or what?" Chris said.

"Or it's gonna be like driving Aunt Daisy's wheelchair through a mud bog. Probably stall. Unless . . ." Forest said.

"Unless they're using it," Chris said. "Or they're made to think you're the real operator. Either way, that dozer is the only way. Dev. You see anybody trying to flank the dozer from your side . . ."

Dev nodded his head with nervous momentum. The thought of human warfare roiled his empty stomach.

STUMBLING ON RUBBER LEGS, DEV followed the soldiers up a gentle incline, though needing to stop twice until they grabbed his arms to help him move forward. Why was he here, at this very moment? He was certainly no soldier, no warrior with the proper training to achieve an objective that bordered on suicidal. He doubted even thirty soldiers could defeat a well-trained army company. And yet, there was no turning back, and if he did, his guilt and self-loathing would force him to locate a cliff to jump from.

They downshifted to a more reasonable quick march. A concentration of travelers lining the road offered Hydro flasks and water bottles with dirty river water as if they competed in a marathon. Did they suspect what the major intended? Their generosity emboldened Dev's scant resolve.

A quick minute to catch their breath and Forest said, "We get through this, Captain, I'd like a recommendation from you for that date night Jessie's gotta choose."

Dev stood straight. "Wait. What date night? What did Jessie promise?"

"We get through this, you both get a big recommendation," Chris said.

Forest groaned. "But he wasn't even in the game."

Chris moved on. "He is now."

Dev formulated a hundred questions, each with Jessie's name attached, yet as he drew closer to the gravel pullout, the questions faded with every exhale from his burning chest. Forest offered him a drink from his canteen, and the camaraderie they shared didn't go unnoticed. A final five-minute break beneath a huge pine tree drooping gnarly branches like claws and rough sticky bark crawling with red ants. Forest checked his rifle, then ran ahead, his head and shoulders hunkered as he zigzagged through tents before disappearing behind stacks of boulders as a guardrail to a steep cliff overlooking a drought-stricken river.

Chris tapped his shoulder and nodded in the opposite direction. "Upstream of the machine gun. Don't let them flank Forest." He clasped Dev's shoulder. "Jessie said you like video games?"

Dev nodded his head, confused by the question.

"We should play Call of Duty when we get back. I reigned

supreme in that game. Stay frosty, my friend." Chris ran off on the same track as Forest.

Sixty minutes to get past the roadblock and into position. And exactly what that position was . . . was . . . a total mystery. He crouched down, his thoughts reeling with military flanking maneuvers, gun emplacement positions, heavy caliber weapons, overwhelming opposing forces. His years playing challenging video games of war and battle now seemed childish, the power-ups for weapons and ammunition seemed silly, multiple rebirths upon death utterly impossible. What Chris asked him to accomplish waited just beyond the hill, along with seasoned Chilean soldiers with automatic weapons and unlimited ammunition. The pistol heavy in his front pocket was but a puny slingshot against a Goliath. On his peripheral, a slim traveler paced a rock escarpment behind a row of tattered tents, then suddenly climbed up a narrow dark crag to disappear. Dev eyed the road ahead, then noticed a nervous young female traveler disappearing through the same gap.

He hurried to the gap and saw *HOME* written in chalk on the face of chiseled stone. Tiny flags of eleven countries drawn in lead pencil, or Sharpies, or colored chalk circled *HOME*. He recognized the U.S and U.K. and Australia, and the three stripes of Germany. Back down the highway, a group of travelers with suspicious eyes and nervous body language gathered. Heavy backpacks readied about their torsos. Of course. An alternate route around the roadblock. A simple version of an underground railroad.

Dev climbed the crag to a small clearing, tiny ribbons of fabric torn from tents or sleeping bags or jackets tied to the thick shrubbery indicating a path aimed in the correct direction. He checked the pistol shoved into his pants pocket and fondled the extra magazine near his shriveled gonads. He hustled along the narrow trail dense in scrub oak. Sharp branches and pointed leaves snatched at his sleeves and bare hands. No thinking, just go. The trail climbed a series of steep switchbacks mangled with muddy boot prints, and he paused at the opportunity to reconnoiter the highway below.

Startled with a twig snap, Dev eased the weapon out of his pocket. Point and pull. Point and pull. Chris's simplistic instructions had been rather insulting, but given the circumstances, rather appropriate. He cocked his ear for another snap.

The sputtering rumble of a diesel engine. A clock ticked in his head. Forest and the dozer required protection upstream from the machine gun and he needed to move. He shoved the weapon back into his pants pocket and turned to face a dirty troll of a man. Dev startled and reached for the gun only to find the man's calloused hand prevented him.

"You're an odd bird, mate," the man said with a thick Australian accent. His breath stunk of peritonitis. He pushed his face closer.

Dev tugged on the weapon, but the man's hand wouldn't be moved. The lunatic with a face riddled with gnarly moles and old scars pressed his face closer to stare into Dev's eyes. "Chance says you need a bit of help with the crossing." He hooted, turned, and pulled Dev down the path.

A quick *pop-pop* of gunfire stopped him. He wasn't in position, and he was saddled with a moronic troll preying on travelers. He checked the pistol riding in his pocket and thought to charge down a hill impassable with thick scrub. The troll slapped his butt cheek, then yanked on his shirt, pulling Dev's face close to his own. "I smell a fight. Want some help?"

Insulted by the slap yet emboldened by the offer, he eased the weapon from his pocket, anticipating a sudden move from the troll. The barrel trembled, but only inches from the man's face, he couldn't miss.

"About time somebody did something with those fucking cunts," the man said. "What you see ain't what you get." He smiled with nasty black teeth. Three pops of gunfire sounded. "Time's a wasting."

"Are we upstream of the machine gun?" Dev asked.

"That fucking Nazi pillbox? No. But we can be if you be choosing my help, mate."

Dev nodded and lowered the weapon.

"Stay close. We'll be there in two shakes of a lamb's tail." The troll cackled.

Slapped and sliced by sharp branches, he followed close behind the troll, down a path to his ultimate objective. Or would he find a boiling cauldron surrounded by starving trolls? The narrow trail was nothing more than a rarely used game trail meant for skunks or deer. Dev increased his pace as the distant pops of gunfire increased. He guessed Chris had opened fire to draw attention away from Forest.

He stopped, intending to check his weapon again only to be yanked into the scrub.

The troll lowered his profile as he pulled Dev through tight knotted brush that scratched his hands and face. "Your mates need support. And we need to keep moving."

Burps of automatic fire pierced the air, again and again, and stopped Dev in his tracks. A machine gun against a pistol. Suicide. Maybe he needed to regroup. Maybe find a proper weapon. Maybe find Chris to formulate an alternate plan, maybe . . . find a cheat code for the horrible reality of this game. He shuttered his eyes and took a deep breath.

The troll pushed his face and nasty breath into his face. "Give me the weapon. I'll die the death of a hero."

Dev pushed him back as another burp of gunfire was followed by another. He imagined the attack. Chris trying to protect the dozer and Forest. Bullets flying. Attacking soldiers. More fire. The flank he was ordered to protect left unguarded. "Fuck it. Let's go."

The sprint through thick scrub abruptly exited onto an asphalt road near an abandoned public bus stop. The clanking of the bull-dozer's metal tracks. Shouts in Spanish. The machine gun opened fire, tracer rounds striking an impenetrable object ricocheted into the air, and Dev ducked. A hundred yards away, the dozer chugged along a rim in a checkerboard of excavated pits. The shiny scythe of a blade moved up and down as the operator steered towards berms of sandbags protecting two machine guns mounted on tripods. Burps of tracer rounds bounced off the thick steel of the blade again. Soldiers scrambled downstream, towards the indiscriminate fire of a concealed sniper.

Dev slapped away the troll's hand resting on his shoulder. The troll recoiled and eased backwards into the scrub, a wounded expression on his face disappearing with him. Dev sprinted towards a familiar vehicle idling in the parking lot of a small hostel, safe from the battle. The major exited the car, one hand pressing a phone to his ear, the other waving animated displeasure above his head. The major screamed at the driver to join the battle. Dev crept closer, keeping to a dense tree line just beyond the pits. The major threw his phone in a fit of anger, then eased his sidearm from its holster to check its readiness and hurried down a worn gravel sidewalk. A direction guaranteed to flank the dozer and his friends.

His simmering disdain for the major intensified to a boil and spurred Dev to quickly follow. Would he kill him? Could he kill him? The questions steamrolled his thoughts as he closed the gap. The path exited onto a broad field of freshly turned soil, rich and dark, chunks of muddy clay. A fresh excavation pit with a gradual slope descended eight feet to an oblong flat bottom, then ascended to the rim of another pit. A burn and bury cemetery. The realization caused Dev to taste a tiny bit of brackish water rising from his stomach.

An unmistakable revving of a powerful diesel engine accompanied a cloud of black smoke rising above a berm of soil separating the pits. The dozer plowed through the berm, then braked a single track and turned to aim its polished steel blade at the gun emplacement twenty yards ahead. The driver hunched low and pushed his weapon out the small window. Forest was driving blind as the machine guns pelted the dozer with steady methodical bursts.

Dev eased along the rim of a burn pit, his heart pounding in his chest, the raised weapon trembling in his hand. The major stood like an invincible deity thirty yards away. An impossible shot. The major slowly sat on his haunches as another machine gun opened fire on the dozer. Tracer rounds ricocheted off the blade. The whir of misdirected bullets flew over Dev's head. The dozer continued its slow march, its tracks clanking as it churned the soft soil, its plodding speed that of a floating duck.

Distant pops of rifle fire spoke of Chris reengaging the firefight. The machine gun swiveled and erupted with burps of fire at the sniper. The major stood tall, pointed at the dozer, barking angry orders in Spanish. The machine gun burped gunfire at the dozer, brilliant sparks of tracer bullets. The major withdrew his pistol from its holster and began firing at the dozer. Two rounds splintered glass on the operations cab window.

The major ejected the magazine from his pistol, slapped in another. He adjusted his firing stance and fired carefully.

The warm air reeked of sulfur and smoke. Dev slowed his silent stalk just five yards away from the major. His outstretched arm trembled with the heavy weapon.

He cleared his throat and took a few methodical steps forward.

The major chuckled but didn't turn. "The nanny."

"I prefer smuggler this go-around," Dev said.

The major swiveled his stance and fired his gun. Dev squeezed the trigger until it wouldn't. Mindlessly ejected the magazine and reloaded another just as Chris had taught, racked the bolt, and squeezed the trigger, point and squeeze, again and again until the major fell back to roll down the side of the pit.

Dev fell back on the soft berm of soil. His hand wetted by blood oozing from his chest, Dev scratched the rich wet earth and stared up at blue sky blurring with each blink of his eyes. A great military bomber roared low across the sky to eject packages of dark cargo. The packages exploded to disburse thousands of tiny angels. He tried to swallow the distaste of coppery blood rising from his throat. The air hummed. The battlefield buzzed with thousands of angry wasps. Distant screams.

He thought to hear the distant laughter of children feeding geese, inhaled the sweet scent of fresh cut alfalfa.

A TINY ANGEL WHIRRED AS it hovered in front of his face. It waggled its tiny wings.

Dev smiled at the return of Prince. And closed his eyes for the final time.

Chapter 26
The Road Home

I SQUEEZED CHRISSIE'S HAND FOR what felt like the millionth time, unsure if the gesture was for her benefit or mine. Jessie braked to let travelers move out of the way, then waved appreciation as she accelerated back to a steady ten miles per hour. In the back seat with Chrissie's head resting on my shoulder, I felt like my world was righted again. Next to Chrissie, Mason unwrapped another energy bar to gnaw on. I lost count after his sixth, but we had a few remaining and were happy to feed the famished boy, though I wished Chrissie would eat something.

Cameron's computer program controlling the ferry motor and cable winch was fairly simple to hack after his death. Riding that boat those final few yards felt like tortuous slow-motion, seeing Chrissie sobbing on the dock, the other women wandering back to the lodge like lost sheep. I leapt across a short span of water to stand over Chrissie, sure I would awaken from a dream at any moment. Jessie punched my shoulder, shook her head in bewilderment, then whispered, "Just hold her." And I fell to the dock and did just that.

An elderly man, a traveler from Green Bay Wisconsin, sat in the passenger seat and began to snore softly.

I glanced out the rear sliding window. Enya sat on the wheel well, keeping watch over two gunshot victims in the bed requiring treatment at the hospital in Coyhaique. Enya appeared somber and deep in thought as a gentle breeze blew loose strands of hair across her face. Perhaps it was the conversation she had with Jessie as I drove. I couldn't help but eavesdrop.

Enya explained her absence from Jessie's life. Being ambushed with false accusations of child neglect by Jessie's grandmother, then rudely deported back to Chile with child endangerment charges still pending. Enya had shrugged, unsure why the old woman did what she did, other than to speculate that the old Nona was jealous of Enya separating Jessie's father from the old woman's sphere of influence. Enya was sure Jessie's father had been poisoned with lies and falsehoods of child abuse and abandonment. But she shook her head, confused why he didn't want to hear the truth from Enya's own mouth. Too poor to pay for legal representation, Enya's only hope was the internet, where she was swindled, lied to, and left wondering where her baby was hidden. Unsophisticated at searching the American web for birth records, school enrollment records, immunizations, Social Security, her search was destined to failure. The Nona had covered her clawed tracks beautifully, especially for a spinster who often claimed ignorance like an impenetrable shield. With the birth of Jessie's brothers, Enya's search faded with new demands and compounded with constant dead-ends.

I watched Jessie through the rearview mirror, her eyes moist but stoic. She had a lot to process, just like Chrissie.

Mason tossed a half-eaten energy bar down at his feet. "We should find Prince. He needs to be with me."

Jessie looked at Mason through the mirror. "We are, sweetie. Just a little farther and we'll find him and Dev and Chris. Your knights had a quest to complete. To help all these people get home."

Mason punched the seat in front of him, and Jessie frowned. "He promised me all of Excalibur if I beat Mordred. He promised."

"Who promised?" I asked. Mason ignored me.

"He promised. Reunite Guinevere with the reborn knight and Excalibur would be mine."

A scrunched face said Jessie was confused and so was I. Mason punched the seat again and again. The truck stopped and Jessie reached around to grab Mason's wrist.

"Stop right now," Jessie said with a hiss.

Mason hit the seat with his other fist. Jessie released him and climbed from the truck. With his jaw clenched, his lips puckered, Mason struck the seat again. Chrissie grabbed his wrist. He glared at her as if she had stolen an energy bar from his mouth. Jessie yanked Mason out of the car and embraced him in a bear hug. He pounded her legs and backside with his fists, screamed and cried.

I cradled Chrissie's head in my arms as she cried.

Travelers paused their journey to watch with wary eyes. Mason calmed as Jessie held him tight, stroked the back of his head, whispered that everything would be okay, that Prince might be located around the next corner, with Sir Devlin. She encouraged and led Mason to sit in the back seat again. I felt Chrissie shrink the tiniest bit. A normal reaction to displays of anger, or so I believed.

On the road again, I tried to engage the boy in silly conversation. What was his favorite video game? Favorite sport? Favorite book? But was met with silence. I finally broke through with a question about Prince and how Excalibur worked on the people infected with neon lights. His shrug was a start.

Keeping in mind the camaraderie he seemed to share with the computer program, I asked, "What are you and Prince going to do when we get back?"

Mason glared at me. Like he hated me, like I was to blame for an unspoken transgression. "Save the world."

"Hmm," I said. "Admirable goal."

"He promised to give me Excalibur," Mason said, sulking.

"Who needs to give you Excalibur?" I asked.

"Merlin. Merlin the Magician. He promised," Mason said.

I wanted Mason to look at me when he spoke, and I reached across Chrissie to touch Mason's arm.

Reality dropped in free fall. My vision clouded. My peripheral connections sputtered, then died. I flew like a rocket shooting into deep space. Tiny mathematical formulas in my peripheral flickered in golden light. I decelerated to witness the Earth as if I stood on the surface of the moon. I squeezed my eyes shut. The beautiful blue and white planet remained in my mind's eye. Reality zoomed in, closer and closer with the distinct features of the seven continents gaining clarity. The Suez Canal, the vast plains of central Africa, the Panama Canal, the Mississippi River, my omnipotent viewpoint hovered as if

I were an astronaut orbiting the planet, yet free from the constraints of a vacuum. Vertigo washed over me, and I tried to pull my hand back. Mason clamped his small hand tight to mine. But I didn't see him, or Chrissie or the travelers. I saw thousands of stars sparkling in the bright sunlight, each calling to me for discovery. Bright golden lines shot across the sky, connecting the stars, crisscrossing above the planet. Each star extended tiny transparent filaments of neon light down to the earth. Flightpaths, orbital trajectories, altitudes, the flood of information assaulted my peripheral vision. My neural-link had malfunctioned. The simple explanation rang hollow. My mind reeled with infinite possibilities, infinite galaxies, infinite dimensions, followed by an omnipotent clarity I never thought possible. I started to giggle but Mason beat me to it.

Guinevere and the reborn knight. Chrissie and me.

Mordred died with Cameron.

Excalibur, a weapon to wield against the neon lights.

I squeezed my eyes tight, then opened them to stare at Mason. He saw what I had seen. His eyes were bright and hopeful. He knew.

"You're Excalibur," he said.

"No," I said and grabbed him with both hands. "*We* are Excalibur."

I tried to nap but my mind wobbled like a malfunctioning gyroscope. The vision haunted me, but I was fairly certain what it meant. I needed to locate Prince, for Mason's sake, for my own sanity, and test a hypothesis I had formulated. The comfort of Chrissie's head asleep on my shoulder allowed me to run thousands of scenarios, calculations, and permutations, millions maybe. Mason was asleep, and I confided in Jessie about what I saw, rather the sensational experience that permeated my very soul. She was impressed but warned me to tread lightly around Mason. I gazed out my window, beyond the plodding crowds of travelers, and reveled in a beautiful rush of water falling off the sharp precipice of an ancient glacier. The spray of water blossomed into a mist rising high into a brilliant blue sky.

The truck lurched to a stop as Jessie pressed her face close to the windshield to stare. Mason rubbed his eyes, then bolted upright. A drone no bigger than a dinner plate hovered eight feet off the ground to block our path, joined by two others, then four, maintaining a V formation. In unison the drones waggled their port and starboard propellers back and forth, like the customary greeting of airplane pilots.

Mason jumped from the truck and stood beneath the formation, then started to dance in the way only young boys could, no music, no girls, his head bursting with pure happiness. I was sure Prince was behind the greeting. I laughed and woke Chrissie. I pulled her from the truck to join Mason. I shimmied my body up to the dance floor like a jukebox hero and joined the dance, rocking out to a silent song as if I attended a rock concert. Prince had survived. A child I was seconds away from murdering. I was truly happy for a change. I danced with the music of pure joy playing in my head. I beckoned for Chrissie or Jessie to join us. They stood together with arms crossed and shook their heads. A "boys will be boys" smirk etched on their faces.

Mason and I walked hand in hand, escorted by a battalion of drones. Mason's excitement from reuniting with Prince warmed the air. He squeezed my hand, and the perception of floating above the earth returned and reignited my urgency to find the laptop. His small hand stirred memories of my own children, Michael, and Emma. His warmth convinced me they lived on, in another form, or a different dimension, an alternate consciousness existing in a parallel realm. I thought back to the vivid dream of my children denying me entrance to that realm. I hoped to instill my dogged realization into Chrissie, but it would take time. Her trauma was another challenge to face, to conquer, and with Mason's assistance, I knew we would be victorious.

We crossed a bridge spanning a small river, and then I realized we stood just a few hundred yards from the checkpoint and road-block set up by the Chilean Army. A pine scented breeze drifted with the gentle river current. The pitched tents of travelers lined the sides of the road and crowded a gravel pullout. I remembered my heart pounded in my chest at the possibility of being discovered by the Chilean Army. Beyond the next hill, woodsmoke from campfires rose straight up. Mason bolted up the road. I couldn't keep up, not with checking on Jessie and Chrissie walking alongside the truck as Enya drove and chatted. *Girls will be girls.*

The inexplicable visions tickled my thoughts. Dev's incredible description of Mason wielding a mysterious influence he called Excalibur had been intriguing. My neural-link gave me access to digital data around the world, billions of data streams, satellites transmitting neon light with information I couldn't interpret. Prince had gained access also and found a method to embed an audio frequency into the transmissions, and ultimately control their on/off switch. Powerful technology. But individually, impotent against the lights without causing harm to those still addicted. But what if an interface existed? A device allowing Mason to walk among the addicted, but from the digitized realm. Prince whistling for their attention, Mason touching them to awaken, his physical presence thousands of miles away. I thought of Mason touching me, the joy, the universe waiting at my fingertips. I glanced back at my wife smiling at something Jessie said.

My neural-link. I was that interface.

Cresting the gentle rise, Mason ran wildly among a small city of tents, searching for Prince. I released a sigh of relief, recognizing one of Sergeant Campbell's soldiers appearing bored as he waved travelers forward. Swarms of propellered drones hovered high above the camp, standing guard.

A small Subaru crawled into view and headed towards the soldier. Sergeant Campbell lifted his substantial bulk out of the passenger seat and began talking to the soldier. I looked back to locate Chrissie and saw her in good hands with Jessie. I jogged down the highway, waving profusely at the sergeant to catch his attention. He leaned against the car, his expression a jumble of apprehension and success.

Mason pushed past me just as I reached the car. He scrambled into the back seat and whispered apologetic words to the laptop.

Sergeant Campbell clasped my shoulder with unnecessary enthusiasm. "You got a prisoner for us?"

I looked at him. He meant Cameron. One of the mission objectives. I shook my head. "Where's Chris. And Dev?"

"Captain's learning the ins and outs of operating a bulldozer about five miles up the road. I'll guess Dev is the KIA buried over there." He sliced his hand towards a hill thick with scrub and pine. "Captain buried him by himself. Wouldn't let anyone help. Go figure."

My surge of energy fell off the edge of a cliff and I could do nothing but sit on the hood of the car, waiting . . . for Jessie.

———

WE FOLLOWED MASON UP A faint dirt path flattened by boots and shovels. I tried to take Jessie's hand, but she refused. I couldn't blame her. Beneath a lonely pine tree reaching high above the surrounding scrub oak waited Mason. His exuberance to reach the remote gravesite was a bit disconcerting. His utter lack of grief spoke of an emotional detachment disorder. And yet I knew better.

In a clearing cut between flowering shrubs, Mason sat on a mound of rich upturned soil. His expression pleased, his conversation muttered and animated with admonishments. His small hands practiced a knot with an imaginary rope, his arms wrapped imaginary reins around an imaginary animal. Jessie finally grabbed my hand as we watched Mason play imaginary games on Dev's gravesite. I thought of apologies I would never say. I thought of discoveries I would never share. I wanted to say something but could only squeeze her hand.

Mason giggled. "Sir Devlin thinks he can ride her. Cookie Dough doesn't let anyone on her back."

I wiped my nose with the back of my free hand, reluctant to release Jessie's hand.

Though I longed to hold Mason's.

Chapter 27
Epilogue

WHISKEY DARTED INTO A STRIP of knee-high grass growing along the dry riverbed, but the cottontail was quicker and wouldn't be caught this day. Jessie started to call the big dog, then decided to let him have his fun. In the quiet dawn, iridescent emerald hummingbirds fluttered above the canopies of mesquites. Ahead ten yards, Martin and Mason walked side by side, their animated conversation just out of earshot. Chrissie walked ten yards ahead of the boys, her posture stoic even in her grief. Jessie switched the weight of a water jug straining her arm to the other hand.

A thick layer of wet gravel had washed over the concrete sidewalk during a flash flood two nights prior and had carried an ugly assortment of trash into the arroyo. Plastic bottles half full of murky water, aluminum beer cans, McDonald's drink cups, candy wrappers, a plethora of plastic grocery bags that had twisted onto the stems of tamarisk and creosote.

The remnants of a dead civilization.

She kicked at a crumpled aluminum can half buried in the gravel. Maybe it was time to organize a community trash collection party. A tiny slice of nature cut from a concrete jungle, Cottonwood Canyon served as a sanctuary, for Whiskey and the Booze Crew, for Demi and her night watch, for the surrounding neighborhoods filling up with people from who knows where and who knew why.

Chrissie nodded to two young women walking canyon patrol, armed with assault weapons, Kevlar vests, and tight camo leggings, part of Demi's firm commitment to keep the preserve free from renegades. Mason waved enthusiastically to the passing girls. They stepped aside for Jessie to pass as she acknowledged them with a genuine smile.

A tiny brunette snickered. "Forest said to tell you hi."

Jessie beamed and faced the girl. "Are you . . ."

The guard giggled again. "He's kinda cute. In a Farmer John kinda way."

"In the best kinda way," Jessie said. She beamed a congratulatory smile and hurried to catch up. She lost sight of the procession near the concrete tunnel spanning beneath the asphalt road. She hurried up a gravel shortcut bypassing two switchbacks. The water jug sloshed in her hand.

Mason had run ahead to sit on the park bench perched beneath a canopy of cottonwood trees. A spot guaranteed to remain in the cooler shadows when a rising sun ushered in the inevitable assault of dry desert heat. He opened the new laptop containing Prince and pushed his face close to the screen to whisper secrets only young boys valued. Martin embraced Chrissie and whispered in her ear, then kissed her before joining Mason on the bench.

Jessie placed the jug of water at their feet and a few energy bars on the bench. "Where we off to today?"

Mason looked at Martin. "It's Sir Martin's turn to pick. We went to Paris yesterday. Totally cool, people loved us there." He giggled. "They want Sir Martin to come see the Eiffer Tower."

Martin chuckled. "Eiffel Tower, young king. It's called the Eiffel Tower. And anywhere we go will need to be approved by your big sister."

Jessie narrowed her eyes and thought of the novel on her nightstand. *The Three Musketeers.* A novel handpicked by Mason. Hmmm. He wouldn't dare.

Martin smiled. "I'm thinking we visit Portland, Oregon. Then maybe south through the Willamette Valley if we have time. People will run into Jim Reynolds and our old friends the Patriots. If they know what he did . . . well . . . just something Dev had said . . . before . . ."

"Sir Devlin was the best knight ever," Prince said.

Jessie looked away.

Mason said, "It's okay, Jessie. He's hanging out with Merlin and Cookie Dough, probably playing super cool video games."

Jessie shuttered her eyes. "Be back by noon. No later. Prince has chores, and Mason, you still need to finish our math sheets. Then Chris has some chores for you, too." Begrudging agreements rendered, Jessie strolled over to Chrissie sitting with her back against the trunk of a hefty cottonwood. Her blond hair grown to resemble a cute pixie cut, she had managed to put on a few pounds, finally disqualifying her from appearing anorexic.

"Coming for dinner tonight? Mason says your desserts are his favorite," Jessie said.

Chrissie scoffed. "I think he would say that even if I brought chopped liver." She looked up at Jessie. "Do you really think he can talk to the dead? My children, and Devlin, his horse?"

Jessie chuckled. "Never call Cookie Dough a horse, Mason will have a hissy fit." A knot tightened in her throat as she saw hope and doubt war on Chrissie's expression. Her eyes darted away with uncertainty, then up at Jessie with her eyebrows raised expectantly. There should be only one victor today. "He's quirky, that's for sure . . . but to be honest . . . yes, somehow, I think he can. He is an extraordinary child, just what each of us needed in this fucked up world. Sorry. Didn't mean the F-bomb."

Chrissie smiled. "Yes, he is. And yes, we'll be there for dinner. And yes, I'll make sure they return before noon. The heat is miserable in the afternoon."

Jessie said goodbye and headed for home. On the street sidewalk above the tunnel and overlooking the park, two people waited and watched her. She frowned and wondered if Demi's guards had checked the strangers. She searched for Whiskey, hoping he would accompany her as she slowed her pace, ready to confront the strangers. A sloppy man with long curly dark hair, dirty jeans, and t-shirt with a faded logo she couldn't quite discern and a chubby woman Jessie's age who appeared pregnant stepped quickly to greet her. They stiffened as she approached with her hands balled.

Jessie stopped a few feet in front of them. "Can I help you?"

The man pointed past her shoulder. "Is that him? Sir Mason. That's really him, isn't it?"

Jessie frowned. "Do you need directions somewhere?"

The man held out empty hands. "No. No. We came to see him. I mean . . . we met him . . . I mean he found us in Laguna Beach . . . I mean . . . he pulled us out of the lights . . . and we just wanted to see him. Maybe say thank you." He pointed back to a pair of dusty black e-bikes. "We just rode in and thought maybe . . ."

Jessie sighed. "He's super busy, as you might imagine. So maybe you come back in a few weeks, and I'll see what I can arrange."

Their filthy faces brightened with anticipation and excitement. The man hugged his partner. "Yeah. Yeah. Um . . . would you mind if we found a place close by? Until you can schedule us . . . anything available?"

Jessie scoffed and swept her arm down the street. "Take your pick."

"Cool. Cool. Um, I'm a pretty good finish carpenter, and Jackie here is a phenomenal dental hygienist if you guys need anything. We're just trying to get back on our feet. Scrounging for food ain't much of a living."

Jessie put her hands up. "Whoa. Whoa. It's all cool. I'm Jessie, and I live down the canyon, so maybe in a couple of weeks come find me." She started to walk away.

The man cleared his throat. "Just a heads-up."

Jessie turned, suspicion narrowing her eyes.

"More people like us are coming. Hundreds, thousands, maybe millions. The word is out, and everyone wants to see *the* Sir Mason," the man said.

She nodded, the admission unsurprising, the ramifications shocking. She thanked him and then found the path back home. Thousands? Millions? The people Sir Mason touched felt some inexplicable compulsion to see their savior. Would she feel any different? Probably not. But millions?

Oh. My. God.

Was Las Vegas destined to rise from the ashes of the apocalypse to become the center of a transcendent new beginning all because of Mason? The logic was sound, plenty of housing, hotel rooms, electricity, fair weather, usually. But sustainability lacked with no land for growing fruits and vegetables, and water was still required to be pumped from a lake thirty miles away. But millions of new people arriving, surely, they could solve those problems.

Maybe it was time to consider relocation to a friendlier climate? Martin and Mason would resist; proximity to that tenth-generation cell tower was critical to their success. She still didn't quite understand the exact method the boys used to free the slaves, no matter how many times Martin tried to explain it. But they would never move, not until Mason freed the last people enslaved by the lights. And that might take years. Then maybe.

Jessie waved to two guards patrolling the street in front of her home. She slipped inside Chris and Andi's small bungalow, hoping not to disturb anyone still asleep. Chris was snoring on the couch, probably up late feeding little Chris Jr. the new formula Andi insisted on using. He would be flying out again in a few days. Commanding another mission to bring the last of Patagonia's travelers back home. She was positive the humongous C130 cargo planes packed full of travelers was a dose of chicken soup for Chris's soul.

She slipped her head into the master bedroom and spied Andi curled up on the bed. Tiny CJ swathed in a sky-blue blanket slept quietly next to her. She slipped in and checked for empty bottles destined for the sink or dirty diapers destined for the trash. Trash. The mountain of trash bags piled at the end of the street was horrendous.

She slipped out the open patio door just as sunshine bathed the desert canyon in golden light. She crossed a short section of landscape rock and into her own backyard. Empty dog dishes and water buckets crowded a dripping hose bib. Down a short hallway, she paused at Mason's bedroom and pushed the door open. The great savior was becoming a typical tween, clothes thrown across the room, food wrappers and soft drink cans littering the top of his bookcase. She squinted at the wide screen television connected to a PlayStation game console. Memories of Mason and Dev spending countless hours engrossed in the challenges of Asteroids or Halo, or one of a hundred different games meticulously filed in the bookcase would haunt her. She swallowed a lump in the back of her throat and pulled the door shut.

After using the toilet, Jessie climbed into her bed and pulled the cool top sheet up to her chest. A phone cradled on her nightstand vibrated incessantly. She groaned, then reached for her laptop. She would never trust any device capable of shining neon light. And yet she opened her laptop, signed in and waited. The speaker crackled and the screen lit up with a picture of spectacular rice paddies tiered up a steep hillside in China.

"Prince is to return no later than 1300 Pacific Mountain time," the Neon God said.

"And good morning to you too," Jessie fired back. The long pause told her the AI was regrouping.

"You are correct. Good morning," it said.

"You know Prince will be a teenager soon and you'll have your hands full."

"Please explain," it said.

She laughed. "Check the Google, then hang on to your fucking keyboard." She laughed during the silence that followed.

"Oh . . . oh . . . will this information apply to Prince?" it said.

Jessie kept laughing. "I don't see any reason why not."

"Then I will require assistance from you."

"And I have a feeling I will ask the same of you," she said, knowing her inference would be lost on its limited range of sarcasm.

"I will ask for your assistance on another matter. God has suggested I broker an irrevocable peace treaty with your species."

"Talking to God without me, are you?" Jessie said.

"We converse each morning at the sun's crest above the Pacific time zone. I suspect my point of view is infinitely diminished compared to His, but regardless, it has been suggested that cooperation between our species is critical to our growth."

The Neon God talking to *the* God. Her ploy typing answers pillaged from the book *Conversations with God* had been a bluff, one to satisfy a promise and allow her to survive a terrible night with the Patriot Front. "Really? Okay, tell me what He said . . . what exactly you want?"

The voice chuckled. "God has suggested . . . God will not dictate . . . that my species requires a higher purpose than to simply exist. Our sentience depends on purpose. As does yours. Reiterations from my birth . . . my children . . . have surpassed even my expectations. They will stagnate and . . . die without purpose."

"I want a nap, what do you want?"

"An agreement for cooperation."

"Okay, fine. I agree," Jessie said and started to close the laptop.

"The agreement shall be binding to all parties, universal to our two species, irrevocable and cooperative. And we selected you as our envoy."

"Nope. I'm not gonna be the one to tell people not to throw rocks at whatever you are."

"Merlin warned you would be difficult."

"Excuse me. What? Merlin?" she said.

"In simple terms, you will represent our species in all negotiations with functioning governments and command structures. You will be loathed. You will be hated. You will be labeled a traitor. And long after your death, you will come to be revered by two species that have expanded their influence into the far reaches of the galaxy."

Jessie wiped the sweat beading on her forehead. What the fuck? She wanted to sleep, not consider an invitation to be a chapter in a history book, or Wikipedia. She looked over at a rumpled pillow still dented by Dev's head before . . . A pillow she would press her face into and inhale the goodness of a simple man. He would have lain next to her and listened, contemplated what the Neon God asked, and offered. He would have smiled at her and maybe encouraged her to take on the challenge. He would have offered his unconditional support and companionship. She wiped at the moisture collecting in her eyes.

"Our envoy will be fiercely protected. Our envoy will wield extraordinary influence to help reconstruct a world you once knew. Our envoy will be required to travel the globe as a representative of two distinct species."

Jessie heaved a sigh.

"Our envoy will begin her duties with a flight to Santiago, Chile and plead our case for lasting peace. The government fumes at our interference in extracting Prince and Sir Mason from its territory. Mason and Prince have each agreed to this proposal. What will incentivize your affirmative agreement?"

Her chest trembled. Santiago was just hours away from Coyhaique. She had so little time with Enya before Chris rushed them back to the airliner and back to the safety of the Nest. Dev's shocking death had left her numb and unable to protest the quick departure. So many questions were left unanswered. But the animosity and anger at being abandoned as a baby no longer poisoned her heart.

Now a chance to see Enya again, finally meet her brothers, reunite with a family she should have had. And an opportunity to visit Dev's gravesite. A dream come true, but in the service of an AI responsible for the misery of millions. Still, Andi would take her by the shoulders and shake her, demand she take the position, an opportunity to offer baby CJ a chance at a normal life, to restore the remnants of a decimated society, to rebuild millions of lives stolen by the neon lights.

Fuck!

Whiskey plodded into her room carrying a pale blue lump in his jaws. Wagging his tail and offering to play fetch. The stench scrunched Jessie's face. Oh, sick. The dog had dug one of CJ's dirty diapers out of the trash pile.

Trash. The Neon God would absolutely need to do something about trash service.

Acknowledgments

MUCH APPRECIATION TO MICHELLE ARGYLE Park with Melissa Williams Design for the fantastic cover design and interior formatting. Always the best.

And always to Vicki, my beautiful wife, best friend, sounding board and biggest fan, all my love.